KNUCKLES AND TALES

KNUCKLES AND TALES

NANCY A. COLLINS

This is a work of fiction. Names, characters, places, and incidents are products of the authors imagination or are used fictitiously and are not to be construed as real, any resemblance to actual events, locales, organizations, or persons, living or dead, is entirely coincidental. The mention of or reference to any companies or products in these pages is not a challenge to the trademark or copyrights concerned.

Biting Dog Publications
P.O. Box 2739
Duluth, Georgia 30096
www.bitingdogpress.com

Copyright ©2003 by Nancy A. Collins
I'm Gonna Send You Back To Arkansaw-Original to this collection,
　©Nancy A. Collins, 2001
The Sunday-Go-To-Meeting Jaw- originally published in Confederacy Of The Dead
　(Roc), ©Nancy A. Collins, 1993
　Seven Devils- originally published in Thrillers (CD Publications),
　©Nancy A. Collins, 1994
　How It Was With The Kraits-originally published in Cold Blood (Ziesing Books),
　©Nancy A. Collins, 1991
　The Pumpkin Child-Original To This Collection, ©Nancy A. Collins, 2001
Raymond –originally published in The Ultimate Werewolf (Dell),
　©Nancy A. Collins, 1991
　Down In The Hole-originally published in More Phobias (Pocket Books),
　©Nancy A. Collins, 1995
　The Serpent Queen- originally published in Strange Attractions
　(Bereshith/Shadowlands Press), ©Nancy A. Collins, 2000
Junior Teeter And The Bad Shine-Original To This Collection, ©Nancy A. Collins, 2001
The Two-Headed Man-originally published in Pulphouse #9, ©Nancy A. Collins, 1990
The Killer-Originally published in Thrillers (CD Publications), ©Nancy A. Collins, 1993
Cancer Alley- Originally published in The Earth Strikes Back (Zeising Books),
　©Nancy A. Collins, 1994
The Worst Thing There Is-Original To This Collection, ©Nancy A. Collins, 2001
Catfish Gal Blues-Originally published in 999 (Avon), ©Nancy A. Collins, 1999
Big Easy-Original To This Collection, ©Nancy A. Collins, 2001
Billy Fearless-Originally published in Ruby Slippers, Golden Tears,
　©Nancy A. Collins, 1995

Cover Illustration ©2003 JKPotter
Interior Illustrations ©2003 Bonnie Jacobs
Book Design by Bonnie Jacobs

ISBN: 0-9729485-1-1

All rights reserved. No part of this book may be used or reproduced in any manner whatsoever without written permission, except in the case of brief quotations embodied in critical articles and reviews.

For information address Biting Dog Publications.

Printed in the USA

Biting Dog is committed to reducing waste in publishing. For this reason, we do not permit our covers to be "stripped" for returns, but instead require that the whole book be returned, allowing us to resell it.

DEDICATION

IN LOVING MEMORY OF IDA MARGARET "BILL" WILLOUGHBY
1910-2002

WELCOME TO SEVEN DEVILS

Sunday Go To Meeting Jaw	3
Seven Devils	21
How It Was With The Kraits	39
The Pumpkin Child	53
Raymond	103
Down In The Hole	117
Serpent Queen	131
Junior Teeter And The Bad Shine	149
The Two Headed Man	179

THE CONFEDERATE STATES OF DREAD

The Killer	195
Cancer Alley	209
The Worst Thing There Is	219
Catfish Gal Blues	225
Big Easy	239
Billy Fearless	249

INTRODUCTION
GONNA SEND YOU BACK TO ARKANSAW

It took me the better part of my life to finally stop being ashamed of my heritage. I don't mean my genetic background, which is largely Anglo-Scots-Irish with the occasional dollop of French and American Indian for flavor. I'm talking about where I'm from, not who I am, although, on a certain level, the two are inextricably intertwined. No, my secret shame lay in geography, not genetics.

I am a third generation Arkansan, or, if you prefer the antique spelling, Arkansawyer. I grew up in the part of the state known as the Ark-La-Miss; those counties located in the far southeastern corner, in the very heart of the Mississippi delta, near the borders of Louisiana and Mississippi.

I remember the day in third grade when the teacher announced to the class that the "official" spelling of our home state was 'Arkansas'. Up to that point, 'Arkansaw' was a legitimate alternative. Either way you spell it, I am an Arkie, born and bred. And for most of my conscious life, I felt like I had to beg pardon for that fact. This shame did not originate within me, but was instilled from without.

I grew up in a couple of small rural communities where the local economy revolved around what was referred to as 'agri-business' and the railroad switching yard. Like my parents before me, my only connection to the culture at large was through the mass media. However, where my mama and daddy only had radio and the movies, I had the television.

To my young mind there was little to differentiate the news and the TV shows from one another; both occurred in foreign places far removed from the world I knew and involved people I did not personally know. I was in the second grade before it occurred to me that the war the newscasters were talking about on the evening news was going on in Vietnam, not the Germany of *Combat* and *Twelve O'Clock High*.

Like all children, television showed me worlds and lifestyles I could never have known in a small, relatively isolated farming community. But like Hispanic, African-American and Asian-American children, I hungered to see something of the world I was familiar with, people and things I could relate to. When I looked to the magic mirror of television, hoping to glimpse a reflection of myself and my family and the lives we lead, all I saw was programs like *The Andy Griffith Show*, *The Real McCoys*, *The Beverly Hillbillies*, *Green Acres*, *Petit Coat Junction*, and *Hee-Haw*.

While there was a recognizable likeness of my world in the fictitious Mayberry and, to a lesser extent, the eccentric farm-folk of Hooterville, for the most part Southerners, and Arkansans in particular, were represented as figure of burlesque: ignorant, raw-boned hillbillies who ate road kill. Jethro Bodine, a flesh-and-blood Li'l Abner minus the social commentary, was as much a symbol of the state in the eyes of others as the University of Arkansas Razorback.

The Southerners of the silver screen weren't much better, either, although there was far more variation, from the realistic milieus of *To Kill A Mockingbird* and *Thunder Road*, the Southern Gothic opera of *A Streetcar Named Desire*, and Grand Guignol of *Hush, Hush Sweet Charlotte*, to such exploitation/ action movies such as *Deliverance* and *Southern Comfort*.

According to the popular culture, Southerners were either slack-jawed hicks, murderous rednecks, corrupt sheriffs, faint-hearted Southern belles, effete alcoholic gentry, or indolent hillbillies snoozing on their ramshackle front porches with a jug tucked in one arm and a pig under the other. It was also a foregone conclusion that none of us wore shoes, had indoor plumbing, and that we all held a grudge about the Civil War.

If being a Southerner wasn't embarrassing enough, being from Arkansas was adding insult to injury. Although Arkansas was a part of the Confederacy, it wasn't home to any noteworthy battles, save for Pea Ridge, which couldn't hold a candle to Manassas or Gettysburg, and

Missouri claimed the Ozark skirmishes between Union forces and rebel guerilla bands such as Quantrill's Raiders and Bloody Bill Anderson.

As tenuous a source of pride the state's past may have provided, its present was nothing to crow about, what with Arkansas perennially hovering in the second-or-third-to-last spots for public education, literacy, and high school graduations. (The standard, half-joking, response of native Arkansans when faced with such depressing statistics has traditionally been: 'Thank God for Mississippi!') The statistics for teen-aged pregnancies and alcoholism in the state during my youth were as high as the illiteracy rates, and in the late 1970s Arkansas had the dubious distinction of being the Unmarried Teenage Mother Capital of the United States.

While I was growing up, Arkansas' favorite sons were Buddy Ebsen, Johnny Cash, Conway Twitty, Charlie Rich, Glen Campbell, Dizzy & Daffy Dean, Lou Brock, and Meadowlark Lemmon. Save for The Man In Black, there wasn't a thimble full of cool to be found.

There wasn't much a young girl, yearning to someday become a writer, could look to for inspiration. It wasn't until I was much older, and had moved way, that I learned that Levon Helm hailed from my home state, as well as such literary and publishing mavens as Charles Portis (*True Grit*), Helen Gurley Brown (*Cosmopolitan*), Maya Angelou (*I Know Why The Sweet Bird Sings*), James Bridges (*The Paper Chase, The China Syndrome,* and *Urban Cowboy*), Ellen Gilchrist, John H. Johnson (publisher of *Jet* & *Ebony*) and Dee Alexander Brown (*Bury My Heart At Wounded Knee*). I guess literary achievements weren't considered as important to state pride as playing the Grand Ole Opry or making the Baseball Hall of Fame (not that there's anything wrong with either of those).

Both my parents and grandparents were proud of their Southern heritage, even though the only reason my mother's family ended up in Arkansas was because my Great-Grandfather Willoughby got drunk on a trip from Illinois to New Orleans and threw all the deck chairs off the river boat and was put out at the first port of call. They tried their best to instill a sense of history in my siblings and I, and to a great extent they succeeded.

But the Mass Media is in constant competition for a child's mind and attention, which was as true then as it is now, and for every lesson in regional pride I received there were numerous movies and television shows telling me that being from the South was either laughably square or something approaching Original Sin.

As I grew up and ventured outside the humble environs of my birth, I found myself experiencing a strange form of discrimination. In this day and age of Political Correctness, where the celebration of Mothers Day can be banned from a private day school for fear of insulting those children who might not have a traditional mother, apparently the only ethnic group its still okay to ridicule and make fun is the Southerner, and White Southerners in particular.

Many of those hailing from the Northern states were surprised to learn that someone as educated and well spoken as myself was not only from the South, but a product of Arkansas in particular. I can not begin to count the number of times some 'Yankee' (as my Grandma would put it), upon learning where I was from, would smirk and say something along the line of: "So, they wear shoes where *you-all* live?" Or, even better: "That means you're white trash, huh?"

Such was my pre-programmed shame of being an Arkansan, it took the better part of a decade for me to stop apologizing for where my parents had chosen to birth me and start getting uppity. Sometimes you have to run away from home in order to appreciate it. After I graduated from high school, I was desperate to shake the dust of my hometown off my heels and get out into the big, wide world I had glimpsed inside the TV set.

However, once I did some traveling, I discovered that the South did not have a monopoly on hicks, rednecks, racists, crackers, good ole boys, hillbillies, peckerwoods and trailer trash. And the more I get to see of the rest of America, with its suburban sprawl and food court culture, the more I have come to appreciate my upbringing in a small rural community. Unfortunately, another of Arkansas' favorite sons proved to be the evil genius who unleashed Wal-Mart, first on his home state, then on the rest of the country, where it has effectively gutted and killed small towns like the ones I grew up in.

It was about that time I began writing the first of my Southern Gothic stories. In my own way I am trying to put down on paper memories of a way of life that was disappearing even as I lived it. The world of my childhood, with both its good points and bad, has all but vanished, and what little still remains is dwindling with each passing day. There is an urgency to try and place on paper a time and a place that, in many ways, seems as ancient and removed from the reality of modern-day America as the flickering images seen in Depression-era newsreels.

There is a kernel of reality lodged in the heart of most of the stories you will find in this collection. *The Sunday-Go-T-Meeting Jaw* was inspired by my Great-Grandfather Collins, who served in the First Alabama Volunteer Militia and had most of his lower jaw blown off during the Civil War, which forced him to wear a wooden prosthetic. *How It Was With The Kraits* was based on an actual mother-and-son team who lived in our town. *Raymond* was sparked by my memories of an old classmate of mine who was, indeed, lobotomized and then was dumped back into the hell of junior high school. *The Pumpkin Child* took seed from fond memories of my Grandfather Willoughby's annual ritual of taking the family out to select jack o'lanterns from the huge pumpkin patch behind the shack of an ancient African-American man who claimed to have been born a slave, and the old Caddo burial mound that was located on our family farm. *Junior Teeter And The Bad Shine* is based on a horrific moonshine party gone wrong my father had to deal with during his stint as a Deputy Sheriff. *Catfish Gal Blues* was born from the countless Sunday afternoons my father drove us out to the levee to look at the Mississippi. *Billy Fearless* is set in the Kentucky of my Grandmother Willoughby's ancestry. And the McQuistion Sisters who appear in various guises throughout these stories were real women—a trio of spinster schoolteachers who lived next door to my family for several years and whose collective age was greater than that of the United States at its Bicentennial.

It's taken me a long time, but I'm no longer ashamed of being from Arkansas, even though the Clinton administration often put my resolve to the test more than once. But you are what you are, and part of what makes you who you are is where you've been. I haven't lived in the state since 1980, and I've resided in numerous places throughout the country in the last 21 years. But Arkansas has placed its mark on me. You can hear it in my voice, my vocabulary, even my sense of humor. Arkansas is in my blood.

But it will always be Arkansaw in my heart.

                Nancy A. Collins
                May 13, 2001
                Atlanta, GA.

WELCOME TO SEVEN DEVILS

Sunday Go To Meeting Jaw

The hungry man squatted in the shadows of the tree-line marking the boundary of Killigrew land, never once taking his eyes off the back of the house. His hot, blood-shot eyes followed the handful of chickens scratching haphazardly in the dirt. Although he had not eaten in three days, the chickens had nothing to fear from him. His hunger could no longer be appeased in such a simple fashion.

He hugged his bony knees with broomstick arms and studied the faded lace curtains that hung in the long, narrow windows of the two-story clapboard house. He stiffened as he caught a glimpse of a woman, dressed in black. He began to sweat and shiver at the same time. Had the fever come back? Or was it something else this time?

The back door slammed open and an elderly Negro woman, her head wrapped in a worn kerchief, stepped out on the porch, drying her wrinkled hands on an voluminous apron that hung all the way down to her ankles. After studying the coming twilight, the old Negress descended the stairs and hobbled toward a small, neatly kept two-room cabin near the house. From the looks of the rest of the half-dozen slave quarters, the old mammy was the only remaining servant on the place

It was getting dark. The family inside the house was no-doubt gathered around the dinner table. If he was going to do what he planned, he'd have to move from his hiding place soon. The starving man's stomach tightened even further.

Hester Killigrew pushed the food on her plate with her fork. Collard greens, roast sweet potatoes, and corn pone. Again. White trash food. Nigger food. Least that's what Fanny Walchanski said.

Fanny's father, Mr. Walchanski, owned the dry goods store in Seven Devils. He was one of a handful of merchants who had benefited from the arrival of the railroad in Seven Devils last year. Mr. Walchanski was very well-to-do, Fanny was fond of pointing out to anyone within earshot. Hester could just imagine what Fanny would have to say if she discovered the Killigrews took their meals in the kitchen instead of the dining room.

Hester looked at her mother, seated at the head of the table, then at her little brother. Francis was busy shoveling food into his rosebud mouth. Francis was only two and a half and couldn't remember how it'd been before the war. Back when there'd been more than just Mammy Joella to see to them. Back when they ate in the dining room every day on proper china.

Hester knew better to complain about their situation. It was sure to make her mother scold her or, worse, break into tears. Hester realized they weren't as bad off as other folks in Choctaw County. They still had a roof over their heads and ate on a regular basis. There wasn't as much red meat as before, and they had a goat for milk instead of a cow, but there were plenty of chickens and eggs.

She remembered how Old Man Stackpole sat in his big old empty mansion until he went crazy and set it on fire before shooting himself in the head. Maybe he got sick of eating greens and corn pone all the time, too.

There was a knock on the back door. Since Mammy Joella had gone back to her cabin for the night, Mama answered it herself. Hester craned her neck to see around her mother's skirts. A tall, thin raggedy man stood on the stoop, his hair long and grimy. He looked—and smelled—like he hadn't washed in weeks. For some reason Hester was reminded of the nutcracker soldier she'd seen in the window of Walchanski's Dry Goods.

"If you want work, I don't have any to give you—and no money to pay you with, if I did." Penelope Killigrew said tersely. In the year since the war ended, ragged, hungry strangers looking for food or temporary work were common. Most were trying to make their way back home the best they could. Others, however, were trouble looking for a place to happen.

The stranger spoke in a slobbering voice that reminded Hester of the washerwoman down the road's idiot son. "Nell—Don't you know me?"

Penelope Killigrew started to cry and shake her head 'no'. Francis, who'd been happily crumbling corn pone with his pudgy little hands, looked up at the sound of his mother's sobs. Hester thought the funny-looking stranger had done something. She jumped from her chair and hurried to the door.

"What did you do to my mama?!?" she demanded. Penelope Killigrew turned and grabbed her daughter's shoulders. She was smiling and crying at the same time, like the time she wouldn't put Francis down. Hester started to get scared. "It's alright, honey! Everything's going to be alright! Daddy's come home!"

KNUCKLES AND TALES: SUNDAY GO TO MEETING JAW

Confused, Hester stared at the half-starved stranger dressed in the tatters of a Confederate uniform. He stared back, his rheumy eyes blinking constantly. Now that she had a good look at him, she realized why he'd reminded her of the nutcracker soldier.

He had a wooden jaw.

○ ○ ○

Hester slammed the door to her room as hard as she could. She didn't care if it shook the whole house. She didn't care if it knocked the house to the ground, for that matter! Mama made her go to her room. Well, that's just fine! She could be just as mad as Mama!

Mama lost her temper because she refused to kiss him. Hester didn't care if she got switched for it later. She wasn't going to kiss him! She didn't care what Mama or anyone else might say!

That man wasn't her Daddy!

Everyone kept insisting that Hester was too young to remember things from before the war. That was stupid. If she could remember their ole dog, Cooter, why not Daddy? She certainly could remember the War—leastwise the occasions it wandered into their lives. Hester didn't know why Mama kept telling the Nutcracker she didn't know better. Maybe it made her feel better about having a stranger in the house. But why did Mama have to pretend he was Daddy?

Daddy was the handsomest man in Arkansaw. At least Choctaw County, anyway. He was big and strong, with shoulders like a bull. He had dark hair with deep blue eyes. He laughed a lot and had a charming smile. Even other men said so.

Hester remembered how she used to sit on the floor in the parlor, playing with her rag doll, listening for the sound of his boots in the hall. Then he'd sweep her up in his arms, swinging her high in the air. Sometimes the top of her head brushed the chandelier and made the crystal drops shake and dance. It sounded just like angels singing. She'd squeal and giggle and Daddy would laugh too—the sound booming out of his chest like thunder. Mama didn't approve of such tomfoolery, though. Hester supposed she was afraid they'd break the chandelier.

Hester was six when Daddy went off to fight for President Davis. Mama cried a lot, but Daddy said it was something he had to do. Hester didn't really understand what was going on at the time, but she thought Daddy looked handsome in his gray uniform. They all went down to Mr. Potter's rotogravure palace down near the train depot and

Daddy had his picture taken. Mama kept it in the family bible, pressed between the pages like a dried flower.

Daddy left in 1861 to go help General Lyon fight General McCulloch at Oak Hills, near Missouri. He wrote letters every day and Mama would read them aloud in the parlor before going to bed. Most of the time he wrote about how much he missed them and how bad the army food was.

In 1862 Daddy's unit joined with General Van Dorn's to keep the Yankees from pushing the Confederacy out of Missouri. That was Pea Ridge. The Confederates lost and the Yankees ended up marching all the way to Helena. Daddy came home for a visit after that. He was skinny and had a beard, but as far as Hester could tell he was still Daddy. He hugged her so hard Hester thought her ribs would bust. He smelled bad, but she pretended not to notice so he wouldn't get hurt feelings. When Mama saw him she started to cry, but Daddy shook his head at her.

"Hush, Nell. Not in front of the child."

He left two days later.

Just before Christmas of that year Daddy fought with General Hindman at Prairie Grove. When they had to retreat to Fort Smith, Daddy was one of the men who didn't desert. He kept writing home, but sometimes they didn't get the letters until a long time after he mailed them. Hester knew sometimes he never got the letters Mama sent him, like the one telling him about Francis being born that winter. The last letter Daddy wrote said he was going with General Holmes to kick the Yankees out of Helena. That was 1863.

They didn't get news of what happened at Helena until a month or two later. Mama found out first. It was a massacre. That's how Mama said it. A regular massacre. Hester didn't know what that meant at the time, but judging from how everyone was carrying on, she figured it had to be real bad. Mama cried a lot and carried Francis around and wouldn't put him down or let Mammy Joella take him. Mammy Joella got upset and begged Mama to eat something. If not for herself, then for "the chirren's sake". All that did was make Mama cry even more.

Things changed after that. Mama took to wearing black and made Hester wear it too, even though it was way too hot for that time of year. Mama cut her hair real short and was sad most of the time. Although they never got an official notice from the army, she was convinced Daddy was dead. Or as good as.

Things at home got hard. Most of the niggers ran off when they heard about the proclamation Mr. Lincoln made freeing the slaves.

KNUCKLES AND TALES: SUNDAY GO TO MEETING JAW

Not that Hester's family had a lot of slaves to begin with, unlike Old Man Stackpole's plantation up the road. The only nigger that stayed behind was Mammy Joella, who claimed she was too old to start someplace new.

Mama sold off several parcels of Killigrew land to keep from being thrown out on the road. After General Lee surrendered, she sold almost all of her fancy dresses, saying she'd never have nothing worth celebrating ever again. She also sold off the dining room set and the good china and silverware.

At first Hester thought Mama was joking about the dirty, foul-smelling man being Daddy. Then Mammy Joella came out of her cabin to see what all the fuss was about. She took one look at the Nutcracker and gave a little scream like she's just seen a ghost.

"It's Mr. Ferris!"

Mammy Joella helped Grandma Killigrew deliver Daddy, long time ago. She'd known Ferris Killigrew longer than anyone outside his own family. But she was old and didn't see or think as well as she used to. Everyone knew that.

o o o

Penelope Killigrew sat on a chair in the kitchen, a clean towel folded in her lap, and silently watched Mammy Joella scrub what was left of her spouse. Ferris Killigrew, her husband of fifteen years and father of her two children, was, like Lazarus before him, back from the land of the dead he'd been so hurriedly consigned to.

The numbness was beginning to fade, like it had years ago, when she'd thought Ferris was dead. Part of her felt guilty for having surrendered hope and resigned herself to widow's weeds so prematurely.

Steam rose from the dented metal tub, wrapping the gaunt figure in a damp haze. His vertebrae stood out like the beads of a necklace. Penelope blinked the tears from her eyes and looked away.

Mammy Joella moved purposefully about her former master, scrubbing his grayish skin, occasionally pouring warm water over his tangled hair with a ladle, clucking under her tongue. Killigrew realized he should have undone the leather straps that held his jaw in place before bathing, but he was not ready to subject Nell to that yet. She'd had a bad enough shock as it was, what with him showing up unannounced on the back stoop. The smell of Mammy Joella's skin and the touch of her calloused hands on his naked flesh reminded Killigrew of how she used to bathe him as a child. The memory was so sharp, so unexpected, he began to cry.

He was both surprised and disgusted by the hot tears rolling down his cheeks and how his sides shook and shuddered from the force of his sobs. He'd never cried in front of Nell before, not even when his mother died. He squeezed his eyes shut, too ashamed to look at his wife.

Mammy Joella's voice whispered in his ear. "Go head an' cry, Mister Ferris. You have yourself a good cry. If anyone deserves one, it's you."

o o o

Hester woke up when her mother screamed.

Although it was dark, the moon outside her window cast a cold, dim light into the room. Hester lay on her bed and held her breath. What was happening? Was the house on fire? Had something happened to Francis?

Then she remembered the Nutcracker and she leapt from her bed and hurried across the narrow hall to her mother's room. She grabbed the doorknob but it refused to turn in her hand.

Hester pounded her fists against the door, shrieking at the top of her lungs. "What are you doing to my mother? Leave her alone! Get out of our house! Get out! Go away! Leave us alone!"

The door jerked open so quickly Hester nearly fell headfirst into her mother's room. Mrs. Killigrew stood in the doorway, her face white and tense—whether from anger or shock Hester could not tell.

"Hester, what are you doing up at this hour? Return to your room, immediately!"

Hester could make out the rail-thin form of the Nutcracker seated on the edge of her parent's bed, his face hidden by shadows. "I heard you yell, Mama..."

"Nonsense, child! You must have been having a bad dream..."

"It wasn't a dream! I heard you." She scowled and pointed at the Nutcracker. "What's he doing here, Mama?"

Mrs. Killigrew frowned and glanced over her shoulder. Her grip tightened on the doorknob. "Come along, honey. Be quiet, or you'll wake up Francis! I'll tuck you back in bed," she whispered, pulling the door shut behind her.

"But Mama, you did scream! I heard you!" Hester protested as her mother herded her back into her room.

"I told you to hush once already, child!" Mrs. Killigrew hissed. "You'll have the whole house up if you're not careful!"

KNUCKLES AND TALES: SUNDAY GO TO MEETING JAW

Hester crawled into bed and looked into her mother's face. "Is that man really Daddy?"

"Yes, honey. It's really him." Mrs. Killigrew drew a quilt over her daughter and smoothed it with trembling hands.

"But why does he look so—funny?"

Mrs. Killigrew took a deep breath, like a woman preparing to jump into a cold stream. "When your father went with General Holmes to try and chase the Yankees out of Helena, he ended up getting himself captured. They sent him to a camp somewhere up North, where they kept Confederate soldiers. He was in that place over a year."

"A couple of weeks before General Lee surrendered, your daddy lead a protest for more food and decent clothing for the prisoners. He got smashed in the face with a Yankee rifle butt for his trouble. The Yankee doctors ended up cutting off his lower jaw to keep the gangrene from spreading. So they gave him a wooden one to replace it and let him go. He's been working his way back home ever since."

"Is he going to stay here with us?"

"Yes, darling. Forever and ever."

"Do people have to see him?"

The slap came so suddenly Hester was too stunned to react. Mrs. Killigrew spun on her heel without another word and slammed the door behind her, leaving her daughter alone in the dark.

Hester lay in her bed, refusing to cry. She pressed her red, stinging cheek against Grandma Killigrew's patchwork quilt and wondered what was wrong with grown-ups. She felt like she was trapped inside a bad dream and that she was the only one who knew she was asleep. It was like everyone was crazy but her. But maybe that was what being an adult was all about; believing things you know aren't so.

Like the Nutcracker being Daddy.

Hester had seen the lie in her mother's eyes, when she'd assured her that the Nutcracker was her father. She knew in her heart, just as Hester did, that whoever this gaunt scarecrow might be, he wasn't Ferris Killigrew. So why did Mama keep pretending?

o o o

Penelope Killigrew stood shivering in the hallway.

She realized she shouldn't have screamed like that, but she just couldn't help herself. When he'd exposed his wounds to her she'd been so overwhelmed... Her relief at discovering Ferris still alive had prevented her from recognizing just how severe her husband's mutilation really was. But now there was no turning away from it.

The half-starved creature that had found its way back home was not the man she'd loved before the war. The Ferris Killigrew that had returned was a mangled, incomplete copy of the husband that had marched off to war four years ago. But she owed it to the memory of the man she'd adored to see to it that what was left be looked after and treated well. It was the least she could do.

o o o

Hester was walking home from school when she caught sight of the wagon in her family's front yard. As she drew closer, Hester recognized it as belonging to the man in town who bought used furniture; the one who'd bought their old dining room set the year before.

"Mama! Mama!"

Hester hurried through the front door, nearly knocking down her mother. Mrs. Killigrew stood in the narrow foyer, Francis resting on one hip.

"Land's sakes, child! What is it now?" she sighed.

"What are these men doing here?" Hester demanded, pointing at the two men in the parlor. One of the men was laying thin blankets on the floor, while the second prepared a heavy wooden crate filled with excelsior.

"They've come to haul off some furnishings I've sold to Mr. Mercer, that's all."

"What are they taking this time?"

"Don't use that tone of voice with me, Hester Annabelle Killigrew!"

Just then there was the sound of a hundred angels laughing, and Hester spun around in time to see one of the packing men lower the crystal chandelier, using the old-fashioned pulley Grandpa Killigrew had had installed decades ago.

"No! No! I won't let you sell it!" shrieked Hester, throwing her books to the floor.

"Hester! Hester, what's gotten into you?!?"

Hester propelled herself at the workman lowering the chandelier, hammering her doubled fists against his ribs. "I won't let you take it! I won't! I won't!"

"Hester!"

The second workman grabbed the girl and pulled her away from his companion. He cast an anxious look over his shoulder at the child's

KNUCKLES AND TALES: SUNDAY GO TO MEETING JAW

mother. "Mebbe we oughta come round later, Miz Killigrew, after she's calmed down some..."

Penelope Killigrew's face was livid. "You'll do no such thing! You'll take the chandelier with you, just as I promised Mr. Mercer! Now if you'll kindly unhand my daughter..."

The workman let go and Mrs. Killigrew snatched her daughter's left ear, twisting it viciously.

"Mama! Owww! You're hurting me!"

"And you're embarrassing me, young lady!" Mrs. Killigrew dragged her daughter down the hall, away from Mr. Mercer's hired men. "How dare you act such a way in front of strangers!" she hissed. "People will think you were raised in a barn! I sold that chandelier to Mr. Mercer to help pay for your father's needs! We have another mouth to feed, and it will be some time before your father is well enough to contribute to the family's welfare! Now, would you care to explain yourself, young lady, as to what brought on that outburst?"

Hester shook her head, her tears finally catching up with her hurt. Francis, distressed by his older sister's sobs, began to whimper.

"Oh, don't you start in as well!" groaned Mrs. Killigrew. "Hester, go to your room! I don't want to see your face until suppertime! Is that clear?"

Hester stormed up the stairs, clamping her hands over her ears to keep from hearing the chandelier's angel-song as it was packed away. She paused and gave her parents' bedroom a venomous look. Before she realized what she was doing, she'd kicked open the door and was shrieking at the Nutcracker.

"It's all your fault! She sold it because of you! I hate you! Why don't you go back where you came from and leave us alone?!?"

Mammy Joella sprang from the corner of the bed, moving faster than Hester had ever seen her move before. "Chile, get outta this room for I bust yore haid!" She flapped her apron at the girl as if she was an errant chicken, a wooden spoon clutched in one arthritic hand. Hester stumbled backward into the hall, but not before she caught a glimpse of the Nutcracker.

He was sitting up in bed, surrounded by pillows, one of Francis's old diapers knotted around his neck. A bowl of yellow grits and a pitcher of goat's milk rested on the dresser next to the bed. A length of rubber tubing hung from the middle of his face, a small metal funnel fixed to its end. A mixture of grits and milk dribbled from what passed for the Nutcracker's mouth.

The tube dangling from the Nutcracker's face reminded Hester of something she'd seen at the traveling circus in Arkansas City before the war.

"He looks like an elephant!" she giggled.

Mammy Joella smacked her with the spoon, leaving a smear of porridge on Hester's forehead. "Don't you be callin' yore pappy names!"

Hester was taken aback by this new affront. As far back as she could remember, Mammy Joella had been a pleasant, if slightly decrepit, servant; loving, forgiving, and slow to anger. "You can't hit me! You're just a nigger!"

"I'm a nigger, awright; but I'm the only nigger y'all got!" Mammy Joella hissed back. With that, she returned her attention to the Nutcracker, closing the door in Hester's face.

o o o

The next day Mrs. Killigrew loaded her husband into the buckboard and went in to town to see Doc Turner. Doc Turner measured Ferris Killigrew's head with a pair of calipers and studied the extent of his patient's wounds before showing them a catalog from a company up north.

"There's nothing they can't make nowadays," he explained cheerily. "Wooden legs, hook arms, glass eyes, tin noses... Course it helps there's such a large demand! Now, what can I do you for, Ferris?"

o o o

The Sunday-go-to-meeting jaw came in the mail a month later. The Killigrew children watched as their mother unwrapped the parcel in the kitchen. While Francis was more interested in playing with the cast-off stamps and string, Hester's attention was riveted on the package's contents.

The Nutcracker's new jaw had its own special case that reminded Hester of the box Mama used to keep her emerald necklace and pearl brooch in, back when she used to have jewelry. The jaw rested on a maroon velvet lining, a network of straps and buckles that resembled a dog's muzzle folded underneath it.

Mrs. Killigrew had sent the artificial limb company one of the few photographs she had of Mr. Killigrew from before the war. The custom fitting cost more, but Doc Turner had assured them it was worth it. Seeing the replica jaw displayed like a watch in a jeweler's window, flustered Mrs. Killigrew somewhat. Outside of noticing it had been painted to mimic European skin tones and was of a distinctly

KNUCKLES AND TALES: SUNDAY GO TO MEETING JAW

masculine cast, it was difficult to judge how closely the people at the artificial limb company had hewed to the photograph.

"Ferris, look! It's here!"

Ferris Killigrew stared at the gleaming piece of hard wood on its velvet cushion but did not move to touch it.

"Let's try it on," Mrs. Killigrew urged.

Killigrew grunted and slowly unfastened the straps that held his army-issue wooden jaw in place. Mrs. Killigrew did not allow her smile to slip as she averted her eyes.

When he'd finished adjusting the new straps, he shuffled over to the cheval glass his wife kept in the corner of the room and studied his new jaw.

He had to admit that it didn't look nearly as fake as the old one. It fit a damn sight better than his old one, too, although it's unnaturally rosy pigmentation made it look like he'd never washed his face above the jaw line.

"Oh, Ferris! It's better than I thought it would be!" Mrs. Killigrew smiled. "It makes you look—like you!" She slid her arms around her husband's waist, pressing her head against his shoulder, like she did in their courting days. "Now you can go to church this Sunday!"

Killigrew clumsily returned her hug, trying hard not to cry again.

"I love you, Ferris," she whispered.

He wanted to tell her that he loved her too; that it had been that love that kept him alive in the prisoner of war camp all those horrible months; that his love for her had drawn him back across four states, despite harsh weather, harsher treatment, and the threat of death by starvation or disease.

He wanted to tell her all these things, but that was impossible now.

As Doc Turner had warned them, weeks ago, the model Mrs. Killigrew had chosen for her husband, while expensive, was purely ornamental. All it was good for was looking natural.

o o o

"But Mama! Everyone will be looking at us!"

"So let them look, then," sighed Mrs. Killigrew, who was busy taking in a pair of her husband's old pants. She frowned at her handiwork. Even after all she'd done, Ferris would still need to wear suspenders and a belt.

"Mama! You don't understand!" The very idea of walking into the First Methodist Church of Seven Devils, Arkansaw, with the Nutcracker made Hester's stomach knot up.

"You're right I don't understand!" Mrs. Killigrew barked. "I don't understand why you're acting like such an ungrateful little monster! Here the Good Lord brings your daddy back from the war—"

"He's not Daddy! He's not!"

"See here, young lady! You're not so grown up I can't take you over my knee! If I hear another outburst like that, I'll cut myself a switch and lash you bloody! You're going to church with us tomorrow even if I have to drag you behind the buckboard like a heifer bound for market!"

"You don't care! You don't care about me at all!" Hester bellowed, knocking her mother's sewing basket off the kitchen table with one sweep of her hand. "All you're interested in is that—that—Nutcracker! You think you can turn him into Daddy and make everything like it used to be! But you can't! Daddy's dead!"

"Hester!" Mrs. Killigrew grabbed her daughter with her left hand, twisting Hester's right arm behind her back. "That's it, young lady! That's all I'm going to take out of you!" she spat, raising her right hand.

"Go ahead! Hit me! Slap me!" Hester taunted through her tears. "Beat on me all you like! It's still the truth!"

Mrs. Killigrew hesitated for a moment then lowered her hand, pulling her daughter to her bosom. Hester struggled for a moment, but her mother's grip was firm. After a few seconds she began to cry—great, wracking sobs—while Mrs. Killigrew held her daughter tight, rocking her like she used to do, not so many years ago.

o o o

The Killigrew family always sat in the third pew on the left hand side of the aisle. It was a tradition that dated back before Hester's birth. For as long as she could remember, her family always sat there during Sunday services.

As they walked down the aisle, everybody turned and looked. Hester's cheeks glowed like hot coals. She could feel Fanny Walchanski's greedy eyes on them, devouring every detail for later recitation. The thought of what she would have to face at school the next day made Hester tighten her grip on Francis's hand. Her little brother began to whine, but she quickly hushed him.

She could hear the members of the congregation mumbling amongst themselves, the ladies agitating the still air with their fans as they craned their necks for a better look. Reverend Cakebread watched

KNUCKLES AND TALES: SUNDAY GO TO MEETING JAW

from behind the pulpit as the Killigrews approached the front of the church. He was a round, pink-faced man with heavy eyebrows the size and shape of caterpillars. Right then the caterpillars looked like they were trying to crawl into his hair.

Aside from being keenly aware that everybody was watching them, the service went as usual, with Francis curling up on the bench for a nap next to his sister halfway into Reverend Cakebread's sermon.

Bored by the minister's nasal drone, Hester found herself looking at the Nutcracker and was startled to glimpse the faint outline of her father's profile. Without realizing what she was doing, she brushed her fingers against his sleeve.

The Nutcracker turned his head and looked at her, breaking the illusion. The sadness in his eyes reminded Hester of the time she found the rabbit in the snare.

And then Reverend Cakebread was saying; "...and if there are any announcements any of you in the congregation would care to make right now..?"

Mrs. Killigrew stood up, nervously straightening the shawl around her shoulders. "I would like to make an announcement, if I could, Reverend." The minister nodded his agreement, and Mrs. Killigrew turned to face the congregation. "As you no doubt already heard, my husband—Captain Ferris Killigrew, who I had thought lost to this world—has been returned to his rightful home, thanks to Our Lord. He is now once more fit to reclaim his place in society. I would like to extend an open invitation to all of you here today to stop by our place after church and help my family celebrate God's mercy. There will be food and drink for everyone."

After Mrs. Killigrew sat down Mr. Eichorn stood up and announced that there would be a Ku Klux meeting that night at the ruins of Old Man Stackpole's plantation house, then they sang the benediction and church was over.

o o o

There was a fly walking on the potato salad. Mrs. Killigrew waved a hand at the intruder, only to have it land on one of the deviled eggs.

"Mama, can't we eat yet?"

"You know better than to ask me that, Hester! You know we've got company coming!" She gave her son's hand a quick slap, forcing him to let go of an oatmeal cookie. "Francis! No!"

Francis plopped down on the floor and began to cry, sucking on his chastised fingers.

Ferris Killigrew sat on the parlor love seat, looking like a well-dressed scarecrow, his hands folded in his lap. He could not bring himself to meet his wife's eyes.

Mrs. Killigrew massaged her forehead, trying to stall the sick headache she knew was coming. All the money she spent on food. Killing one of their best chickens. And no one had the decency to show up. Not one. She retreated into the kitchen, where Mammy Joella was grinding Ferris's evening allotment of grits and blackstrap molasses into a fine mush.

"An'one show up yet?"

"Not yet. No, I take that back. Reverend Cakebread came by just after church."

"Tha's a preacher-man's job; payin' visits on folks no-one else wants t'mess wif."

"That's not true! Ferris was born and raised in Seven Devils! He has plenty of friends! You know that!"

The old woman sighed wearily but did not halt grinding the grits into baby food. "Tha's fore the war. Things different now. Folks hereabouts used to thinkin' Mr. Ferris daid. They mo' comfortable wif him that way, I reckon."

"What are you babbling about?" snapped Mrs. Killigrew.

"If'n he'd come back whole stead'a crippled-up, things might be different. Mebbe. But he ain't. He reminds folks things ain't ne'er gonna be th' same. Like us black folks. He's embarassin'. He reminds folks of what they done lost."

Mrs. Killigrew stared, dumbstruck, at the gnarled old Negress. In the fifteen years since she'd become a member of the Killigrew home, this was the only time Mammy Joella had spoken to her about something besides housework and childcare. It was as if the doorstop had suddenly taken to spouting prophecy.

The moment his mother left the room, Francis got off the floor and helped himself to the oatmeal cookies. After satisfying his hunger, he waddled over to his father and offered him a cookie.

Killigrew accepted the offering, nodding his thanks and trying his best to smile around the jaw. It wasn't easy. He ruffled his son's curls and allowed his hand to linger, caressing the boy's cheeks and smooth brow with his trembling fingers.

KNUCKLES AND TALES: SUNDAY GO TO MEETING JAW

When he looked up, he saw Hester standing in the parlor door, watching him the way you'd look at a bug.

o o o

He was found the next morning, hanging from the chandelier hook in the parlor, still dressed in his nightshirt. His face was darkened with congested blood while his lower jaw seemed to glow with rosy health. Although the Sunday-go-to-meeting jaw wasn't any good for eating or talking, it had proved adequate for suicide.

Mrs. Killigrew found him. She stared at her husband's body for a long moment then went upstairs and woke Hester. She told her daughter to take the mule and ride into town and fetch Mr. Mouzon, Seven Devil's undertaker.

After she made sure Hester had left by the back door, Mrs. Killigrew went to her room and dressed. When she returned to the parlor to await the undertaker's arrival, she discovered Mammy Joella standing in the doorway, staring up at her former master.

"Mammy Joella?"

The old woman grunted to herself and turned, brushing past her mistress without looking at her.

"Joella!"

Her only answer was the slamming of the back door.

o o o

Hester sat on the love seat and watched the wax trickle down the sides of the thick white candles burning at either end of the Nutcracker's coffin. She was dressed in her best black dress, her hair fixed with a black velvet ribbon. She swung her feet back and forth, watching the tips of her shoes disappear then reappear from under the hem of her skirt.

She could hear her mother talking in hushed tones with Reverend Cakebread and Mr. Mouzon in the kitchen. Francis was crawling on his hands and knees on the worn Persian carpet, pushing his little wooden train round and round in circles. Hester knew she should tell him to stop grubbing around on the floor in his good suit, but she also knew that would only make him cry, and she really didn't want to deal with that right now.

Hester wished Mammy Joella was still around so she wouldn't be expected to keep an eye on her little brother all the time. But Mammy

Joella had disappeared the same day the Nutcracker hanged himself, walking away from her cabin with nothing but the clothes on her back, a gunny sack full of bread, some goat cheese and a fruit jar full of sassafras tea.

Mama had complained to Sheriff Cooper about it, but he hadn't been of much help.

"What do you expect me to do about it, Nell? Set th' hounds on her? Niggers can leave whene'er they see fit, now."

Still, Hester thought her mother was holding up well, under the circumstances. In many ways she seemed more tired than grief-stricken. To Hester's knowledge, her mother had yet to shed a tear. Whenever she responded to the condolences offered her, there was hollowness in her voice. Hester knew that, secretly, her mother was relieved that it was all over; that she no longer had to pretend that the Nutcracker was her husband. Better to bury him and get on with the business of living. She wondered what new schoolyard taunt Fanny Walchanski would dream up to commemorate the event and was surprised to discover she no longer really cared what Fanny Walchanski thought or did.

Hester stared at the Nutcracker, stretched out in his narrow pine box, a lily clamped to his motionless chest. Mr. Mouzon had done a good job, for once. The Nutcracker's face was now the same color as his jaw, giving his appearance a continuity it had lacked in life.

As she stared at the Nutcracker's profile, a weird feeling crept over her, like the one in church two days earlier. For a moment she found herself looking at the face of her father, Ferris Killigrew. Then the vision wavered and was gone. In its place was the dead Nutcracker; only now the rabbit was free of the snare.

Hester felt something on her face and touched her cheek. She stared at the tears for a long time before she realized she was crying.

SEVEN DEVILS

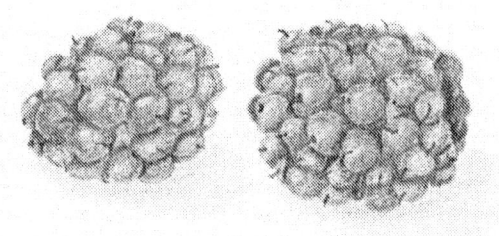

It was 1925. Eunice McQuistion was five, going on six. Her parents lived in Little Rock, but that summer her mother was experiencing a particularly troubled pregnancy, so her paternal grandparents volunteered to look after Eunice until the baby came.

Eunice's Grandpa Junius and Granny Lucille lived in Choctaw County, in a small town called Seven Devils. Eunice had never really been to Seven Devils before, although her parents claimed they'd taken her down on the train to visit her grandparents when she was just a baby. Eunice didn't remember any of it, so as far as she was concerned it never really happened.

One morning in May Eunice's daddy took her down to the train station and put her on the train to Seven Devils. He gave her an apple to eat and a dime to buy soda pop along the way and kissed her goodbye, telling her the next time he saw her she'd have a brand-new baby brother or sister, then handed her over to the conductor. Eunice tried to be brave and not cry too much.

When the train pulled up to the station at Seven Devils, Eunice saw a old man waiting on the platform. He was tall and skinny, with white hair and wire-rim glasses. Although she had never seen him before, she knew he had to be her Grandpa Junius.

As she got off the train, the old man stepped forward to take her bag, smiling down at her with his cornflower-blue eyes. Hidden within the folds and wrinkles of his face, she could glimpse the likeness of her father.

"You must be Eunice. Wait until Mother sees you! Why, you're the picture of your Aunt Gladys when she was a girl!"

After collecting her luggage, they walked to end of the train platform, where his buckboard waited. Eunice's father drove a Model T, but Grandpa Junius preferred mules to horse-power.

If there was ever love at first sight, that was what happened between Junius McQuistion and his granddaughter.

NANCY A. COLLINS

Grandpa Junius and Granny Lucille lived outside Seven Devils proper, their house being located on what was known as Plantation Road. As they bounced along the ruts, Eunice's basic impression of the area was that it was very, very flat and very, very green, with huge fields of cotton and sorghum interspersed with bayous and forests. It was also very hot and humid, the chirping of the cicadas becoming a persistent, distant hum the farther they got from town.

Granny Lucille was waiting patiently for them on the front porch glider, shelling peas into a big metal bowl in her lap. The elder McQuistions lived in the same house in which they had raised their five children. They had added on a couple of rooms and had the building wired for electricity, but it still lacked indoor plumbing. There was a privy in the back yard, along with a old barn that housed their brace of mules and a milk cow, as well as a fenced-in chicken coop. Further back was a small truck garden, where Junius tended neat rows of tomatoes, corn, cabbage, watermelon, and snap-peas. And when Eunice saw the fine old oak tree in the front yard and the brand-new swing hanging from its lowest limb, she knew this was going to be her best summer ever.

o o o

Junius McQuistion was sixty-six years old and in astonishing health for a man who had come of age amidst great hardship and deprivation.

His parents came to America from Scotland in 1855, settling in the hills of Tennessee, where they struggled to make a living as farmers, only to lose what little they had during the Civil War. Orphaned at fifteen, the family home and holdings lost, Junius made his way to Memphis, where he worked on the dock, loading cotton onto the riverboats that traveled up and down the Mississippi. In 1876 he fell in love with and married Lucille Cavanaugh, the foreman's daughter.

While he was a good, conscientious worker, there was little promise of advancement at his job. Then, in 1879, he met Ezra Stackpole, a wealthy land-owner from Arkansas desperate to find reliable, educated employees to help him convert his family's plantation, Sugar House, into a sugar refinery. Stackpole offered him a job as Sugar House's dock foreman and he took it, bringing his wife and young family with him.

Forty-six years and five children later, he and his wife were was still there and, thanks to the arrival of the railroad and timber industries in

KNUCKLES AND TALES: SEVEN DEVILS

Choctaw County at the turn of the century, both of which showed interest in property Junius had acquired over the years, the McQuistions were the second wealthiest family in town, just after the Stackpoles.

Not that Eunice knew any of this at the time of her arrival in Seven Devils. All she was aware of was that Grandpa Junius and Granny Lucille were her father's parents and that they sent her presents on her birthdays and Christmas. The history of Seven Devils, not to mention its arcane social hierarchy, belonged to the world of grown-ups and had nothing to do with her.

But not for long.

o o o

They were in Badinger's Grocery, Grandpa Junius mulling over his wife's shopping list. Although his eyesight had begun to fail in the last few years, Junius was loathe to admit it. Eunice's job on these excursions was to "decipher" her grandmother's perfectly legible handwriting.

While they were waiting to be waited on, a middle-aged heavy-set man dressed in a rumpled seersucker suit, the armpits sodden in the July heat, entered the store. While Eunice had never seen the stranger before, she found herself clutching her grandfather's pants leg in fear. Junius stiffened slightly at the sight of the large, florid-faced man.

"Afternoon, Asa."

The bigger man grunted something approximating a response as he brushed past Junius. Mr. Badinger stopped midway through filling Mrs. Winthrop's order, a nervous smile on his lips.

"Good day, Mr. Stackpole! I'll be right with you!"

"Well, I never!" Mrs. Winthrop sniffed, drawing herself up to her full height of 5'2".

Asa Stackpole pulled a large, black cigar from the breast pocket of his seersucker, bit the end off and spat it onto the floor, fixing the retired school teacher with a cold stare, his eyes as small and greedy as a pig's. Mrs. Winthrop quickly averted her gaze and busied herself with checking and re-checking her half-filled order.

Five minutes later, Asa Stackpole left Badinger's Grocery with a box filled with various groceries and sundries, a trail of foul-smelling cigar smoke hanging in his wake.

"Sorry about that," Mr. Badinger said weakly, mopping his wide brow with a handkerchief he fished from his back pocket. "But you know how those Stackpoles get when they have to wait."

"Like father, like son," Mrs. Winthrop sniffed. "You shouldn't cater to that brute, Caleb! Even if he is the richest man in Choctaw County!"

"What can I say, Miz Winthrop? He holds the note on this place. I'll be another five years paying him off."

Mrs. Winthrop shook her head in disgust, nearly unseating her sunbonnet. "I like to think of myself as a good Christian, but I'll be blessed if I can find a single kind word for Asa Stackpole and his family."

While Mr. Badinger finished filling Mrs. Winthrop's order, a small black boy hurried into the store, grabbing Junius' wrist. Eunice watched as her grandfather bent down so the child could whisper hurriedly into his ear.

Mr. Badinger, who had climbed a ladder to retrieve a bolt of cloth, frowned down at the wide-eyed negro child. "What are you doing in here, boy? You know you're not allowed in here...!"

Junius straightened up, folding the grocery list and stuffing it in his pocket. "It's alright, Caleb. The boy's on an errand." He turned to address the black child. "You tell your ma I'll be there directly." He took his grandchild's small, smooth hand in his large, wrinkled one. "C'mon, Eunie."

"Where we going, Grandpa?"

"We're going to see Ash, child. He's bad sick."

Ash was the small, bald banty-rooster of a man with skin the color and consistency of crepe paper who did odd jobs for Grandpa Junius. Granny Lucille said Ash had been born a slave and was a full-grown man when Grandpa Junius first met him, forty-five years ago.

Ash lived in Niggertown, Seven Devils' shadow community. According to the public census, it was part of the same township, but in reality the negroes had their own grocery, their own churches, and their own restaurants.

Ash's two-room shotgun was situated on the far end of Railroad Street, close enough to the tracks that its foundations shivered every time a train passed. There was a small crowd gathered on the front stoop that spilled into the yard. Eunice pressed herself against her grandfather when the dark, sweating faces turned to stare at them as the buckboard drew to a halt.

A black man in a frayed frock coat stepped forward, a dog-eared Bible tucked in the crook of his right arm, as Junius climbed down from the buckboard.

"Afternoon, Mr. Junius."

"Afternoon, Deacon Pike."

KNUCKLES AND TALES: SEVEN DEVILS

"He been asking for you."

Junius reached to lift Eunice from her seat. "That a fact?"

"He won't let me bring in th' preacher." This came from a short, squat woman the color of teak. Her heavy arms were locked under her sagging bosom. The thin, frightened pickaninny who had approached her grandfather in the grocery peeped out at Eunice from behind her faded gingham skirts. "Every time I try sneakin' him in, he gets to squawkin' like a mad hen and cussin'—! Lord, you wouldn't believe the nastiness that comes out of that ol' devil's mouth!"

"Then I guess I ought to go see what he wants, Cordelia."

The crowd moved aside to let them pass as he moved toward the front porch. Eunice could feel their silent gaze sliding over him like water drawn from the well. She tightened her grip on her grandfather's hand. She'd never been around so many black people before at one time in one place. Eunice was familiar with Ash and Jericho, the coloreds that helped her daddy during planting, and Queen Esther, the woman that helped her mama with the heavy lifting, but these broad, dark faces were alien to her.

The front room of the shotgun was close and incredibly hot. A pot belly stove squatted in the corner like an ancient god from warmer climes. The odor of wood smoke, black-eyed peas, and fatback was thick in the air. A double mattress and two smaller sleeping pallets filled what was left of the floor, leaving only a narrow pathway to the second of the two rooms.

The back room was dark, the light shuttered by curtains made from flour sacks and burlap bags. An iron bedstead dominated the room, which was littered with empty patent-medicine bottles. The smell was foul and Eunice felt her grandfather hesitate. Something moved in the bed.

"You bring him? You got him like I told you?"

"I'm here, Ash." Her grandfather let go of her hand and moved closer to the bed. Unnoticed, Eunice ghosted closer for a better look.

Ash looked like a tiny doll with the face of a dried apple swaddled in threadbare quilts and blankets, his head and shoulders supported by a mound of pillows. His long, knotted hands lay atop the covers, fingers plucking blindly at the pattern of the quilt.

"Cordelia says you won't let her bring in a preacher," Junius gently chided.

"Don't need no preacher-man tell me I've sinned," Ash rasped. "I know that. Lord knows that, too. I know I'm dying. Been long time comin'. Mebbe too long, for some." He shot his yellowed eyes toward his great-grandchild, standing in the doorway.

"Lissen to that trash, Mister Junius! Lord, you'd think I ain't lifted a hand t'feed and clothe his black heinie!"

"Clear off, woman. I got things that must be said."

Even though his voice was so weak it was little more than a whisper, Eunice could hear the echo of the man Ash must have been when he was young. Cordelia opened her mouth then snapped it shut with an audible click. She gave the old man a glare that was both angry and fearful, then turned and left the two whites alone with her great-grandfather.

"You shouldn't talk to Cordelia like that, Ash."

A weak smile wrinkled the dying man's seamed face even further. "I know that. But that woman's so bull-headed—! Just like her great-granny!" The smile disappeared amongst the creases in his face. "What you know about 'fessin', Mister Junius?"

"You mean confessing? Like to a priest?" Her grandfather looked lost for a moment. "I was raised Presbyterian, Ash..."

"It don't make no never mind," the old black man gasped. "I heard once that 'fessin' be good for the soul—lettin' out the bad things you done so's they can be aired. Mebbe if you 'fess up to what you done, long time ago, you don't have to go to Hell for doing it. Mebbe that's true. Mebbe not. I never had me the education to know them things. But, I know what I know. And that's I can't go to my grave carryin' what I got locked up 'side me." He tapped his ribcage weakly with one broad, spatulate finger.

Junius eased himself onto the edge of the bed, his attention focused on its occupant. "Ash—what is it that's botherin' you? I've known you almost as long as I have my wife. You're no sinner; no more than any man born."

Ash's eyes clouded and tears leaked onto his cheeks. "I should have told it sooner, but I was always scared. Scared of that man. Old Man Stackpole. When he died I thought I could come forward and say my piece. But the boy—lord, the boy's worse than his daddy! If I'd knowed back then I'd live to be so old—mebbe I'd have kilt the old bastard and his whelp then and there, even if it got me lynched!

"It was Stackpole's idea. Not mine. I didn't want no part of it, but he threatened t'shoot me if I didn't help him. But I reckon I was used to crazy white folks tellin' me to do things I didn't want to do. Me and him and that boy of his went out after them folk..."

"Wait a minute, Ash..." Her grandfather's voice had become so hard it was alien to her. "What folks?"

KNUCKLES AND TALES: SEVEN DEVILS

"Them folks that left all them years back. Mister and Miz Newburg, the Rialls, and the Haldemans..."

Junius McQuistion's face paled and a muscle in his jaw jumped.

"We set out after 'em after Mister Stackpole thought everyone was asleep. It didn't take us long to find them, either. They hadn't got too far, what with them young'uns... They had pitched camp near Bayou Beelzebub. They was asleep when we came up on 'em. Old Man Stackpole, he said we should surround 'em, in case any of 'em trys to escape. Then they commenced firin' into the camp! They didn't have no chance! No chance at all!

"I was too sacred to do nothin' but fire up in the trees. The young'uns—I could hear them cryin' after the shootin' stopped. Old Man Stackpole and that boy of his were walkin' through what was left of the camp, an' I seen Old Man Stackpole bend over like he was tyin' his shoe, then I seen the knife in his hand. He was—he was killin' the young'uns, just like some injun! Then he comes up to me and hands me this shovel and says 'Git to work, nigger!'

"I ended up diggin' those poor folks graves. And he had me bury 'em deep, on account that he didn't want no animals scatterin' their bones where anyone might find 'em. After I finished buryin' them, Old Man Stackpole looks me straight in the eye and he says, 'If you ever tell anyone about this, nigger, I'm gonna kill you and that flock of pickaninnies you got'. So I kept what I'd seen and done to myself. I was scared that if I did say anything, folks would think I was just some crazy nigger and I'd still end up dead.

"But I couldn't die with all that horrible truth trussed up in me. All that blood and sin—I couldn't tell that to no preacher-man—not one young enough to be my grandson, leastwise. You know what Old Man Stackpole was like. You know I'm tellin' you God's own truth."

Junius stared at the low ceiling of the sick room as if trying to decipher a message written in the rafters. Eunice noticed her grandfather's hands were trembling. Somehow that frightened her far more than Ash's talk of blood and sin. Junius drew in a deep breath and lowered his gaze. Ash's brittle frame lay silent and unmoving, his yellowed eyes already glazing.

Eunice was suddenly aware of her grandfather watching her. She stood rigid in his gaze, the sweat soaking through her cotton dress. Their eyes locked and Eunice took her first step into the secret world of grown-ups.

"This never happened, you understand?" His voice was so hard. He didn't sound like her grandfather anymore. "You didn't hear a word."

She nodded vigorously, her voice stolen by an unexpected rush of tears. For the first and only time in her life Eunice was frightened by the tall old man with the sharp blue eyes.

"Good lass." Her grandfather rose from the deathbed and went into the front room, leaving her alone with Ash. Eunice watched as a fly landed on the dead man's withered cheek and sipped the tears and sweat trapped in the folds of his skin. She was vaguely aware of Cordelia's braying sobs, signaling that the official mourning could now begin. Was this what it was like to be grown-up? Knowing things others shouldn't? Everything seemed so different now, viewed through the veil of secrets drawn about her.

They went home without the groceries that evening. Although Granny Lucille blessed him out three ways to Sunday, Grandpa Junius never explained what had happened that afternoon.

Later that night Ash's shack caught fire and burned to the ground. Cordelia and her seven children, including the tiny little black boy who had summoned them to his great-great-grandfather's deathbed, died in the blaze. Grandpa Junius commented that it was odd that Cordelia's shanty could catch fire during the dead of summer, but said nothing else about the matter.

Two weeks later, Eunice's mother went into labor. Unfortunately, the baby—a boy—became tangled in the umbilical cord and strangled. The doctor tried to remove the stillborn boy-child trapped inside her. Towards the end they were forced to dismember the unborn infant and remove it, piecemeal, from her womb. Three days after her second child's aborted delivery, Eunice's mother died of childbed fever.

Eunice's father was distraught, and it was decided that Eunice would remain with her grandparents until he was capable of handling her. So summer lengthened, became indian summer, turned into autumn, and Eunice was still living in Seven Devils.

o o o

The McQuistion's land abutted that of the Stackpole's. The massive white pillars of the Stackpole's ancestral antebellum mansion—Sugar House—could be glimpsed through the grove of trees that separated their respective lots. One of the first things Eunice had been told never to do was wander onto the Stackpole's property. Both Grandpa Junius and Granny Lucille had been adamant on the subject.

"You must never climb the fence in the north pasture, is that

KNUCKLES AND TALES: SEVEN DEVILS

understood? The woods on the other side belong to Mr. Stackpole. And the Stackpole's don't take kindly to trespassers. I know for a fact he's got traps set out there..."

"Junius! There's no need to frighten the child!" Granny Lucille whispered.

"There's no need in the child losin' a hand or a foot in one of Asa's cursed man-traps, either!" he returned sharply. "Those woods are dangerous; understand, young lady?"

She understood. But simple understanding soon turned into curiosity, and it wasn't long before she was sneaking over the fence into the Stackpole's land. It was on one of these forbidden ventures into the neighboring property that she met Asa Stackpole's first-born son and heir, Enos.

In was early September and Eunice was wandering through the woods when she came upon a dead rabbit caught in a snare. The rabbit lay twisted and stiff in the grass, a thin loop of silver wire pulled so tight about its neck it had sliced through its fur. There was dried blood crusted about it mouth and nostrils. Both fascinated and repulsed, Eunice knelt to study the dead rabbit.

"Don't touch that!"

Eunice gasped and turned around, surprised to find herself being watched by a boy dressed in brown wool knickerbockers and a matching vest and cap. He was twelve or so, with a spotty complexion, bad teeth, and nervous, watery eyes. Even though he was taller and heavier and a good six years older than her, Eunice couldn't find it in her to be scared of the strange boy.

"Why not?"

"Because its ours."

"Why do you want a dead bunny?"

The boy blinked, looking confused. Obviously no one had ever asked him such a question before. "Because its ours," he repeated. "So don't you go touchin' it!"

Eunice stood up, hands on her hips. "Why would I want to touch your ol' dead bunny, anyways?" she asked indignantly. "So who are you anyway, tellin' me what to touch and what not to touch?"

"I'm a Stackpole! Enos Stackpole! Asa Stackpole's my daddy! And you're not supposed to be here! You're trespassin'!"

"I'm not tres—tres—that word you said! I'm just walking through the woods!"

"Are not! You're trespassin'! And trespassers ain't supposed to touch nothin' that belongs to us—which means the trees, flowers, rocks, animals and everything!"

"If that's how you feel about it, you can just keep your stupid ol' dead bunny!"

Before Enos could generate a reply, there was a bellowing sound from the direction of the Stackpole residence.

"Enos! Where the hell are you, boy?"

A look of pure terror crossed the boy's face, helping Eunice decide that now was a good time to go home. As she ran towards the split rail fence that marked the division line of McQuistion and Stackpole territory, she looked over her shoulder in time to see Enos' father emerge from the surrounding bramble, his face even redder than before, a leather strap clutched tightly in one hand.

"I told you to see to them chores, boy! When I tell you to do something, by damn, I expect it to be done!"

Enos turned his head and lifted one hand to fend away the blow he knew was soon to follow. The sight of his son cringing in front of him seemed to enrage Stackpole even more.

"Flinch away from me, will you? Well, by damn! I'll sure as hell give you something to flinch about!"

"No, daddy! No! I'll be good!"

"Who are you to be tellin' me 'no', boy?"

Eunice grimaced in sympathy as the strap fell across the hapless boy's shoulders, shaking her from her temporary paralysis. She was already over the fence and running as fast as she could in the direction of her grandparents' house before Mr. Stackpole could land another blow.

Later that night, as her Grandpa Junius was tucking her into bed, Eunice brought up the subject of the Stackpoles for the first time since that hot summer afternoon in Ash's shack.

"Grandpa—?"

"What is it, sweetness?"

"Can I ask you something?"

"I reckon so."

"Why is Mr. Stackpole mean to his son?"

Grandpa Junius stopped smiling and gave her a funny look.

"What do you mean, Eunie?"

"Why does he whup on him?"

"You saw Mr. Stackpole beat Enos?"

Eunice nodded, her manner very serious. "With a big ol' leather strap, like the one my daddy uses to sharpen his razor!"

Grandpa Junius winced slightly and shook his head. "You saw this?"

"I saw them out in the woods. Mr. Stackpole was whippin' Enos and yellin' and cussin' him out."

KNUCKLES AND TALES: SEVEN DEVILS

"Eunice, you know you ain't supposed to go near those woods..."

"I wasn't," she lied slightly. "I was on our side of the fence! But why is Mr. Stackpole mean like that?"

"Honey, I know this might be hard to understand, seein' you're so young. But some folks—well, some folks just seem to be born with a mean streak in 'em. Asa Stackpole's one of those kind of people. So was his daddy, who you've never met and never will, thank the Lord."

"Was he always mean, Grandpa? Like he is now? Even as a baby?"

"I never knew Asa when he was a baby, but I'm willing to say he didn't start off that way. When I first met him, he was eleven years old. Your granny and me, we'd come down from Memphis so's I could work for Old Man Stackpole—Asa's pappy.

"Old Man Stackpole was ornery as a bag full of rattlers. He wasn't used to having white help—he got his start with slaves and he sure resented having to pay out wages. At first he treated me and the others he hired to help get Sugar House back on its feet like white niggers. He even took a buggy whip to one of the foremen who talked back to him! Although, as bad as we got it, I know his family must have got a whole lot worse.

"Although he paid us good, some of the workers had enough of Old Man Stackpole as they could stand and struck out on their own, taking their families and belongings with 'em. They were going to head towards Ashley County and land jobs in the sawmill." Grandpa Junius shook his head, smiling grimly. "Lord, was Old Man Stackpole mad when he found out! You'd think they were slaves turned rabbit!"

"Is that when he killed those people?"

The smile disappeared from his face and he fixed Eunice with a hard stare. "Child, don't you *ever* tell anyone about that! Never *ever*, do you understand? Some things ain't safe to know; leastwise, not in a town as small as Seven Devils."

"But what about those people? The ones he and his daddy killed back then?"

"Sometimes its better to just let things lie, Eunice. I don't expect you to understand all what I'm sayin' to you. Ezra Stackpole died thirty years ago, but his son is still very much alive. And Asa Stackpole is a dangerous, bad man. Old men and little girls don't mean a thing to him."

o o o

Two weeks after Eunice saw Asa Stackpole beat his son, Granny Lucille decided it was time to start putting up preserves for the winter.

So Grandpa Junius took Eunice out to pick blackberries.

According to her grandfather, the best blackberries in all of Choctaw County could be found in the marshy brambles of the surrounding bayous.

On the map, the names of the seven streams sounded arcane, even foreboding: Bayou Asmodeus, Bayou Astaroth, Bayou Baphomet, Bayou Beelzebub, Bayou Leviathan, Bayou Lucifer, and Bayou Mammon suggested dark, evil trees dripping Spanish moss, infested with owls and bats. In reality, they were simply seven interconnecting creeks that emptied into the nearby Mississippi River and, during the rainy season, contributed to the town's continued isolation from the surrounding communities.

Eunice and her grandfather left the house that mild September afternoon, dressed in old clothes, wearing canvas gloves and rubber galoshes, carrying tin pails. It was such a nice day, Grandpa Junius decided to leave the mule in the barn, so they set out for the blackberry patch near Bayou Beelzebub on foot.

Eunice looked at the surrounding underbrush nervously. "What about snakes, Grandpa? There won't be any snakes, will there?"

"Not this late in the year, honey. Most of 'em are hibernatin' by now. They're sound asleep and won't be interested in botherin' us," Grandpa Junius replied reassuringly.

The blackberries weren't exactly black—more a deep purple—but they smelled nice and tasted even better. Grandpa Junius had to scold Eunice more than once about eating more berries than they picked. Not that he was averse to sampling the pickings, either.

"You haven't lived until you've tasted your Granny's blackberry pie!" Grandpa Junius exclaimed as he plucked the ripe berries from their prickly vines. "She makes a mighty fine conserve, as well. In the forty-eight years since I first married your grandmother, she's yet to serve me a meal that wasn't fit for a king—even when we was poorer'n church mice!" He straightened up, massaging the small of his back, grimacing slightly. "Oof! Cold weather must be on the way! Whenever my back gets to achin' like that, it's a sure sign there'll be frost of the pumpkin in day or two, you can take my word for—"

There was a loud, sharp sound, as if someone had broken a green tree branch over their knee, and Grandpa Junius suddenly collapsed to the ground. There was a hole in the side of his head the size of a quarter and his swan-white hair was now the color of red wine.

"Grandpa?" Eunice clutched her half-filled pail to her chest, her eyes huge. "Grandpa?"

KNUCKLES AND TALES: SEVEN DEVILS

Her grandfather remained both motionless and silent. A twig snapped, causing her to turn and face her grandfather's killer.

Asa Stackpole stood behind her, dressed in the red plaid flannel shirt and canvas trousers of a hunter, a deer rifle held in the crook of one meaty arm. He stared down at her with dark, unreadable eyes. Enos, dressed and outfitted in a similar manner, stood in his father's shadow.

Mr. Stackpole clucked his tongue and shook his head slightly. "Will you look at that…What a shame. What a horrible shame…"

"You hurt my grandpa!" Eunice wailed.

Mr. Stackpole opened the breech of his rifle, jettisoning the spent shell. He acted as if he couldn't hear Eunice's sobs as he casually reloaded. "Such a tragic accident. It happens at least once a year, though: some poor soul shot while in the woods, mistaken for a deer. Who would have thought it would happen to Junius McQuistion, of all people?" He snapped the rifle shut, fixing Eunice with his cruel, piggish gaze. "It's just a cryin' shame what happened to him and his sweet, innocent little granddaughter…"

"You killed him! You killed my grandaddy! You did it on purpose!" Eunice screamed. "I hate you!" With that she hurled her pail at Mr. Stackpole, striking him in the shin.

Mr. Stackpole's smirk disappeared, to be replaced by a look of such sheer, unrestrained anger it frightened Eunice into silence. Mr. Stackpole grabbed Enos by the collar with his free hand and dragged him forward.

"Shoot her!" he snarled.

Enos was sweating and twitching like he had a fever, holding his rifle the way a man might handle a serpent. He licked his lips nervously, his eyes focused on the red mess leaking out of Junius' head.

"Daddy—"

"*I said shoot the little bitch!*" Mr. Stackpole roared. "Is that too much to ask, you little shit? You didn't have any trouble slittin' the throats of them pickaninnies when I told you!"

Enos shook his head as if trying to dislodge an earwig. "But—but they was niggers, Daddy! This is different—I *can't!* I can't do it!"

Mr. Stackpole gave his son a withering look of disgust. "I might as well cut off your John Thomas and put you in a dress, for all the good you're to me!"

"I don't want to do this, daddy—"

Mr. Stackpole silenced his son with a cuff to the ear. "*Want?* Since when does what anyone *wants* have to do with what has to be *done?* You think I '*wanted*' to kill the Haldemans, Rialls, and Newburgs forty-five years ago? No! But my daddy told me to do it, so I *did* it! It *had* to be done! You didn't hear *me* whinin' about what I did and didn't want! Now, do as I say, boy! Or it's the strap!"

Enos lifted the rifle to his shoulder, trembling even harder than before. Tears and snot ran freely from his eyes and nose as he struggled to restrain his sobs.

Mr. Stackpole rolled his eyes in disgust. "Stop blubberin' and do it!" he snapped.

Eyes squeezed into slits, teeth set, Enos fired into the branches overhead. Somewhere a mockingbird called out in alarm.

"Useless little shit!" Mr. Stackpole snarled, backhanding Enos hard enough to knock him to the ground. "If I want something done, I gotta do it myself!" He stepped forward, shouldering his rifle in one smooth movement. Mr. Stackpole cocked the trigger, looking down the barrel of his gun into Eunice's tear-washed face. "Your grandaddy shouldn't have taken you with him to that nigger's shack, little girl. It's his fault I gotta do this."

Something beneath the litter of dead leaves and windfall under Eunice's feet twitched. Even with certain death in the form of Mr. Stackpole's rifle scant inches from her face, part of her worried that it might be a snake.

Mr. Stackpole frowned and lowered the rifle a bit, scowling down at his boots. "What the hell—?"

The ground beneath Eunice's feet shuddered just like her grandaddy's mule did when it was cold and burst outward, sending clods of dark, damp earth in every direction. Mr. Stackpole swore as the earth continued to undulate and shiver underneath his boots. His coarse shouts abruptly turned into a shriek of terror as the first skeletal hand burst from the ground.

Eunice lifted her arms to protect her face and cried out, tripping over her grandfather's cooling body. Sprawled atop Junius' corpse, she stared in mute horror as three, then six pairs of hands clawed their way free of the dirt. Soon their heads emerged from the soil, like hideous flowers striving to greet the sun. Some of them still had a little withered flesh clinging to them, and almost every skull sported a hole in its temple or forehead. Eunice closed her eyes against the sight, but deep inside herself she could hear Ash's voice, echoing and re-echoing:

"They had pitched camp near Bayou Beelzebub...he had me bury 'em deep, on account that he didn't want no animals scatterin' their bones where anyone might find 'em..."

KNUCKLES AND TALES: SEVEN DEVILS

Mr. Stackpole was screaming now, flailing with his rifle butt at the dead things clutching his legs. He put the stock of the rifle through the skull of one of them, but it didn't seem to either notice or care. Eunice shut her eyes as tightly as she could and clamped her hands over her ears and stayed that way until Mr. Stackpole stopped making noise.

When she reopened her eyes, the ground was whole and unmarred. There was a large circle, over fifty feet in diameter, that was swept clear of leaves and other forest detritus, but other than that there was no evidence of anything out of the unusual having occurred that afternoon. There was also no sign of either Mr. Stackpole or his rifle.

Eunice found Enos on her way to get help. He was wandering on his own, smiling vacantly at the trees overhead. The front of his pants were wet and he smelled like Granny Lucille's compost heap. He smiled at Eunice the same way he smiled at the trees and didn't protest when she took him by the hand and lead him back to her grandparents' house.

o o o

Junius Gordon McQuistion's death was ruled an accident. While out hunting with his father, Enos Stackpole had mistaken the old man for a deer and shot him in the head. Then Asa Stackpole, while attempting to fetch help, apparently lost his way and wandered into quicksand, meeting his death before his son's eyes. Enos would never be the same again, poor boy.

Eunice returned to Little Rock after her grandfather's funeral. She never once told the adults what truly happened that day—not even her Granny Lucille. She knew they wouldn't believe her. And part of her did not want to be believed.

It wasn't too hard to convince herself that the official account of what transpired that September afternoon was what actually happened. But sometimes she had dreams. Dreams of being trapped deep within the dark, damp earth. Dreams of being held in bony arms dressed in tatters of rotten flesh and desiccated muscle, her mouth filled with dirt and screams.

She always woke from these dreams to find herself smiling.

HOW IT WAS WITH THE KRAITS

They're tearing down the old Krait house today. I reckon half the town will turn out to watch the bulldozer knock it down. Not that most folks here still remember anything about the Kraits, but in a place like Seven Devils, you got to get your thrills where you can.

There was a time, back before the Second World War, when the town centered on the Kraits and their comings and goings. That was because Old Man Krait owned it, right down to the last pair of raggedy underwear on the skinniest cropper's ass. I can still see him in my mind, clear as day, although I wasn't more than five or six when he died.

He was a long drink of water with wide shoulders and a face like an angry owl's. He'd suffered some kind of illness as a child and wore a funny-looking shoe with a heel as thick as my pa's work boot. I remember how he used to clomp down Railroad Street—which was Main Street back then—clutching that cane of his, and my pa and the other men-folk would take off their hats to bid him good day. I don't recollect him saying anything back. My mama, bless her soul, once slapped the bejesus out of me for asking why Old Man Krait wore such a funny shoe while he was still within earshot. I was only three or four and didn't know nothing about mortgages and the difference between bank presidents and dirt farmers.

While Old Man Krait might not have been much to look at, he had himself a pretty wife. Eugenia Krait was a fine-looking woman, no two ways about it, and Old Man Krait married her before she was out of school. She was fifteen and he was fifty, so you know tongues wagged about that. It was five years before they had themselves a kid. Jasper Krait and me was born in 1920; that's how I can keep most of what went on straight.

Jasper wasn't a well baby. He had the colic and cried all the time. I reckon Old Man Krait was too set in his ways to put up with having a little baby in his house. My mama found out from some of their help that Old Man Krait had his son's bottles doctored with cognac so he wouldn't cry.

When Jasper started to walk and get into things, Old Man Krait's way of handling it was to send his wife and child off to visit her kinfolks in Biloxi. For three years. Sometimes he'd take the train to spend holidays with them, but usually she would come to him. Without the boy, of course.

Then in 1925 Old Man Krait up and died while taking supper at his home. The day of the funeral everyone in Choctaw County, if not the whole of Southeast Arkansas, turned out on Railroad Street to watch the fancy hearse with etched glass and black plumed horses make its way to the Baptist church. My pa even put me up on his shoulders so's I could get a better look. Hell, it was almost as good as the time the circus came to town!

Everyone figured Eugenia would up and marry again right quick, what with her being beautiful, young, and rich to boot. But she never did. And she stayed put in Seven Devils, even though her folks were in Mississippi. Turned out she learned a lot from Old Man Krait in the ten years they was married. The gal had a head for business, as Choctaw County soon discovered when she took over running her husband's bank. But although she was good at driving hard bargains, the one thing Widow Krait was bad at was raising her son.

My mama was a tenderhearted woman by nature, and she felt sorry for Jasper, what with him losing his daddy and all; so she decided to invite him to my birthday party. The day of the party there comes this knock on our back door. When mama answered it she found one of Widow Kraits' niggers standing there holding a big box wrapped in a fancy ribbon. The nigger told mama that Widow Krait regretted that Jasper would be unable to attend my birthday party, but wanted me to have a present anyway.

The box was a wooden case full of painted tin soldiers laid out on a velvet lining. They were the finest toys I'd ever seen—much less owned. Since I couldn't have cared less if Jasper Krait came to my birthday party, I couldn't understand why my mama got her nose so far out of joint. She wanted to send the toy soldiers back, but I kicked up such a fuss she let me keep them. However, she made me put them in the closet so's the kids too poor to bring nothing but oranges or pecans wouldn't feel shamed. My mama was good that way. Afterwards, I overheard her tellin' my pa that it'd be a cold day in July before she'd extend another kindness to the Kraits.

I started first grade in '26 and went to the old three-room schoolhouse that used to stand where they got the Burger Bar now.

KNUCKLES AND TALES: HOW IT WAS WITH THE KRAITS

That's where I met up with Heck Jones, the Wilberforce Twins, Freddie Nayland, and the gal I ended up marrying. If Jasper Krait ever saw the inside of that school, I never heard tell about it. Hell, far as I know, he never set foot in a real school at all. His mama hired some fancy-pants tutor from the college over at Monticello to teach Jasper at home. The tutor came in on the train early each morning and left late every afternoon. I don't recall ever hearing his name.

The Widow Krait was still visiting her folks in Biloxi every summer and during Christmas. Her usual custom was to leave Seven Devils just before Decoration Day and stay gone until the first week of September. But for some reason, no one knows why, Widow Krait came home in July 1928, and never went to Biloxi again.

It wasn't long after that the rumor started that Widow Krait had bought a little nigger boy as a "companion" for Jasper. Not that anyone was surprised, mind you. By that time Jasper was already on his way to being, well, Jasper. He was the kind of young'un you'd have to hang a hambone on just to get the dog to play with him.

Every so often me and the gang would catch a glimpse of Jasper and his pet nigger playing in the Kraits' fenced-in backyard, but we couldn't have cared less. The gang didn't have much use for sissies, and you couldn't get much sissier than Jasper Krait. Why, his ma used to dress him up in Little Lord Fauntleroy outfits, just like Mary Pickford! Hell, any self-respecting boy would have gone to church nekkid rather than be seen dressed like that! As it was, the only time folks in Seven Devils got an unobstructed view of Jasper was during Sunday services, and even then the Kraits had a pew all to themselves.

Things pretty much kept on like that until '32. That was the year the Widow Krait got herself a beau.

She'd been having business dealings with some fella out of Memphis, who came down on the train to get her to sign some papers. Once he got a good look at her, he stayed a week. It was all proper, of course. He stayed at the Railroad Arms, which was a right nice hotel back in them days. No one was surprised, truth to tell. Eugenia Krait was still young and had her looks, and the fella from Memphis was real handsome and polite. Not a thing like Old Man Krait.

The fella from Memphis started paying more and more calls on Widow Krait, and it was plain to see she enjoyed his company. My pa commented on how it'd do Jasper good to have a man around and once his ma remarried she wouldn't spend so much time fussing over the boy. Mr. Svenson, the barber, nearly took off Pa's earlobe agreeing with him.

NANCY A. COLLINS

When the Choctaw County Squib social page announced that the Widow Krait was planning to take a trip to Memphis without Jasper, all Seven Devils was abuzz with the news. To the best of anyone's memory, it would be the first time since Old Man Krait's death that mother and child had been separated. Widow Krait was to take the train to Memphis early that Friday and return by Sunday evening.

She never made it past the depot.

Just as the porters were smashing her baggage, Jasper's pet nigger rode up on a mule. Seems Jasper fell out of the hayloft in the barn in back of the house and busted his collarbone. Widow Krait went straight home to look after her boy.

Turned out Jasper smashed a sight more than his collarbone; his right knee was hurt so bad the doctors couldn't mend it properly. He ended up with a permanent limp and had to use his daddy's cane to go up and down stairs.

When the doctors told her that her son would be a cripple, Widow Krait had the old barn destroyed. No one saw the fella from Memphis again; although someone said he'd gone on to open a chain of dry goods stores.

To tell the truth, Jasper Krait was pretty much a non-person as far as the citizens of Seven Devils were concerned. I had my own interests and entertainments and Jasper never once figured in them. Come the Second World War, his trick knee kept him out of the draft. I ended up in the Infantry and saw action in France. In '42 I married my gal, Nadine, while home on leave. I didn't see her again until '46.

During that time Jasper was workin' in his mama's bank. Or was supposed to be. He'd picked up a taste for gambling and spent more time than not in Hot Springs, playing the ponies. When the track was shut, he'd hop a train down to New Orleans and waste his time in the casinos on River Road.

In '44, while I was gone fighting the war, there was some kind of hoo-ha over at the bank. My Nadine was working as a teller at the time, which is how I come to know about it. Seems that when the banking authorities came in and audited the books there were some—'irregularities'. Things got settled—exactly how I don't know—but the upshot was that Jasper got "laid off" and put on an allowance. He never did a lick of work from there on in.

When I got home in '46, the last thing on my mind was the Kraits. I had me a wife I hadn't seen in four years, a three-year-old boy I was a stranger to, and a G.I. loan. But when I got back to Seven Devils I

KNUCKLES AND TALES: HOW IT WAS WITH THE KRAITS

found the whole county gossiping about Jasper Krait having himself a girlfriend. Her name was Bessie Lynn Haig and she wasn't exactly what you'd call glamorous. I'm not saying she was ugly, mind you. The girl was as plain as butcher-paper, that's all. Bessie Lynn was the organist at the Baptist church and the Lord only knows how she and Jasper ever got together.

But as homely as she was, she seemed to exert a good influence on Jasper. He stopped drinking and gambling and took to bathing regular and actually doing things like telling folks 'howdy' when he saw them on the street. The change was monumental.

One Sunday in '47, Reverend Cakebread got up in front of the congregation and said that it was his pleasure to announce that Jasper and Bessie Lynn would be tying the knot in a month's time.

On the day of the wedding everybody in town turned out to see what had once seemed as likely as men on the moon: Jasper Krait marrying a decent, god-fearing woman. Bessie Lynn was dressed up in a fancy bridal gown that almost made her look pretty. The men-folk took Jasper out by the privy behind the church for some last-minute "fortitude" for his nerves. I was one of them, and as we stood around smoking roll-yer-owns, sipping white lightnin' out of fruit jars, and cracking wedding-night jokes, it was like Jasper had always been part of the group.

I felt happy for Jasper, in my way. I was enjoying being a husband and a daddy after all the killing I'd seen and done over in Europe; and I wanted other folks to know being part of a family heals all wounds, if you have a mind to let it.

I forgot that families have a way of creating wounds, too.

When Jasper's pet nigger showed up on the mule, I saw the happiness drain from Jasper's face like someone had pulled a plug in the back of his head.

It was the Widow Krait. She'd fallen down the stairs. Jasper went straight home and never made it back to the church that day. After the first thirty minutes Bessie Lynn was anxious. After an hour had gone by she got mad. By the time the third hour rolled around, she was crying. I couldn't take no more and left not long after. I can still see poor, plain Bessie Lynn standing in the vestibule, boo-hooing into her bouquet. It was not a pretty sight.

Bessie Lynn was too ashamed to show her face in Choctaw County after that, so she went to live with a maiden aunt somewhere in the Ozarks. No one ever saw her again. I guess that's when Jasper really started in drinking. He'd always been one for the bottle, but once Bessie Lynn was gone he ended up being the town drunk.

In '53, Sheriff Campbell retired and, seeing how I was one of the few white men left under thirty who'd seen military service living inside the town limits, I ended up with the badge.

Mostly my job consisted of making sure Rial's Package Store wasn't selling to minors and hosing off the highway after wrecks. It wasn't like they show it on television; no car chases or bank robberies or nothing exciting like that.

I tell you, being the Law for twelve years opened my eyes to a lot of things. Most of them not so good. I ended up knowing more about my neighbors than either them or me wanted. It was one thing to gossip about Mordecai Simpkins' drunken rages, but another to lock him up for putting his baby's eye out with a coat hanger.

I guess it was—what? 1960?—when it happened. It was a nice spring day and Heck Jones gets a knock on his door. He's kind of surprised to see Jasper Krait standing there, pretty-as-you-please, even though the Kraits were his neighbors. Heck sees Jasper's got a stack of records—them hi-fi long-players—under his arm.

"Afternoon, Heck," says Jasper, as if he come calling every day.

"Afternoon, Jasper. What can I do you for?" Heck was nonplussed by Jasper stopping by unannounced and smelling like the Jack Daniels plant, but he was curious to find out what the richest man in town was doing on his front stoop.

"Well, Heck, I was hopin' you'd do me the favor of keepin' these here record albums for me while I go outta town."

Heck thought that was mighty peculiar at the time, seeing how the passenger trains didn't stop at the depot no more and he knew Jasper didn't have no driver's license, but he let it pass.

"You going outta town? Where to?"

Jasper looked nervous and shrugged. "Just outta town, that's all. Look, you gonna keep these records for me or not?"

"Sure, I'd be happy to oblige, Jasper. But why can't you leave 'em home?"

He commenced to sweating and for a moment Heck was afraid Jasper was gonna puke all over his wife's tulip bed. "I just can't. That's all." He started to get this belligerent look on his face, like a mule that's decided it don't want to move, that was a watered-down version of what Old Man Krait used to give folks who were late paying their notes on account of their crops got washed away. So Heck ended up taking in Jasper Krait's records.

KNUCKLES AND TALES: HOW IT WAS WITH THE KRAITS

Later on, I found out Jasper made similar spur-of-the-moment visits on his other neighbors that day, asking each of them the "favor" of boarding a particular cherished object of his while he was "outta town"; he left his paperback book collection with Mamie Pasternak, his prize shotgun with Carlton Tufts, his good Sunday-go-to-meeting suit with Sam Wilberforce, and his fishing rod and tackle with Freddie Nayland.

The next night the Krait house caught fire.

I'd just come in from a hard day of plowing the south forty when the call came in. The volunteer fire department was already on the scene, the old hook and ladder pulled up on the Krait's front lawn. Reverend Thurman, who took over the Baptist church after Brother Cakebread passed on, was standing there in his braces and oilcloth coat, an axe in one hand and soot on his face, as if he'd just come back from freeing souls from Hell.

"How is it, Reverend?"

"Not too bad. The back porch got burnt up real good, but we got the worst of it."

"Anyone hurt?"

"See for yourself."

Just then Heck Jones and Sam Wilberforce come out the front door, carrying the Widow Krait between them. She was in her sixties and getting on the frail side, but she still had her dignity. And she weren't bad looking, as old ladies go.

"What kept y'all so long?" fumed Brother Thurman.

"She wouldn't come out 'till she put on her housecoat and got her teeth in, Reverend! Said she refused to stand in front of every soul in Choctaw County in nothing but her flimsies and her bare gums," Sam explained.

I could tell Reverend Thurman wanted to let fly with a few choice words on the vanity of Eve, but the look the Widow Krait shot him made him shut his mouth before he got started.

Jasper showed up the next day, asking the neighbors what had happened to his mama. When Heck Jones told him she was over at St. Mary's in Dermott, being checked out for smoke inhalation, Jasper looked more surprised than relieved.

Everyone knew it was arson. Hell, even Granny Simple—who was blind in one eye, deaf as a post, and hadn't had her wits about her since Hoover was in office—could see that. Someone turned up a bunch of oily rags and an empty can of gasoline under the floorboard's in Jasper's pet nigger's shack and there wasn't much I could do except arrest him.

Now, I ain't a nigger-lover, but I ain't proud of what I done. I knew that nigger didn't do it—or if he had, it was on orders—but I arrested him anyway. I still feel bad about that, but I had a few more years to go on paying my note and my oldest was fixing to go off to Fayetteville and major in business. There wasn't much of a trial and Jasper's pet nigger got sent to Cummins for seven years. When the state troopers came to take him, he looked kind of relieved. I got the impression he was happy to go anywhere, so long it was away from the Kraits.

After that, things quieted down some. It was easier for folks to believe that Jasper's pet nigger, full of Martin Luther King and cheap shine, got it into his head to burn down the Kraits' house, than for them to think about the truth.

Widow Krait hired a mess of carpenters to fix up the house and got shed of everything that had smoke or water damage. Most of the time Jasper laid low, drinking even harder than before. My own mama, bless her, passed on that winter, so I was more preoccupied than usual.

Then, about a year after the fire, I get this call before Nadine left the house for Sunday school. It was the Kraits' nigger maid, Amberola. Seems she found Widow Krait unconscious at the foot of the stairs. I told her to stay put and called Doc McFadden then phoned the ambulance service over in Desha County. Turned out the Widow Krait took herself one hell of a bad spill. She came to for a spell while Doc McFadden was checking her over and asked to see Jasper.

I found him sleeping it off in his bedroom. When I told him his ma was hurt and asking for him, he looked real funny—like he's swallowed his chaw—then puked all over his bed.

Doc McFadden rode with her to St. Mary's over in Desha County, since Choctaw didn't have a hospital back then. He told me later that she'd busted her hip, collarbone, and a couple of ribs, and that it was a testament to God's mercy she'd lived to tell about it.

She was in the hospital for a long time. Most of the women-folk in Choctaw County paid her a visit while she was stuck in bed. My Nadine took her some Upper Rooms and a couple of crossword puzzles. She said that the Widow Krait was quite gracious, even with her hip in a plaster cast, but acted like she was the queen of England granting an audience. Nadine said that seeing her that way helped her understand Widow Krait. She didn't like her any better, mind you, but it made things clearer, at least woman-to-woman wise.

It was six months before the Widow Krait came back to Seven Devils. She couldn't do for herself too well, thanks to that busted hip,

KNUCKLES AND TALES: HOW IT WAS WITH THE KRAITS

so Amberola pushed her in a wheelchair whenever she had to visit the bank. An electrician came in from Pine Bluff and installed a special elevator seat so's she could get up and down the stairs on her own. Funny how the Kraits seemed to run to cripples: first the Old Man, then Jasper, and finally Widow Krait.

Doc McFadden and me knew a lot of things that most folks hereabout wished we didn't. Things like that happen when you're the only doctor and the only law in a town this size. So it was only fittin' he'd call me that night.

"Jimbo? You set down to dinner yet?"

"Just gettin' ready to, Doc. What is it?"

"It's the Kraits. You better get on over here. I'll be calling Dewar's Funeral Home next."

I felt my guts cinch up. The last thing I wanted to do was go and look at Eugenia Krait's corpse, but I got in the truck and drove over anyway.

I was a tad surprised to see the Widow Krait sitting in her front parlor, Amberola hovering over her like a huge shadow. She glanced up when I entered the house then quickly looked away.

Doc McFadden took my elbow and started leading me to the stairs. "Come on up. It's Jasper."

The only son and heir of Josiah Krait was sprawled across his bed, dressed in a pair of dirty boxer shorts and socks that didn't match. There were a couple of empty Jack Daniels bottles on the nightstand and a beat-up dime novel with a picture of a woman being tortured by Nazis laying face-up on the floor. Jasper was colder'n a wet mackerel in January.

"Shit, he's dead, alright. What was it—did he die in his sleep?"

Doc shrugged. "Can't rightly tell. I wouldn't be surprised if it turns out he drank himself to death. Anything's possible." He looked at me when he said that and I knew what he was getting at.

Anything's possible.

Amberola looked at me like I was a mealie in the cornbread when I entered the parlor. She'd been with the Widow Krait since before the Old Man died, and I knew she wouldn't have me upsetting her mistress, but I had my job to do, nigger maid or no.

I cleared my throat and held my hat close to my chest with both hands, gripping the brim like a steering wheel. The Widow Krait looked up and frowned for a second, as if trying to place me.

"Sheriff Turner," she said, her voice tired but far from weak.

"Yes, ma'am."

"Is he dead?"

I gripped my hat tighter. Lord, I hated that part of my job more than hosing off the highway. "Yes'm. I'm afraid so."

She nodded her head and sighed to herself but didn't offer to say anything else.

"Uh, Miz Krait—when was the last time you saw your son? Alive, I mean. I hate to be asking you these questions, ma'am, at a time like this..."

"I understand, Sheriff. It's your job. I know what it's like when something has to be done." She looked up at me again, and I could see her eyes were as clear and blue as a summer sky. "I reckon the last time I saw Jasper was last night. He brought me some hot cocoa and we sat and drank it in the sitting room. Yes, that was the last time, I'm pretty certain of it. When he didn't show up for dinner this evening, I had Amberola go up and fetch him. It wasn't that uncommon for him to stay in his room most of the day, on account of his...condition, but he usually came down for supper. That's when Amberola found him..."

"Yes, sir. I found him like that." Amberola folded her meaty arms as if daring me to try and wrassle any more information out of her.

I left them sitting in the front parlor, the Widow Krait looking as delicate as a china doll. But I knew the porcelain was hiding a cold steel core.

When Doc McFadden pumped Jasper's stomach he found a Moon Pie, some cocoa, and enough whisky and painkillers to kill a team of mules. Doc recognized the painkillers as being those he'd prescribed Widow Krait for her hip. I asked him if he thought Jasper had committed suicide.

"Ain't saying no such thing, one way or another. Could have been accidental. Jasper had arthritis in that bum knee of his. Maybe he dosed himself with his mama's pain pills. That, on top of his drinking, would have done the trick. Anything's possible. As it is, I still owe the bank for my car."

Jasper's death was listed as heart failure and a day later he was cremated. Reverend Thurman was scandalized that the Widow Krait had her son stuck in an urn instead of buried, like the Good Lord intended. It just didn't seem Baptist.

Jasper's ashes hadn't cooled on the mantelpiece before Eugenia moved to Florida, taking Amberola with her. I don't know if she took Jasper's urn, though. If she ever came back to Seven Devils, I never heard of it. Talk has it she lived in a retirement community near Boca Raton and became a mean hand at shuffleboard.

KNUCKLES AND TALES: HOW IT WAS WITH THE KRAITS

Over the years the gossip surrounding the Kraits slacked off. And once the state banking authorities took over running things in '64, people didn't have any real reason to think about 'em any more. The Krait house, once the biggest and finest home in all Choctaw County, fell into disrepair.

A couple of years ago word got out that Eugenia Krait had died. A niece in Biloxi ended up inheriting the estate and she drove up from Mississippi last summer to look things over. I reckon she didn't like what she found, since they're tearing the place down.

I guess I'll go and watch 'em bulldoze the house. I'm the only one left who remembers how it was with the Kraits, now that Doc McFadden's retired and moved to Arizona, and Heck, Reverend Thurman, and even my Nadine, bless her, are gone.

Still, I can't help but wonder what it was like for them in that big, fine, lonely house. Spending all that time together, needing each other so bad love and hate became one and the same thing. I'd like to think he was the one who put the painkillers in the hot cocoa, and that she switched the cups when he wasn't looking.

Anything's possible.

THE PUMPKIN CHILD

Part One: 1946

"Next stop Seven Devils!" the train conductor said in a controlled bellow. "All out for Seven Devils, Arkansas!"

Hollis Railsback, recently a Corporal in the United States Army, started awake at the sound of his hometown's name and glanced at the wristwatch he picked up at the Honolulu PX. It was six in the morning. Right on time.

He quickly stood up, reaching for the canvas duffle bag in the rack over his seat. After spending two and a half years trying not to get killed, he'd learned to wake up fast and clean. He looked around the coach car to see who else might be getting off at his stop, but judging from the snores, he was the only one disembarking. Shouldering his duffle, Hollis hurried towards the conductor, who stood at the exit with his pocket watch in hand.

"Welcome back, soldier," the conductor said, eyeing Railsback's dress greens. "Been away from home long?"

"Nearly three years, sir."

"See any action?"

Hollis shifted about, trying not to show his irritation with the question. Barely a week out of the service and he was already growing weary of curious civilians.

"I got my share," he said with a shrug. "Mostly in the Pacific. I've just spent the last six months recovering' from malaria and beriberi I picked up out in the jungle. Now I'm going' home."

"Well, you're almost there now," said the conductor.

The train hissed like a great iron serpent as it put on its brakes, sending a brief, jarring shudder along its length as it came to a full stop. A porter in a white jacket appeared at Hollis' elbow, carrying a large metal step stool.

"Move back, sir," the conductor said, motioning for Railsback to clear the way. "Let George here make sure everything's safe for you to leave the train."

The porter stepped into the narrow open stair well and then hopped down, setting the step stool securely onto the station platform.

"There y'go, cap'n," the porter said, removing his red cap as he smiled up at Railsback.

Hollis smiled and shook his head as he exited the train, tipping the porter a quarter. "I'm just a corporal."

"Whatever you say, cap'n."

The porter picked up the stool and hopped back into the rail car. The conductor leaned out and waved to the engineer, and within seconds the train began to move again, its wheels squealing like steel banshees as it pulled away from the station.

Hollis turned his back on the departing train and looked up and down the deserted platform. Not even the tiny one-room ticket office was open. Railsback frowned. He hadn't exactly been expecting a brass band or anything, but he had, at the very least, thought his father would be waiting for him.

Hollis had wired his father from Kansas City the day before, when he switched trains, to let him know when he was supposed to arrive.

Puzzled, he went down the platform stairs that exited onto Railroad Street. As he walked down Railroad Street towards the main business district, he felt strangely disconnected, as if he was in a play, walking through carefully crafted sets designed to replicate the places and things of his youth. His first impression was that nothing about the town was different, and, to a certain extent that was true: the iron clock outside the First Federal was still five minutes off; the bandstand was still in the park opposite the Bijou; Bayou Baphomet still wound its way through the center of town, funneled through a network of carefully maintained drainage ditches. Hollis looked closer, he could see subtle signs of change, such as the sign outside Parker's Drug Store now reading Parker and Sons Pharmacy, and Tibbit's Dry Goods having been replaced by a Ben Franklin Store.

As he strolled down First Street, it suddenly occurred to Railsback that perhaps his father had stopped by the office before heading over to the rail station and got sidetracked by some paperwork, as was so often the case. As he neared Railsback Seed & Feed, he peered in through the front window, hoping to catch sight of his father silhouetted behind the counter, but all there was for him to see were

KNUCKLES AND TALES: THE PUMPKIN CHILD

shadows and bags of hog feed. Hollis's puzzlement gave way to genuine concern and he hurried towards his home, five blocks away.

The house Hollis Railsback grew up in was a modest affair, with a wide front porch, wooden siding, green shingles, and a glider hung from rusty chains, where he had spent countless summer nights idly swinging back and forth, watching the fireflies come out with the twilight.

He tried the door, but it refused to turn. Hollis's concern now became full-fledged fear. He could never, in his memory, recall his father ever locking the door. He leaned on the doorbell set and heard its strident buzz echoing throughout the house.

"Daddy! Open up!" Hollis shouted, banging the door so hard it rattled the front parlor windows. *"It's me! Open up!"*

"Gracious! Who's making such a racket this early in the day—?" An older woman dressed in a pink housecoat, curlers still in her hair, peered over the hedgerow from next door. "Here now!" she said sharply. "What're you up to? I'll have the law on you if you don't settle down!"

Railsback stepped towards the hedge, a look of relief on his face. Up until that moment, part of him had been secretly afraid the town was deserted. "Miz Eunice! Where's Daddy gone off to?"

Eunice McQuiston, the Railsbacks' neighbor for the last thirty years, halted her harangue and squinted at him. "Hollis—? Hollis Railsback?" She fished in her cleavage and retrieved a pair of cat-eye glasses. "Lord A' mighty—that *is* you! God in Heaven, boy! Every one hereabouts gave you up for dead six months ago!"

"I'll admit I got close to dying', but I ain't dead, Miz Eunie."

"So I can see, son."

"Miz Eunie, I sent Daddy a telegram letting him know I was coming home today…"

Miss Eunice's face grew sorrowful. "Oh, Hollis, I'm *so* sorry, darlin'."

"What? You're sorry for what? What's happened to Daddy? He ain't dead, is he?"

"No, Hollis. Horace ain't dead…but I don't doubt he'd rather be than where he is now. Your pappy's over at Twin Oaks."

The words struck Hollis like a closed fist; Twin Oaks was the sanitarium. Hollis fought to keep from staggering as the meaning of what Miz Eunie said sank in. "No," he whispered. "That can't be so…Not my daddy…"

"It came on him sudden," Miz Eunice said gently. "About a month ago. He was down at the store, one minute he's talking to Jake Carlton, and the next minute he's laid out on the floor. Doc Bocage said it was a stroke, brought on from stress and over work."

"Over work? How's that? He's got three employees under him."

"Not anymore," Miz Eunie said, shaking her head. "He had to let Tim and Jack go awhile back. The only person he still has working for him is Mamie."

Hollis couldn't believe what he was hearing. Tim Tullis and Jack Fortenberry had worked for his father as far back as he could remember.

"Why would Daddy fire Tim and Jack?"

"On account of the competition he was getting from Bright Star Agricultural."

"Bright Star Agricultural? Never heard of them."

"They opened up a year ago, just after the state finished with the new highway. Virgil Bayliss owns it. You remember Virgil, don't you, Hollis?"

"I remember him, awright," Hollis replied, his voice as hard as bone.

Miz Eunie's cheeks colored as she belatedly realized her faux pas. "Well, yes, ahem, I reckon you *would*, wouldn't you? Well, I best get back to my breakfast before my toaster catches fire. It's good to have you back home, Hollis."

Hollis watched Miz Eunie disappear back into her home, then turned and walked around the back of his father's house. The Railsbacks' '37 Packard sat inside the unsecured garage, a patina of dust obscuring the back windshield. Hollis took the old Folgers can down from the shelf over his father's workbench and upended it, dumping the spare set of house and car keys into his hand, then walked back and let himself in through the front door.

The house was profoundly silent and smelled of stale, closed air. A small drift of unopened mail and unread magazines, including the telegram he had sent from Kansas City, lay piled just below the mail slot in the door. Hollis bent to pick up one of the letters and saw it was a past due notice from one of the feed store's suppliers. He threw the bill back down onto the pile.

Talk about a hell of a homecoming. It was clear now that his father had been hiding his business troubles in his letters. No doubt the old man didn't want to worry his son while he was recovering in the hospital. Hollis had wondered why he hadn't received a letter from his father over the last month, but had simply charted it up to delays in the mail. After all, Honolulu was a far way aways from Seven Devils, Arkansas. And, to make matter worse, Virgil Bayliss wasn't content with simply stealing his girl; he had to steal Daddy's business, too.

KNUCKLES AND TALES: THE PUMPKIN CHILD

Hollis and Virgil had grown up together, attended school together, sung in the church choir together, even played on the high school football team together. Despite this, Railsback could not recall a time when he did not detest the bastard.

He couldn't really pinpoint the exact reason for his intense dislike of the man; Virgil Bayliss had never once shown the slightest animosity towards him. Perhaps his resentment arose from how easy everything seemed to be for Virgil, who had been born with matinee idol looks and a strapping physique. With his a crown of wavy golden hair, Virgil Bayliss looked like how Jack Armstrong, All American Boy sounded on the radio: clean-cut, wholesome and virile. Virgil was gifted with a sharp and inquisitive mind and was also an all-round athlete. Basketball, baseball, football, tennis, chess, debate squad…you name it, Virgil Bayliss was its captain.

However, while Hollis was a good student, he was nowhere near as smart as Virgil, nor as gifted. No matter what it was Hollis tried his hand at, he had to fight to attain what little success he could claim, while Virgil Bayliss seemed to glide along through life with as much effort as a swan.

The one area that Hollis had enjoyed unqualified success, though, was with Joslin Simms. Hollis had known Joslin all of his life, and he had loved her since the first time he realized she wasn't a boy. Joslin was the fairest, most perfect example of womanhood Choctaw County had ever produced. With her long, blonde hair, smoky violet eyes, and pale, translucent skin, she looked more like a porcelain doll than a flesh-and-blood woman. While her beauty drew men to her, it was her fragility that kept them in her thrall. There was a precious delicacy to her that always seemed on the verge of being ruined, like hothouse orchids in danger of a blast of cold air from a carelessly opened door. To quote his father, Joslin was not just a girl or even a woman; she was a *lady*.

And throughout their high school years, the lady was incontestably his.

Hollis's plan for the future had been to go the University of Arkansas up in Fayetteville, get a degree in Agricultural Engineering, go to work in the family business, then marry Joslin. But then the war happened, and all his plans went out the window. He could still see her standing on the train platform, wrapped in his letter sweater, clutching a hanky to her tear-swollen eyes as the train pulled away from the station.

Joslin started out writing him every day for the first three months. Then she started writing every week. Then it was once every two weeks. By the time he was gone a year, her cards and letters arrived one a month.

Then, two years into his tour, he got a Dear John. In the letter, Joslin told him she had fallen in love with Virgil Bayliss, who was given a deferment because he had blown out his knee playing football his senior year of high school.

Hollis's mouth twisted into a bitter smile as he recalled the intense satisfaction he had felt as he watched from the sidelines as Virgil writhed in pain on the playing field, clutching his ruined kneecap. At the time it had secretly pleased him to know, for once, something had not gone perfectly for Seven Devil's golden boy.

Of course, Hollis had no way of knowing that Virgil's injury would keep him out of the draft, while he would be sent halfway across the globe to fight for possession of a chain of god-forsaken islands scattered between Honolulu and Rangoon that were not only infested with Jap soldiers, but with every possible biting fly and poisonous snake as well.

Still, Hollis wasn't really surprised that Joslin had dumped him for another man. He had always known she was overly dependent on others for her strength, both physically and emotionally. After all, it was one of the things that had drawn him to her. .No, what galled him was that she had dumped him for Virgil Bayliss, of all people. If she had chosen anyone else, at least Hollis could have comforted himself by knowing she had settled for someone inferior to him.

Was this what he had fought for in the Pacific? For Virgil Bayliss to steal his girl? Had he slogged through those damned swamps, up to his armpits in slime and leeches, to have Virgil Bayliss wreck his family business and put his father in the old folk's home?

Welcome home, soldier boy.

o o o

Horace Railsback sat in a high back convalescent's wheelchair parked in the middle of a pool of sunlight like a potted plant. The left side of his face hung from his skull like wet laundry, and his left arm was twisted inward on itself, tucked near his chin, in parody of deep thought. Although he appeared clean and well cared for, Hollis could not help feel like his father was in bad need of dusting.

It took Horace a disturbingly long moment to recognize Hollis. It wasn't until the orderly prodded the old man by telling him his son had come to see him that a glimmer of recognition could be glimpsed in his right eye.

"Son..? My son..?" Horace said, his voice as dry as a paper rose.

"Hi, Daddy," Hollis said in a low shout, as if by raising the volume he could somehow reach the place his father's mind had retreated to." I'm back. I missed you."

KNUCKLES AND TALES: THE PUMPKIN CHILD

"Back? From where? Where did you go, son?"

"To war, Daddy. I went off to war. But I'm back now. I'm back to help you run the store."

Horace Railsback nodded his head as if it might topple from his shoulders. "My boy is in the service, you know. Fightin' Japs."

o o o

Mamie Joyner, his father's long-time secretary, burst into tears when Hollis walked into the back office. Mamie was a short, squat little woman who bore a strong resemblance to a pot-bellied stove, if said stove wore cranberry-red lipstick, cardigan sweaters and kept its hair in a bun.

"Oh, Mr. Hollis!" she boo-hooed into his shoulder. "I can't tell you how glad I am that you're back!"

"I know, Mamie. It's good to see you, too," he said, patting her on the back.

"I've been coming in every day since your father took ill, answering the phone and seeing to it that things were in kept in order. To tell the truth, I didn't know what else to do with myself! If only Mr. Horace was here..!" A renewed series of sobs shook her compact frame.

"That can't be helped, Mamie. You and I both know that. But now that I'm home, I'm going to see to it that things get back to the way they used to be."

"Oh, Mr. Hollis!'

"Don't cry, Mamie—please, stop crying! You're no use to me when you cry." Hollis gently pried the weeping woman from him and pointed her in the direction of the filing cabinets. "Now, I need you to fetch me the books for the last year or so, so I can get an idea of what's happened to the business and what needs to be done. Can you do that for me, darlin'?"

"Of course, Mr. Hollis," Mamie sniffled, daubing at the corners of her eyes with a tissue.

"That's my girl. Just put them on Daddy's desk. I'll go over them this evening."

Come midnight, Hollis Railsback had finished going over the accounts, and he had to admit that things were not as bad as he had thought they were. They were a far sight worse. Railsback Feed & Seed was not just teetering on the verge of bankruptcy; it had already fallen headlong into the hopper while no one was looking.

When he'd gone off to war, the new highway was just talk, nothing more. But in 1944 there was a nice, new two-lane blacktop located a mile from the older, narrower road that cut through town. Now travelers headed to Little Rock in one direction, or Greenville in the other, no longer had to drive through the business district, with its two separate sets of railroad tracks and five traffic lights. Still, no one gave much thought about what the new highway might mean, since the war was still on and gas was rationed and most everyone traveled by train. So when Virgil Bayliss opened up his Bright Star Agricultural Supply out on the new highway, everyone in town figured him for a fool.

But the farmers and ranchers who bought feed and seed weren't town folk. They had to drive into Seven Devils to make their purchases, which meant they regularly dealt with the railroad crossings, which had freights on them at least three times a day, if not more, as well as the traffic lights and the limited free parking spaces on First Street. By being out on the highway, Bright Star Agricultural was able to offer convenience and ample parking to men who viewed coming into town as a tedious chore. The result was a slow but steady loss of customers for Railsback Feed & Seed.

Hollis's father had managed to hang on to some of his old clients—mostly those farmers to whom he had extended credit during the boll weevil infestation—but, for the most part, the younger farmers who were taking over from the previous generation were taking their business to Bright Star.

To make matters worse, Horace Railsback had taken out a second mortgage on the house simply to see to it that the lights stayed on in the store and Mamie was kept on the payroll. But most of what Horace had gotten from the bank was being rapidly eaten away by his medical bills. Within a month's time the bank would foreclose on both the business and the house, and after that it was only a matter of time before Twin Oaks either kicked his father out or sent him to the State Hospital over in Benton.

Try as he might, Hollis could not puzzle his way out of the trap his father's sentiment and the state highway department had constructed for him. So he took the bottle of Old Granddad his father kept in the bottom filing cabinet and got drunk.

o o o

Hollis woke up with a start when Mamie unlocked the store. He had passed out at his father's desk, his head resting on an open ledger.

"Mr. Hollis! Were you here all night?" Mamie asked, clucking her tongue.

KNUCKLES AND TALES: THE PUMPKIN CHILD

Railsback blinked and looked around, rubbing the gum from his eyes. "I suppose I was."

"That's not good for your back, you know."

"So you tell me," he grunted as he got to his feet. His lower back ached and his neck was so stiff the muscles creaked. "Mamie, you tidy things up here. I'm going home to change my clothes, splash some cold water on my face. I'll be back in a hour or two."

"Very well, Mr. Hollis."

Hollis flinched as the morning sun hit his unshielded eyes as he left the feed store. The bitter tackiness of his mouth was enough to make him decide to grab a quick cup of Joe before heading home.

The Sip-N-Sup was across the street from the First Federal. It had booths, tables and a lunch counter, as well as a room in the back where the local Kiwanis and Rotarians held their meetings. The breakfast rush had just ended and Jesse, the short order cook, was cleaning the grill in anticipation of the clerks and accountants from the bank across the street hurrying over for their lunch break. Hollis had spent much of his young life eating at the Sip-N-Sup. After his mother's death, he and his father had taken nearly every meal there. If ever there was a home-away-from-home, it was the Sip-n-Sup.

As Hollis entered the restaurant, a tiny bell over the door rang, announcing his arrival. Mary-Margaret, the Sip-N-Sup's all purpose waitress and cashier, jumped down from her perch behind the register.

"Well, I'll be! Mr. Hollis! How long you been back?"

"Couple of days."

Mary-Margaret turned around on her stool and shouted at the top of her lungs in the direction of the short order station. "Jesse! Looky who's come back from the war! It's Mr. Hollis!"

"Hey, Mr. Hollis!" Jesse said, glancing up from the grill he was cleaning. "You kill some Japs while you was gone?"

"I reckon I did. Never got close enough to see how many, though."

"Glad to hear it," Jesse replied, and returned to his polishing.

"Don't you mind Jesse none," Mary-Margaret said with a laugh. "You know how he is when it comes to that grill! He ain't satisfied until he can see his face in it! Now what can we do you for?"

"Coffee. Black. And some dry toast."

"Looks to me like someone's been out celebratin'," Mary-Margaret said with a wink.

"I wouldn't call it celebrating, exactly."

Mary-Margaret gave one of her patented horselaughs as she poured fresh coffee into a white ceramic mug. "Still the same old Mr. Hollis!"

He sipped at the hot, bitter brew, trying his best to quiet the drums thumping behind his eyes. Despite his hangover, and the problems heaped upon his shoulders, it was still good to be back home, surrounded by people he had known since before he could talk. After so much change, all of it chaotic and more than a little dangerous, the presence of familiar faces and things was a comfort in itself.

Just as he was finally beginning to feel that things were nowhere near as bad as they looked, the bell over the door rang again, and Joslin Simms walked in. The breath left his body as if he'd been sucker punched. Although he knew that he would eventually run into her, it hadn't occurred to him it would be so soon, and in one of their old haunts.

When he left Seven Devils, Joslin was seventeen-year-old girl who wore bobby socks and saddle oxfords. Now, nearly three years later, she was a woman of twenty who dressed in pullover sweaters, tight skirts and patent leather pumps. As much as it pained him to look at what was no longer his, he could not find it in himself to feel anything but awe in the presence of her beauty.

When he saw who she was with, his stomach cinched itself into a seething bag of bile. Virgil Bayliss followed Joslin across the open threshold and into the restaurant's main room, favoring the leg he had damaged so heroically in the final game of the season, back in '42.

Hollis looked down at his hands and realized that he had twisted his cloth napkin into a garrote.

The twosome selected a table near the picture window facing the street, and Bayliss held out a chair for Joslin. As she placed herself in the seat, Virgil looked up and stared right at Hollis. A frown crossed his chiseled features.

"Hollis? Hollis Railsback?" Virgil stepped forward, smiling broadly, his hand held out in greeting. "I'll be damned, it *is* you!"

A pained rictus that might pass for a smile appeared on Hollis' face as he rose from the booth and moved to intercept Virgil's greeting. "Hello, Virgil."

Virgil grabbed Hollis' hand with both of his, pumping his arm vigorously. "You old son of a gun! How long you been back?"

"Not long," he replied, trying hard to fight the urge to ram a coffee spoon through the bastard's right eye.

Virgil finally let Hollis' hand drop and turned to smile in Joslin's direction. "Honey! Look who's here!"

The Joslin Hollis had known was easily flustered in dodgy social situations and invariably looked to her date to set the tone for her reaction. Judging from how she was trembling like a deer, an anxious smile plastered across her face, it was clear to him that aspect of her personality had not matured with her taste in clothes.

"Hello, Hollis," she said in a wispy, little-girl voice. "It's great to see you again."

"It's great to see you, too, Joslin," he replied, trying his best to hide the hurt in his eyes, not so much for Joslin's sake than to keep Bayliss from catching on

"How's your father doing?" Bayliss asked, an edge of concern in his voice.

Hollis took a deep breath and shrugged his shoulders. "He's doing, I guess."

"Well, when you've got yourself squared away, come out and see me. I got a few things I'd like to discuss that could be to y'all's advantage. The Railsback name means a lot to farmers in this neck of the woods. Your daddy's done more than his fair share for o Choctaw County, and folks don't forget that."

"That's kind of you to say, Virgil."

"Pshaw! It's the truth, ain't it? Promise me you'll come out and see me in a couple of days?"

"I'll let you know. I best be going...I've got a lot of things to catch up on, now that I'm home."

o o o

Son a bitch simply couldn't let him go and be done with it. No, he had to make him writhe and twist like a worm on a hook. And to top it off, he had the audacity to try and work business into it on top of everything else. 'The Railsback name means a lot to farmers in this area.' Damned right it did. Everyone knew Horace Railsback was a friend to farmers, and could be counted on for sympathy and understanding when it came to boll weevils, droughts, and the runs on the bank. The Railsback name not only meant something, it was worth something, too. He could see where Bayliss was headed. He wanted to buy up the Railsback name and the last of their trade. And judging from how butter wouldn't melt in his mouth, Virgil probably figured he could get what he wanted for a song.

Hollis felt as if there was a hornet's nest wedged between the folds of his brain, and every time he thought of Virgil Bayliss, it was like stirring the hornets with a stick. And just as it felt as if couldn't get any worse, he stepped onto the front porch of the house and saw the newspaper, *The Seven Devils Advocate*, lying on the welcome mat.

He automatically bent over and picked up the paper, glancing first at the headline then flipping it over to see what was printed beneath the fold. He found himself staring at a photograph of Virgil Bayliss dancing in the Mammon Bayou Country Club's ballroom with Joslin, both of them smiling to beat the band. Underneath the picture was the headline: *Bayliss-Simms Engagement Announced.*

Hollis closed his eyes to shut out the sight, but he could still see Virgil Bayliss' bland, self-satisfied smile swimming before him, accompanied by the buzzing of hundreds of angry hornets

o o o

Choctaw County was a dry county, at least in theory. But being dry never kept folks from getting drunk. Hollis Railsback, like every county boy over the age of thirteen and man under the age of dead, knew exactly where to go and who to see about acquiring liquor.

If you wanted the kind with labels and screw-top lids, you went to Miz Maybell's Honky-Tonk, out on the old Monticello Highway, where you could either get it by the drink or by the bottle. But if you wanted moonshine, then the man to see was Pappy Pritchett, out on Indian Mound Road. Pappy's liquor came with a screw top, too, but that's because it was in Mason jars.

The Pritchett's place was a sprawling amalgamation of rusted-out tractors, gutted jalopies, sagging outbuildings, the center of which was the large, ramshackle shack that had served as the clan's homestead since before the Civil War. The only visible concession the Pritchetts had made to the modern world was the Coca-Cola machine parked on their front porch.

As Hollis drove up the rutted, mud-and-gravel drive, a pack of skinny-shanked coonhounds poured out from under the stoop, baying so lustily you'd think Sherman was on the march again.

Pappy was working on one of the trucks parked in the dooryard, buried up to his waist in the engine. Upon hearing the dogs, he pulled himself free of the truck and stared at the approaching vehicle, idly rubbing his hands with a rag only slightly less oily than the engine he'd been working on.

The coon dogs boiled around the Packard, barking loudly and scratching at the doors with muddy paws. One hound got onto its hind legs and, supporting its upper body on the hood of the car, glowered balefully into the driver's side window at Hollis.

"Y'all dawgs, hush up!" Pappy said, flapping his hands at the pack

KNUCKLES AND TALES: THE PUMPKIN CHILD

as he waded through their number, sending a hound or two flying with a sharp kick. "G'wan, y'all mangy critters! Git!"

The dogs looked at Pappy, then at the Packard, before retreating en masse. Hollis opened the car door and got out, nodding a greeting to the moonshiner.

"Hey, Pappy."

"Hey, Hollis. My boy Ezra tells me you been off to some war or t'other," Pappy drawled as he tucked his rag back into the hip pocket of his greasy overalls.

"Yes, sir. That I have."

Pappy sucked on his teeth and nodded his head for a couple of seconds. "Did y'all win?"

"Yes, sir. That we did."

"Good enough, then," Pritchett replied. "So, how much y'all want?"

"Gimme a six pack," Hollis said, handing over six dollars. Pappy took the money and diligently counted it before tucking it into the front pocket of his overalls. He stepped into a nearby shed and returned with a cardboard box with six sealed Mason jars inside.

"Y'all havin' a party?"

"No, sir."

"Y'all havin' a wake, then?"

"Not exactly. But you ain't far off."

"Well, whatever th' occasion, I'd kindly appreciate you don't commence to drankin' until yore off my property. Last time some good ole boy got his-self likkered up he knocked over my outhouse. That weren't too bad, except that Mam-Maw was inside at the time."

Hollis took the box from Pappy and carefully placed it on the passenger side floor. "Can I get to the levee takin' this road?"

"Sure, but it ain't th' easiest way. Keep on down th' road apiece—when y'all come to a fork in th' road. Th' right fork goes to the levee. Th' left fork don't go nowhere but to the injun mound an' Granny Grimes' place."

"Granny Grimes? That old witchy-woman still around?"

"Granny Grimes always been 'round," Pappy said darkly, spitting to ward off the evil eye. "Reckon she always will be. Funny how some things grow old, but they never die."

o o o

The levee was built by the Army Corps of Engineers following the disastrous Flood of 1910, which sent Mississippi river water into literally every home in Choctaw County, leaving catfish stranded in front yards and alligator garfish flopping on curbstones. Where once the Father Of All Waters ran free and unbridled through the delta, it now was channeled behind a winding wall of quarried stone, covered with a protective layer of dirt and sod.

Hollis remembered the shock he'd experienced when he learned in the third grade that the levee was not a natural phenomena, but a man-made structure, not unlike the Caddo burial mounds that dotted the area. Although the river was no longer free to invade the surrounding countryside with every hard rain, which did not mean the Mississippi had been erased from the consciousness of those who lived nearby.

As a teenager, whenever things got too much for him to handle, Hollis used to come out to the levee and watch the river. There was something about how the muddy waters rolled along in majestic indifference to mankind's attempts to tame it that calmed his inner demons. Hollis had seen a lot of water in the last three years, but none of it held the same mystery and romance for him as the Mississippi.

Hollis sat on the hood of his car and passed the day by alternating staring at the murky brown water with drinking shine straight from the jar. Somewhere halfway through the afternoon and his third jar of squeeze, he passed out. When he woke up the sun was gone and the stars were out, and the last of the shine he had spilled was taking the paint off the hood of the Pontiac.

Earlier that the day the drive out to the levee hadn't seemed that bad, but now the sun was down it was like driving down a coal mine, with precious little in the way of landmarks to go by. After what seemed like an eternity, he finally reached the fork in the road and turned in what he believed was the direction of town.

After a couple of minutes, when he had yet to pass the Pritchett's homestead, Hollis realized he must have taken a wrong turn. Cursing vigorously, he slowed down to look for a place to turn the car around and saw a light ahead in the darkness. As he got closer, he saw a small shack set a hundred yards or more back from the road, next to which was the largish pumpkin patch he'd ever seen. With a start, Hollis realized he was looking at the cabin of Granny Grimes.

Granny Grimes was a living legend in Choctaw County, and was as much a local fixture as the river. Hollis had heard tell about the Granny Grimes since he was a little boy; yet he had never once laid eyes on the woman, as she refused to set foot in town. According to the stories, Granny Grimes was a midwife, of sorts, who helped the blue-

KNUCKLES AND TALES: THE PUMPKIN CHILD

gummers deliver their babies. But she was better known for her hexing. Some in town called her a 'folk doctor', while others less prone to charity called her a witch. But, rumor was, there wasn't a man or woman born in Choctaw County who hadn't found their way to her cabin, one time or another, in search of a charm or a spell, including the Baptist minister.

Hollis pulled his car up in the yard, picked up the cardboard box with its three remaining jars of shine, and walked up the drive towards the old woman's house. As he drew closer, he spied the figure of a woman with white hair, wearing a shawl draped about her hunched shoulders, and puffing on a corncob pipe, sitting in a rocker on the front porch, a Coleman lantern resting at her feet.

"*Hey there!*" he hollered, in case the old lady was deaf. "You on the porch! You Granny Grimes?"

The old woman halted her rocking and looked in his direction, apparently unconcerned by the sudden appearance of a drunken stranger in her dooryard. "I be Granny Grimes, jest as ye be Hollis Railsback."

Hollis felt a cold finger travel down his spine. "How'd you know who I am?"

The old woman chuckled, amused by his reaction. "Ain't that why ye come out to see ol' Granny? On account I got witchin' ways? Besides, jest cause I never go t'town don't mean I don't know who's who in Seven Devils." She leaned forward in her rocker and gestured with a gnarled hand for him to come forward. "Step on up, son, so's I can get a good look at ye. My eye sight ain't what it used to be."

As Hollis neared the shack, there came a low, guttural growl and two eyes, red as blood and bright as fire, blinked open in the shadows under the porch. He stopped in his tracks and swallowed hard, unable to look away from the baleful gaze.

"Old woman, you got you a dog under there?"

"Somethin' like a dawg," Granny Grimes said, rapping the bowl of her pipe against the arm of her rocking chair.

"Will it bite?"

"If'n I tell it to." She studied him for a second. "I reckon ye ain't no trouble. Least not far as I'm concerned. Hush now, Sathan," she said, apparently to the thing under the stoop. "Y'all can come up on the porch, Mr. Hollis."

Hollis did his best to ignore the creature under the stairs as he stepped onto the porch. Now that he was close enough to get a good look at her, Hollis realized Granny Grimes was the oldest woman he'd ever seen outside a pine box. She was ugly as a mud fence, with sparse hair whiter than a bar of Ivory soap, and skin like a dried apple. She was bent over with widow's hump, and arthritic hands dangled like the claws of a bird from her stick-like arms. Given her advanced age, it was impossible to tell if she was Black, White, or Indian, or a mix of all three.

"You live out here all by yourself?" Hollis asked.

"That I do," Granny said, nodding her snow-white head. "Been on my own since th' Flood. Not that it bothers me none, although I admit I don't chop wood and draw water like I used to. But ye ain't here to chaw th' fat with an ol' woman. Ye come here cause ye got yerself crossed."

"Beg pardon?"

"I'm talkin' about yer luck, boy! I can tell jest by lookin' at ye! Ye got yerself bad luck in money an' love, am I right?"

"Are you sayin' someone's hexed me?"

"It's possible, but sometimes a man don't need to have someone curse him to make his luck get all cattywumpus. Sometimes it's on account of bein' born under bad stars. I reckon thas yore problem."

"Is there a way to fix it?"

Granny Grimes shook her head. "I cain't fix bad luck. If thas what the stars have in store for a man, then thas his luck. However... I *can* deflect it."

"Could you do that for me?"

"Perhaps. It depends on whether you can pay my price."

"I can't afford much, I'm afraid. I got less than twenty dollars to my name, since I bought this shine."

"There's more than one way to pay me for my services," Granny said with a cackle. She pointed to the pumpkin patch growing beside the cabin. "I need ye to go out in th' punkin patch yonder an' pick out th' nicest, plumpest, prettiest punkin ye can carry under yore arm and set it on the porch." Granny nodded at the lantern sitting on the edge of the porch. "Take some light with ye, so's ye can see what yore doin'."

"Yes, ma'am," Hollis said, picking up the lantern.

In dark of night, the pumpkin patch was as silent as a graveyard and just as inviting. As he moved amongst the humped rows, lantern held high to light his way, Hollis imagined the round fruits scattered about him looked like mounds of skulls. Sensing that he was being watched, he turned up the flame on the lantern and was startled to see a vast, dark bulk loomed before him. He gasped and took a step back before realizing he was looking at the old Caddo burial mound that gave the road Granny lived on its name.

KNUCKLES AND TALES: THE PUMPKIN CHILD

After five minutes, Hollis found a nice, fat pumpkin the size of a cured ham that was as golden as a harvest moon. Using his army-issue pocketknife, he severed it from its vine. In the stark shadows thrown by the lantern, the sap that leaked onto his hands looked like blood.

Hollis took the pumpkin back to the cabin and set it on the porch, at the old woman's feet. Granny Grimes nodded in approval and puffed on her pipe.

"Thas a fine 'un, no two ways about it. Now I needs ye t'go out and find th' most dried-up, blighted punkin and bring it back as well."

"What's' this have to do with gettin' my luck uncrossed?" Hollis grumbled.

"It's not yore place to ax me such questions!" Granny Grimes replied tartly. "Now go out and fetch me a sick punkin!"

Hollis wasn't used to having folks that weren't exactly white talking to him in such a manner, but there was something in the way the old woman's eyes flashed that made him hold his tongue this time. He trudged back out into the patch and, after a few minutes of searching, returned with the second pumpkin.

Where the first pumpkin was nice and firm and glowed with health, the second was lopsided and covered with scabby gray patches that had eaten quarter-sized holes in its rind. Granny Grimes grinned, extremely pleased by the selection.

"Yes, these will do nicely! Now, be a dear boy and help me get 'em into the house." Granny took the lantern from Hollis as he stooped to gather up the pumpkins and walked ahead of him into the darkened cabin.

The interior of the shack was cramped and smelled strongly of sassafras and turnip greens. An ancient Ben Franklin stove dominated the center of the cabin's single room, and the plank walls were covered with makeshift shelves filled with jars and rusty coffee cans. Dried herbs, roots and wildflowers hung upside from the rafters like clusters of bats. The only furniture inside the cabin was a rickety chair set beside the stove, a workbench that was placed against the far wall, and a narrow mattress stuffed with straw and covered with a tattered hand-made quilt.

Granny pointed a gnarled finger at the workbench littered with candle stubs and unguent jars. Hollis placed the pumpkins on the table and glanced around the close confines of the shack, a look of apprehension on his face.

"Gimme yore hand, boy." Holding his hand with a surprisingly firm grasp, the old woman produced a hatpin from the folds of her shawl and pricked the meat of his thumb.

"*Oww!*" Hollis jumped back, snatching his hand away from the old woman. A large drop of blood, as red as a ruby, rose from the puncture wound. "Why'd you do that?"

"Squeeze a drop of yore blood onto th' sick punkin,' Granny said in way of explanation. "And while yore doin' it, say 'this is th' luck of Hollis Railsback'."

Hollis stretched his arm out and squeezed the ball of his thumb with the knuckle of his index finger. The drop of blood grew bigger, trembled, and fell like a crimson tear, splashing onto the diseased rind of the sick pumpkin.

"This is the luck of Hollis Railsback," he intoned. Although the words sounded foolish coming out of his mouth, he could not find it in him to laugh.

"Now do th' same thing over the other punkin, except you give the name of the person who's luck you want for yore own."

"What do you mean whose luck I want?"

"Like I said, there's no destroyin' bad luck—but I *can* make it go somewhere's else. This spell will swap out yore luck for another's. Now who will it be?"

A slow, nasty smile pulled on the corners of Railsback's mouth as he squeezed the second drop of blood from his thumb onto the good pumpkin. "This is the luck of Virgil Bayliss."

Granny Grimes gave a little cackle and clapped her hands together. "Step aside, son! Ye jest set by the fire and have yerself a drank. I got conjure-work to do."

To his surprise, Hollis saw that the remaining three jars of shine neatly arranged beside the chair, although he did not remember bringing them inside the shack. Suddenly weary from wandering the pumpkin patch and eager to dull the pain in his thumb, he dropped down into the chair and picked up the nearest jar, unscrewing the lid as he watched Granny Grimes busy herself at the table.

Muttering a sing-song cadence under her breath, the old woman took a large, sharp knife and plunged it into the healthy pumpkin, sawing the top off and scooping out its guts as if she was making a jack o'lantern, setting the pulp aside in a neat mound. Then she took the knife to the sick pumpkin, pulling out dark and slimy innards that smelled of rot, and then put them inside the first pumpkin. She then took the pulp from the healthy pumpkin and dumped it inside the diseased pumpkin, and sealed the tops of both gourds shut with a stick of beeswax. By the time she'd finished, Hollis was well into his second jar of shine.

KNUCKLES AND TALES: THE PUMPKIN CHILD

Granny Grimes hobbled from her workbench over to a washbasin on the windowsill, dipping her gnarled hands into the water to cleanse them of the juice and pulp from the pumpkins.

"It is done. Yore luck's been put on another, and his luck is now yore's. All that is left to take care of is my fee."

"Like I said...I don't have much in the way of money..."

"I don't want yore money, boy."

"What do you want, then?"

"Jest some company, is all. Like I said, I been livin' out here on my own-some for nye onto forty years." She took one of the jars down off the shelf and removed something from it, handing it to Hollis. "Here. Swaller this."

Hollis had a hard time focusing his eyes on the pill Granny Grimes held out to him: it was the size of a man's thumb and as black and shiny as a lump of anthracite coal.

"What is it?" he slurred.

"Just swaller and be done with it."

Hollis dutifully popped the pill into his mouth, grimacing as he washed it down with a sip of Pappy Pritchett's shine. Whatever it was, it tasted like floor sweepings, with a hint of manure for flavor.

Whether it was the pill or the liquor he'd been consuming, Hollis' head began to swim and his vision blurred. He opened his mouth to say something, but his jaw muscles no longer seemed to work. With a flash of insight that was as useless as it was belated, he realized that the old witch had drugged him. He tried to stand up, but his legs were made from boiled spaghetti. The last thing he remembered before the darkness claimed him was the sound of weird, high-pitched giggling that seemed to be coming from more than one person.

o o o

When Hollis awoke it was almost dawn. He was lying on his back on a straw mattress and something was poking him in the side. He rolled over and saw Granny Grimes curled up beside him. Her skin was so withered and wrinkled he at first didn't realize she was naked.

"Merciful God!"

Hollis leapt to his feet in a single bound. He looked down and saw, to his disgust, that he was missing both his trousers and his drawers. "You filthy old witch! What did you do?"

Granny Grimes sat up, her dugs hanging flat against her chest like empty leather wineskins. "Ye needn't carry on so! I only claimed my payment, is all I did. Ye got what ye wanted, and I got what I needed."

"Oh, sweet lord…" Hollis moaned, fighting the urge to vomit as he struggled into his discarded trousers. "That pill you gave me…"

"It's an old family recipe," she said, displaying her toothless gums in a lewd grin.. "Guaranteed to put starch in yore flag, no matter what the circumstances."

Hollis grabbed his shoes and dashed out of the cabin, choking on the bitter mixture of bile and half-digested alcohol filling his throat. He tripped as he hurried off the porch and sprawled headlong in the yard. The thing that wasn't exactly a dog issued a brief growl but did not offer to leave its hiding place.

Granny Grimes emerged onto the porch in all her obscene glory, her gnarled hands planted on her heavy hips, her white hair hanging about her hunched shoulders like a fall of snow. In the gray light of early morning her skin looked like a dried up riverbed. She laughed as she watched Hollis stumble back onto his feet, the sound of her voice like fingernails on a chalkboard.

o o o

It took three baths, the last one using carbolic soap and a boars bristle scrub brush, before Hollis felt clean again. As he toweled off his pink, bleeding torso, he filed what had happened out at Granny Grimes cabin into the same mental lock box where he kept the memories of what enemy artillery had done to his best friend's face and the eyes of the Jap soldiers who died on the end of his bayonet.

At first he felt numb, as if someone had shot him up with Novocain, but after a couple mugs of coffee he was starting to feel his old self. By the time he headed off to work he had talked himself into believing the whole thing was just a crazy bad dream. As he entered the back office, he saw Mamie behind her desk, talking on the phone.

"Yes, I'll be sure to tell him as soon as he comes in," she said, then quickly hung up.

"Tell me what, Mamie?"

Mamie gasped and jumped in her seat. "Good heavens, Mr. Hollis!" she said, placing a hand to her breast. "You scared me out of a year's growth!"

"I'm sorry. Now, what is it you're going to tell me?"

Mamie pursed her cranberry-red lips in consternation. "It's Mr. Bayliss."

KNUCKLES AND TALES: THE PUMPKIN CHILD

"What about him?"

"He's...he's had some kind of fit. Collapsed at the Country Club last night. They sent an ambulance from Drew County to take him to St. Mary's Hospital in Dermott."

"That's...that's a real shame," Hollis said, wondering if his voice rang as hollow in Mamie's ears as it did in his own.

o o o

The doctor at St. Mary's diagnosed Virgil with polio, and the country club's swimming pool was immediately shut down for sterilization. Within a week of his collapse, Virgil's condition had worsened to such an extent he had to be moved, via train, to Baptist Hospital up in Little Rock.

A couple of days later, Joslin called up Virgil and asked if he could drive her to the capital. Hollis said he would be more than happy to help out any way he could. So when the doctors told Joslin that Virgil would have to be placed in an iron lung, possibly for the rest of his life, Hollis was on hand to catch her as she fainted. It would not be the first time his hands would be full thanks to Virgil Bayliss' misfortune.

The phones at Railsback Seed & Feed were ringing off the hook with orders from former Bright Star Agricultural customers. Within two weeks Hollis was able to rehire all this father's old employees, and by the time three months had passed he hired two new men. To make things even better, Hollis received a call from the doctors at Twin Oaks announcing that his father was recovering from his stroke.

Hollis saw Joslin on a regular basis, since he drove her up to Little Rock to visit with Virgil every weekend. After three months, Virgil released Joslin from their engagement, speaking as best he could between the timed gasps of the ventilator. Joslin wept all the way home from Little Rock, but when by the time they reached her parents' home she confessed to Hollis that her tears were caused by the guilt she felt for feeling relieved. She felt bad for Virgil, but was happy for herself, for now she realized just how foolish she had been to let her loneliness get the better of her while Hollis was off fighting the war.

As he pulled Joslin into his arms, Hollis was too happy to feel guilty about his good luck. Besides, he deserved to be as happy as the next guy, didn't he? Assuming the next guy was Virgil Bayliss.

NANCY A. COLLINS

Part Two: September, 1957

Hollis Railsback thumbed through the April, 1953 issue of *Photoplay* like a Catholic working a rosary. Over the last few years, the interior of the clinic had become all too familiar to Hollis, but at least he had to count his blessings. Before Lester Bocage came to town in 1950, the nearest medical facility was St. Mary's in Dermott, nearly thirty miles away.

Hollis sighed and tossed the movie magazine back onto the stack of other outdated periodicals that littered the coffee table set in the middle of the room. It was just past midnight by his watch, and he'd been sitting in the waiting room for the better part of an hour. He wondered how much Bocage was going to stick him for opening the clinic for an after-hours emergency.

"Hollis—?"

Lester Bocage stood in the doorway of the waiting room, dressed in his white doctor's coat and clutching a clipboard under one arm, his free hand resting on the doorknob.

"How is she, Doc?" Hollis asked, getting to his feet.

"She's resting," Bocage said, smiling wearily. "Come on back to the office, will you? We need to talk."

Hollis nodded and followed the physician down the hall. Bocage's inner sanctum was crowded with bookcases overflowing with reference books and medical models, including a fully jointed human skeleton that hung from a hook in the ceiling like a gruesome piñata. The skeleton sported a pair of wool socks "so he won't catch cold", as Bocage was fond of quipping.

Bocage dropped into the leather chair behind his desk and motioned for Hollis to take the seat opposite him. "I noticed you didn't bother to ask about the child."

"Is it dead?"

"Yes. Yes, it is. Although I wouldn't exactly have called it a baby," Bocage fished a pack of Chesterfields out of his coat pocket and offered one to Hollis. "Smoke?"

"Don't mind if I do," Hollis said. He took one of the cigarettes, lighting it with his old PX Zippo.

"Hollis, how important is it that y'all have children?"

"What do you mean?"

Bocage leaned forward, his brow knit and voice stern. It was the face he wore whenever he wanted his patients to understand the gravity of their situation. "This was Joslin's *fifth* miscarriage. She's what? Thirty-

KNUCKLES AND TALES: THE PUMPKIN CHILD

two? Have you given any thought to what this is doing to her, emotionally as well as physically?"

"Are you saying there's something wrong with my wife?" Hollis asked, his spine stiffening.

"I'm *telling* you that Joslin can't take another miscarriage. She's never been a strong woman—you know that better than anyone. Have you given any consideration to adoption?"

Hollis sighed and relaxed his shoulders. There was no denying the truth of what Bocage was saying. "No," he said, shaking his head. "We want it to be *our* child, not someone else's. What should I do?"

Bocage shrugged and ground his cigarette out in a ceramic ashtray shaped like a set of lungs. "Unless you can guarantee her next pregnancy comes to term and produces a healthy baby, I recommend you sleep on the couch."

o o o

Joslin lay curled in a ball on the back seat of the Cadillac, mumbling to herself like a child awoken from a deep sleep as Hollis drove back to the house. He couldn't help but reflect on how the sterling luck that had carried him for so long and so far suddenly seemed only to fail him when it came to producing an heir.

In 1947 Hollis closed the old in-town office and relocated Railsback Feed & Seed in the former Bright Star Agricultural building. The move out to the highway proved so profitable Hollis was able to marry Joslin in 1948, confident he could keep her in the style she was accustomed to.

Freed of the confines of downtown Seven Devils, Hollis decided to expand the business to include farm equipment, and in 1951 Railsback Seed & Feed changed its name to Railsback Agricultural Supply. 1953 saw the Railsbacks buying his-and-hers Cadillac cars. In 1955, following Horace Railsback's fatal heart attack while waterskiing, Hollis moved his lovely wife into a brand-new home near the Mammon Creek Country Club.

It was about this time Hollis began to grow concerned he had no one to hand the Railsback fortune over to when the time came. By keeping track of Joslin's menstrual flows, body temperature, and estrus cycles, the Railsbacks were able to pinpoint the exact time when intercourse was most likely to result in conception. Although making love to his wife under these conditions was as enjoyable as being forced to eat a heavy meal on a full belly, Hollis was willing to do whatever it took to insure his posterity. However, getting pregnant and staying that way are two different things.

The first time Joslin miscarried, she was barely six weeks along. The second miscarriage also occurred during the first trimester, as did the third and fourth. According to the doctors, Joslin suffered from a 'nervous uterus' that expelled fetuses at the first sign of stress. Of course, the more she miscarried, the more anxious and stressed-out she became. With this, her fifth pregnancy, Joslin barely managed to reach the second trimester, despite taking to bed the moment the rabbit died.

Doc Bocage was right: Joslin couldn't take much more of this. After her previous miscarriage she had plunged into a depression so deep Hollis had been afraid to leave her alone around sharp objects. If things did not improve soon, he was going to be forced to take desperate measures.

o o o

In the eleven years since he last drove down Indian Mound Road, many things had changed. Granny Grimes' cabin, however, was not one of them. The pumpkin patch was also still there, although in the light of day it seemed far less menacing than he remembered, the Caddo burial mound sitting in the middle of it like a loaf of bread left behind by a forgetful giant.

Hollis approached the cabin slowly; wary of what might leap out from under the porch to greet him. As he drew closer, he could make out the sound of someone chopping wood on the side of the cabin opposite the pumpkin patch. Circling around he saw a young boy, roughly ten years old, dressed in a pair of tattered overalls, splitting cordwood with an axe.

"Excuse me, son..."

The boy halted in mid-swing and turned to regard Hollis with a stare as flat as paving stones. From the set of his mouth and the shape of his nose it was clear that the boy was some kin to the old woman. There was something familiar about the jut of the boy's jaw and the shape of his cheekbones, but given the amount of promiscuity and inbreeding amongst the hicks of Choctaw County, such family resemblances tended to be fairly strong and wide spread. No doubt the boy was some variant of Pritchett.

"I'm looking for Granny Grimes...is she still living?"

Before the boy could answer a familiar voice spoke from behind him. "Of course I'm still amongst th' livin'. I t'ain't daid yet, and don't expect to be for some time to come. "

KNUCKLES AND TALES: THE PUMPKIN CHILD

Granny Grimes stood at the corner of the house, leaning on a hoe, her trembling head covered by a faded sunbonnet. Like her shack and surrounding property, the old woman seemed little changed from the last time Railsback had seen her.

"Ye needn't look so spooked, Mr. Hollis," Granny Grimes said with a dry, rasping laugh. "I seen ye drive up in that fancy Cadillac car while I was out tendin' th' patch." She fished a tattered rag from the pocket of her skirt and mopped at the perspiration dripping from her wrinkled face. "I see ye made Jasper's acquaintance," she nodded at the boy, who turned his back on them and resumed chopping wood without saying a word.

"I need to speak to you about something—personal."

"I didn't think ye jest come out here for the first time in 'leven years jest to see how I was doin'," the old woman snorted. "Come on in and set a spell."

The interior of the cabin was just as dark and cramped as Hollis remembered it, although he noticed that the old woman's bed seemed larger than it had the last time he was there. Hollis caught himself before his mind could wander further, and forced himself to turn his attention back to Granny.

"What do you know about babies?" he asked.

Granny Grimes smiled crookedly. "Thas what most folks come t'me for—th' begettin' or gittin' rid of young'uns. And it's fair t'say, without me braggin', that I done forgot more about chirrun than ol' Doc Boo-Cage will ever know on the subject."

"My wife and I have been trying to have us a kid—but the pregnancies won't take. I'm afraid she can't take much more stress. She feels like its all her fault, her not being able to give me a child."

"It ain't her fault. The fault lies with *ye*, not her. When ye come out here that last time, ye axed me t' put yore luck on another and have his luck put on ye. Well, thas exactly what happened. It simply weren't Virgil Bayliss' luck t'have young'uns."

Railsback flinched at the sound of Virgil's name. It had been nearly a decade since he had heard the name spoken aloud. Joslin didn't like talking about Virgil, and all of their employees and friends at the Country Club knew better than to bring up the subject. Not that there was any reason for Virgil's name to come up in casual conversation. Last Hollis heard, Virgil was still stuck inside an iron lung at the State Hospital.

"But, ain't there some way of getting around that? Some kind of spell you can work?"

"Ye don't know what yore axin'. Ye got what ye wanted, but to get it ye had to give up whatever it was ye once had. Now ye come to me sayin' ye want yore old luck back."

"I don't want *all* of it back, just some of it."

"Luck ain't like water in a rain-barrel! Ye can't just take what ye want and leave the rest behind!"

Hollis's frustration level had always been low, and eleven years of having things his way had done nothing to raise his threshold of tolerance. He grabbed Granny by one of her broomstick arms and spun her around to face him.

"*God-damn you, old woman—! Can you do what I asked or not?*"

Something struck Hollis's right shoulder hard enough to make him stagger a few steps and let go of the old woman. The boy Jasper stood in the doorway, breathing hard, a split of wood clutched in one hand.

"You little son of a bitch!" Hollis snarled, his eyes narrowing into slits. "How *dare* you strike me?"

The boy bared his teeth like a feral dog and charged forward, the wood raised over his head.

"Jasper! No!" Granny cried, but it was too late.

Hollis disarmed his young attacker using his old commando training, sending the boy crashing into the wall, knocking down shelves and sending their contents flying. Jasper lay dazed amongst the dried herbs and preserved foodstuffs, a thin trickle of blood creeping across his upper lip.

"There was no call for ye to do that! He's jest a chile!" Granny snapped at him as she knelt beside the boy.

"The little bastard shouldn't have hit me!" Hollis snarled, massaging his shoulder. "Now, are you going answer me, woman, or am I going to have to get rough with *you*, too?"

There was a growling sound from underneath the house. Railsback glanced down and saw a pair of eyes looking up at him from between the loosely fitted floorboards, red as fresh-banked coals. Whatever the eyes belonged to, it was not a dog. Hollis let his fists fall open and stepped away from the old woman and the boy, his mouth suddenly too dry to spit.

"Y'all townies is all alike," Granny Grimes said in disgust. "Always comin' out here, demandin' 'this,' orderin' that, as if havin' flush toilets and 'lectric lights make y'all something special! But for all yore gadgets and gee-gaws, y'all *still* come out to see ol' Granny for yore hoodoo! Very well, I'll do as ye ax. I'll fix it so's ye and yore woman can get a young'un. But it don't come cheap. Ye pay me what it's worth."

"How much?"

KNUCKLES AND TALES: THE PUMPKIN CHILD

"Well, I'm a simple woman used to simple ways, and there's no changin' me this far along. But th' boy...th' boy got his life ahead of him. I would like to see him get his-self a proper education..."

Hollis cast a dubious glance in Jasper's direction. "What for? To study to be a half-wit? The child can't even speak!"

"Oh, Jasper can talk, awright," Granny said, patting the boy's head like she would a dog's. "When he has a mind to. But thas besides the point. I reckon ten thousand dollars will do jest fine."

"Ten thousand dollars?" Hollis shouted, the blood rushing to his face. "Are you out of your senile old mind?"

"Be that as it may," Granny replied evenly. "But it is still th' price. Take it or leave it."

Hollis fumed for a long minute, trying hard to figure some other way of getting what he needed from the witch without coughing up the money, but he was over a barrel and she knew it. He grimaced and reached inside his jacket. "Very well...can you take a check?"

"What use do I have for a piece of paper with yore name on it?" Granny replied, spitting on the floor. "It's cash on th' barrel-head or nothin'. Thems th' terms."

"I don't have that kind of money on me. It'll take a couple of days for me to get together the funds."

"That suits me just fine. It'll take a couple of days for me to mix up th' necessary potions. Come back out here in three days with th' money, and I'll have everything ready."

Hollis did as he was told and returned in three days. But as he pulled up in front of Granny Grimes shack, he was alarmed to see the old woman talking to a man standing on the porch. The man was in his late thirties and thin as a rake, dressed in nothing but a pair of busted-out overalls and a filthy homespun shirt, holding a croaker sack in one hand. Hollis did not recognize the man, but he stayed put in the Cadillac, just to be on the safe side, until Granny's visitor vacated the property, leaving her with the sack he'd been carrying.

"Who the hell was that?" Hollis snapped.

"That there was Waddy Creek. Lives on t'other side of th' patch from me. He was seein' about his young'un, Naddy. Seems the gal got herself in the family way. Waddy wants me to tend to th' chile when her time comes. He was payin' me in advance for my services." She pointed to the sack lying on the porch, which twitched feebly, as if whatever was inside wasn't through dying. "Speakin' of which, ye got my money?"

"Here it is," he said sullenly, handing over a shoebox held shut with a thick rubber band. "You want to count it?"

"I think ye got enough sense not to try an' cheat me," she replied over her humped shoulder. Inside the cabin Jasper was tending a pot of foul-smelling liquid bubbling atop the stove. The boy glanced up long enough to fix Hollis with a sullen glare, and then returned to stirring.

"I gots what ye need," Granny said, holding a small leather pouch out for his inspection. Inside the bag was a finely ground powder the color of dirty snow. "Sprinkle this on her food and mix it up in her drank for the next week, but do not spend yore seed with her. Then, on the night when the moon is dark, go to her bed as her husband."

"Are you sure this will work?"

"That mixture can make a mule drop kittens! Jasper here is proof of that," Granny replied

Hollis didn't exactly know what to make of that last statement, or the way the boy looked at him. He wasted no time leaving Indian Mound Road and heading back into town.

o o o

"So, Doc...what's the verdict?"

Dr. Bocage looked over the top of the lab report at the Railsbacks. They were seated side-by-side, Joslin's hand folded inside Hollis's bigger one, their eyes alight with a mixture of hope and dread that had become all too familiar.

"Well, according to these results, Joslin, you are, indeed, pregnant."

Joslin's tight, anxious grimace melted into a genuine smile, and a tear slipped from the corner of her eye. "Praise Jesus," she said. "When am I due?"

"Judging from what you've told me, I'd put your delivery date at the end of October. Looks like y'all might have yourself a pumpkin child."

"You *really* think so, Doc?"

"I don't' want you to get your hopes up *too* high, Joslin. But I *am* encouraged your color's improved, and that your blood count is much better than those during your previous pregnancies. However, I want you to avoid *anything* that might possibly lead to stress! Stay in bed as much as possible. Let the maid handle the heavy lifting and the laundry. You just worry about making sure that baby has a happy Halloween."

o o o

"Mister Hollis..?"

KNUCKLES AND TALES: THE PUMPKIN CHILD

"Yes, Willie-Jo?" Railsback said, looking over the top of the evening paper at the maid, a compact, middle-aged Negro woman, who was standing in his doorway. "What is it?"

"It's 'bout Miz Joslin," Willie-Jo replied uneasily.

Hollis folded his paper and set it aside. "Is something wrong?"

"Thas just it, Mister Hollis," Willie-Jo said. "I can't rightly say. Perhaps if you come and take a look for yourself."

Hollis followed Willie-Jo from his study into the kitchen. Several plates were arranged alongside the counter next to the sink. On the plates were the chewed bones of various cuts of meat, some of which still had bits of gristle clinging to them. Hollis readily recognized a T-bone steak and a couple of pork chops, as well as a chicken drumstick. A fourth plate was smeared with a dark, viscous semi-liquid that looked like congealed blood.

"When Miz Joslin went to lunch today with her mama, I took the opportunity to clean up her room. I found these here dishes shoved under her bed."

"I don't see any cause for alarm, Willie-Jo," Hollis shrugged. "After all, she's three months along now, and she's eatin' for two."

"That's not what I'm gettin' at, Mister Hollis," the maid said, her voice growing tighter. "I didn't cook *none* of this food. Neither did Miz Joslin or anybody else! Everything here was et raw! And I can't find the calves liver I had wrapped in butcher paper for tonight's dinner. She can get herself poisoned doin' like that—!"

Hollis reached into his wallet and pulled out a handful of bills. "Here's some money. Phone Seaman's Grocery and have them deliver whatever you need to make dinner. And don't fret, Willie-Jo. I'm sure Miz Joslin's just fine—she'd just craving iron, is all."

"Yes, Mr. Hollis," Willie-Jo said, without much conviction, as she took the offered cash. "As you say, sir."

o o o

That night, as they dined on chicken and dumplings, Hollis found himself watching Joslin eat. Funny how he hadn't noticed it before, but his wife had undergone a significant sea change with her sixth pregnancy. She had gained weight and her china doll complexion was now as ruddy as that of a washerwoman's. Where once Joslin had been an orchid, subsisting on nothing but sunlight and air, she now seemed firmly rooted in the earth, like a flowering plant...or a fruit-bearing vine.

"What are you staring at?" Joslin asked as she ladled another helping of dumplings onto her plate.

"Nothing, really," he said, flashing his best reassuring smile. "I was just noticing how...healthy...you look. How are you feeling, honey?"

"Ravenous!" she said, with a girlish giggle. "Honestly, sometimes I wonder if I can *ever* eat enough! But Doc Bocage tells me that's a good sign...he says I was probably underweight during my earlier pregnancies."

"That a fact?" Hollis replied, pushing a dumpling around the edge of the plate with his fork. "Have you been, um, experiencing cravings lately?"

"Cravings? What kind of cravings?" she asked, cocking her head like a spaniel.

"Oh...ice cream and pickles, that kind of thing."

"Heavens, no!" she said with a laugh. "That's just an old wife's tale, Hollis! Although, now that you mention it, I *do* have a hankering for pumpkin pie..."

o o o

He was standing on top of the Caddo burial mound, staring down at the pumpkin patch, spread out before him like a minefield. With the knowledge that comes with dreams, he knew something was waiting for him out there in the pumpkin patch. Although he was not sure exactly what it might be, he knew, whatever it was, it was most definitely evil and meant him harm.

Knowing these things, he realized that he was safe as long as he remained atop the mound and did not enter the pumpkin patch. Just as he started to relax, secure in his inviolability, he heard a baby cry. The sound seemed distant and yet close at hand, twisted by echo until it was somewhere between the wail of an infant and the yowl of a cat.

Although he realized it was impossible, since his child was still twenty weeks from being born, somehow the crying baby was his own. His son was lost somewhere in the pumpkin patch, helpless and afraid. And with the certainty born of nightmares, he knew that whatever it was lurking in the pumpkin patch was hunting for the child.

Suddenly he was no longer atop the burial mound, but down in the pumpkin patch. The pumpkins were unnaturally large and extremely orange, with vines as thick as snakes, the leaves as wide as napkins. Something grunted somewhere in the darkness, and he caught the rank smell of almost-animal on the night wind.

KNUCKLES AND TALES: THE PUMPKIN CHILD

The baby cries again, and although he can tell it is somewhere nearby, it's wail seemed muffled. Desperate to find his child before the thing in the darkness did, Hollis pushed aside the flowering vines, peered under drooping leaves...until he realized that something was wrong with the pumpkin at his feet.

He stared at the swollen orange fruit for what seemed like an eternity before noticing the fruit nearest the stem had been cut away with a knife, then carefully replaced, just like a jack o'lantern, except no face was carved into the rind. Although he did not know why or how, he was certain beyond any doubt that his son was inside the pumpkin. So he lifted the lid and peered inside.

The thing inside the hollowed-out pumpkin was not so much a child as a half-formed fetus, with an oversized head, an undeveloped body, and tiny matchstick extremities. Its eyes were huge and dark, like almonds painted black and pressed into the head of a marzipan doll. It had a lizard's tail growing from the base of its spine, which wiggled like a worm in fresh-turned earth, and split feet like that of an ostrich. As Hollis stared in horror and loathing at the thing that he had made, his son opened a lipless mouth and mewled like a kitten.

Something in the darkness coughed like a lion at a watering hole, and he realized that the horror in the pumpkin shell had conspired with the thing that was stalking him to lure him away from the mound. He ran back in the direction of the Indian mound, but the geography of his dream had turned into that of a nightmare: no matter where he turned, the mound was nowhere to be found.

He charged blindly through the pumpkin patch, like a rabbit pursued by a hound, his heart thundering wildly in his chest, his eyes bugging in terror. He ran and ran until he collided headlong with something that knocked him to the ground. Trembling in fear, he looked up at the shadowy figure looming over him, expecting it to be the monstrous lurker from the shadows, ready to pounce on him with its razor-sharp claws and teeth.

Instead, the figure blocking his path simply stood there, motionless and speechless, its arms spread wide, like a fisherman demonstrating the size of the one that got away. With a sudden start, he realized what he was looking at is neither man nor monster, but a scarecrow.

He allowed himself a relieved chuckle at his own expense...until he saw the effigy's face. Although its head was a burlap bag stuffed with straw, with shoe buttons for eyes and a crudely stitched mouth, there was no mistaking the seamed and wrinkled features of Virgil Bayliss staring down at him.

NANCY A. COLLINS

o o o

Hollis awoke choking on a scream. He lay there beside his wife, breathing fast and hard, uncertain whether he had cried out in his sleep. Joslin muttered something in her sleep and rolled over on her side, pushing her swollen belly against him. Hollis jerked away as if he'd touched a live coal, quickly pulling on his bathrobe.

Careful not to awake Joslin, he tiptoed out of the bedroom and headed downstairs to his den and its liquor cabinet. There he sat in his favorite easy chair and drank bourbon, staring out the window at the darkened landscape, until the rising sun chased away the last shadows of night.

o o o

Although he had long since moved his business out onto the highway, Hollis still took lunch "in town" at the Sip-N-Sup. That particular day downtown was more crowded than usual, so he had to park his Cadillac car a little further down the street than usual and walk back up the block to the restaurant.

As he headed in the direction of the Sip-N-Sup, Hollis saw the strange figure of a man moving towards him. The other man was dressed in dark, loose-fitting clothes and walked with the aid of aluminum arm-crutches, dragging his legs behind him like afterthoughts. Hollis stared so long at the stranger's wasted lower extremities he did not think to look into his face until he was almost upon him. A horrible wash of vertigo overcame him, like that of a mountain climber whose handhold has unexpectedly crumbled in his grip.

"Hollis! Hollis Railsback!" Virgil Bayliss said. "Remember me?"

"Sweet Jesus! Virgil—is that *you*?" The shock and amazement that crossed Hollis' face was indeed genuine. The golden boy of their shared youth was long gone, replaced by an emaciated stick figure with the sunken eyes and translucent skin of an invalid.

"Yes, it's me—or, rather, what's left of me."

"How did you get out? I mean, I thought the doctors said your case was..."

"Incurable?" Virgil finished the sentence for him with a bitter smile. "So did I. But, the strangest thing happened about four, almost five months ago...I suddenly started to recover."

"Is that a fact?" Hollis said, trying to keep his smile from turning into a rictus grin. "After all this time? Well, don't that beat all."

KNUCKLES AND TALES: THE PUMPKIN CHILD

"I've never been one to question my luck," Virgil said, without apparent irony, "And I'm not about to start now. The doctors say I'll never be what I was, but within a few years I might be able to walk with just a cane."

"Well, that's just...*wonderful*, Virgil. Glad to hear it. Where you staying in town?"

"I'm living with my sister and her family, for the time being. And old friend of my father's set me up with a job as a notary public at the courthouse. It ain't much, but at least I'm earning my keep..."

"I'm happy things are lookin' up for you, Virgil. Truly I am."

"I reckon I should be the one offerin' the congratulations," Bayliss said, with a crooked smile. "I hear you and Joslin have a young'un on the way."

"God willin' and the creek don't rise," Hollis replied, crossing his fingers. "We had our share of troubles there, but it looks like our luck has finally changed in that department."

"Amen to that," Virgil said solemnly, nodding his head. "I'd offer to shake, but I'm afraid that's out of the question." He held up his right crutch, gripped in a pale, knobby hand. "I got to get back to the courthouse. This is my first day at work. Maybe we can meet for lunch at the Sip-N-Sup sometime soon? Just like old times."

"Yeah," Hollis said emptily. "Just like old times."

o o o

"Hollis, honey? Are you coming to bed?"

Railsback glanced up from his desk and stared at his wife for a long moment as she stood in the doorway of his study. She was wearing a long nightgown made from some semi-sheer fabric that would have, normally, been enough for him to quit what he was doing and turn in for the night. Now, however, it made her swollen belly look like a moon glimpsed through a scrim of clouds.

"You go on up to bed, darling," he said, smiling wanly. "I'll be up after I deal with this paperwork."

Joslin frowned. She could sense he was lying to her, but couldn't figure out why. As she left the room she paused and turned back to look at him. "Hollis..?"

"Hmm?"

"I was talkin' to Suzie Huckabee today, and she said she saw Virgil Bayliss over at the courthouse. Is that true?"

"If she says so, then I reckon it is."

Joslin flashed a smile brighter than any Hollis could remember being turned in his direction in a long time. "Oh, Hollis! Isn't it *wonderful* that Virgil's out of the hospital?"

"If you consider him bein' crippled up an' poorer'n Job's turkey 'wonderful', then, I guess, yes, it's wonderful," he snapped.

"I was just saying how nice it must be for Virgil to be out of that horrid iron lung and finally able to come home…" Joslin said, clearly baffled by her husband's attitude.

"I *know* what you're saying," he replied tersely. "Now go on up to bed."

Hollis waited a couple of seconds after Joslin closed the door of the study to make sure she wasn't coming back, then took the bottle of bourbon out of his desk drawer.

Virgil Bayliss. Virgil goddamn Bayliss. First in his dreams, now on the fucking sidewalk on his damned cripple-sticks. He thought he had gotten that bastard out of his life twelve years ago, only to wake up and find him back again.

He especially didn't like the fact Virgil started recovering from his polio around the exact same time Joslin became pregnant. That *really* bothered him. What if his old luck had found him and was coming home to roost? Granny Grimes warned him he was stirring fire with a sword, but he had been too obsessed with his need for a son to listen to her warnings.

Still, there was no true cause for alarm on his part. The Virgil Bayliss he spoke to today was as much the old Virgil Bayliss he had so keenly resented as the man in the moon. Indeed, he actually felt pity for the cripple. After all, his good looks were ruined, his health broken, his fortune lost, and he was reduced to living with his kid sister and taking charity from his father's old cronies up at the state house. What was there to envy or resent…?

No, Virgil was the one envying *him* now. How galling it must be for him to come back home, only to find his place of business and former fiancée claimed by the same man? How bitter must Virgil's heart be, knowing that the house Hollis lived in, the cars he owned, and the woman who shared his bed could have all been his? How must it pain him to lie there, in his sister's spare bedroom, and think about how the child in Joslin's belly should have been his?

No, strike that last part.

Still, as much as it made Hollis feel good thinking about how much better he had it than Virgil, he could not shake the feeling that, somehow, as miserable as his life might be, Virgil Bayliss did not have dreams of being hunted in the pumpkin patch by something that wasn't quite an animal, but was most certainly not a man.

KNUCKLES AND TALES: THE PUMPKIN CHILD
Part Three: Halloween, 1958

The first contractions occurred one minute after midnight, although Hollis was no longer sharing a bed with his wife. As Joslin's belly continued to expand, and his drinking had grown worse, Hollis had gradually surrendered his marriage bed in favor of sleeping on the sofa in his study. Despite this, Joslin's initial howl of pain was loud enough to wake him.

Hollis sat bolt upright on the sofa, looking around blearily, his senses still blunted by the bourbon he used to put himself to sleep. It took him a long second before realizing the cries of pain, for once, were not part of his nightmare, but coming from upstairs.

He took the stairs two at a time, his heart banging like a tractor cylinder. He found Joslin sitting up in bed, her hands resting on her swollen stomach like a swami's crystal ball. Her features were drawn and she bit her lower lip in pain as another contraction hit her.

"Is it time?" he asked, trying to keep the fear out of his voice.

"It's time," she replied, smiling through her discomfort. "You better go call Doc Bocage and tell him our lit'l punkin child is on his way."

Hollis nodded dumbly and hurried back downstairs to phone the doctor. So many thoughts were fighting for room and attention inside his head: he had to find his shoes, pull the car around, make sure Joslin didn't forget the little overnight case packed with a change of clothes, then call Joslin's family and let them know what going on, get a message to Edna, who had replaced Mamie as his personal secretary when she retired in '53, that he wouldn't be in the office in the morning...But, first, he had to call Lester and let him know that Joslin was in labor and that they were on their way to the clinic.

His hands were trembling so fiercely it took three tries for him to get his index finger in the rotary dial. The phone on the other end of the line rang once, twice, thrice...

"Hello?" The voice on the other end was blurred by sleep, but Hollis recognized it as belonging to Bocage's wife.

"Tess? It's me, Hollis Railsback. Can you put Lester on the horn? Joslin's gone into labor."

"I'm sorry, Hollis, but Lester's not here."

"*What?*"

"He's in Lake Village."

"What the hell is he doing in Lake Village at this time of night?"

"Ginger Teeter went into premature labor earlier this evening.

Lester followed the ambulance to Lake Village General. I don't expect him back until daylight."

"Jesus Christ on the cross, Tess! What am I supposed to do here? Joslin's in labor!"

"Try and keep your head, Hollis. You won't do Joslin or yourself any good gettin' upset. Babies don't just fall out on the floor. Joslin's got at least six to twelve hours to go before she'll be ready to deliver. I'll put a call into Lake Village, that way Lester can swing by your place on his way back into town."

"But, what should I do?"

"There's not much you *can* do right now, except hold her hand, give her some ice chips so she doesn't get dehydrated, and make sure she's comfortable."

Hollis hurried into the kitchen and grabbed one of the ice trays out of the freezer and wrapped the ice cubes in a hand towel and whacked it a few times with the tenderizing mallet, then dumped the busted ice into a small bowl. He wasn't sure what good cracked ice would do, but at least it kept him busy.

When he got back upstairs, he found Joslin sprawled on the floor between the bed and the closet, moaning in pain. He dropped the bowl, ice chips instantly forgotten, and scooped up his wife and placed her on the bed.

"Baby, are you alright? What happened?"

Joslin's head rolled from shoulder to shoulder, her eyelids fluttering as she fought to regain consciousness. "I was going...to get...the overnight case...but the pain...it was too much...I must have fainted...Did you call the doctor?"

"I called him, alright. Look, honey, I got some bad news. Doc Bocage had an emergency call that took him out of the county..."

Joslin's eyes widened with fear as what he was telling her registered. "Hollis, what are we gonna do?"

"I spoke to Lester's wife, and she said that you've got a few more hours to go before the baby comes. Lester should be back by then. Everything will be awright. I fetched you some ice chips..."

"*To hell with ice chips!*" Joslin snapped, her eyes flashing with pain. "And to *hell* with Tess Bocage! There's something wrong, Hollis!" She grimaced as another spasm gripped her abdomen, leaving her panting like a winded animal. "It feels like I got knives inside me. It's not supposed to feel like this, Hollis. Something's wrong—bad wrong. You gotta get some help."

KNUCKLES AND TALES: THE PUMPKIN CHILD

"But, the doc's in Lake Village..."

Joslin dug her nails deep enough into Hollis's forearm to draw blood, the corners of her mouth pulled so tight her lips disappeared. *"Get help!"*

o o o

Although it was well after midnight, there was still a light burning in the window of Granny Grimes' shack. Hollis made the porch in a single bound, unmindful of what might lurk beneath its stoop, and pushed open the front door without knocking.

A solitary Coleman lantern hung from a hook in the ceiling, casting its lambent glow about the tiny one-room cabin. Jasper sat in front of the stove, perched atop an upended orange crate, reading a dog-eared funny book, but Granny was nowhere to be seen.

"Where is she?" Hollis demanded, stepping towards the boy, his hands closing into fists. "Where's the old woman?"

Jasper stared silently at Hollis for a long moment, then returned his gaze to the tattered copy of Archie Comics.

"You pay attention when I'm talkin' to you, you little fuck!" Hollis bellowed, boxing the boy's ears hard enough to knock him onto the floor. "Where's the old witch?!? Answer me, or I swear by Almighty God I'll kick you yeller, boy! And don't think I won't do it, too!"

Jasper wiped his lower lip, stared at the smear of crimson on the back of his hand, then looked up at the man towering over him.

"She's off deliverin' the Creek baby," he said sullenly. Hollis was slightly surprised to hear the boy speak, as he wasn't sure the boy was not a mute.

"Well, you go an' fetch her! Tell her my wife's gone into labor and is in a bad way, but the doctor's been called outta town! I need her help with the baby! Tell her there's money in it for her." He took a piece of paper and a pencil from his pants pocket and scribbled down his address and shoved it into the boy's hand. "Here's where I live. Tell her I'll leave the front door unlocked." When Jasper didn't instantly leap up and bolt out the door, Hollis lifted back his left foot, in preparation of putting a boot in the gut. "You heard me, boy! If I tell you 'frog', you jump!"

Jasper scrambled to his feet and dashed out the door into the chill autumn night without once looking back. Hollis shook his head in disgust as he watched Jasper run through the pumpkin patch in the direction of Waddy Creek's place. Apparently the only way to get through to the boy was with a strong right hand and the threat of violence. With that, Hollis drove back home to await Granny Grimes' arrival.

o o o

When Hollis pulled up to the front of the house, he could hear Joslin screaming, even though all the windows were closed. He hurried upstairs and found Joslin looking much worse than when he left her. Her hair was plastered tight to her skull with sweat, and the lines in her face were etched so sharply they looked like scalpel wounds. The bedclothes were twisted and snarled, and the bottom half of the mattress was soaked with fluid.

"My water broke," Joslin gasped by way of explanation. "Where did you go? Did you get help?" Her eyes darted around the room, hoping to spot signs of an ambulance crew or a doctor.

"I sent for a midwife."

"Midwife—?" Joslin frowned. "Where is she?"

"She'll be here shortly. She was off delivering another baby, but don't you worry. I had her..." Hollis paused, uncertain of exactly what relation Jasper was to Granny "...I had her boy fetch her."

"Are you sure it'll be safe?" Joslin asked.

"We've got nothing to fear," Hollis said, patting her hand. "After all, Granny Grimes has delivered more babies than Lester Bocage has hair on his head."

"*Jesussssss!*" Joslin shrieked and grabbed the corners of the mattress, baring her teeth in a grimace.

"I'll go get you some water," Hollis said, and quickly hurried back downstairs, eager to excuse himself from the room. He returned to the freezer to make more ice chips, only to realize he hadn't bothered to refill the trays he had emptied earlier.

"*Son of a bitch!*" Hollis shouted, hurling the aluminum ice cube trays across the kitchen. He angrily pounded the kitchen table several times with his balled-up fist. After a minute or two of swearing and beating the hell out of the furniture, he stepped back and took a deep breath, trying to regain control of himself.

He had never expected to be this involved in the birthing of his child. He had imagined his role would be limited to driving Joslin to the clinic and pacing the waiting room, chain-smoking cigarettes until the doctor stuck a little bundle wrapped in a blue blanket in his arms and said, "Congratulations, it's a boy!" He certainly hadn't bargained for any of this.

KNUCKLES AND TALES: THE PUMPKIN CHILD

There was nothing he could really do to help Joslin except hold her hand and tell her the doctor was on his way over and over again like a goddamned broken record. If there was anything Hollis hated more than Freedom Riders and Johnson Grass, it was feeling helpless. And right now he was about as much use as handles on a house.

If he was going to face what the rest of the night had to offer, it would require a little Dutch courage. He went into his study and retrieved a fresh bottle of bourbon from his desk. All he needed was a little belt, that was all, before going back upstairs to his groaning, sweating, laboring wife. There was nothing wrong in taking a drink to steady his nerves, right? He was no use to Joslin and the baby if he panicked, right?

He was a quarter-way through the bottle when he heard what sounded like hoof beats headed towards the house. Hollis went to the window and peered out through the curtains. Granny Grimes was coming up the drive on a mule, a carpetbag satchel clutched in one hand. As the mule got closer, Hollis saw the boy Jasper riding behind Granny, his arms wrapped about her waist. Hollis was glad it was the middle of the night and that his house was set a quarter mile back from the road. It wouldn't do for the neighbors to see the local witchy-woman walking through the front door of the richest man in town.

Hollis stepped out of the study just as Granny crossed the threshold into the house. She paused in the foyer, staring up at the crystal chandelier blazing over her head, a look of disdain on her wizened face.

"Hmph. So that there's 'lectricity," she said. "Don't seem that special, if ye ask me."

"Thank God you're here!"

Hollis had never thought he would ever be glad to see Granny Grimes again, but now it was all he could do to keep from bursting into tears. The same obviously could not be said for Granny, who regarded Hollis as if she'd just scraped him off her shoe.

"Gawd ain't got nothin' to do with it," she replied. "Where's yore woman?"

Before Hollis could reply, a scream of pain loud enough to cause the pendants on the chandelier to rattle came from upstairs. Granny glanced up at the ceiling and nodded. "Well, I reckon that answers that question. I'm gone head on up and see what's what."

"What about me? What do you want me to do?" Hollis asked as he watched the old woman climb the stairs to the second floor.

"I'm gone need fresh towels. Ye can show Jasper here where y'all keep 'em."

Hollis glanced over the boy, who was still standing on the stoop, staring warily about the foyer. "C'mon inside," he said, motioning for Jasper to enter the house. "I'll show you the linen closet."

Hollis lead the way down the hall to the first floor closet, from which he removed an armload of towels and handed them to Jasper. As he stood in the open doorway, he realized for the first time he was still holding the bottle of bourbon.

"What the hell?" he muttered. "I can afford to relax now."

Hollis tilted back his head as he lifted the bottle to his lips, taking his eyes off the boy. Suddenly the door slammed shut, sending him staggering backward, spilling most of the content of the bottle onto his shirt. He grabbed the doorknob, but it refused to turn.

"Let me out of here, you little shit!" he shouted, pounding his fist against the doorjamb. *"What the hell are you playing at?"*

If Jasper gave an answer, Hollis could not discern what it was. He pressed his ear to the door and strained to hear if the boy was giggling at his little prank, but all he could hear was his own heart, rabbiting away in his chest. No doubt the little bastard pulled the stunt to get back at Hollis for slapping him around earlier. Well, by damn, the little son of a bitch was *really* going to catch Billy Blue Hill now! Hollis gulped down the remaining bourbon, narrowing his eyes as he plotted his vengeance on the nappy-headed wood's colt.

o o o

Hollis was not aware he had drifted off until the sound of the closet door slowly swinging open started him awake. Despite the awkwardness of his situation, the combination of alcohol, darkness, and silence had somehow managed to lull him into a state of unconsciousness. Hollis stumbled out of the closet, but there was no sign of anyone in the hall.

"That's right, you lit'l pissant!" Hollis shouted. *"You better run an' hide! Cause when I catch you, boy, you're gonna have to part your hair to sneeze!"*

As his own voice echoed through the house unchallenged, two things suddenly occurred to Hollis: all the lights had been turned off, and except for the ticking of the grandfather clock in the front parlor and his own ragged breathing, the house was as silent as a morgue.

Joslin.

He took the stairs three at a time, his mouth so dry he couldn't work up enough spit to lick a stamp. As he reached the second floor, the bedroom door was standing wide open. A sick dread, as clammy as a dead man's hand, closed about his heart.

KNUCKLES AND TALES: THE PUMPKIN CHILD

"Joslin?" he whispered as he stepped into the darkened room. "Joslin, honey—are you there?"

The bedroom was darker than the rest of the house, as its drapes were still drawn against the inevitable arrival of the morning sun. Still, the smell is enough to tell him something has gone horribly, horribly wrong. The last time he smelled anything like it was during the war, when one of the guys in his platoon caught shrapnel in the gut, causing his bowels to spill out of his body like grotesque party streamers. Although Hollis knew he didn't want to see what lay in wait for him on the bed, he automatically turned on the bedside lamp.

The first thing he saw was bread knife from the kitchen lying on the bloodstained mattress, its blade still wet. Then he saw Joslin, lying in a rapidly cooling pool of blood, her arms and legs tangled amongst the soiled sheets. Despite the volume of blood spilled, there were only two identifiable wounds on her body: a severed jugular and the gaping wound that ran from her pubic bone to her sternum. Whoever killed her had also removed several laps of gut, neatly arranging them onto her left breast and shoulder, as if hollowing her out like a jack o'lantern.

He wanted to cry, vomit, and tear his hair. He wanted to scream loud enough and hard enough to punch a hole in the roof of heaven and let God know the injustice done unto him. He wanted to do all these things, but the best Hollis could do was a blubbering sob.

"Joslin—Jesus, baby, I'm so sorry! I'm so sorry..!"

"Yore sorry, awright."

Granny Grimes was standing just inside the bedroom door, holding her carpetbag in front of her with both hands.

"You murderin' witch! I'll kill you for this—!" Hollis snatched the knife up and advanced on Granny Grimes, ready to plunge the blade into her withered breast.

The old woman did not seem the least bit concerned for her safety. She shook her head, more contemptuous than fearful. "Ye townies is all alike! Just cause me an' Jasper come t'town two onna mule don't mean I ain't got sense t' protect myself." Granny spat out of the left side of her mouth and said in a loud, resonating voice; *"Sathan: show thyself."*

There appeared before Granny Grimes a creature the likes of which Hollis Railsback had never seen before, yet whose scent was all too familiar. The beast was six feet in length and stood three feet high at the shoulder, with yellow-gray fur. It had long forelegs in comparison to its hindquarters, and the back feet sported four toes capped with non-retractable claws. Its head, which hung low between its hunched shoulders, was hairless, with a prominent brow and patches of bright blue ribbed skin marking its cheeks, as well as a long, bright scarlet snout. As it took a step towards him, Hollis realized the creature's forelegs ended in something resembling hands.

The thing Granny called Sathan fixed Hollis with eyes red as a murderer's hand and peeled its lips back in a vicious snarl that revealed fangs as long and as sharp as the blade he carried—and far more numerous.

Hollis screamed in terror at the sight of the thing from under the porch and dropped the knife. "Keep it away! Keep it way from me!"

Granny Grimes smoothed her familiar's neck ruff with a gnarled hand and clucked her tongue. "Ye jest couldn't leave things be, could ye? It weren't enough swappin' out poor ole Virgil Bayliss' luck for yore own, was it? Ye had to have his luck, and yore own as well. But now yore payin' th' price for such folly."

"Why did you have to kill my wife?" Hollis blubbered. "She had nothing to do with this..."

"What was yore woman t'me?" Granny snapped. "I give her to ye in th' first place, I figger I got th' right to take her away. Her and th' young'un, too."

Hollis lowered his hand from his face and stared at the old woman. He had forgotten about the child. There had been no sign of a baby amongst the blood and spilled entrails on the bed. "Where's my baby—? Damn you, witch, what have you done with my son?"

"I got yore baby right here, Mr. Hollis," she said, patting the satchel made from carpet scraps. "It's more of my makin' than y'all's, anyhow. That remedy I give ya'll? Th' one that put th' seed in yore woman's belly and kept it there? That there was a left-hand charm. Anything sowed by th' left-hand is marked to serve the Dark One. Yore baby ain't got a soul, Mr. Hollis. Not now, not ever. And as for yore son...well, I raised him up as best I could."

"Thas right, 'Daddy'," Jasper sneered as he stepped out of the shadows and pressed the cold muzzle of a gun to Railsback's right temple.

The last thing through Hollis Railsback's mind before the bullet was whether or not any of Virgil Bayliss' luck might follow him into the afterlife.

o o o

Naddy Creek woke up wondering where her baby was.

One of the last things she could remember was Granny Grimes giving

KNUCKLES AND TALES: THE PUMPKIN CHILD

her a cup of something warm and funny-tasting to drink to help her with the pain. Just as she was falling asleep, she thought she saw Daddy take the baby from where it lay beside her in the bed and hand it over to Granny, who then popped it inside her satchel.

"Daddy—?" Naddy called out from her bed. "Daddy? You home?"

There was no answer, but Naddy knew that didn't mean nothing. She struggled out of bed, grimacing as she swung her feet onto the hard-packed dirt that served as their floor. Her lower half felt like she'd been laid into with a two-by-four, but the need to find her baby was strong enough to keep her upright.

Naddy pushed back the old horse blanket that separated the bedroom from the rest of the house and peered out into the front room. Waddy Creek, her father and sole remaining relative, was seated at the table, staring hard into the hurricane lamp before him, his left hand wrapped around a jar of Pappy Pritchett's shine. Naddy moved towards him in a mincing shuffle as if she was carrying an apron full of eggs.

"Daddy...didn't ye hear me callin' ye?"

Waddy Creek twitched as if she'd pricked him with a pin. He looked up at his daughter with unfocused eyes. "Should ye be up an' about so soon, gal?"

"Daddy—whare's th' baby?"

The corners of Waddy's mouth pulled down, as if he'd bit into something sour and he quickly looked away. "Baby's daid."

"But—but, I heared it cry."

"Yore mistaken, girl," Waddy said, downing another scalding gulp of shine. "It ne'er drew breath. It was born daid."

Naddy was only thirteen years old, and she might not have had any book learning, but she knew enough to realize when her father was lying to her. Like the time he told her putting his thing in her wouldn't hurt, and now, with him saying her baby was dead.

"Yore lyin' to me, Daddy," she said, her voice hard and angry. "Ye give Granny my baby t'get rid of, didn't ye?"

Waddy whipped his head around so fast he nearly over turned in his chair. "Ye callin' me a liar, girl?"

"I'm callin' ye *worst* than a liar, Daddy."

"Why ye mouthy lit'l slut!" Waddy slurred, pushing himself away from the table. "After all I done for ye..." He clawed blindly at his waist, his fingers fumbling with the buckle to his belt. "I'll teach ye t'have proper respect for yore daddy..."

However, Waddy was thwarted by his own drunkenness, and he collapsed onto the dirt floor in a sodden stupor. Naddy stepped over her snoring father, picked up the hurricane lamp from the table and then went outside.

She paused on the stoop and shivered as the cold night air cut through her. All she was wearing was her flannel nightie, but she couldn't waste the time getting dressed. She had to go to Granny's and get her baby back. Naddy wasn't sure what Granny wanted with her young'un, or what it might take to get it back, but she at least had to try.

Cutting through the punkin patch was the shortest way to the old woman's shack, although she normally avoided traveling that way, since the patch was alive with snakes during the warm months. But now that it was cooler, she figured she should be safe. Naddy set off in the direction of Granny's cabin, holding the lamp up high to light her way.

As she neared the dark hump of the Caddo mound, Naddy tilted her head to one side, straining to catch a sound she wasn't sure she had heard the first time. It was a tiny cry, as weak and frail as the mewling of a half-drowned kitten. She frantically cast her gaze about, trying to find where the baby's cries were coming from, and found a large pumpkin that that been severed from its vine, the top of which had been cut off, then carefully replaced.

Groaning in pain, Naddy slowly knelt beside the pumpkin, setting the lamp down beside her. She lifted the lid and stared inside at the newborn baby girl, curled inside the pumpkin shell as if still inside her mother's womb. The baby was covered in blood and slick with pumpkin guts, a length of umbilical cord hanging from her belly like a hank of purple yarn.

"Don't cry, baby," Naddy said, smiling down at her little pumpkin child. "Mama's here."

o o o

When dawn came to Seven Devils that cool, crisp Halloween morning, it brought to light horrors so extreme it put to shame the frights at the Bayou Drive-In's Dusk-To-Dawn Spooktacular. Indeed, the events of that day would be whispered about for decades to come by successive generations of local children, until they lost the sordid shine of scandal and acquired the high polish of myth.

The shocking horror began when Dr. Lester Bocage, returning from Lake Village following the delivery of the Teeter twins, stopped at Hollis Railsback's house. Doc Bocage figured that he would either ferry the pregnant Mrs. Railsback back to his clinic or, if she was too far along to be moved, simply deliver the Railsback baby at home.

KNUCKLES AND TALES: THE PUMPKIN CHILD

As one of the few physicians practicing in the county, Lester Bocage had seen more than his fair share of car wrecks and farming accidents. But nothing he had ever encountered before could have prepared him for what he found in the house on Mammon Bayou Road.

During the inquest, Sheriff Renfield Boyette voiced the opinion, judging from the information available at the crime scene, that Hollis Railsback had attempted to deliver his child by himself. Seeing that he was shit-faced drunk at the time, all he managed to do was gut her like a trout. It was thought Hollis slit Joslin's throat in a bizarre show of mercy, once he realized what he had done.

To make matters worse, the child Hollis Railsback ripped from his wife's belly was horribly deformed, with a deeply cleft palate, crossed eyes and webbed fingers and toes. In a drunken, grief-fueled rage, it appeared Railsback had crushed his monstrous offspring's skull, and then blew his own brains out with a gun he kept in the bedside table.

The entire community was deeply shocked by what had happened to the Railsbacks. After all, Hollis was Seven Devils' fair-headed boy; a man who had it all and for whom nothing was impossible, if he set his mind to it. He had wealth, the respect of his community, and the love of a good woman. And yet it seemed his legendary good luck had literally soured overnight.

"It makes you think," as more than one saddened citizen of Seven Devils was heard to say in the days following the inquest and the funerals.

As if that wasn't a year's worth of excitement for the county, things got even stranger when a barefoot Naddy Creek, dressed in nothing but her nightie, walked into town carrying a newborn baby in a pumpkin-shell.

Mary-Margaret had just opened the Sip-N-Sup for the breakfast trade when she looked out the front window and saw the thirteen-year-old walking down the middle of First Street. Mary-Margaret promptly ran out the door and grabbed the poor child, hurrying her into the restaurant, where she removed the baby from its bizarre carrying-case and wrapped it in a tablecloth. While she poured Naddy some hot cocoa, Jesse fried up an Early Bird skillet for the girl, who looked like she could use some looking after, poor thing.

It was nearly two hours before the sheriff and doctor showed up, since they were both out at the Railsback place, but Naddy didn't particularly mind the wait, since she'd never been into town before, much less eaten in a genuine sit-down restaurant.

When Sheriff Boyette finally showed up, he listened carefully to what Naddy had to say, occasionally writing things down in a little note pad. As hard as it might be to believe the story, there was no denying the truth of it—after all, there was the pumpkin Naddy found the baby in sitting on the table in front of him.

It was clear to Sheriff Boyette that Waddy Creek had paid Granny Grimes to dispose of Naddy's baby, hoping to get rid of the physical evidence of the incest. There had been rumors about Granny Grimes and her pumpkin patch dating back to when Sheriff Boyette was in knee-pants, but this was the first hard evidence of the old woman being a 'baby farmer', as it was called.

After sending Naddy and the baby to Doc Bocage's clinic for looking after, Sheriff Boyette called in a couple of his deputies and told them they were driving out to Waddy Creek's place. When they arrived, they found Waddy passed out cold in a pool of his own piss. The sorry son of a bitch was so drunk he barely opened his eyes when the deputies hauled him up by the armpits and threw him in the back of the patrol car.

The next stop was that of Waddy Creek's nearest neighbor, Granny Grimes, which proved to be in keeping with the rest of the day's unpleasantries, as they found the old hoodoo-woman stretched out on her bed, her head laid open like one of her prize pumpkins. Despite Waddy's incoherent babbling about a boy named Jasper, there was no sign of anyone else ever having lived in the shack.

Waddy Creek ended up found guilty of the murder of Granny Grimes and the attempted murder of his daughter/grandchild, not to mention the crime of incest, and was sentenced to life without parole at Cummins Prison. Three years into his sentence he made the mistake, while on farm detail, of calling an extremely large, particularly mean convict by the name of Tyree Solomon a nigger, whereupon Tyree promptly put a hoe blade between Waddy's eyes.

As for Naddy, her baby was taken away by Social Services and she herself was placed in a foster home in a county on the other side of the state. Neither child was seen again, at least to anyone's knowledge.

But you shouldn't think that Halloween 1958 was all murder, mayhem, and depravity. For it was that very day, or so he later claimed, that Virgil Bayliss began to get the feeling back in his legs.

KNUCKLES AND TALES: THE PUMPKIN CHILD
Epilog: Atlanta, 2001

Jack and Lauren Crowne held each other's hands as they sat in the waiting room, too anxious to even pretend to look at the stack of glossy magazines spread across the coffee table before them. Jack was a software engineer, Lauren an elementary school teacher. They were thirty-seven and thirty-three, respectively, had been married for nine years, and although they desperately wanted children, they had yet to conceive. They had been to numerous other fertility specialists, but nothing had seemed to work. It had taken three months for them to secure a consultation with the gynecologist they were now waiting to meet. But from what the Crownes had read on the various infertility support newsgroups, if anyone could help them, it was this man.

The frosted pane of glass that separated the receptionist's desk from the waiting room slid back and a pretty young woman with cornrowed hair and cafe-au lait skin peered out at them. "Mr. and Mrs. Crowne?"

"Yes?" they said in unison, their eyes alight with hope and expectation.

"Dr. Grimes will see you now."

RAYMOND

I remember the first time I saw Raymond Fleuris.

It was during Mrs. Harper's seventh grade homeroom; I was staring out the window at the parking lot that fronted the school. There wasn't anything happening in the parking lot, but it seemed a hell of a lot more interesting than Old Lady Harper rattling on about long division.

That's when I saw the truck.

Beat-up old trucks are not what you'd call unusual in Choctaw County, but this had to be the shittiest excuse for a motor vehicle ever to roll the streets of Seven Devils, Arkansas. The bed overflowed with pieces of junk lumber, paint cans, and rolls of rusty chicken wire. The chassis was scabby with rust. It rode close to the ground, bouncing vigorously with every pothole. The front bumper was connected to the fender by a length of baling wire, spit, and a prayer.

I watched as the truck pulled up next to the principal's sedan and the driver crawled out from behind the wheel. My first impression was that of a mountain wearing overalls. He was massive. Fat jiggled on every part of his body. Thick rolls of it pooled around his waist; straining his shirt to the breaking point. The heavy jowls framing his face made him look like a foul-tempered bulldog. He was big and fat, but it was mean fat; no one in their right mind would have ever mistaken him for jolly.

The driver lumbered around the front of the truck, pausing to pull a dirty bandanna out of his
back pocket and mop his forehead. He motioned irritably to someone seated on the passenger's side, and then jerked the door open. I was surprised it didn't come off in his hand. His face was turning red as he yelled at whoever was in the passenger's seat. After a long minute, a boy climbed out of the truck and stood next to the ruddy-faced mountain of meat.

Normally I wouldn't have spared the Fleuris's a second look. Except that Raymond's head was swaddled in a turban of sterile gauze and surgical tape and his hands were covered by a pair of old canvas gloves, secured at the wrists with string.

Now that was interesting.

Raymond was small and severely underweight. His eyes had grayish-yellow smears under them that made it look like he was perpetually recovering from a pair of shiners. His skin was pale and reminded me of the waxed paper my mama wrapped my sandwiches in.

Someone, probably his mama, had made an effort to clean and press his bib overalls and what was probably his only shirt. No doubt she'd hoped Raymond would make a good impression on his first day at school. No such luck. His clothes looked like socks on a rooster.

By the time the lunch bell rang, everybody knew about the new kid. Gossip runs fast in junior high, and by the end of recess, there were a half-dozen accounts of Raymond Fleuris' origins floating about. Some said he'd been in a car wreck and thrown through the windshield. Others said the doctors up at the State Hospital did some kind of surgery to cure him of violent fits. Chucky Donothan speculated that he'd had some kind of craziness-tumor cut out. Whatever the reason for the head bandages, and the gloves, it made Raymond Fleuris, at least for the space of a few days, exotic and different. And that means nothing but trouble when you're in junior high.

Raymond ended up being assigned to my homeroom. Normally, Mrs. Harper had us sit alphabetically; but in Raymond's case, she assigned him a desk in the back of the room. Not that it made any difference to Raymond. He never handed in homework and was excused from taking tests. All he did was sit and scribble in his notebook with one of those big kindergarten pencils.

Raymond carried his lunch to school in an old paper bag that, judging from the grease stains, had seen a lot of use. Once I accidentally stumbled across Raymond eating his lunch behind the Science Building. His food consisted of a single sandwich made from cheap store-bought white bread and a slice of olive loaf. After he finished his meal, Raymond carefully flattened the paper bag, folded it, and tucked it in the back pocket of his overalls.

I felt funny, standing there watching Raymond perform his little after-lunch ritual. I knew my folks weren't rich, but at least we could afford paper bags. Maybe that's why I did what I did when I saw Chucky Donothan picking on Raymond the next day.

KNUCKLES AND TALES: RAYMOND

It was recess and I was hanging with my best friend, Rafe Mercer. We were talking about the county fair coming to town next month. It was nowhere near as big or as fancy as the State Fair up in Little Rock; but when you're stuck in a backwater like Seven Devils, you take what you can get.

"Darryl, you reckon they'll have the kootchie show again?" Rafe must have asked me that question a hundred times already. I didn't mind, though, because I was wondering the same thing. Last year Rafe's older brother, Calvin, got in on the strength of some whiskers and his football-boy physique. Not to mention a dollar.

"I don't see why not. It's been there every year, ain't it?"

"Yeah, you're right." Rafe was afraid he would graduate high school without once getting the chance to see a woman in her bra and panties. He looked at the pictures in his mama's wish books, but that wasn't the same as seeing a real live half-naked lady. I could understand his concern.

Just about then Kitty Killigrew ran past. Both me and Rafe were sweet on Kitty, not that we'd admit it to her—or ourselves—this side of physical torture. She was a pretty girl, with long coppery-red hair that hung to her waist and eyes the color of cornflowers. Rafe went on to marry her, six years later. That fucker.

"Hey, Kitty! What's going on?" Rafe yelled after her.

Kitty paused long enough to gasp out one word. "Fight!"

That was all the explanation we needed. Schoolyard fights attract students like shit draws flies. Rafe and I hurried after her. As we rounded the corner of the building, I could see a knot of kids near the science building.

I pushed my way through my schoolmates in time to see Chucky Donothan kick Raymond Fleuris' feet out from under him.

Raymond flopped onto his back in the dirt and lay there. It was evident that the fight—if you could call it that—was pretty one-sided. I couldn't imagine what Raymond might have done to piss off the bigger boy; but knowing Chucky, the fact Raymond had weight and occupied space was probably insult enough.

"Stand up and fight, retard!" Chucky bellowed.

Raymond got to his feet, his eyes filled with pain and confusion. His bandage-turban was smeared with dirt. With his over-sized canvas gloves and shit-kicker brogans, Raymond looked like a pathetic caricature of Mickey Mouse. Everyone started laughing.

"What's with the gloves, retard?" Chucky sneered. "What's the matter? You jerk off so much you got hair on your palms?"

Some of the girls giggled at that witticism, so Chucky continued pressing his attack. "Is that your big secret, Fleuris? You a jag-off? Huh? Huh? Is that it? Why don't you take 'em off so we can see, huh?"

Raymond shook his head. "Paw sez I can't take 'em off. Paw sez I gotta keep 'em on alla time." It was one of the few times I ever heard Raymond speak out loud. His voice was thin and reedy, like a clarinet.

The crowd fell silent as Chucky's naturally ruddy complexion grew even redder.

"You tellin' me no, retard?"

Raymond blinked. It was obvious he didn't understand what was going on. It dawned on me that Raymond would stand there and let Chucky beat him flatter than his lunch bag without lifting a finger to protect himself. Suddenly, I didn't want to watch what was going on anymore.

"Chucky, leave him be, can't you see he's simple?"

"Butt out, Sweetman! Less'n you want me to kick your ass, too!"

I cut my eyes at Rafe. He shook his head. "Hell, Darryl, I ain't about to get the shit knocked outta me on account of Raymond Fleuris!"

I looked away.

Satisfied he'd quelled all opposition, Chucky grabbed Raymond's left arm, jerking on the loosely fitted glove. "If you ain't gonna show us, I guess I'll make you!"

And that's when the shit hit the fan.

One second Raymond was your basic slack-jawed moron, the next he was shrieking and clawing at Chucky like the Tasmanian Devil in those old Bugs Bunny cartoons. His face seemed to flex, like the muscles were being jerked every which-way. I know it sounds stupid, but that's the only way I can describe it.

Raymond was on the bully like white on rice, knocking him to the ground. We all stood there and gaped in disbelief, our mouths hanging open, as they wrestled in the dirt. Suddenly Chucky started making these high-pitched screams and that's when I saw the blood.

Chucky managed to throw Raymond off of him just as Coach Jenkins hustled across the playground, paddle in hand. Chucky was rolling around, crying like a little kid. Blood ran from a ragged wound in the fleshy part of his upper-arm. Raymond sat in the dirt, staring at the other boy like he was from Mars. There was blood on Raymond's mouth, but it wasn't his. The bandage had come unraveled in the brawl, giving everyone a good look at the three-inch scar that climbed his right temple.

KNUCKLES AND TALES: RAYMOND

"What the—blazes—is going on here!" Coach Jenkins always had trouble refraining from swearing in front of the students, and it looked like he was close to reaching critical mass.

"Donothan! Get on your feet, boy!"

"He bit me!" Chucky wailed, his face filthy with snot and tears.

Coach Jenkins shot a surprised look at Raymond, still sitting in the dirt. "Is that true, Fleuris? Did you bite Donothan?"

Raymond stared up at Coach Jenkins and blinked.

Coach Jenkins' neck pulsed and he looked at the ring of now-guilty faces. "Okay, who started it?"

"Donothan did, sir." I was surprised to hear the words coming from my mouth. "He was picking on Raymond."

Coach Jenkins pushed the bill of his baseball cap back and tried to keep the vein in his neck from pulsing even harder. "Did anyone try to stop it?"

Silence.

"Right. Come on, Donothan. Get up. You, too, Fleuris. We're going to the principal's office."

"I'm bleeding!"

"We'll have the nurse take a look at it, but you're still going to the office!" Jenkins grabbed Chucky by his uninjured arm and jerked him to his feet. "You should be ashamed of yourself, Donothan!" He hissed under his breath. "Pickin' on a cripple!"

I stepped forward to help Raymond. It was then that I noticed one of his gloves had come off in the fight.

"Here, you lost this."

Raymond snatched his glove back, quickly stuffing his bare hand into it. But not before I had time to notice that his ring finger was longer than the others.

When I was a kid, Choctaw County was pretty much like it was when my daddy was growing up. If not worse. Sure, we had stuff like television and a public library by then, but by the time I was twelve the old Malco Theater went belly-up; another victim of the railroad dying off.

One of the biggest thrills of the year was going to the county fair. For five days in late October the aluminum outbuildings dotting what had once been Old Man Ferguson's cow pasture became a gaudy wonderland of neon lights.

If you went to the fair every night, you'd eventually see the entire population of Choctaw County put in an appearance. It was one of the few times the various ethnic groups and religious sects congregated at the same place, although I'd hardly call it 'mingling'.

The blacks stayed with the blacks while the whites stayed with the whites. There was also little in the way of crossover between the Baptists, Methodists, and Pentecostals. Families came by the truckload, dressed in their Sunday-go-to-meeting clothes. I never knew there were so many people in the county.

Rafe and I were wandering the booths lining the midway, looking for the kootchie show. Rafe hadn't shaved in three weeks, hoping he could build up enough beard to pass for sixteen. We bumped into Kitty, who was chewing on a wad of cotton candy and contemplating a banner that showed a dwarf supporting a bucket of sand from a skewer piercing his tongue.

"Hey, Kitty. When'd you get here?" I asked, trying to sound casual.

"Hey, Darryl. Hey, Rafe. I rode over with Veronica about a half-hour ago. You just get here?" There was a strand of pink candyfloss stuck at the corner of her perfect mouth. I watched in silent fascination as she tried to dislodge it with the tip of her tongue.

Rafe shrugged. "Kind of."

"Seen the World's Smallest Horse yet?"

"No."

"Don't bother. It's a rip off; just some dumb old Shetland Pony at the bottom of a hole dug in the ground." She poked her half-eaten cotton candy in my face. "You want the rest of this, Darryl? I can't finish it. You know what they say; sweets to the sweet."

"Uh, no thanks, Kitty." People keep saying that to me on account of my last name, Sweetman. I hate it, but short of strangling everybody on the face of the earth, there's no way I can avoid it. And no one believes me when I tell them I can't stand sugar.

"I'll take it, Kitty." Rafe was a smoothy, even then. Did I mention he ended up marrying her after high school? Did I mention I haven't talked to him since?

Kitty frowned and pointed over my shoulder. "Isn't that Raymond Fleuris?"

Rafe and I turned around and looked where she was pointing. Sure enough, Raymond Fleuris was standing in front of the "Tub-O-Ducks" game, watching the brightly colored plastic ducks bobbing along in their miniature millrace. Although his hands were still gloved, he no longer wore his bandage on his head, and his dark hair bristled like the quills of a porcupine.

Rafe shrugged. "I saw his daddy shoveling out the livestock barn; the carnival lets the temporary workers' families ride for free."

KNUCKLES AND TALES: RAYMOND

Kitty was still looking at Raymond. "You know, yesterday during recess I asked him why he had brain surgery."

I found my voice first. "You actually asked him that?"

"Sure did."

"Well, what did he say?"

Kitty frowned. "I dunno. When I asked him, he looked like he was trying real hard to remember something. Then he got this goofy grin on his face and said 'chickens'."

"Chickens?"

"Don't look at me like I'm nuts, Rafe Mercer! I'm just tellin' you want he said! But what was really weird was how he said it! Like he was remembering going to Disneyland or something!"

"So Raymond Fleuris is weird. Big deal. C'mon, I wanna check out the guy who cuts a girl in half with a chainsaw. Wanna go with us, Kitty?" Rafe mimed pulling a cord and went rup-rup-ruppppp!, waving the wad of cotton candy like a deadly weapon.

Kitty giggled behind her hand. "You're silly!"

That was all I could take. If I had to stay with them another five minutes I'd either puke or pop Rafe in the nose. "I'll catch up with you later, Rafe. Okay? Rafe?"

"Huh?" Rafe managed to tear his eyes away from Kitty long enough to give me a quick, distracted nod. "Oh, yeah. Sure. Later, man."

Muttering under my breath, I stalked off, my fists stuffed in my pockets. Suddenly the fair didn't seem as much fun as it'd been ten minutes ago. Even the festive aroma of hot popcorn, cotton candy, and corndogs failed to revive my previous good mood.

I found myself staring at a faded canvas banner that said, in vigorous Barnum script: Col. Reynard's Pocket Jungle. Below the headline a stiffly rendered redheaded young man dressed like Frank Buck wrestled a spotted leopard.

Lounging behind the ticket booth in front of the tent stood a tall man dressed in a sweat-stained short-sleeved khaki shirt and jodhpurs. His hair was no longer bright red and his face looked older, but there was no doubt that he was Colonel Reynard: Great White Hunter. As I watched, he produced a World War Two-surplus microphone and began his spiel. His voice crackled out of a public address system, adding to the noise and clamor of the midway.

"Hur-ree! Hur-ree! Hur-ree! See the most ex-zotic and danger-rus ani-mals this side of Aff-Rika! See! The noble tim-bur wolf! King of the Ark-Tik Forest! See! The wild jag-war! Ruth-less Lord of the Am-A-Zon

Jungle! See! The hairy orang-utang! Borny-Oh's oh-riginal Wild Man of the Woods! See! The fur-rocious Grizz-lee Bear! Mon-Arch of the Frozen North! See these wonders and more! Hur-ree! Hur-ree! Hur-ree!"

A handful of people stopped and turned their attention toward the Colonel. One of them happened to be Raymond Fleuris. A couple came forward with their money. Raymond just stood there at the foot of the ticket podium, staring at the redheaded man. I expected the Colonel to make like W.C. Fields, but instead he waved Raymond inside the tent.

What the hell?

I didn't really want to see a bunch of half-starved animals stuck in cages. But there was something in the way Colonel Reynard had looked at Raymond, like he'd recognized him, that struck me as curious. First I thought he might be queer for boys, but The Great White Hunter didn't look at me twice when I paid for my ticket and joined the others inside the tent.

The "Pocket Jungle" reeked of sawdust and piss. There were raised platforms scattered about the tent, canvas drop cloths covering the cages. Colonel Reynard finally joined us and went into his pitch, going on about how he'd risked life and limb collecting the specimens we were about to see. As he spoke, he went from cage to cage, throwing back the drop cloths so we could see the animals trapped inside.

I hadn't been expecting anything, and I wasn't disappointed. The "jaguar" was a slat-thin ocelot; the "timber wolf" was a yellow-eyed coyote that paced the confines of its cage like a madman; the "grizzly" was a plain old black bear, its muzzle so white it looked like it'd been sprinkled with powdered sugar. The only thing that really was what it was supposed to be was the orangutan.

The ape was big; it's wrinkled old man's features nearly lost in its vast face. It sat in a cage only slightly larger than itself, its hand-like feet folded in front of its mammoth belly. With its drooping teats and huge girth, it resembled a shaggy Buddha.

Just as the Colonel was wrapping up his act, Raymond pushed his way from the back of the crowd and stood, motionless, gaping at the "timber wolf". The coyote halted its ceaseless pacing and bared its fangs. A low, frightened growl came from the animal as it raised its hackles. The Colonel halted in mid-sentence and stared first at the coyote, then at Raymond.

As if on cue, the ocelot started to hiss and spit, flattening its ears against its sleek skull. The bear emitted a series of low grunts, while the orangutan covered its face and turned its back to the audience.

KNUCKLES AND TALES: RAYMOND

Raymond stepped back, shaking his head like he had a mite in his ear. The muscles in his face were jerking again, and I imagined I could smell blood and dust and hear Chucky Donothan squealing like a girl. Raymond staggered back, covering his eyes with his gloves. I heard someone in the crowd laugh; it sounded like was a short, sharp, ugly bark.

Colonel Reynard snapped his fingers once and said in a strong voice; "Hush!"

The animals grew silent immediately.

He then stepped toward Raymond. "Son..."

Raymond made a noise that was somewhere between a sob and a shout and ran from the tent and into the crowds and noise of the midway. Colonel Reynard followed after him, and I followed the Colonel.

Raymond made for the cluster of aluminum outbuildings that served as exhibition halls. The Colonel didn't see Raymond dodge between the Crafts Barn and the Tractor Exhibit, but I did. I hurried after him, leaving the light and activity of the fairground behind me. I could dimly make out Raymond a few dozen yards ahead.

I froze as a tall, thin shadow stepped directly into Raymond's path, knocking him to the ground. I pressed against the aluminum shell of the Crafts Barn, praying no one noticed me lurking in the darkened "alley".

"You all right, son?" I recognized Colonel Reynard's voice, although I could not see his face.

Raymond shuddered as he tried to catch his breath and stop crying at the same time. The carny helped Raymond to his feet. "Now, now, son... There's nothing to be ashamed of." His voice was as gentle and soothing as a man talking to a skittish horse. "I'm not going to hurt you, boy. Far from it."

Raymond stood there as Colonel Reynard wiped his face clean of tears, dirt and snot with a handkerchief.

"Let me see your hands, son."

Raymond shrank away from the stranger, crossing his gloved hands over his heart. "Paw sez if I take 'em off he'll whup me good. I ain't ever supposed to take 'em off ever again."

"Well, I say it's okay for you to take them off. And if your daddy don't like it, he'll have to whup on me first." The carny quickly untied both gloves and let them drop. Raymond's hands looked dazzlingly white, compared to his grimy face and forearms. Colonel Reynard squatted on his haunches and took Raymond's hands into his own, studying the fingers with interest. Then he tilted Raymond's head to one side. I could tell he was looking at the scar.

"What have they done?" The Colonel's voice sounded both angry and sad. "You poor child...What did they do to you?"

"Here now! What you doin' messin' with my boy?"

It was Mr. Fleuris. He passed within inches of me, but if he noticed my presence it didn't register on his face. I wondered if this was how the first mammals felt, watching the dinosaurs lumber by their hiding place in the underbrush. The big man reeked of manure and fresh straw. Raymond cringed as his father bore down on him.

"Raymond—Where the hell's yore gloves, boy? You know what I told you bout them gloves!" Mr. Fleuris lifted a meaty arm, his sausage-sized fingers closing into a fist.

Raymond whimpered in anticipation of the blow that was certain to land on his upturned face. Before Horace Fleuris had a chance to strike his son, Colonel Reynard grabbed the big man's wrist. In the dim light it looked as if the Colonel's third finger was longer than the others. I heard Mr. Fleuris grunt in surprise and saw his upraised fist tremble.

"You will not touch this child, understand?"

"Dammit, leggo!" Fleuris' voice was pinched, as if he was both in pain and afraid.

"I said 'understand'?"

"I heared you the first time, damn you!"

The Colonel let Fleuris' arm drop. "You are the child's father?"

Fleuris nodded sullenly, massaging his wrist.

"I should kill you for what you've done."

"Here, now! Don't go blamin' me for it!" Fleuris blustered. "It was them doctors up at the State Hospital! They said it'd cure him! I tried to tell 'em what the boy's problem was, but you can't tell them big-city doctors squat, far as they're concerned! But what could I do? We was gettin' tired of movin' ever time the boy got into th' neighbor's chicken coop."

"Now he'll never learn how to control it!" Reynard stroked Raymond's forehead. "He's stuck in-between the natures, incapable of fitting into your world...or ours. He is an abomination in the eyes of Nature. Even animals can see he has no place in the Scheme!"

"You like the boy, don't you?" There was something about how Fleuris asked the question that made my stomach knot. "I'm a reasonable man. When it comes to business."

I couldn't believe what I was hearing. Mr. Fleuris was standing there, talking about selling his son to a complete stranger like he was a prize coon dog!

KNUCKLES AND TALES: RAYMOND

"Get out of here."

"Now hold on just a second! I ain't askin' for nothin' that ain't rightfully mine, and you know it! I'm the boy's pa and I reckon that calls for some kind of restitution, seeing how's he's my only male kin..."

"Now!" Colonel Reynard's voice sounded like a growl.

Horace Fleuris turned and fled, his fleshy face slack with fear. I never dreamed a man his size could move that fast.

I glanced at where Reynard stood, one hand resting on Raymond's shoulder. Colonel Reynard's face was no longer human, his mouth fixed in a deceptive smile. He fixed me with his murder green eyes and wrinkled his snout. "That goes for you too, man-cub."

To this day I wonder why he let me go unharmed. I guess it's because he knew that no one was going to listen to any crazy stories about fox-headed men told by a pissant kid. No one wanted to believe crap like that. Not even the pissant kid.

Needless to say, I ran like a rabbit with a hound on my tail. Later I was plagued by recurring nightmares of a fox-headed animal-tamer dressed in jodhpurs that went around sticking his head in human mouths, and of a huge orangutan in overalls that looked like Mr. Fleuris.

By the time Christmas Break came around everyone had lost interest in Raymond's disappearance. The Fleuris family had moved sometime during the last night of October to parts unknown. No one missed them. It was like Raymond Fleuris had never existed.

I spent a lot of time trying not to think about what I'd seen and heard that night. I had other things to fret about. Like Kitty Killigrew going steady with Rafe.

Several years passed before I returned to the Choctaw County Fair. By then I was a freshman at the University of Arkansas at Monticello, over in Drew County. I'd landed a scholarship and spent my weekdays studying in a bare-ass dorm room while coming home on weekends to help my daddy with the farm. I had long since talked myself into believing what I'd seen that night was a particularly vivid nightmare brought on by a bad corndog. Nothing more.

The midway didn't have a kootchie show that year, but I'd heard rumors that they had something even better. Or worse, depending on how you look at it. According to the grapevine, the carnival had a glomming' geek. Since geek shows are technically illegal and roundly condemned as immoral, degrading, and sinful, naturally it played to capacity crowds.

The barker packed as many people as he could into a cramped, foul-smelling tent situated behind the freak show. There was a canvas pit in the middle of the tent, and at its bottom crouched the geek.

He was on the scrawny side and furry as a monkey. The hair on his head was long and coarse, hanging past his waist, as did a scraggly beard. His long forearms and bowed legs were equally shaggy, coated with dark fur that resembled the pelt of a wild goat. It was hard to tell, but I'm certain he was buck-naked. There was something wrong with the geek's fingers, though that might have been on account of his four-inch long nails.

As the barker did his spiel about the geek being the last survivor of a race of wild men from the jungles of Borneo, I continued to stare at the snarling, capering creature. I couldn't shake the feeling that there was something familiar about the geek.

The barker finished his bit and produced a live chicken from a gunnysack. The geek lifted his head and sniffed the air, his nostrils flaring as he caught the scent of the bird. An idiot's grin split his hairy face and a long thread of drool dripped from his open jaws. His teeth were surprisingly white and strong.

The barker tossed the chicken into the pit. It fluttered downward, squawking as it frantically beat the air with its wings. The geek giggled like a delighted child and pounced on the hapless bird. His movements were as graceful and sure as those of a champion mouser dispatching a rat. The geek bit the struggling chicken's head off, obviously relishing every minute of it.

As the crowd moaned in disgust and turned their faces away from what was happening in the pit, I continued to watch, even though it made my stomach churn.

Why? Because I had glimpsed the pale finger of scar tissue transversing the geek's right temple.

I stood and stared down at Raymond Fleuris crouched at the bottom of the geek pit, his grinning face wreathed in blood and feathers.

Happy at last.

DOWN IN THE HOLE

BASED ON AN IDEA BY WILLIAM P. MYERS

I wake from unwelcome dreams, wrapped in an envelope of cold sweat, the bitter taste of fear in my mouth. I look to my wife. She's still asleep. Good, I didn't wake her up this time. Coming out of a nightmare is bad enough, but feeling guilty for disturbing someone else's night makes it worse.

My wife is a wonderful woman. Very understanding. She tries to comfort me whenever I have particularly bad dreams—the ones that wake me up screaming. But I know it must be coming wearisome to her. Lord knows, I find it annoying.

She recommended that I see a therapist about my—problem. But my father was a minister—an old-fashioned hard-line Calvinist, to be exact—and he didn't hold with doctors who didn't cut you open. If something was wrong inside your head and heart, then that was God's province, not Man's. Although I turned my back on my father's beliefs during college, old attitudes like that are hard to shake.

Besides, I don't need an analyst at one hundred dollars an hour, three sessions a week, to ferret out the childhood trauma that shaped my adult nightmares. I know all too well where my dreams come from. All I have to do is close my eyes, and it all comes rushing back to me—in far too much detail for my own tastes.

It was back when my family lived in Choctaw County. My father was assigned pastor to the Methodist church there. I was six years old when our family first moved there—my brother Dale was five. Seven Devils was a small isolated Arkansas town located in the Mississippi Delta region. It was too hot in the summer and too cold in the winter. There wasn't much of a public library, and if you wanted to see a movie you had to drive outside the county to nearby Monticello.

In some ways, Seven Devil's quietude made it the ideal place "to raise the kids up". On the other hand, in a town where there were as many liquor stores as brands of Baptists, teen pregnancy and alcoholism were through the roof. My friend Rich, who I attended school with all the way through senior high, used to say there wasn't anything to do in Seven Devils "except drink beer and hate niggers".

It was summer when it happened. It was 1965 and the Beatles were in America, the Stones not far behind them. Viet Nam was percolating away and civil unrest was breaking out in cities on both sides of the Mason-Dixie Line. However, none of this managed to penetrate the placidity that enveloped Choctaw County. In fact, nothing much in the way of social change had occurred since World War Two. I was playing with my brother, Dale, and our friend, Rich.

"You're dead!"

"No I'm not! You were dead a while ago!"

I clambered out of the tall yellow grass and lofted a thin bamboo stick at Rich. Rich ducked as the shaft drifted down beside him.

"You can't do that! That's your rifle, not your spear!" Rich was only arguing for form's sake. We'd been playing War for an hour or so, and this was always how it ended.

Dale appeared suddenly off to the right, standing up so his head and shoulders could be seen above the long grass. Dale and I may have been brothers, but our ideas about War were entirely different. Dale preferred to hide out as long as possible without being caught, while I loved the tense thrill of a chase. The vacant lot behind the old church was the best place for either strategy.

Like I said, Rich was our best friend, although we often got into squabbles as to whose best friend he really was. It didn't matter that Dale was a year younger than me; we couldn't remember a time when we weren't all doing something together. But that's how it was in Seven Devils. There were fewer than a thousand people in the whole town, all of them stranded in the butt hole of Arkansas. Friends had to last

I leapt on my bamboo rifle-spear and pulled it out from under my foot before the others could reach it—just in case the game wasn't really over yet. "I wouldn't have to spear you if you were playing fair!"

"Yeah, yeah, yeah!" Rich grinned.

I chased Rich half-heartedly out onto the gravel driveway, where Dale joined us. We stood around for a moment, unsure of what to do next.

Rich looked down the drive and nodded across the street. "What do you think Ray's been doing all day?"

Ray Burns was a big kid who rarely spoke to us, since we were just fourth and fifth graders. We didn't talk to Ray much either, since he never paid us any attention unless he was trying to pull some kind of

KNUCKLES AND TALES: DOWN IN THE HOLE

gag. But there he was, bare-chested and sweaty, digging a hole where Mr. Jenning's house used to stand.

It was weird seeing someone actually doing something in our neighborhood. Nobody did much of anything, since most of the people who lived there were poor and old—except for Ray's family, who were just poor. Mr. Burns, Ray's dad, spent most of his time driving trucks and left Ray on his own a lot. I thought that was kind of neat. I wondered what it would be like to not have someone telling you to do your homework, what to wear, how to cut your hair, or when to go to bed.

"Maybe Mr. Jennings buried his money there?" Dale whispered. Dale was always interested in buried treasure—even more than War.

"Hey, I think he's coming over here!" Rich whispered anxiously. "Let's go!"

I watched Ray coming up the drive and tried to think of what else we could do besides stand around like a bunch of dummies. "We'll just talk to him for a second and then go, okay?"

We shuffled our feet in the gravel and looked around uneasily as Ray crunched towards us. I didn't particularly dislike Ray. Sometimes I actually wished we could be friends. Ray was always doing things and he always seemed to have kids around him, but he never had any real friends. That was probably on account of his taste for cruel practical jokes. Like the time he pantsed that crippled kid at the roller skating rink. I wondered what would make Ray act so mean. Maybe it had something to do with him not having a mom

Well, that wasn't exactly true. Ray did have a mom, but she was locked up somewhere. I once overheard my mother discussing Mrs. Burns during one of her bridge parties. She'd called Mrs. Burns a "dipso", whatever that was. Rich said that was another name for dork or wimp, but somehow I doubted that.

"Y'all finished playing War? Who won?"

"Nobody," Rich said a little warily. "What're you digging for?"

"Nothing in particular. I just started finding stuff and kept going."

"So what'd you find?" I heard myself ask.

Ray cocked his hip and stretched his back. "Some arrowheads and pieces of an old gun."

Dale brightened with interest. Even Rich became curious.

"Can we see?" I asked eagerly, thinking of my own small collection of fossils and arrowheads.

Ray looked steadily at us. "Sure, but only if you promise not to tell anyone anything about it."

We nodded but Ray made us promise out loud before leading us down the drive and across the small asphalt road onto the old lot.

We climbed down into the neck deep hole and started digging around. The earth fell apart in our hands like wet tobacco and smelt of dirt and cut roots. We looked around for a while but the hole was no different from the ones we dug to play War—nothing but dirt.

"Where's the arrowheads and the gun?" I asked.

"Yeah, I thought you said you were finding stuff," Dale said accusingly.

"It's in the house. Just keep looking and I'll be back with the gun." Ray turned and left without waiting for a response.

We looked at one another and when no one said anything we went back to sifting the dirt with our hands. Soon Ray came back out of the house, wrapped in an old red blanket and sporting a leather headband with a dirty feather stuck in it.

Ray smiled and pulled the blanket tight around his shoulders. "You want to see the gun?"

Dale nodded.

Ray opened up the blanket and showed us a nickel-plated snub-nosed revolver. He held a bit of the blanket between the pistol grip and his left hand and hand his finger around the trigger. In his other hand he held a bottle of cheap whiskey, which he hoisted for a drink

I could whiff the sour smell of the liquor even in the hole. The space around me suddenly grew smaller and my mind started to scramble for the words that would get them out of this mess.

"You didn't find that gun here!" Rich blurted.

I didn't wait for Ray to respond to that one. "We gotta go, we were supposed to be home two hours ago." And the three of us rose as if the bluff would actually work.

Ray jumped sideways and pointed the gun at Rich. "No one leaves 'till Big Chief Red Feather say so! White man steal land, now white man pay! No move! Sit! If squaw want you, squaw come get you!"

Dale started to cry. I looked hard at Ray's narrow skull and wondered if there really was any Indian in him—probably not.

We sat quietly and waited for whatever would come next. Ray tilted back another swallow of alcohol and stared out across the rooftops. His eyes grew dull and emptied out into the distance only to fill with a truly transcendent hate when he returned his gaze to us, huddled together in the hole like frightened pups.

"White man kill squaw and child! Only me left now! Now I kill white squaw and child!"

KNUCKLES AND TALES: DOWN IN THE HOLE

Dale was so scared he wet himself. Rich wiped at his eyes, trying hard not to let his lower lip quiver. I felt as if my lungs and heart were trying to jump out of my chest.

"Ray, we *really* have to go home. Mama's gonna get *real mad* if we're late for dinner—"

"*Shut up!*" Ray screamed, his spittle striking me in the face. "I told you my name's not Ray! It's Big Chief Red Feather! You understand me?"

I was too frightened to do anything more than nod.

"Then let me hear you say it! Say my name!"

"B-big Chief Red Feather." My throat was so tight it felt as if I was going to choke on the words.

Ray smiled crookedly and sat down on the edge of the hole, dangling his legs over the side. "That's better." He took another long pull. "I *hate* this town." His voice had taken on a definite slurring sound. He hefted the whiskey bottle, scanning the surrounding houses. "I *really* fuckin' hate it!"

I flinched at the sound of the f-word. In our house, nothing made my dad reach for his belt faster than cuss-words. Especially high-octane dirty ones like shit, goddamn, and the Big F.

"Wassamatta, kid? Haven't you ever heard anyone say fuck before?" Ray sneered.

I squared my shoulders and tried not to look too scared. "Sure I have. I'm in the fifth grade."

"I'm *so* impressed." Ray pointed the gun at me like it was a shiny finger. "Yeah, but have *you* ever said it?"

"Said what?"

"Fuck."

"Sure. Lots of times."

"Then let me hear you say it."

Rich and Dale were watching me with huge, frightened eyes. Dale started to whimper.

"*Shut him up!*" Ray snapped, waving the gun at Dale. "He sounds just like a damn girl! It's bad enough I gotta sit here and smell his piss, I don't want to listen to him whine, too!" He returned his attention to me. "Okay, let me hear you say fuck."

"I don't want to say it."

"Why? You too goody-goody? Afraid you'll go to hell if you say it?"

"I just don't feel like saying it, that's all."

Ray leveled the gun right between my eyes. "Big Chief Red Feather tells white man to say fuck or white man dies!"

"Fuck," I muttered.

Ray cupped a mocking hand to his ear. "What's that? Speak up!"

"Fuck."

"I can't hear y-o-o-u-u-u!"

"*Fuck!*"

The intensity of my shout made Rich and Dale jump. I met Ray's slightly out-of-focus gaze. The older boy nodded then looked away. "God, I hate this stinkin' place." He was back to staring at the sky, although the gun remained pointed into the hole. "Ain't nothin' to do, nowhere to go, no one to see that you don't already know. Or think they know you. Everybody already got their minds made up 'bout how things are and how they're gonna be. Bunch of stuck-up jerk wads, that's all they are."

He peered down into the hole with angry, bloodshot eyes. "You should get down on your knees and *beg* me to kill you! Kill you before you grow up and get like *them*! I'd be doin' you guys a *favor*, y'know that?"

"What the hell's going on here?"

Ray jumped at the sound of an adult voice. The whiskey bottle and gun disappeared inside the blanket faster than a conjurer's doves.

"Uh, hello, Reverend Thayer! Me and the boys was just playin' cowboys and injuns, that's all!"

My father scowled at Ray over his spectacles. "Aren't you a little *old* to be playin' at that, Ray?"

Ray shrugged, careful not to dislodge the blanket. "They asked me, so I figured why not?"

My father didn't look terribly convinced. He frowned down at Dale and me, cowering at the bottom of the hole. "What the devil are you boys doin' down there?"

"We was just playin'," Ray piped in. "*Right*, Mike?"

"Y-yeah, Dad. Just playin'."

"Well, get on outta that hole! Your mother's about ready to have kittens! She sent me out looking for you cause she's afraid her tuna casserole's gonna go cold."

Ray was backing his way toward the house as we clambered out of the hole. He caught my eye and mouthed the words *'don't tell'* while my father wasn't looking.

"Just look at your clothes!" my dad scolded. "Your mama's gonna be fit to be tied when she sees those stains!"

When they got back to the house, Dale started crying and couldn't stop. I told my father what had happened in the hole.

KNUCKLES AND TALES: DOWN IN THE HOLE

At first he got real quiet, then his face lost its color, then it came back in spades. For a moment I thought he was going to get his gun and shoot Ray.

"It's about time something was done about that boy! Emma, call Doc Sutter and have him come over and check the boys! Better tell him to stop by the Winters' place, too, and see to Rich!"

"Honey, what are you going to do?"

"Don't worry. I'll see to it everything's taken care of."

My father went into his study and made a long phone call with the door shut. Mom made us wash and put us to bed, even though it was still light outside. Dr. Sutter came by and examined us later, although he wouldn't tell me exactly what it was he was looking for. Dale ended up getting a shot that made him sleepy because he wouldn't stop blubbering.

I sat on my bed and looked out the window in the direction of Ray's house. Just after it got dark I saw flashing red and blue lights and heard the sound of car doors slamming and men shouting. I'm not sure, but I think I recognized my father's voice. I wondered if Ray would tell about me saying fuck to get back at me for spilling my guts about the gun? My stomach knotted up at the thought of my father finding out about what I'd said.

The next day I walked over to the empty lot next to the Burns house to look at the hole, only to find that it filled in. When I asked my father what had happened to the hole, he told me not to ask questions that might upset people.

No one in Seven Devils ever saw Ray again. A month after Ray disappeared, Mr. Burns signed on with a trucking company in Wichita and moved away. Three weeks later, their empty house caught fire and burned to the ground.

When I tried to talk about what had happened in the hole with my parents, they pretended I was making it all up. Rich joked that my father killed Ray and buried his body in the hole, and that's why everybody pretended nothing had happened. I got mad and punched him in the nose hard enough to make it bleed. After that, Rich was Dale's best friend more than mine.

The months turned into years and me and Rich and Dale grew older. Rich and Dale continued being close friends, even going so far as to going in together on an old car they drove to school and football games. I kept more and more to myself, preferring to sit alone in the high grass behind the old church, drinking contraband whiskey while contemplating the empty lot across the street and the secret it held locked in its belly.

Rich was first of our merry group to meet the Reaper. We weren't even out of high school yet. He developed a serious drug problem while in ninth grade. Crank. Downers. Coke. Whatever. His dad bought him a moped for his graduation, sort of as a consolation prize for him not being able to go to college. The week before commencement, he rode it straight into a semi. They didn't leave the casket open at his service. It was so weird—like they were burying this box they said Rich was in, but there was no way of seeing if he was really in there or not.

Everyone thought it was an accident. Everyone but me. Rich had told me, a couple of days before he got run over, that he'd been having the weirdest feelings. Like wanting to steer his bike into the headlights of cars, like a moth to a flame. The day after I graduated from high school I packed my bags and bought a one-way ticket to Memphis.

No one in Seven Devils ever saw me again.

My father expected me to attend a divinity school and study to become a minister. I had other plans. My father refused to pay for my education, so I struggled for several years, working any number of shit jobs while I attended art school. Then I managed to land a job working for an advertising agency, where I ended up making a lot of money.

Now I'm successful, moderately wealthy and married to a wonderful woman. I'm light-years removed from the stagnant hellhole of my youth. But my dreams...my dreams are another matter altogether.

They always start the same way. I'm at work, desperately trying to sort out one of the bigger accounts. The intercom buzzes. It's my secretary.

"Someone here to see you, Mr. Thayer."

Before I can tell her I'm too busy to see anyone today, the door to my office swings open and Ray Burns walks in. He's dressed exactly the same way as the last time I saw him, except that the blanket is muddy and full of holes and the feather stuck in his headband is muddy, too. He reeks of cheap whiskey and when he gets closer I can see that his face is smeared with dirt and the skin is flaking away, revealing the bone beneath. He grins at me and a worm crawls out of his nose.

"No ones leaves until Big Chief Red Feather say so! White man steal land, now white man pay! Get down on your knees and beg me to kill you! Fuck-fuck-fuck-fuck!"

And then he pulls out the gun—the nickel-plated revolver—and points it right at my head and pulls the trigger. And I wake up just as the bullet enters my forehead. Sometimes I try to wake myself up before that happens—sometimes I succeed. But only sometimes.

KNUCKLES AND TALES: DOWN IN THE HOLE

They say that dreams reveal our deepest fears and hopes. If this is true, what do mine reveal? Am I frightened of failure? Am I worried that, should I not succeed in my business, I'll find myself back where I started; doomed to spend my mortal span in Seven Devils, Arkansas? Or is there something else hidden inside the symbols, waiting for me to crack the code and solve the riddle?

I told you about what happened to Rich, and what happened to me. Now its my turn to tell you about Dale.

Dale graduated from high school a year or so after I did. Like myself, he high-tailed it out of town the first chance he could. Unlike me, he agreed to our father's demands and went to divinity school. He was kicked out during his sophomore year, however, when he was discovered in the men's room of the campus library, performing oral sex on a fellow student. My father disowned him, refusing to allow him to set foot in the family home ever again.

By this time our father was retired from the active ministry and living in Hot Springs. The last time my father and brother saw each other was in 1987, when they both attended my wedding. I hadn't seen either of them in a long time, and it was dismaying to see how much they had in common—they were both alcoholics. If they spoke to one another during the wedding, neither of them ever mentioned it to me. My father died of cirrhosis of the liver in 1990. Dale did not attend the funeral.

The last time I spoke to my brother was three months ago. He was drunk and he apologized for waking me up.

"That's okay, Dale. What's wrong?"

"Wrong? What makes you think something's wrong?"

"If nothing's wrong, why the hell are you calling me at two in the morning?"

There was silence on his end of the line. I could picture him chewing on his thumbnail, just like he used to do when we were kids.

"I'm having trouble sleeping. Dreams."

"Nightmares?"

"Kinda. Remember Ray?"

Silence on my end now.

"Mike? You still there?"

"Yeah. I remember Ray. What about him?"

"You ever read about Delayed Stress Syndrome? It's usually used to describe Viet Nam vets or hostages. It's when the events of something traumatic finally start to hit home, both physically and emotionally. Sometimes it can take years before the person starts to suffer the effects of what happened to them. And in cases where people have been made to pretend it "never happened", the side effects can be especially damaging. I'm thinking maybe that's what I have—Delayed Stress Syndrome."

"Dale, maybe you need to see a doctor..."

He laughed then, because he knew I had the same aversion to psychiatrists as he did. "Yeah, sure. Dad would really love that."

"Dad's dead, Dale."

"You think he killed him?"

"Who?"

"Dad. Do you think Dad killed Ray?"

"Dad was a minister. Minister's don't kill people."

"Ministers aren't supposed to be drunks, either."

"Look, Dale, why don't you try and get some sleep—? Try and relax—draw yourself a nice hot bath or something?"

"Yeah, right. Talk to you later, Mike. Night."

Later that week my brother Dale drew himself a nice, hot bath, climbed in, and opened his wrists. He was twenty-nine.

Now I'm standing here, staring out my bedroom window, frightened of returning to bed. Returning to sleep. Terrified that if I sleep, I'll wake up and kill myself. Just like Rich. Just like my brother.

I look at my wife, wrapped in her own private world of dreams. She frowns in her sleep and murmurs something. Maybe it's my name. I know she's been worried about me since my brother's death and the subsequent arrival of the nightmares. She has every right to be. As I watch her, I suddenly realize what my course of action must be.

I get dressed as swiftly and as silently as I can. As I write the note telling her not to worry, that I'll be back soon, I realize how crazy this all is. But it is something I must do. If I don't go through with it, I'll find myself eyeing the headlights of on-coming cars and contemplating the edges of straight razors very soon.

Seven Devils is a nine-hour drive from where I now live. But first, I must take a side-trip, to the storage locker where Dale and I moved what remained of our parents' household after dad died and mom moved to the retirement community in Arizona.

It takes me a solid hour of shifting boxes, but I finally find my father's tools. I take one of the shovels—one of the old ones—and place it in the trunk of my car.

It's noon by the time I reach Choctaw County. The town of Seven Devils seems to have dwindled even more than when I last saw it

KNUCKLES AND TALES: DOWN IN THE HOLE

twelve years ago. The buildings look more run down, the streets emptier. It seems as if the town fathers are no longer bothering to pretend that this place has a future.

It takes me awhile to find our old block, since all the neighborhoods look dilapidated now. I only succeed in locating it because I spot the Methodist church my father used to preach at. I pull up and stare around, shielding my eyes from the sun. I have to use my memory to try and place where the Burns' house used to be.

I get out of the car and open the trunk, retrieving my father's shovel. I walk over to the empty lot. It has been twenty years, but I can still make out where the hole once was. I begin digging.

Although Seven Devils is a very small town, no one comes over to see what I'm doing or who I am or why I'm here. I dig for three hours, laboring under a sweltering delta sky. Sweat runs down my back and brow, making my eyes sting. Blisters blossom and burst on my hands, but I keep at it.

What was I expecting to find? Evidence of murder? Suicide? Ray Burns' worm-eaten skeleton, grinning up at me from its unhallowed resting place? In the end, all I found was a rotted leather headband, an old liquor bottle and what might have once been a feather.

I stared at the detritus that was all the physical evidence that remained of the ordeal Rich, Dale and I underwent two decades ago. Wherever Raymond Burns may have ended up, it wasn't in the bottom of this hole.

I still don't know what made Rich and Dale kill themselves. Then again, I don't know what made our dad drink and why our mother spends her free time obsessing over her toy poodle—which she talks to more than any of her children. Maybe it was guilt. Maybe it was stress. Maybe it was unhappiness. Maybe it was from being raised up-tight white Anglo-Saxons protestants. Or perhaps it was the taint from being in such a soul-killing town as Seven Devils. I'll never know.

All I know is that within minutes of my finishing the hole, I fell asleep. And I dreamed. I dreamed about being in high school and being late for a test for a class I never once attended and when the bell rang everyone came out into the hall and I suddenly noticed I wasn't wearing any pants.

It was the best dream I ever had.

SERPENT QUEEN

For more than fifty years, the Choctaw County Fair has been held the week after Labor Day. But that year, for some reason, the second week of September came and went, without a single ring-toss booth to mark its passing.

With October came autumn, setting the trees ablaze with a fire that did not burn. The air was cool and crisp and clear after the torpid, pollen-laden summer breezes, carrying with it the hint of smoke from distant bonfires. At night the winds held a hint of the coming winter, as if Mother Nature was content right now in merely flashing the edge of the scythe she carried at her waist. By the time the carnival arrived in Choctaw County, the harvested fields boasted more stubble than a drunk's cheek.

Unlike the previous carnivals the county had played host to, the caravan of trucks and trailers came without fanfare. One day the county fairgrounds were empty, the next they were crowded with thrill-rides, gaudily painted canvas banners and stuttering neon signs

If the citizens of Choctaw County found this sudden appearance of the strangest of strangers more than passing odd, they kept it to themselves. After all, the county fair was one of the few times farmers and townsfolk alike were allowed to put aside the drudgery of their proscribed routines. Why run the risk of ruining one of their few chances for fun by looking the horse in the mouth?

o o o

"The carnival seems different this year."

Barry paused in gnawing on his corn-dog to glance up and down the midway. The wide shoulders of his letter jacket shrugged indifferently.

"Yeah, kinda," he grunted. "I don't think it's the same one as the last couple of years. Maybe that's why it was so late."

"That's probably it," Cindy replied, plucking half-heartedly at a wad of fluorescent pink cotton candy. It was hard to put her finger on exactly what was unusual about the carnival, but there was something. And she was certain that the weirdness, for once, lay in something beside herself.

At first glance, the midway seemed no different from any of the others she had seen over the years: games of chance; thrill rides; concession stands peddling cotton candy and curly fries. But then again, there was the old-fashioned carousel with its ornately carved mythological characters in place of champing ponies, the House of Fun with its maniacally laughing clockwork harlequin capering on the balcony, and the equally antique Ferris wheel. These old-timey amusements seemed strangely out of place amidst the garishly painted Tilt-A-Whirl, Octopus, and Zipper, with their flashing colored lights and blaring sirens.

Barry's eyes suddenly widened and his corn dog fell, half-eaten, from his hands onto the sawdust-strewn track of the midway. "Wow! Check it out, Cindy!" he said excitedly, pointing at a line of banner. "A freak show!"

Cindy blinked, jarred from her reverie. "Freak show? When did they start having one of those?"

A line of large banners was arrayed along the front of a dirty white-and-red striped tent. At the top of the banner-line was a large sign, written in classic circus script: *Dr. Oddbody's Gallery of Living Wonders.* Each of banners depicted, in garish colors and doubtful scale, such human marvels as The World's Smallest Couple, a bearded fat lady, and some thing called a Human Ostrich and a Serpent Queen. The drawings were crudely done, but possessed a compelling vitality that made it hard to look away from them.

The first banner depicted a tall man in a white lab coat—no doubt Dr. Oddbody himself— standing with his hands held up to either side, palms flat. In one hand he held a tiny, perfectly formed woman, while in the other he held an equally small man. The tiny man was smoking a cigar.

The second banner depicted a very fat woman with a dark, heavy beard that nearly obscured her ample bosom. An ermine cape was draped over her ample shoulders, her oddly dainty hands clutched a jeweled scepter, and a crown rested on her head

The third banner showed an ostrich with the head of a man. The ostrich-man had what looked like the outline of a pipe wrench stuck in his elongated throat. The image was so grotesquely ludicrous; Cindy couldn't help but giggle at it.

KNUCKLES AND TALES: SERPENT QUEEN

The fourth and final banner depicted what was supposed to be a beautiful, half-naked woman —at least from the waist up. From the waist down she was a coiled snake.

"Aw, man! This is *so* cool!" Barry whispered, barely able to control his enthusiasm.

There was a man standing behind the tall, coffin-like ticket booth beside the front entrance. He looked to be in his late forties, lean with dark hair and a pockmarked face. He was dressed in a white lab coat, with a stethoscope wrapped about his neck and a physician's mirror strapped to his brow. In one hand he held a wheel of pasteboard tickets the color of blood, in the other he clutched an electric bullhorn. As he spoke into the mouthpiece, the parabolic mirror flashed like a Cyclops's eye.

"Hurry! Hurry! Hurry! Step right up, ladies and gentlemen, to Dr. Oddbody's Gallery of Wonders and be amazed, shocked, startled and amused unlike you've *ever* been before, *all* for the paltry sum of one dollar, four quarters, ten dimes, one hundred pennies—the price of two candy bars! See for yourself the *grandest*, most *astonishing* collection of prodigies and monstrosities gathered together in one place since the days of ancient Rome!

"I, the one and *only* Dr. Oddbody, have traveled to the farthest corners of the globe to bring back marvels for your entertainment and enlightenment! From the heart of darkest Africa, to the headwaters of the Amazon, to the cannibal isles of the South Pacific I have risked *everything* and dared *all* to bring these wonders back to the United States, for the delight and education of *you*, my fellow man!

"I have spared *no* expense in searching every nook and cranny of the world to provide this banquet for the brain and feast for the eye! *Step up!* Step up and see the amazing Gobbles, the Human Ostrich! Captured in the savannas of Nairobi, where he was raised from early boyhood by the mighty running birds of the plains! See him *swallow* a light bulb *whole*—then cough it back up again!

"*See!* Smidgen and Midgen, the World's *Smallest* Couple! They're tiny as can be, but oh, how does their love grow! *See!* Duchess Harrietta, the World's Fattest Bearded Lady! *See!* Lamia, the Serpent Queen! Where does the *girl* end and the *snake* begin? Only *Lamia* knows for sure! Step up, ladies and gentlemen! *No* waiting, *no* delays! Step up, and avoid the rush! Tickets now selling in the doorway!"

Cindy scanned the banners, feeling the same kind of mixture of curiosity and anxiety that had marked her first peek at her older brother's stack of porno mags. "I don't know about this... Its like paying to look at deformed people."

"Aw, c'mon!" Barry chided, shooting her a sour look. "*You're* the one always complaining about how boring things are around here! Now there's a chance of doing something different, and you're chickening out! Maybe you really *are* just like your mama, after all?"

That last nettle stung, just like he knew it would. Cindy straightened her shoulders, resolve replacing her previous timorousness. "Okay. Let's *do* it, then."

Barry stepped forward, thrusting a couple of crumpled bills at the ticket-seller.

Dr. Oddbody set aside his bullhorn to glance down at the young couple. His gaze slid across Barry's raw-boned farm boy's face and came to rest on Cindy. Although the carny said nothing, she could feel his eyes weighing her like a heifer on the auction block. Her cheeks turned red and she quickly looked away.

"Move ahead and keep to the right," Oddbody said, smiling like a croupier as he took their money and ushered them inside the tent.

As they stepped inside, Cindy could feel the freak show proprietor's eyes on her back. She reached out for Barry's hand, but he had already moved away from her.

The interior of the tent smelled of sawdust and was divided by a series of canvas half-walls. Each exhibit had their own special booth, with a painted backdrop and a wooden platform that enabled the paying customers to an unobscured view of the performer.

The first display belonged to Smidgen and Midgen. The World's Smallest Couple were not, in fact, pocket-sized, but they *were* small, roughly the size of toddlers. Their cubicle was designed to resemble a front parlor, with a sofa, easy chairs, and a coffee table scaled to accommodate the owners. Despite their child-like builds, Smidgen and Midgen affected adult hairstyles and clothes tailored to fit their small builds. With their high-pitched voices they could be easily be mistaken as children playing an elaborate game of dress-up— until you saw their wrinkled, knowing faces. On their tiny, baby-like hands were matching bands of gold.

As Barry and Cynthia stepped up, the midget couple smiled and welcomed them to their "home", then launched into well-rehearsed spiel recounting their individual origins, how they met, and their life together as a professional couple. They were particularly proud of their son, who played basketball for Indiana.

KNUCKLES AND TALES: SERPENT QUEEN

The second stage housed an exceptionally large, bearded woman dressed in a tent-like purple muumuu and matching velvet cape trimmed in blatantly faux-ermine. The bearded fat lady explained, with an accent redolent of the Bronx, that she had once been the wife of the Duke of Ultima Thule—but was forced to step down when she grew a beard better than her royal hubby's.

While the royalty angle was a nice touch, the Duchess was nowhere near as imposing as her banner had represented her. Granted, she was indeed fat, and she *did* have a beard, but she weighed a mere three hundred pounds, with a sparse growth of scraggly chestnut-colored hair that barely covered her double chin. Except for the little crown and ermine robe, there was little to differentiate the Duchess from any number of women Cindy had seen shopping at the local Wal-Mart.

Gobbles the Human Ostrich was seated on a stool, reading a newspaper as Barry and Cindy approached his stage. He was a rather ordinary looking man dressed in a black leotard and tights, and the only decoration in his performance space was a smaller version of the banner than hung outside and a wooden table that boasted an array of inedible objects, such as razor blades, a light bulb, a long-stemmed rose and a can of nails.

As they drew near, the Human Ostrich took a page of the newspaper he'd been reading, tore it in two, wadded it up into a ball, then stuffed it into his mouth and swallowed it whole. Cindy grimaced and made an uneasy noise as she watched the Human Ostrich's throat bulge.

Unlike the previous exhibits, the Human Ostrich did not seem to feel obligated to launch into an elaborate account of his supposed origins and behavior. As it was, his act was pretty much self-explanatory. As they watched, he picked up the long-stemmed rose and bit off its head, munching on it like a contented cow. Then he proceeded to consume the thorny stem in the exact same manner.

"*Dude!*" Barry said, by way of approval.

When the Human Ostrich reached for the razor blades, Cindy cringed and moved toward the fourth and final stage in the tent, leaving Barry to gape at Gobbles ingest metal implements.

Unlike the others, an old-fashioned theater curtain, like the ones in the high school auditorium, obscured the final stage. They were the color of good wine and were made from heavy velvet, with golden tassels on the hem. Cindy wondered what they could be hiding. Then, without a sound, the curtains were pulled back and music began to play. It was the high-pitched sound of an exotic flute, like the ones snake charmers play.

She glimpsed something white and gold partially hidden in the shadows at the back of the stage. With a start, Cindy saw that it was a woman, naked save for a heavy golden rope wrapped about her torso and limbs in a Gordian knot.

When the golden rope began to move of its own accord, Cindy realized that she was looking at the woman known as Lamia, the Serpent Queen.

The snake charmer moved forward as the music began to play, the great serpent wrapped about her like a living stole. The snake's skin sparkled like a wet sun, dappled by irregular patches of darkness. Cindy recognized it as being some kind of python, perhaps it was an anaconda, said to be the largest snake in the world. In any case, it was certainly bigger than the baby boa constrictor back at the Life Sciences lab back at school.

The snake's blunt-nosed head, which was perched on the dancer's shoulder, facing the audience, was easily the size of a large dog's, its eyes as dark as a closet. With a start, she realized the serpent was looking right at her with an unwavering gaze, its forked tongue furiously tasting the air. The intensity of its gorgon-like stare made something in her chest squeeze her heart as firmly as a hand, then let go. Cindy gave out with a tiny cry—part gasp, part scream—and took an involuntary step backward.

So riveting was the python's size and appearance, it took her a moment to realize that the dancer was just as unique and unusual as her monstrous pet. Her flesh was as pale as a mermaid's, her eyes as carefully painted as those of the Egyptian pharaohs. Her heavy chestnut locks were piled atop her head and held in place by a golden diadem in the design of a sunburst. She was both voluptuous, yet surprisingly fragile-looking, not unlike the portraits of Mary Magdalene.

Save for the diadem, a few golden upper arm bracelets, and silver bangles on her ankles and wrists, Lamia was otherwise naked, although what would have been otherwise public private parts were conveniently concealed by the coils of the snake wrapped about her.

While Cindy was so self-conscious as to her appearance she could not bring herself to wear anything but a one-piece swim suit, Lamia stood there, naked as an egg, dressed in nothing but her own skin and yards of living scales, without apparent shame nor undue pride. Instead, she held herself with all the dignity of Caesar's wife before the Senate.

"Holy shit!"

Barry had finally finished gawking at the Human Ostrich and walked

KNUCKLES AND TALES: SERPENT QUEEN

in on the middle of Lamia's act. He watched the snake charmers gyrations with a jaw that hung like a dead weight on a delicate scale.

"What's she doing?"

"*She's dancing,*" Cynthia replied in a hushed voice, as if the freak tent had become a cathedral. Trying her best to ignore her companion, she returned her attention to the stage.

Despite her feminine charms, it was clear from the muscles that tensed and rippled underneath her pale, smooth skin, Lamia was as strong as a lioness. She had to be, if she could carry such a prodigious living weight about her neck and still move, much less dance.

If the snake's bulk hampered her as she swayed to the music, she did not show any of it. The snake moved in concert with her movements, sliding its body along her limbs and torso, lifting its snout skyward and following the movements of her hands. She coached and prodded the great serpent as she would a lover as it caressed her trembling white flesh.

Lamia took the creature's inhuman head in her hands and stroked it as she would a cat's, kissing its blunted snout. In return, the python's tongue darted forth and touched her own.

"Aw, man! That's *sick!*" Barry said with a loud, somewhat nervous guffaw, the words striking Cindy like an open hand. "That bitch is *twisted!*"

Cindy glanced up at Lamia as she moved with a fluid grace, her hands turned out flat, palms up, like a Balinese dancer. If she heard what had been said, it did not show. The serpent queen's face was as impenetrable as a porcelain mask, regarding her audience with a placid indifference, almost as if she had emptied her eyes of sight.

Cindy turned and shot Barry a withering look. "Don't you know *anything*—?" she hissed.

There was a look of dumb incomprehension on Barry's face—one that she had become all too familiar with.

"What did *I* say?" he demanded, more defensive than contrite.

The thing within her chest squeezed again, and she saw her future with Barry laid out before her, like bolt of cloth unrolled for inspection: marriage six months after graduation; a couple of kids before their third anniversary; a drinking problem for him, a weight problem for her; divorce by their seventh anniversary. The images were too vivid, the future hurts and disappointments too sure, to be anything but true.

Fighting to hide the claustrophobic panic rising with her, Cindy turned and fled. The thought of spending another minute in his company enveloped her in despair as heavy as a horse blanket. She burst from the tent's exit, gasping like a swimmer staggering free of strong surf, Barry's steps thundering close behind. She glanced around anxiously, looking for some place to hide, but it was too late.

"Hey! What's got *into* you?"

Barry grabbed her upper arm and turned her to face him none too gently. That, too, had become all too familiar as well.

"What did you mean by running off like that?"

Cindy looked at her feet rather than meet his angry, confused gaze. How could she tell him that being near him was like being slowly suffocated? That his kisses had all the passion of underdone bacon? That whatever future she might have with him was worse than no future at all? With a sob of anger and frustration, she yanked her arm free of his grasp and fled into the milling crowds of the midway.

"*Cindy! Cindy—come back!*" Barry yelled as he gave half-hearted chase. After a half-dozen running paces he gave up his pursuit, flapping his arms in disgust. Barry shrugged his shoulders and headed off in the direction of the Hit-The-Cats booth. "Fuckin' basketcase," he grumbled under his breath. She'd come back, if she didn't want to walk back to town at the end of the night. Besides, even if she managed to find her own way home, she'd make her way back to his door sooner or later. After all—where else was there to go?

o o o

Cindy gasped, despite herself, when the lights of the midway switched off. With the darkness came silence, as all the portable generators that powered the various thrill-rides and other amusements shut down.

The House of Fun ceased its maniacal laughter, the taped calliope music came to a halt, and the pounding beat of heavy metal and hip-hop that served as the aural backdrop for the more adrenaline-charged thrill-rides cut off in mid-note. After enduring the amplified roar of the carnival all night, the silence made Cindy's eardrums throb like ghost limbs.

She had spent the last couple of hours dodging in and out of the various exhibition halls, trying to avoid being spotted by Barry, before finally ending up behind the metal outbuilding that housed the prize-winning quilts and canned peaches.

Now that she was certain that the locals had all left for the night, Cindy abandoned her hiding place and took a tentative look around. The only illumination came from the moon, which looked down on

KNUCKLES AND TALES: SERPENT QUEEN

the carnival from its place in the sky, as white and perfect as a magnolia floating in a bowl.

All of the concession stands and game booths were shut up tight, nor was there any sign of the carnies who manned the controls of the rides. It was as if the carnival workers had sealed themselves up within their individual fiefdoms to sleep away the daylight hours.

The stillness was eerie. She had not expected it to be so—lifeless— once the townspeople had gone. She thought the carnies might gather together to drink and play cards and tell stories after the fair shut down.

Cindy gave out with a short, high shriek as a hand closed about her shoulder, squeezing it firmly. She spun around, her heart beating like a blind man's cane, and found herself staring into the smirking face of Dr. Oddbody. There was craftiness in the barker's eyes, though it lacked a sense of ill will—as if treachery was as natural to him as storms on the sea or lighting from the sky.

"Lamia wants to see you," he said, his message couched in a cloud of second-hand bourbon.

"*Me?*" she managed to squeak. "Are you sure?"

"I'm sure all right," Oddbody said, flashing a smile as sharp and unexpected as a knife in a bishop's sleeve. He pointed with one long, tobacco-stained finger at a small silver-skinned trailer located behind the freak tent. There was a light burning in the solitary window.

Cindy glanced back at Dr. Oddbody, but the barker had somehow managed to disappear. She swallowed and returned her gaze to the squalid little trailer with its beckoning light in the window.

She felt as if she was watching herself in a movie as she strode across the deserted midway, past the shuttered ring-toss and cotton candy booth. Even through she knew she should leave right away, she could not bring herself to do so. It was as if she was fastened to the snake charmer by an invisible cord, one that was being shortened with the steady ratchet of a windlass. It was like a dream, where she was being lead by unseen and irresistible forces towards dark and dangerous places she was not sure she truly wished to go.

Her heart was thumping like a pagan's drum—something she had never experienced, even in her most intimate moments with Barry. All she knew was that she must see Lamia, speak to her—perhaps she would have an answer for the strange throbbing that was like a toothache in her heart.

On closer inspection, the snake charmer's trailer was no less grungy than it had appeared from a distance. Stepping onto the chipped cinder block that served as the trailer's front step, Cynthia rapped her knuckles against the doorframe. Although there was no voice raised in response, the door opened inward. Mustering her courage, she stepped inside.

The interior was barely big enough for an adult to stand up in, and was crammed with steamer trunks and cardboard boxes filled with the odds and ends of a traveling life. Adding to the discomfort, the heat within the tiny trailer was thick as jelly. What little open space in the trailer was dominated by a large vanity table lined 20-watt bulbs and cluttered with jars of cold cream and tubes of lipstick and mascara.

It was in front of this altar to illusion that Lamia was seated, dressed in a silk kimono embroidered with black and gold Chinese dragons battling on a scarlet field, her back to her visitor. The serpent queen's unfastened hair hung flat against her body like a living cloak as she stared into the vanity's oval mirror, languidly rubbing cold cream onto her face.

Cindy cringed as she caught sight of her own acid-washed jeans and feathered hair reflected back at her. She wanted to run away and hide in embarrassment, but she had come this far, and there was no use in turning back. "H-hello? Lamia?" she managed to stammer. "Dr. Oddbody said you wanted to, um, see me—?"

Whatever reaction she had expected from the serpent queen, it was certainly not the one she got.

Lamia did not bother to turn around, but merely looked at Cindy's reflection, regarding her with eyes as lifeless as the skin on a stagnant pond. With a thrill of revulsion, Cynthia noticed a long spindle of drool hanging from one corner of the snake charmer's slackened mouth.

Baffled, Cindy moved closer, meeting and holding Lamia's uncomprehending gaze. The dancer cringed and made a whimpering sound, her expression as dumb and anxious as a dog's. Was this the same woman who had transfixed her with such fluid grace and unearthly beauty? As Cindy reached out to touch Lamia's shoulder, the snake charmer jerked away clumsily, making a pathetic noise like that of an animal in distress.

Cindy drew her hand back as if it had been burned. Where was the snake? She did not remember seeing upon entering a tank or box the huge python could be resting in. She glanced back up at the mirror before her and saw something emerging from the clutter of steam trunks and cardboard boxes behind her, its skin shimmering like jewels laid against black velvet.

Panic rose within her, thick as honey and blood, and she tried to scream, but it stuck in her throat like a wad of cotton. She did not want

KNUCKLES AND TALES: SERPENT QUEEN

to turn to face it, but watching its reflection as it raised itself up behind her, its great head waving back and forth as if to some unheard tune, was even more horrible. Slowly she turned to face the monster snake.

It sat there, coiled about itself, as proud as an idol, blocking her escape route, watching her with eyes as deep and dark as mountain nights.

She had known the creature was huge, but there was no way it could have been this big. It was as if the snake had doubled its width and length in a matter of hours. It peered down at her from a height, the top of its skull nearly pressed against the low ceiling of the trailer.

Cindy wanted to look anywhere but at the mammoth serpent coiled before her, but she could not look away. The great snake emitted power, which stank like blood and hot metal, as if underneath the dabbling of gold and shadow, under the muscle and scales, lay secrets undreamed of.

And then, to Cindy's surprise, the snake spoke to her, its voice as quiet and dry as wind in high grass.

"*Yesss*. Oddbody was correct. I wish to meet with you."

A sea change rippled through the serpent's upper body, remolding it into the likeness of a human woman. Although the features were classically beautiful, there was a slyness to the face, like that of a child forced to grow up fast.

Cindy watched the transformation in stunned silence, both transfixed and terrified by its beauty. She knew now, however belatedly, that Lamia was not the name of the woman seated before the mirror.

"Be not afraid, my child," whispered the serpent queen. "I mean you no harm. Indeed, I have but the kindest of intentions towards you. I can offer you many things, my dear. I can give you lifetimes, and a chance to die in beauty, like a flower snapped from its stem in fullest bloom."

"W-why me?"

The snake woman smiled with her lipless mouth. "Ah! Such courage! There is a tragic daring about you, like that of a moth chasing flame. I knew you were suited to my needs when I first saw you. You are bold, in your way, my dear. Bold as a dying saint. And we gods must have our saints."

"G-god? You're a god?"

"*Godesssss*," Lamia corrected, the word escaping like air from a tire. "There was a time when I was worshipped throughout the civilized world, in lands far distant and more warmer than this one I am now condemned to wander. It is like a long hopeless homesickness... missing those young days.

"Mine were the healing arts and the secrets of fertility. Libations of milk and sweet wine were poured in my honor. Brides prayed to me to fill empty cradles. My temples were filled with the perfume of burning braziers.

"My priestesses writhed, boneless as poured water, as my divinity merged with their mortality, transported into ecstasies unknown by the priests of this age's pale carpenter. And, as befits a goddess, there were blood sacrifices. The child-flesh I gorged upon wed me to your kind, linking me forever to this world, even long after my worship ceased.

"Time has its way with us all, gods and mortals alike. I have watched over the centuries as my followers were overcome by invaders, my religion debased, and I was turned from goddess to demon to monster to, finally, myth. However, while I may no longer be worshipped in every house, that does not mean I am without my servants."

"Is that what she is?" Cynthia asked, pointing at the woman seated before the vanity. Despite all that was going on, the dancer seemed unperturbed, still rubbing cold cream into her face. She acted as if she was alone and not sharing the cramped confines of the trailer with a snake-woman and a teen-aged girl.

Lamia's face lost its slyness and something like the affection crossed the demon-goddess's features.

"*Yesss,*" she sighed. "Poor Thea. It is within my power to grant those who serve me eternal youth. Unfortunately, even gods and goddesses have their limitations. While I can bless my priestesses with physical immortality, I cannot prevent the ravages of age from affecting their minds. My sweet, loyal Thea has served me faithfully for over one hundred and twenty-five years—but she now suffers from profound senility. For the last few years I have guided her movements with my own. It is I who dances with her, not the other way around. Without me to ride her shoulders, she's little more than an animated husk. The time has come for her to be...retired from duty."

"And—you expect me to replace her?"

Lamia's inhuman eyes sparkled with a strange light, like fire kindled within ice. "Long centuries ago, my priestesses were scattered to the four corners of the world by cruel invaders who feared my power. Over the years, my prodigal daughters bred with the sons of man. On the outside, their descendants are no different from any other mortal woman—save that they hold within their hearts an unborn snake. The moment these prodigal daughters are finally brought before my divine presence, the serpent inside uncoils."

KNUCKLES AND TALES: SERPENT QUEEN

Lamia's eerily beautiful face moved closer, bobbing gently on its endless neck like a helium balloon, until she was mere inches from Cindy's own. The goddess smiled, her forked tongue flickering forth and caressing the tip of the girl's. The touch was as light as that of a butterfly's wings.

"Did you not feel a strange stirring within your breast the moment you first laid eyes on me? Did not your very heart ache, as the snake within you hatched? If not, then why did you flee the male's touch? Why did you come to this place—if not to receive my blessing—?"

Cindy shook her head in confusion. "You're trying to hypnotize me…"

"If you do not believe me, then look to your heart, and see the truth that lies within."

Cindy closed her eyes, took a deep breath, and reached within herself, like reaching inside a sack. What she found within herself was cool and scaly to the touch. As the fingers of her soul closed about the snake inside her heart, it was as if the heavens were showering her with light in its purest form.

She opened her eyes and saw Lamia's half-human face, shrouded by a nimbus of holy fire. The awe she felt in the presence of the snake goddess was both ecstatic and crippling, dropping her like a baton to the back of the knees. She fell before the coiled splendor of the goddess, prostrating herself before her living god.

"Look upon me, my child," Lamia whispered.

Cindy raised her head and stared into the eyes of the goddess. Lamia smiled and, with the swiftness of a striking cobra, looped itself about the young girl, holding her tight within her gleaming coils. Instead of being afraid, the young girl's heart lifted like a wave at her mistress's smooth, dry touch.

"*Sssindy—*" Lamia whispered. "The love of a god is a transforming thing. Once experienced, you can never go back to what—or who— you were before. There are but two choices open to you—to serve me or die. Do you understand and accept this truth?"

Where a few minutes ago, such an ultimatum would have sparked fear and horror within her, what she felt was as strong as the sun, as deep as the sea—and more certain than any truth she had ever been told. There was no hesitancy, no fear, and no anxiety to her actions.

Cindy lifted one hand and stroked Lamia's cheek. The goddess's eyes dimmed as an inner lid slid across her dark orbs. The serpent queen's coils tightened, and although Cindy knew that the slightest increase of pressure could turn the embrace into a suffocating death grip, she was unafraid. The goddess smiled at her new acolyte, exposing fangs as delicate and exquisitely formed as pieces of white jade.

Lamia struck so swiftly there was no time but for anything but a tiny cry of surprise, as the dripping fangs sank into the soft flesh of Cindy's throat. She could feel the venom spread through her like ink dumped into a well, but instead of paralysis and pain, there was an ecstasy as warm and rich as wine. Then the darkness claimed her.

o o o

Cindy did not know how long she lay unconscious on the floor of the trailer, but when she finally opened her eyes, she was greeted by the sight of Thea's bare feet disappearing down Lamia's gullet as the serpent-queen realigned her jaw and swallowed convulsively one final time, pushing the contents of her meal down into her midsection.

Cindy did not experience any revulsion or horror at the sight before her. Indeed, it seemed only right that one who had served Lamia so loyally and so well for so many years would join with her in such a fashion. Indeed, Cindy prayed that one day she, too, could serve her mistress in such a primal fashion.

Cindy staggered over to the vanity, dropping into Thea's recently vacated seat to stare at herself in the mirror. Outwardly, she seemed little changed from the girl who had entered the trailer earlier that night. The only obvious difference were the twin puncture marks on her neck, clotted with blood and a thick, yellowish fluid. The bite throbbed dully, but she did not mind the pain.

Cindy smiled crookedly and glanced over her shoulder at. Lamia. She did not need to be told what to do next or how to go about it. The knowledge was part of her, transferred to her by her mistress in her kiss.

She stripped herself of her clothes and took a pair of sharp scissors to her driver's license permit and Social Security card, turning it into laminated confetti. Come the dawn the carnival would be on its way to somewhere else, and Cindy Crockett would be no more. She paused in her destruction of her identity and cocked her head to one side.
She would need a new name to go with her new self. Cassandra was a good choice. had not Cassandra been given the gift of true sight when a serpent kissed her ears?

There was a flickering tickle at her heel. She glanced down and saw Lamia, who had shed her divine aspect and reverted to her earthly avatar, coiling her way up her bare leg.

KNUCKLES AND TALES: SERPENT QUEEN

Of course. It was time for Lamia to go for her nightly ride on the Ferris wheel. The one that never stopped to let its passengers on or off. Smiling indulgently, she reached down and lifted the monstrous python onto her shoulders. Although it was incredibly heavy, she did not grimace or grumble under her burden. After all, it was a great honor to serve as the serpent queen's arms and legs. Without any further hesitation, she stepped into the night, naked save for her god.

JUNIOR TEETER AND THE BAD SHINE

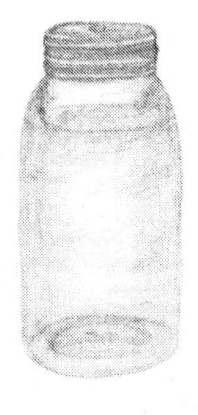

When most folks think of Arkansas, they think of the Ozark Mountains and hillbillies sitting on the front porch with a pig under one arm and a jug of moonshine under the other. If they're political minded, they might think of President Clinton. Or if they're sports-minded, they might think of the University of Arkansas Razorbacks.

But one thing they never think of is swampland. Nestled down in the far butt-end of the state, flanking Mississippi and Louisiana, is what is referred to as "the Ark-La-Miss". What isn't bayou is farmland—cotton and rice, for the most part. And fertile land it is, too. As part of the Mississippi River Delta it's some of the choicest, richest soil this side of the Tigris and Euphrates.

There's not many places on God's green earth more out-of-the-way than Choctaw County, Arkansas. There's little in the way of industry in the area, since most of the jobs are in agriculture or what's referred to as "agribusiness"—tractor dealerships, fertilizer salesmen, feed-n-seed stores and the like.

Hard times and skinny wallets have always been common to this part of the country. Things weren't much different in Choctaw County before the Depression and they haven't gotten much better since. That's not to say there aren't rich folk in Choctaw County—far from it. But them's that poor outnumber them's that rich four to one—and them's that poor tend to stay that way.

Seven Devils is the county seat. The reason its called Seven Devils is because of the seven bayous that surround it. When the area was first settled, the founding fathers dubbed the bayous "the Seven Brothers"—but come the first flood season, they got to calling them something else entirely.

Indeed, Bayou Baphomet cuts through the very middle of town. The old city hall was built on a brick and iron platform so the bayou could flow right underneath. Which is one reason city hall smells like a mildewed sock.

Since it is the county seat, Seven Devils serves as a defacto hub of business, including those that have nothing to do with agri. It has the Bijou, a couple of restaurants, a honky-tonk, a corresponding number of churches and package liquor stores, three gas stations, a switching yard, a couple of car dealerships, a Wal-Mart and a fast-food joint. So, if you live in Choctaw County and you're looking for something to do on the weekend, then odds are you end up in Seven Devils. It's no Babylon, but it's the best they can do, Cradle of Civilization wise.

Most of the people living in town were born in Seven Devils, grew up in Seven Devils, and most likely than not, will die in Seven Devils as well, if they don't move away after graduating from the local high school. But that doesn't mean they don't know their ass from a teakettle when it comes to how the world works.

People who live in the suburbs and big cities have real funny ideas of what does and doesn't go on in small towns like Seven Devils. They expect it to be what they see on TV—like Mayberry RFD or Smallville, USA. In their minds rural America consists of slow-moving, slow-talking, slow-thinking folks with nothing better to worry about but the Fourth of July Parade and apple-pie judging at the County Fair. And, to a certain extent, that's true.

But there is a dark side to small town life, just like every rock has its dirt-side. But for some reason, the worms that come crawling out when you turn over that rock always seem a lot more disgusting. People expect crime and sin to be in big cities like New York and New Orleans and Houston—but it's hard for them to understand that the seven deadly sins are no respecters of clichés. And they certainly don't give two hoots for the size of a town.

Take Junior Teeter, for instance.

The Teeters had lived in Seven Devils since fish had legs. At least, that's how it seemed. Harald Senior was a hard-working sort. Not the sharpest knife in the drawer, but a good man for the most part. His wife, Jo-Lynne, was a nice woman, from all accounts. But after the doctor told her that Junior was going to have to do her in the young'un department, she got a tad strange. She doted on the boy like he was God's gift to the world, and Harald Senior let her have her way. So it was small wonder Junior turned out as useless as teats on a boar.

The boy had absolutely no ambition or drive. He was so accustomed of others doing for him, he didn't know how to do for himself. He couldn't hold down a job, couldn't keep a wife, but he *had* taken up drinking, which was about the only thing he'd shown much of an aptitude for.

KNUCKLES AND TALES: JUNIOR TEETER AND THE BAD SHINE

After Junior's folks died, he was pretty much adrift, even though he was well into his thirties, and it wasn't long before he frittered his way through what little he'd inherited. Still, as useless as Junior may have been, everyone was shocked when he took up with Merla Pritchett.

The Pritchetts have been a carbuncle on Choctaw County's ass since before the Civil War. In its time, the clan has been in charge of bootlegging, floating crap games, pimping, and fencing and hot cars rackets. If there is something low-down, sleazy, and crooked going on in the county, chances are it involves a Pritchett somehow.

Well, it wasn't long before loud music started blaring out of Junior's house all hours of the day and night, and all sorts of riffraff started coming and going. The neighbors weren't exactly sure what was going on, but it was suspected the Teeter place was being used as a distribution point for Pappy John Pritchett's moonshine. No one was thrilled by all this, but they largely turned a blind eye to it, and tried to turn a deaf ear, out of respect for Junior's folks. But such things can only go so far for so long.

o o o

As Edna McQuistion had gotten on in years, sleeping through the night had become harder and harder for her. The slightest disturbance was often enough to wake her up and keep her up until cockcrow. But the music that came blaring out of Junior Teeter's house at 4:30 am that morning was far from a "slight disturbance". Even though her boarding house was across the street and two doors down, the volume was enough to make the windowpanes rattle in her bedroom.

As she squinted at her bedside clock, Edna—better known to the young and old citizens of Seven Devils alike as Miz Eddy—decided she had put up with enough out of respect for Harald and Jo-Lynne Teeter.

o o o

"Police Department."

"Royce—that you?"

"Sure nuff. What you calling about, Miz Eddy?"

"It's Junior Teeter. He's got that music of his turned up loud enough to wake the dead! You know I don't like complaining—"

"Don't you fret, Miz Eddy. You ain't the only one that's called in to complain about Junior this morning. I was just getting ready to head on over there."

"Thank you, Royce."

"It's my job, ma'am."

Since she was up and there was no question of getting back to sleep, Miz Eddy decided to get an early start on breakfast for her boarders. As she headed for the landing, Boyd Tilberry stuck his head out of his room.

Even on the best of days Boyd was something of a sore bear in the morning. It usually took three cups of coffee and a plate of flapjacks to turn him into civil company.

"What in Sam Hill's going on?" he growled. "Can't a man get some peace and quiet?"

"I've already called John Law on him, Boyd," Miz Eddy assured her oldest boarder. "There's not much else you or I can do about it."

Boyd grumbled something under his breath and yanked his head back into his room, slamming the door behind him. When Miz Eddy got to the kitchen, she was surprised to find the Dunlevy girl already sitting at the table, sipping a glass of orange juice.

Caroline had only been with Miz Eddy for a week or so, but she'd already taken a shine to the child. She was young and pretty and employed by the County Extension Office as a social worker. Since Seven Devils was hardly the kind of community with a lot of pre-fab apartment complexes for rent, she had ended up at the boarding house for the time being.

"Hope you don't mind me helping myself, Miz Eddy," Caroline smiled sheepishly. "I couldn't sleep, what with all the noise—"

"Don't you never mind, honey. But as long as you're up, could you do me a favor and reach me down the percolator? Boyd will be needing his coffee soon enough."

Ten minutes later, the coffee was perking away and Miz Eddy was heating up the griddle while Caroline mixed the batter for flapjacks. Suddenly the thunderous music coming out of Junior's house stopped in mid-blare.

"Thank heaven for small favors," Miz Eddy sighed, wiping her hands on a tea towel as she stepped away from the stove. "Sounds like the cavalry has finally arrived."

Caroline and Miz Eddy put aside what they were doing and hurried to the front parlor in order to look out the window. From where they were standing they could see Royce Boyette's squad car pulled up in front of the Teeter place. Royce was nowhere to be seen, but the bubble-gum machine on the roof of his car was still slowly flashing red.

KNUCKLES AND TALES: JUNIOR TEETER AND THE BAD SHINE

As Miz Eddy looked to the house, she noticed that there was a pickup with over-sized wheels parked behind Junior's Camaro in the driveway.

"I should have known Tommy-Lee would be over there," she sighed, letting the curtain drop back into place.

"Who's that?" Caroline asked.

"The Shackleford boy," Miz Eddy answered, heading back to the kitchen. "Talk about trash that won't burn! I really shouldn't call him a boy, though. I reckon he must be about thirty-five by now. That's his mud-buggy parked in the drive. Him and Junior have been friends since junior high. He's the one that introduced Junior to that Pritchett girl. Lord, Jo-Lynne must be spinning like a 45 rpm record by now."

Miz Eddy went back to making breakfast without giving a second thought to Junior Teeter. No doubt Royce had pulled the plug on Junior and Tommy-Lee's little party and was reading them the riot act. While Junior and Tommy-Lee liked to play at being rough and tough, they were pretty much all talk, and Royce Boyette was hardly the type they picked to mouth off to. Leastwise not more than once.

As she was preparing to ladle a second serving of pancake batter onto the griddle, Miz Eddy was surprised to hear what sounded like her porch door slam shut, followed immediately by someone hammering on the front door.

"Caroline," she said, frowning as she tightened the cinch on her house-robe. "There's someone at the door. Could you keep an eye on those flapjacks for me and make sure they don't burn?"

"Sure thing, Miz Eddy."

Miz Eddy scuffed her way to the foyer in her slippers and peeped through the side-window. She was startled to see the sheriff standing on her porch, looking white as a frog's belly. She opened the door and waved him in.

"Royce—Lord A' mighty, boy! What's wrong—?"

"I—I—need to use your restroom, Miz Eddy," he said, his voice tight as a drumhead.

"Help yourself," she said, pointing to the water closet under the staircase.

"Thank you, ma'am." Royce didn't waste any time. The moment the door closed behind him, she could hear him getting sick. Miz Eddy headed back into the kitchen to find Caroline was standing in the doorway, looking down the hall.

"Was that Sheriff Boyette I heard talking?"

"Sure was."

"Where is he?"

"Being sick in the downstairs privy," she explained. "Caroline, could you do me a favor and reach me down that crystal decanter? The one on the high boy over there? Something tells me Sheriff Boyette's going to be needin' a little Irish in his coffee. Thank you, honey."

A couple of minutes later Royce Boyette emerged from the downstairs bathroom, his hair damp from the water he'd splashed on his face. He stood in the kitchen door, turning his battered Stetson around in his hands and looking somewhat embarrassed. Although Royce was a physically intimidating man, whenever he got around women he became as awkward as a farm boy at high tea.

"Thank you for letting me use your, um, convenience, Miz Eddy," he said. "If it's not too much of a imposition, could I borrow your phone? I need to put a call into the Barracks."

"Help yourself, Royce." Miz Eddy gestured to the phone resting on its very own little table in the hallway.

"Oh—we took the liberty of fixing you some coffee, sheriff," Caroline said, stepping forward.

"Thankee kindly," he smiled weakly, taking the proffered mug. Royce sniffed the coffee and glanced at Miz Eddy, but she pretended not to notice. However Miz Eddy couldn't help but notice how Caroline's cheeks flushed as she returned Royce's smile. She had the look on her face of a woman who wished she had the foresight to wake up with her hair done and make-up already applied.

Royce returned to the hall and picked up the phone. He frowned at it for a moment, momentarily baffled by the rotary dial, and then took it back into the privy, closing the door behind him.

"What do you think happened?" Caroline whispered.

"I haven't the foggiest—but it must be something serious if he's having to call the State Police Barracks over in Chicot County."

"Well, I'm going to run back up stairs and get some clothes on," Caroline stated, trying her best not to sound too excited. As she hurried up the stairs, she nearly collided with Boyd, who was still in his robe and slippers.

"Mind where you're going, gal!" he snapped. "This ain't no Stairmaster!"

"Sorry, Mr. Tilberry!"

Whereas Caroline was Miz Eddy's newest boarder, Boyd was the oldest. He'd been a lodger ever since the early sixties, when she and her

KNUCKLES AND TALES: JUNIOR TEETER AND THE BAD SHINE

sister Mabel first converted the old homestead into a boarding house. Back then Boyd was still working for the railroad, and after he retired in the mid-Eighties he elected to stay on, largely because no one else would have him, and lived off his pension from the Brakeman's Union. Boyd wasn't the sweetest of the Lord's peas, but Miz Eddy had grown accustomed to him over the years. It was her theory Boyd was such a grouch because he was missing fingers—or parts of fingers—on both hands from his years of knocking boxcars in the switching yard.

"If this don't beat all!" Boyd grumped as he entered the kitchen. "Gettin' woke up before the chickens and folks runnin' up and down stairs like th' damned house was on fire! All account of that worthless Teeter brat!"

"And a bright and cheery good morning to you, too, " Miz Eddy shot back. "Coffee's ready."

"Well, praise God for small favors," Boyd grumbled, making a beeline for the percolator. Just then Royce stepped out of the downstairs privy and replaced the phone on its table in the hall.

"Thank you for the use of the phone, Miz Eddy."

"What in tarnation is he doin' here?" Boyd demanded.

"It's official business, Boyd—now sit down and have your coffee! How about you, Royce? You got time for another cup?"

Royce hesitated, glancing in the direction of the front door, but it was clear he was in no hurry to get back to Junior's place. "Well, the Smokies will be here in thirty minutes, give-or-take. And it ain't like anyone's going anywheres... So, yes, I reckon I got time for another cup."

Miz Eddy stared at Royce. So did Boyd, who for once didn't seem to have anything to complain about.

"Heavens, Royce—what's happened over there?" she asked in a shocked whisper. "Is Junior—?"

"Daid? Yes, ma'am, I'm afraid he couldn't get much more if he tried." Royce glanced about the kitchen. "Where'd Miss Dunlevy go?"

"Back upstairs. She'll be down directly," Miz Eddy explained as she refilled his coffee cup. "Now what's this about Junior being daid—?"

"It's not just Junior, Miz Eddy. There's three others in there with him."

"Land's sake!" Miz Eddy pulled out one of the chairs from the kitchen table and sat down. Four people dead in one house—at least at one time— wasn't very common in Choctaw County. "Do you know who they are?"

"Yes, ma'am. I know for certain that two of them are Tommy-Lee Shackleford and Merla Pritchett. And I think the third is Lyla Burnette."

"That lit'l gal that waits tables out at the Dixie Belle?"

"Yes, sir, Mr. Tilberry. I believe so."

"I *knew* it!" Boyd grunted, shaking his head. "It's them gang-bangers what did it! It was one of them drive-bys!"

"How can it be a drive-by shooting if they were all in the house, Boyd?" Miz Eddy snorted.

"Miz Eddy's right, Mr. Tilberry. I don't think it was a proper killing. From what I seen, it looks to be an accident. I think they were poisoned."

"Poisoned?" This came from Caroline, who had made her reappearance in the kitchen outfitted in a blue dress, her hair freshly brushed and with just a hint of make-up on her face. Royce made to get up from his chair, but she waved him back down. "Don't get up on my account, sheriff. Now—what's this about poison?"

"All I know is what I saw over there, Miss Dunlevy—and what I saw was awful, no two ways about it!" Royce sighed and rubbed his face— he was trying hard to keep his hands from shaking. "When I pulled up in front of the house, the music was so loud I knew there was no point knocking—no one inside would hear it. So I tried the front door, and it was unlocked.

"The moment I set foot in the house I noticed something strange— something beside the music going full blast, I mean. The place smelt like someone was fixin' barbecue! Then I see this brand spanking new expensive sound system with speakers the side of steamer trunks sitting in the front room. So I go over and turn it off so's I could hear myself think.

"Now, I fully expected Junior to come reeling downstairs cussin' a blue streak and wantin' to know what happened to his music, but instead there's just silence. I give a shout out for him and Tommy Lee, but don't hear a peep. Not even a snore. I look around the front room and I can tell that someone had themselves a party no long before. There's one of Pappy Pritchett's jars of shine sittin' on the coffee table in front of the sofa along with a few of them Scooby-Doo jelly jar glasses, not to mention an ashtray full of cigarette butts and marihuana leavings. So I head upstairs, thinking they might be passed out in one of the bedrooms. Well, I was right. Sorta.

"What got my attention when I made the second floor was this god-awful stench, although it took a moment for me to catch wind of it, what with the barbecue smell so heavy in the house. There's three of them in the master bedroom. They're all naked and piled together on the bed like gators on a riverbank. And daid as doornails. I didn't need

KNUCKLES AND TALES: JUNIOR TEETER AND THE BAD SHINE

to touch 'em to tell that. Lord! There was vomit everywhere—all over the bed, the bedclothes, the floor around the bed!

"I get close enough to see that the bodies were those of Tommy Lee and the two girls and that they're stone cold daid, each and every one of them. But I couldn't find Junior. I check the second bedroom and the bathroom, but he's not in either one of them. So I go back to stand on the upstairs landing, trying to figure out where he could have got off to. Then I glance down and see a small pool of vomit that's soaked its way into the hall runner. I must have walked right through it earlier, but didn't notice. Then I see some more splotches of puke on the stairs below me.

" I followed the trail back downstairs. I could see it went through the living room and into the kitchen through the dining room. So I push open the swingin' door that separates the kitchen from the dining room and the smell of roasted meat is so strong it all but knocked me down. It was like someone was roastin' a pig: hair, guts and all."

"Royce, remember that time Fanny Stockard borrowed my stove to roast that rabbit her husband shot without gutting it first? Lord, I thought we'd never get the smell out of those drapes!" Miz Eddy interjected.

"Yes, ma'am," Royce agreed. "It was just like that, only a hundred times worse. Well, the first thing I see in the kitchen is Junior Teeter's hairy heinie pointed in my direction. The man's slumped, buck naked, over the top of the kitchen range. It looked to me like Junior was tryin' to fix some coffee to sober him and his friends up when he succumbed to whatever it was kilt the others. I say that on account of the big old-fashioned coffee pot layin' on the floor and water and loose grounds spilt all over the linoleum—not to mention more of that nasty-lookin' vomit. The kind that's green and yellow with blood mixed in.

"I call out Junior's name real loud, hopin' maybe he ain't as far gone as the others, but he don't stir. So I step forward and reach out to roll him over, to see if he's still alive—and—and—" Royce's face lost what little color it had regained as he replayed the event in his mind. "And his arm come off in my hand."

Everyone gathered around the table gasped if someone had stolen all the oxygen in the kitchen. Royce took a long swallow of coffee before finally continuing.

"Junior, he must have turned on the range top—it's electric, you see—and then he blacked out and fell across the eye. He...he was done all the way through, from shoulder to mid-chest. He must have been cookin' like that for hours. His arm came away as easy as a turkey leg."

"Lord—how awful!" Miz Eddy said as she patted Royce's hand. It wasn't much comfort, but it was best she could do under the circumstances. "If it had been me, I'd have fallen out on Junior's drive in a dead faint!"

"Don't think I didn't come close," Royce said with a weak chuckle. "I've seen my share of stuff, hosin' off the highway after wrecks—but nothing quite like that! I just let Junior's arm drop on the floor and stepped away, kinda dazed like. Then I turned round and saw the icebox standin' open with the jars of shine inside. I figger Junior and them got hold of a bad batch." He glanced at his watch. "I best get back there. The Smokies are gonna be pullin' in soon, along with th' meat wagon. I appreciate the coffee, Miz Eddy and the, um, use of your facilities."

"Are you sure you're going to be all right, sheriff?" Caroline asked.

Royce actually blushed. He smiled and bobbed his head, and for a moment the horror of what he had just gone through was a thousand miles away. "I'll be fine, Miz Dunlevy. Although its kind of you to ask. I've learned to try and not let these things get to me, if I can."

Miz Eddy snagged the lawman's arm as he stepped out of the house and onto the porch, causing him to turn back to look back at her. "Royce—?"

"Yes, ma'am?"

"If Junior and the others was long daid by the time you got there...who was it that turned on the music?"

"That's a good question, Miz Eddy," he replied grimly. "One I've been askin' myself as well."

o o o

The rest of that morning was one of the busier ones in the neighborhood's history. Once the State Troopers and the undertaker's hearse showed up, the neighbors came out of their houses and stood on their lawns in their robes and slippers, watching from a safe distance as the official types hurried in and out of the Teeter place.

Once Miz Eddy finished with breakfast, she threw on a housedress and a pair of slippers and took up a vigil from her porch. Boyd soon joined her, still in his bathrobe and slippers. Since he was working on his fourth cup of mud, he was half-decent company.

"Lord, wouldn't Jo-Lynne have a fit if she was here to see them walkin' through her flowerbeds like that?" Miz Eddy sighed, shaking

KNUCKLES AND TALES: JUNIOR TEETER AND THE BAD SHINE

her head as the umpteenth police officer tramped through what was left of the tulips.

"What do you reckon they'll do with the bodies?" Boyd asked, craning his neck as best he could as the last of the dead was shoehorned into Josiah Wallace's hearse. Since Choctaw was such a small county, and without a proper hospital of its own, the funeral parlor served as the county morgue, when need be, with Josiah the coroner of record, although he was without proper forensic schooling. Whenever the sheriff or the state police needed tests done, they usually brought in a pathologist from the university in Monticello.

"They'll have to autopsy them, I reckon." Miz Eddy frowned and peered over the top of her spectacles at Boyd. "Funny thing, though. When's the last time you heard of someone poisoned by shine?"

Boyd sucked on his dentures for a long moment. "Can't rightly say. It's been awhile, that's for certain. I haven't heard tell of any bad squeeze since the War. Those Pritchetts might eat their peas with a knife, but they sure know their way round a still. Then again, accidents *do* happen."

"I reckon so," Miz Eddy sighed, although something about the way she said it made it clear she wasn't convinced.

Boyd glanced up in time to see Sheriff Boyette break away from talking to Josiah Wallace and trot towards the boardinghouse. "What's *he* want *now*?" the old man commented sourly.

"Hey, Miz Eddy. Hey, Mr. Tilberry," Royce said, touching the brim of his Stetson in greeting.

"Hey, Royce," Miz Eddy replied. "Something wrong?"

"No, ma'am. I was just hopin' I might impose on you one more time. Since Junior didn't leave no kin, I was wonderin' if you would be good enough to pick out something for him to be buried in? Normally, Josiah would handle it, but he's up to his ass in alligators, what with this being a multiple death and all."

"Sure thing, Royce. It's the least I can do for his mama and daddy, rest their souls."

"Thanks, Miz Eddy. I'll have my deputy escort you through the house once everyone's had their fill of fingerprintin' and photographin'." As Royce prepared to leave the porch, he paused for a second and looked about. "Um—where's Miss Dunlevy?"

"Caroline had to go on to work, I'm afraid. She said she had to give evidence in a domestic abuse case being heard over in Monticello."

"Oh. That a fact?" Royce said, nodding his head so as not to show his disappointment. "Leastwise Choctaw County's keeping her busy.

Well, tell her I asked about her."

"Sure thing, Royce."

Boyd made a sound like a horse shooing flies as he watched the sheriff make his way back to the crime scene. "What's with all this pussyfootin' around? Why don't the boy just come out and ask that gal for a date?"

"You know how shy Royce is, Boyd. Always has been. And it didn't get any better after the way Didi done him."

"Well, pardon me but 'boo-hoo'!" Boyd snorted derisively. "It's been dog years since she run off with that truck driver! He should have got over that long ago!"

"How would you know, Boyd Tilberry?" Miz Eddy snapped. "You ever have anyone break your heart into a hunnert different pieces and then grind it under their heel? Cause that's exactly what Didi did to that poor boy! I swear, if he hadn't lucked into that deputy job right about then, I don't know what would have happened to him."

"Jeezus, woman! Pull your horns in!" Boyd grunted. "The way you stand up for him, people would think you was a mama hen and he was your chick!"

"Sorry, Boyd. But I can't help bein' defensive," Miz Eddy sighed. "It's just that he reminds me so much of Renny at times it just ain't funny."

o o o

Royce's deputy, Garland, came to collect Miz Eddy around noon. By that time all the ambulances and State Troopers were gone, leaving only their boot prints and what looked to be a mile of yellow crime scene tape wrapped about the Teeters' lawn.

"You okay, ma'am? I'm not going too fast for you, am I?" Garland asked as he walked the old woman across the street, steering her by the elbow as if she was going to tip over in mid-step.

"Sweetie, I know you mean well and all," Miz Eddy said, pulling her arm free. "But if there's one thing I *despise*, it's folks treating me like I'm made outta egg-shells! I didn't get to be seventy-five by being too frail to withstand a high wind!"

"Yes, ma'am," Garland mumbled, his ears turning bright red. "Sorry, Miz Eddy."

The front door of Junior's house was unlocked—as were most doors in Choctaw County. The first thing that struck Miz Eddy as she entered the house was the odor. Royce was right: it sure smelt like

KNUCKLES AND TALES: JUNIOR TEETER AND THE BAD SHINE

someone had had themselves one hell of a pig roast. The second thing that caught her attention was the stereo system in the front room.

Granted, she had never had much interest in such things—she made do with that old variable speed hi-fi stereo Mabel bought her back in '65 just fine—but even an admitted old fogy such as herself recognized an expensive sound system when she saw it. And one such animal was sitting right next to Junior's butt-sprung old sofa. The speakers were as tall as she was and connected to what looked like a CD player, audio cassette machines, a radio receiver and a digital clock, with a whole bunch of flashy green lights and blinking red ones thrown in for good measure.

"Mercy!" she gasped. "Where did Junior get the money for such a thing?"

"That's what Sheriff Boyette was wondering," Garland said. "It sure is a beaut, ain't it?"

"If you like those kind of things, I reckon it is," Miz Eddy sniffed. "Wherever he got it, he couldn't have had it very long, because the boxes it came in are still stacked in the corner. If you ask me, Junior would have been better off spendin' his money on fixin' this place up."

Miz Eddy hadn't set foot inside the Teeter place since Harald Senior's funeral, three years ago. Jo-Lynn had been gone a year by that time, and the house was already starting to slide. From the looks of it, Junior hadn't run a vacuum since then, much less dusted. There were cracks in the plaster and the wallpaper was starting to fade and peel. The furniture was badly dinged up, with cigarette burns and stains on all the upholstery. When Miz Eddy thought of how house-proud Junior's mama had been, she shook her head and sighed. Sometimes she wondered if her turning out an old maid wasn't a blessing in disguise.

"I best go pick out Junior something decent to get buried in—assumin' he has anything decent."

"You need me to follow you upstairs, Miz Eddy?"

"No thank you, Garland. I reckon I can handle that on my own."

Miz Eddy made her way up the narrow stairs to the second floor. Judging from what Royce had told her, it sounded like Junior had moved into his parent's old room, so she'd look in those closets first.

Upon reaching the top landing the reek of sick nearly knocked her down. Even though the door to the master bedroom was standing wide open, she stood on the threshold for a long moment, doing her best to accustom herself to the smell. The bodies were long gone, and the bed had been stripped, but she could clearly make out dark stains on the mattress and on the nearby carpet.

Miz Eddy found what she recognized as the suit Junior had worn at his daddy's funeral hanging in the corner closet and quickly bundled it up. As she folded the suit jacket over her arm, she felt something stiff in the inside breast pocket. She checked for herself and saw an envelope with a printed return address. Probably some bill left over from Harald Senior's funeral Junior never got around to paying. Miz Eddy removed the envelope and slipped it into the pocket of her housedress. She then snatched a pair of socks and a clip-on tie out of the dresser, but didn't bother trying to locate a pair of shoes. After all, it wasn't like Junior was going to be walking anywhere.

When Miz Eddy returned downstairs, Garland was still standing in front of the stereo, studying it with the same intensity her papa would have given a top-of-the-line combine.

"I've got what we came for, deputy."

Garland acted like he'd been startled from a daydream. "Hmm-? Oh! Sorry, Miz Eddy! I was just lookin' at this critter. Like I said, it's a real hum-dinger. It's got all the bells and whistles: graphic equalizer; dual audio cassettes; fifteen disc CD player; a CD-ROM digital recorder...hell, it even has an alarm clock thrown in for good measure!"

"Alarm clock?"

"Sure nuff." Garland pointed at the digital clock display that read 12:07pm.

"Is it set to go off?"

"I dunno. All we got to do is punch a button to find out." Garland pressed a small black rubber button and the display went from 12:08 PM to 4:30 am.

"Well, I'll be dipped," Miz Eddy muttered. "That's when the music started this morning! But why would Junior set an alarm for four-thirty in the morning? That boy wouldn't set foot outside before two in the afternoon unless the house was on fire!"

"That's *another* good question, Miz Eddy," said a voice from behind them. They turned to stare at Sheriff Boyette, who stood in the open door of the Teeter place with his arms folded. "A *very* good question indeed."

o o o

Miz Eddy couldn't remember a time when there was a quadruple viewing at Wallace's Funeral Parlor. There were double-headers every now and again, but usually Josiah's business was steady, not brisk.

KNUCKLES AND TALES: JUNIOR TEETER AND THE BAD SHINE

Which was fine by her. Sometimes it seemed all she ever did anymore was go to funerals.

The Wallaces had been undertakers in Choctaw County since the Spanish-American War. Josiah took over the business from his daddy, Jeroboam, back during the Viet Nam War. Josiah had upgraded the parlor considerably, adding on extra viewing parlors as well as expanding the casket and monument showroom.

Over the last twenty years Miz Eddy had become far more familiar with the interior of Josiah's family business than she ever thought she would. Boyd told her that was the price she had to pay for being too cussed to catch cancer.

Josiah Wallace was standing in the foyer of his establishment, dressed in his trademark dark suit, his face respectfully somber. Although he looked rather haggard—which was understandable, as he had performed four restorations in just under three days—he still kept his mask of professional commiseration securely in place.

In the fifty-six years Miz Eddy had known the man, she couldn't remember ever seeing him crack a smile. Not even as a young'un. Then again, when you're born into a family of undertakers, looking serious comes as natural as climbing trees does to other kids.

"Hey, Miz Eddy."

"Hey, Josiah."

"I take it you've come to pay your respects to Mr. Teeter Junior?"

"Where have you got him?"

"Mr. Teeter Junior is reposing in Slumber Room Number One," Josiah replied, opening the door for her.

Miz Eddy stuck her head into the viewing parlor. An open casket rested on a bare dais and a guest book sat open and unsigned on a postern nearby. There were no other mourners in the room. Nor was there any music or flowers. Miz Eddy turned and frowned at Josiah.

"Is that it? Aren't you even going to play any music?"

Josiah looked a bit embarrassed. "As Mr. Teeter Junior left no instructions as to how he wished to make his final departure, and there were no surviving family members to discuss arrangements or financing, I'm afraid I had little choice but to be, shall we say, *minimalist*. As it was, his restoration was *quite* labor intensive…"

Miz Eddy clucked her tongue as she opened her clutch purse, removing a fifty-dollar bill. "I never had much use for Junior Teeter alive, but the Good Book says we should do unto others as we would have them do unto ourselves. I'd like to put this towards flowers and some music for the room. Bach, if you got it. And, if you don't mind, Josiah, I'll sit with Junior, seeing he has no folks of his own."

"You are a *true* Christian lady, Miz Eddy," Josiah said, taking the offered bill with the stately grace of the professional mourner. "Would that the world had more like you."

"Perish the thought, Josiah!" she chuckled dryly. "If it's all the same to you, I'll go ahead and pay my respects to the others while you see to Junior."

"As you wish, Miz Eddy. Miss Pritchett is in Slumber Room Two, Mr. Shackleford is in Slumber Room Three, and Miss Bartlett had to be placed in the Smokers' Alcove ."

"Gracious!"

"I'm afraid it could not be helped," Josiah sighed by way of explanation. "We're simply unequipped for such high volume business." With that, he quickly retired to the back of the parlor, where none of the amateur mourners were ever permitted, and left Miz Eddy alone in the foyer.

While she couldn't abide either Merla Pritchett or Tommy Lee Shackleford while they were drawing breath, she felt honor-bound to see them off on this, their last public appearance. After all, part of living in a town as small as Seven Devils was being connected to folks whether you cared for them or not. After muttering eeny-meeny-miney-moe under her breath, she decided on saying goodbye to Tommy Lee first.

Slumber Room Three was slightly smaller than the one Junior was in, but at least there were floral displays around the casket and music playing in the background. Seated on a plush-velvet folding chair near the casket was Tommy Lee's father, Wiley Shackleford, dressed in a dark suit shiny at the cuffs and elbows, and, doubtless, the butt.

"Hey, Miz Eddy," Wiley said, his voice rusty from cigarettes and crying. Wiley looked like he really needed a drink, and for once Miz Eddy couldn't blame him for it.

"Hey, Wiley," she said softly as she signed the guest book. Hers was the second name, below that of Wiley's. "How you holding up, sugar?"

"I'm doin' all right, given the circumstances," he sighed, returning his rheumy eyes to where his son lay.

Miz Eddy looked down at Tommy Lee Shackleford one last time. She almost didn't recognize him with his hair washed and without his Jack Daniels gimme cap and two-day growth of beard.

"My! Don't he look natural!" she lied.

KNUCKLES AND TALES: JUNIOR TEETER AND THE BAD SHINE

Wiley got up to stand beside her. "Josiah did a mighty fine job on my boy. Much better than what that butcher in Flyjar did on his granny." He pulled a pack of Lucky Strikes out of his breast pocket then stopped. His eyes darted around, like those of a trapped animal. "I really need a smoke, but they've got that lit'l Burnette gal stuck in the alcove…"

"Go ahead, Wylie. It's not like Tommy Lee's in any position to mind."

Wiley lit his cigarette and gave her a grateful smile. "I appreciate you stoppin' by, Miz Eddy. I don't reckon there'll be many more visitors, what with all his other friends daid, too. Well…at least he's with his mama now."

Miz Eddy merely smiled and nodded. This was not the time to remind Wiley that Tommy Lee's mama was live and well and had been shacked up with a mannish woman in Memphis for the last fifteen years.

"I tole Tommy Lee drinkin' squeeze was gone lead to grief, but he wouldn't pay me no never-mind," Wylie continued. "I warn't him it'd eat up his belly and brain, but he jest kept on with it. I never could understand that boy." He shook his head sadly "Hell, it weren't like he couldn't afford store-bought!"

○ ○ ○

After she took her leave of Tommy Lee Shackleford, Miz Eddy paused and peeked into the alcove. It had originally been set aside for nursing mothers, but when the city was finally forced to implement the state smoking ordinances, Josiah had moved in a couple of sand-filled ashtrays and renamed it the "smoking alcove".

In order to accommodate Lyla Burnette's casket, Josiah and his assistant had been obliged to remove the ashtrays and the folding chairs, which left barely enough room for a grown person to stand beside the casket and view its occupant. Miz Eddy had never met the Burnette girl, but she was surprised at how young she was. Too young to be a client of Josiah Wallace's, that was for certain.

When she entered the viewing parlor that held the remains of Merla Pritchett, she had to fight to keep from gasping for air. The room was so full of floral tributes that it was like breathing through a bouquet of roses.

There was a man sitting in one of the folding chairs near the casket—but he wasn't a Pritchett, that much was certain. The stranger sitting with Merla wore a nondescript suit with an equally nondescript hair cut. He stood up quickly upon seeing her.

"Are you Mrs. John Pritchett?"

"No!" she replied with a great deal more heat than she'd intended. Whoever this fellow was, he sure as hell wasn't from Choctaw County if he couldn't tell her from a Pritchett.

The stranger resumed his seat as Miz Eddy signed her name in the viewing book then peered into the casket. It looked to her that Merla was being sent into the Great Beyond with a great deal less in the way of make-up than usual.

Josiah emerged like a stage magician from the heavy tapestry hanging behind Merla's casket. "Ah, there you are, Miz Eddy! I've done as you requested. Oh, and Agent Torrance? The Pritchetts have arrived."

"Oh, my," Miz Eddy said, turning her gaze onto the stranger in the dark suit. "Are you with the federal government, young man?"

"Yes, ma'am. Department of Alcohol, Tobacco and Firearms."

Miz Eddy pulled back one of the drapes that covered the windows in the viewing room and peered out at the parking lot. Pappy John's ancient electric-blue Cadillac convertible, its sagging bumper splashed with mud, was sitting in one of the slots marked for family members. She glanced over her shoulder at Josiah, who was standing beside Merla's casket, nervously dry-washing his hands.

"How many of them are there, Josiah?"

"Enough," he replied, trying his best to keep his own anxiety under control. It was families like the Pritchetts that made the Wallace's' business as successful—and grueling—as it was.

The door of the viewing room flew open as the Pritchetts came in to pay their last respects to their kin. The first one through was Pappy John, of course. Miz Eddy hadn't clapped eyes on the man in six years, but he seemed little changed. He was still bandy-legged and sinewy as whipcord, with long white hair slicked back with a fistful of wild root and his beard combed out so it framed a face burned red from the sun. He was tricked out in a suit that was short in the sleeves and rode high on the shin, and a shoestring tie held in place by a bolo made from turquoise and hammered silver. With his broad forehead, strong nose and piercing dark eyes, Pappy John Pritchett could almost pass for an Old Testament prophet instead of a moon shiner.

In Pappy's wake were a half-dozen Pritchett boys, ranging in age from forty to fifteen, outfitted in overalls and shit-kickers and not much else, save for their deer rifles and shotguns.

Josiah's eyes looked like they were going to spring out of his head at the sight of the Pritchetts' weaponry. "Pappy! I thought I made

KNUCKLES AND TALES: JUNIOR TEETER AND THE BAD SHINE

myself perfectly clear on the phone—Firearms are *not* allowed on the premises!"

"I understood you well enough, Josiah—I jest ignored you is all. Good thing, too, seein' how y'all didn't tell me about this here bastard," Pappy snarled, glowering at the ATF agent. "I don't intend to find myself in no Ruby Ridge sitchy-ation."

"I assure you, Mr. Pritchett, that I am unarmed," Torrance said as he got to his feet. "However, I *do* have a warrant for your arrest, signed by a federal court judge…"

Upon hearing the word 'warrant', the assembled Pritchetts chambered and cocked their respective weapons in unison. Pappy John scowled and held up his hand, signaling for them to hold their fire.

"*Arrest?* On what charge?"

Agent Torrance's cool facade was beginning to crumble. It was clear he was not used to hard-bitten swampbillies like the Pritchetts. "S-second Degree Murder in the deaths of Harald Teeter, Jr., Thomas Lee Shackleford, Lyla Burnette and Merla Jane Pritchett…"

"You Yankee sumbitch!" Pappy John thundered. "You accusin' *me* of poisonin" my own grand-baby?"

Miz Eddy lifted an eyebrow. She'd known Merla was a Pritchett, but ignorant as to her exact relation to the old man. Then again, sorting out which Pritchett was related to which was difficult, if not impossible, given their habit of "marrying in".

"Cain't a man come into' town to bury his kin decent without some Yankee revenuer tryin' to stick his nose in where it don't belong? "

"Mebbe we should show this here Yankee what happens t'folks that go pokin' their noses into places they don't belong, Pappy?" grinned one of the Pritchett boys, displaying an impressive array of misaligned, chaw-stained teeth.

"You got something' thar, Billy-Jim," the old man said, rubbing his chin thoughtfully. "But y'all ought to hold off on it until we's outside. After all, we ain't here to raise a ruckus. We's here to pay final respects to Merla. Less'n this Fed has a problem with that. I tell you what, Mr. Fed, you want to serve me with them papers and take me into custody, you're free to do so—or try, at least—once I'm done tellin' my grandchile goodbye."

Agent Torrance, now sweating profusely, made for the door, but a couple of the younger, more loutish Pritchetts blocked his way. The ATF agent turned to look at Pappy, panic in his eyes.

"Byron! Jasper!" Pappy John barked. "You boys heared me! Leave him go!"

The boys moved aside, allowing the ATF agent to pass. The moment the door closed behind Torrance, the boys burst out into raucous laughter. Pappy John's face turned bright purple and he spun around and cuffed the nearest Pritchett so hard the boy staggered.

"Hush! You hush up laughin' right this second!" he bellowed. "I ain't gone have no carryin' on! Y'all got better manners an' that—so use 'em! We's here to say good-bye to Merla, not bray like a string of jackasses!" The assembled Pritchetts grew instantly somber at the mention of their kinswoman's name.

One of the older Pritchetts—a raw-boned fellow in his late forties with a lantern jaw and hair the color and texture of straw—abruptly sobbed out loud. The Pritchett called Jasper leaned his shotgun against the wall in order to pat his weeping relative on the shoulder.

"There ain't no shame in cryin' for yore daid," Pappy John said soothingly. "Merle, you go first—you go tell yore baby-girl good-bye."

Merle Pritchett nodded as he wiped the tears from his eyes with the back of his hand. He stepped forward and looked down at his daughter, stroking her hair and muttering something under his breath that only he and the dead could understand.

"I'm real sorry you was here to see that fracas, Miz Eddy," Pappy John said. "We didn't come here to start no trouble."

"I understand that, John," she replied. "You're just doin' right by your family, that's all."

"That's God's honest truth," the moon shiner agreed. "If'n a man don't got his family, he got nothin' in this world—or the next. And speakin' on behalf of the Pritchetts, we appreciate yore stoppin' by, Miz Eddy. That's right kindly of you."

"We're all God's children, John."

"Amen t'that, Miz Eddy. Although some of God's children don't seem to see it that way." Pappy John shook his silvery head, a look of genuine distress on his weathered face. "Believe you me: if I thought fer a moment that my shine was responsible for killin' those young'uns, them bastards—pardon my French—at the ATF Bureau wouldn't have to go wakin' up no judge to sign any fancy papers. I'd have stuck my shotgun in my mouth and blowed my own head clean off. It would be bad enough havin' something like that to answer fer—but my own grand-baby? I couldn't live with it! No sir!

"Wherever they got that bad shine, it weren't from me! I run a tight ship, Miz Eddy. I check and double-check everythin' that comes out of the stills. I seen my uncle get struck blind during Prohibition, and I

KNUCKLES AND TALES: JUNIOR TEETER AND THE BAD SHINE

sweared then and there I weren't never gone pass that grief on if'n I could help it. I know folks in Choctaw County got a low opinion of us Pritchetts—but I know better than to pass on bad shine in my own back yard."

The door to the viewing parlor opened again and Royce Boyette stepped into the room. Upon seeing the sheriff, the assembled Pritchetts swung their weapons at him.

"Pappy! Call your boys off!" Royce looked more exasperated than concerned.

"Damn it—Jasper! Lester! Billy-Jim! Maddox! What did I tell y'all?!?"

The Pritchett Boys grudgingly lowered their weapons, mumbling under their breath.

"I'm glad I caught you here, John," Royce said, shouldering his way across the room. "I just got through talkin' to Agent Torrance out in the parking lot..."

"Whatever he tole you is a bald-faced lie, sheriff!"

"It don't matter either way, Pappy. Because what *I* told *him* was enough for him to tear up his warrant and head back to Little Rock."

"Come again?"

"I just got the toxicology reports back on Merla and them and from the samples of shine taken from Junior's icebox. Turns out that they was poisoned all right—but by strychnine! And from the tests run on the jars in the icebox, only *one* jar was tainted. The one that was sitting on the coffee table in the living room. It also happened to be the only Mason jar in the house that *didn't* have Pappy's finger prints on it."

"Well, I'll be dipped in shit and shot fer stinkin'!" Pappy said. "So, what yore tellin' me is it *weren't* no accident?"

"It was murder. No doubt about it. Someone—we don't know *who* just yet—snuck into Junior's house and deliberately planted a tainted jar of moonshine in his icebox. That answers some questions, but opens up a whole different can of worms. Such as: who the hell would want to murder Junior Teeter and why?"

Miz Eddy coughed into her fist, causing everyone in the room to look in her direction as she reached inside her clutch purse and retrieved a folded envelope.

"I'm not sure if this is of any help—but I found this in the suit I picked out for Junior. I didn't think anything about it until I was getting ready to come here this evening. It looks like some kind of paperwork from a lawyer up in Little Rock. I'm not sure, but I think Junior might have been comin' into some money."

Royce took the envelope and frowned at the return address. "Looks like I'm gonna need to take me a little road trip."

o o o

According to the letterhead found in the suit Junior Teeter was buried in, Jesse Craddock's law office was located on a side street within ten blocks of the state capitol. It was one of several dozen such satellite businesses, including bail bondsmen and notary publics, which orbited the state capitol and courthouse.

Royce Boyette sat in his unmarked Ford LTD and double-checked the address. The building he was parked in front of looked more like a converted garage than a lawyer's office. It was hardly impressive, even to someone from Seven Devils. However, according to the shingle on the door, *"Jesse Craddock: Attorney at Law"*, this was indeed the right place.

The reception area of Craddock's law office consisted of a couple of chairs lined against the wall. The only decoration, besides a general-issue battery-operated wall-clock, was a sofa-sized piece of art depicting seagulls that Royce recognized from the annual Starving Artist Bazaar held at the War Memorial Stadium parking lot, where they sold pictures by the square foot.

The secretary's desk was empty, although the file cabinets were standing half-open, and just beyond the reception area he could see a door with Jesse Craddock's name on it standing open.

Royce paused and frowned, listening to what sounded like snoring coming from the lawyer's office, then checked his wristwatch. It was ten thirty in the morning—which didn't qualify as "early" in his book, even in the state capitol.

"Hello? Anyone t'home?"

There was an abrupt strangling sound, followed by the sound of papers being crumpled and tossed quickly aside. A few seconds later, a red plastic razorback stuck its snout out of the door of Craddock's office, soon followed by the rest of the hog, which was strapped to the head of a paunchy, balding man in a rumpled suit the color of spilled blood.

"Can I help you?" grunted the man with the plastic pig on his head.

"Are you Jesse Craddock?"

"Yes, that's me." Craddock said as he removed his headgear. "Please excuse my appearance—I was celebrating my law school's twentieth class reunion."

KNUCKLES AND TALES: JUNIOR TEETER AND THE BAD SHINE

"My name's Royce Boyette, Mr. Craddock—"

"What is it can I do for you, Mr. Boyette—?"

"Well, actually, it's *Sheriff* Boyette."

"*Sheriff?*" For someone whose business was the law, the realization he was talking to a lawman seemed to discomfort Craddock quite a bit.

"Yes, sir. I'm from Seven Devils, down in Choctaw County..." Royce pulled his wallet out of his back pocket and flipped it open so the lawyer could see his badge. "Sorry about droppin' in on you unannounced like this, but when I tried to call the number I had for you, I didn't get an answer..."

"No need to apologize, Sheriff Boyette," Craddock sighed. "My secretary up and quit on me last week without any warning and I haven't been able to replace her yet and, to add insult to injury, my answering machine's busted. Come on into my office—we can talk in there."

The interior of Craddock's office seemed even more cramped than the reception area, thanks largely to the bookcases that lined the walls. A sofa littered with newspapers and empty fast-food wrappers was shoved against the far wall. Craddock's desk was wedged in between a filing cabinet and under the stuffed and mounted head of an eight-point buck.

"This is about Junior Teeter, am I right? Horrible business, that. Can't say I'm surprised, though." Craddock noticed Royce was staring at the deer. "Nice taxidermy job, don't you think? Bagged that old boy a few seasons back. He's one of the few things my wife left me after the divorce." He laughed, but there was no humor in it.

"Is that a fact? Sorry to hear that, Mr. Craddock. But, as you guessed, I'm here to ask a few questions about Junior. By the way—how is you heard about what happened? I wasn't aware it'd made the news in Little Rock."

"I've got a subscription to the *Choctaw County Courier*," Craddock explained. "It was a present from Junior's folks, years back. I'm more than happy to help you with your inquiries, Sheriff. But I really don't know how much light I can shed on the subject. I didn't really know Junior all that well. I was more his daddy's lawyer..."

"You've been handling Harald's estate?"

"Yes, sir. What there was of it. Mostly some property out in Texas that had been in the family for awhile."

Royce reached inside his front shirt pocket and took out the envelope Miz Eddy had found. He carefully removed the letter inside it and handed it to Craddock. "It was my understanding from this letter that

Junior had an appointment with you on what proved to be the day following his death. Something involving a great deal of money."

Craddock scanned the letter and handed it back to Royce. "Yes, sir. That's right, sheriff. Junior was supposed to come in to sign a lease with Bobcat Petroleum. Seems that property in Texas has oil on it."

"Oil—? Well, I'll be damned! How much do you figure that's worth?"

"Well, from what I understand, even in today's market, I'd say Junior was lookin' at a guaranteed income of twenty-five thousand a month."

Royce gave a low whistle and shook his head in amazement.

"My feelings exactly," Craddock chuckled dryly. "Of course, if ever there was a case of pearls before swine..."

"How so?" Royce asked, lifting an eyebrow quizzically.

"Well, I don't mean to speak ill of the dead—and especially of my own client—but Junior was one of the least deserving souls to have that kind of money dropped in his lap. I first got to know the Teeters nineteen years ago. I was clerking for a law firm that handled a lot of DWIs and the like, and Junior had gotten himself in trouble with some underage drinking and driving. By the time I split from the firm, and took the Teeters as clients along with me, I'd kept Junior out of the jug on four occasions. Like I said, I handled Harald Senior's probate. Too bad he and his wife didn't live long enough to see this money. Junior was sure to piss it all away —"

"If he'd lived."

"Yes. Of course. Poor luck, there. But, like I said—I'm not that surprised that's how he ended up, even knowin' as little as I did about the man."

"Well, I can't argue with you there. Junior was careless with everything, whether it was money, women, drinkin', or drivin'. But I don't think he can be blamed for how he died—"

"Of course not! I didn't mean to infer that!" Craddock said quickly. "It was just the luck of the draw. Getting hold of a bad batch of moonshine like that—But accidents will happen."

"Yes, sir. That they will. But I'm afraid that's not the case with Junior."

"Beg pardon?" Craddock said, looking somewhat startled. "B-but didn't he die from alcohol poisoning?"

"Oh, he was poisoned, all right. And not just him—there were those three friends of his as well."

"F-friends?"

"Yes, sir. I reckon you didn't read the other obituaries, then?"

KNUCKLES AND TALES: JUNIOR TEETER AND THE BAD SHINE

"N-no. Just Junior's. His was the only name I recognized."

"I can understand that. Anyways, it weren't alcohol poisoning that kilt him. It was strychnine."

"Strychnine?"

"Yes, sir. Which means it weren't no accident. Not by a long shot. It's murder, sure as I'm standin' here. The thing is, I couldn't figger for the life of me who on God's green earth would want to go to such bother to murder Junior Teeter. I'm not sayin' Junior was without an enemy in the world. Far from it. It's just that if any of his crowd was aimin' to do such a thing, they'd just haul off and stab or shoot him. But now that I know money's involved—well, that makes things a damn sight easier to understand."

"Does it?"

"Oh, yes, sir!" Royce said, smiling broadly. "Next to sex, money's the surest motive there is! Well, I appreciate you takin' the time to talk to me, Mr. Craddock, but I best be headin' on home. I got my deputy holdin' down the fort while I'm gone. He's a good ole boy, but still a tad wet behind the ears."

As Boyette reached the door of the office, he paused and turned to give Craddock one last look. The lawyer's face was as gray as liver and dripping like he'd just stepped out of the shower.

"By the way, councilor—now that Junior's dead, who does the estate go to?"

"I-it falls to the executor."

"And that would be —?"

"Me."

"That's what I thought," Royce said, nodding his head. He touched the brim of his Stetson and smiled at Craddock the way a coondog smiles up at a treed possum. "Y'all take care, now, y'hear?"

o o o

Miz Eddy was sitting on the glider on her front porch, gently swinging back and forth as she enjoyed the evening air, a pitcher of iced tea sweating on the TV tray beside her. There was still enough daylight to see by, but the sun was rapidly fading. She always enjoyed that magic hour of dusk, when the lightning bugs came out to court and before the skeeters got too bad.

She waved a hello to Royce, who was walking up the sidewalk in her direction. The sheriff returned her wave.

"Hey, Royce."

"Hey, Miz Eddy. Mind if I come sit a spell with you?"

"You bathed lately?"

"Yep. Two days ago."

"Then I reckon I can tolerate you," she chuckled, patting the seat beside her. "Help yourself to some tea, if you like."

"Thankee kindly, ma'am," Royce smiled as he poured himself a glass. He then joined her on the glider, the chains groaning with the added weight. He pushed his hat back on his head, pressing the cool glass against his forehead.

"You look tuckered out," Miz Eddy observed matter-of-factly.

"It has been one hell of a day, I'll give you that," Royce sighed. "But I got some good news—looks like the Teeter case is solved."

Miz Eddy's ears all but pricked. "Is that a fact?"

"Yes. ma'am, it 'tis," Royce replied, sipping at his tea. He lowered the glass and looked about. "Miss Dunlevy wouldn't happen to be around, would she?"

"Damn you, Royce Boyette! Don't you do me like that!" Miz Eddy snapped, jabbing a bony finger in his ribs. "Now tell me what's gone on or get your heinie off my porch!"

Royce gave a short whoop of laughter. "Now-now, Miz Eddy! I was just funnin' ya!"

"So—you got that whole mess with Junior and them solved?"

"In a fashion. I just got word from the Little Rock PD that they found my main suspect swingin' from the lighting fixture in his office. Lawyer by the name of Craddock."

"The lawyer did it?"

"Well, Junior didn't have himself a butler, did he? Turns out this Craddock fella was up to his neck in hock. His wife cleaned him out when she left him—for another lawyer, no less. Turns out his filing cabinet was full of shut-off notices and his car was about to be repossessed. His secretary walked out on him because he kept bouncin' checks on her. She's th' one who found him, by the way. She'd gone back to try and wrangle her pay out of him.

"I'd gone up to Little Rock earlier today to talk to him. I could tell he had something to do with it from the get-go." Royce's shook his head in disgust. "He tried to feed me a line of B.S. about reading about Junior's death in *The Courier*, as if I was too big a cracker to go over to the paper and check their subscription list! I'll be damned if I understand why folks lie about things like that, but they always do.

KNUCKLES AND TALES: JUNIOR TEETER AND THE BAD SHINE

"The reason he knew about Junior bein' daid was on account of him killin' him. But he didn't know about the others. When I told him there'd been three additional deaths, you'd have thought he'd seen his own lookin' over my shoulder at him. Mebbe he did at that.

"Anywho, the LRPD called me up on account of the note he left where he confessed to drivin' down from Little Rock and sneakin' in through Junior's back door and puttin' that doctored jar of shine in the icebox the day before he was supposed to come to his office and sign those papers. Course, Craddock had no way of knowin' Junior would invite his buddies over to celebrate his good fortune or that he'd blow what he had left in his bank account on a new stereo system for the occasion..

"Not that I needed Craddock's confession to prove that he did it. The fingerprints I lifted off the letterhead you found in Junior's suit match those on the jar of bad shine. I reckon he had to type it up his own self, seeing that his secretary had quit on him.

"I reckon Junior's money was just too much temptation for an unsuccessful lawyer like Craddock to wrestle with. The way Craddock must have seen it, Junior comin' into that kind of money was as good as throwin' it down the well. And he was probably right. But that didn't give him the right to kill Junior, worthless trash or not.

"In the end, I reckon Craddock preferred doing himself in to spendin' the next decade in the death-house, waiting his turn for the Big Fix. Probably a good thing he chose as he did, seein' how many Pritchetts there are in Cummins Prison. He wouldn't have lasted a week before he got a toothbrush in the eye."

"That's some mighty fine sheriffin', Royce," Miz Eddy said, giving his hand a squeeze. "Your uncle would be proud of you."

"Thank you, ma'am," Royce said softly, his ears turning pink as he blushed. "That means a lot to me, Miz Eddy."

"Renny Boyette was one of the best sheriffs this town ever had. You're a lot like him, Royce. You could pass for his son."

Royce gave the old woman sitting beside a sidelong glance. "You still miss him, don't you, Miz Eddy."

She took a deep breath and held it for a second, staring out across the yard into the early evening dusk. "Royce, there's not a day that goes by that I don't think of your uncle at least once. Sometimes I wake up and have to remind myself it's been thirty-odd years since he got shot trying to stop that gas station hold-up. Had it happened an hour or two later, you'd be callin' me Aunt instead of Miz Eddy. But I try not to dwell on such things—Renny certainly wouldn't have wanted me to."

Miz Eddy glanced over at the Teeter house—now empty and dark for the first time in recent memory—and gave a tiny sigh. "You know, if it hadn't been for Junior blowin' his savings on that stereo system to celebrate his good fortune in advance, then settin' that alarm of his the way he did to make sure he was up and dressed in time to drive to Little Rock to sign those papers, and puttin' that letterhead in his one good suit so he wouldn't lose the address, no one would have been the wiser."

"More an' likely," Royce agreed. "And if he hadn't invited folks over to party with him, I wouldn't have felt it necessary to have an autopsy conducted—or test the shine. But that's where Craddock messed up—he didn't even know enough to mix antifreeze in the shine, instead of strychnine. Granted, it ain't as quick, but it does the job.

"If he'd done that, no one would have any reason to think it wasn't anything but what Craddock intended it to be mistook for in the first place: some ne'er-do-well cracker who had the poor luck to get hold to bad shine, and Pappy Pritchett would be sitting in the pokey facing reckless endangerment or whatever the hell they call third degree murder nowadays."

"Well, I reckon I'm woman enough to admit I was wrong."

"How so, Miz Eddy?"

"I used to say Junior Teeter was one of the most useless men that ever drew breath. But since he helped solve his own murder, in his own way, I reckon Junior wasn't completely useless after all. Of course, he had to get kilt first in order to *be* of any use."

"Yep," Royce said, rattling the ice cubes at the bottom of his glass. "Life's funny that way, ain't it?"

After agreeing that, yes, life was indeed funny, they fell quiet, each wrapped in their own thoughts, and sipped their ice tea, watching the fireflies dance in the gathering dark.

THE TWO HEADED MAN

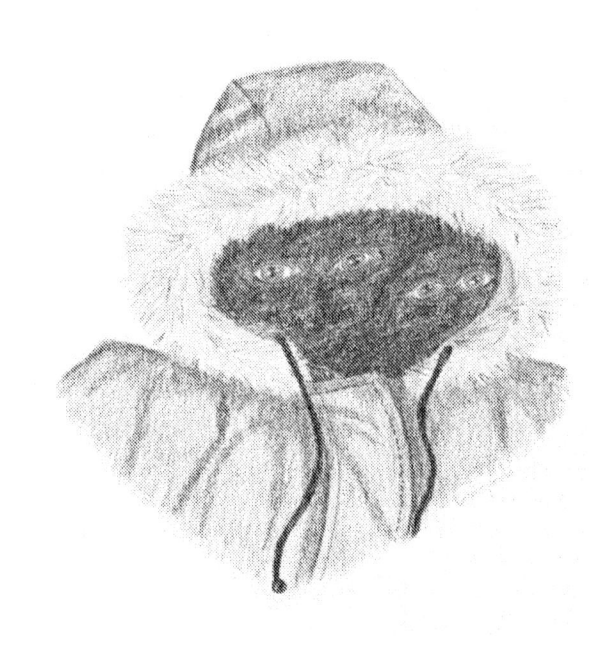

It was going on midnight when the two-headed man walked into Kelly's Stop.

The short-order cook glanced up when the short burst of cold air rifled the newspaper spread across the Formica serving counter. The man stood in the diner's doorway, the fur-fringed hood of the parka casting his face in deep shadow. He tugged off his mittens and stuffed them into one pocket, flexing his fingers like a pianist before a recital.

"You're in luck, buddy," said the cook, refolding the newspaper. "We was just about ready to call it an early night."

The waitress stabbed out a cigarette and pivoted on her stool to get a better look at the stranger. She tugged at her blouse waist, causing her name, LOUISE, to twitch over her heart.

"Car had a flat...up the road..." came a voice from inside the shadow of the parka's hood. "We don't...have a spare..."

The cook shrugged, his back to the stranger. "Can't help you there, bub. Mike Keckhaver runs the Shell station down the road a piece, but he don't open up 'till tomorrow morning."

"Then we'll...have to wait."

" 'We'?" Louise moved to the front window and peered out between the neon Miller Hi-Life and Schlitz signs. The gravel parking lot fronting the diner was empty. "You got somebody with you, mister?"

"Yes...You could say that," answered the stranger as he unzipped the parka and tossed back the hood.

Louise gasped and clamped a hand over her mouth, smearing lipstick against her palm. The cook spun around to see what was going on, butcher knife in hand: late-night truck-stop robberies were not uncommon along Highway 65.

The stranger had two heads. One was where heads are supposed to be. And a damn fine one at that. It was the handsomest head Louise had ever seen this side of a t.v. screen. The stranger's hair was longish and curly and the color of winter wheat. It framed a face designed for a movie star; straight nose, strong and beardless chin, high cheekbones, and eyes bluer than Paul Newman's.

The second head looked over the stranger's left shoulder, perched on his collarbone like a parrot. It wasn't a deformed or even an unsightly head—just average. But its extreme proximity to such masculine perfection made it seem...repulsive. The second head was dark where the other was fair, brown-eyed where the first was blue. It regarded Louise with a distant, oddly disturbing intelligence then turned so its lips moved against it's fellow's left ear. The stranger laughed without much humor.

"Yeah, guess I did scare 'em some..." The stranger shrugged off his coat. "Sorry, didn't mean to startle you like that."

Now that the parka was all the way off they could see that the stranger really didn't have two heads. A padded leather harness, like those worn by professional hitchhikers, was strapped to his shoulders and midsection. But instead of a bed roll and an army surplus dufflebag, he carried a little man on his back.

The stranger seated himself on one of the stools, leaning slightly forward under the weight of his burden.

"What is he? A dwarf or something'?" The cook ignored the look Louise shot him.

The man did not seem at all insulted. "Nope. Human Worm."

"Huh?"

"Carl's got no arms...or legs."

"That so? Was he in Viet Nam?"

"No. Just born that way."

"How about that. Don't see that everyday."

"No, you don't," he agreed amiably. The Human Worm leaned closer and whispered into his ear again. The stranger nodded. "Okay. Why not, long as we're here. We'll have two orders of bacon and eggs...one scrambled...one sunny-side up...two orders of toast...and two coffees. Got that?" The stranger pulled a cloth hankie out of his pants pocket and draped it over his left shoulder.

"Uh, yeah. Sure. Comin' right up."

"Name's Gary. This here's Carl," the stranger jerked a thumb to indicate his piggyback passenger.

"Pleased t'meetcha," the cook grunted.

Carl bobbed his head in silent acknowledgment.

Louise stood near the end of the serving counter, debating on whether she should try to talk to the handsome stranger with the freak tied to his back.

Talking to the various strangers that found their way into Kelly's Stop was one of the few perks the job had to offer. The trouble with

KNUCKLES AND TALES: THE TWO HEADED MAN

the locals was that she knew what they were going to say before they even opened their mouths. She hated living in a pissant little town like Seven Devils. She envied the strangers she met; travelers from somewhere on their way to someplace. She liked to pretend that maybe one of them would be her long-awaited Dream Prince and take her away from Kelly's Stop—just like Ronald Coleman rescued Bette Davis in Petrified Forest. But if her Prince was going to put in an appearance, it was going to have to be pretty damn soon. Her tits were starting to sag and the laugh-lines at the corners of her eyes were threatening to become crow's feet.

She studied the two men as they waited to be served. It was sure as hell a weird set-up. But that face...Gary's face...was the one she'd pictured in her fantasies. It was the face of the Prince who would deliver her from a lifetime of bunions, corn plasters, varicose veins and cheap beer.

The more she thought about it, he wasn't really that strange. It was kind of sweet, really, the way he carried the crippled guy on his back. It wasn't that much different than pushing a wheelchair.

The cook plopped the eggs and bacon onto the grill, slammed twin slices of bread into the toaster and returned his attention to the spitting bacon.

"Louise! Get th' man his coffee, willya?" The command made her jump and she scurried over to the Bun-O-Matic coffee-maker.

"How you like it?" she asked, hoping she didn't sound shrill. Her hands were shaking. She took a deep breath before she poured.

"Black. Cream and sugar."

She slid the cups across the counter and located a sugar dispenser. She felt his eyes on her as she moved to get the cream from the cooler, but she wasn't sure which one of them was doing the looking.

Gary picked up the cup of black coffee with his left, blew on it a couple of times, then lifted it over his shoulder. Carl lowered his head and noisily sipped from the lip of the cup while Gary stirred his coffee with his right hand.

"Wow. Neat trick." She kicked herself the minute she said it. What a hick thing to say!

Gary shrugged, causing Carl to bounce slightly. "Helps if you're ambidextrous."

"Ambiwhat?"

"Carl says that's being good with both hands," he explained, gesturing with a piece of bacon. Carl leaned forward, grasping the proffered strip with surprisingly white, even teeth before bolting it down like a lizard.

Louise watched as Gary fed himself and his rider, both hands moving with unthinking grace. He acted as if it was as natural for him as breathing. Carl wiped his mouth and chin, shiny with grease and butter, on the napkin draped over his companion's shoulder. His eyes met Louise's and she hastily looked away.

There was something hot and alive in those eyes; something hungry and all too familiar. Her cheeks burned and she dropped a bouquet of clean flatware onto the floor.

"Look, mister, I'm gonna be closin' shop real soon. Like I said, the Shell station don't open 'till seven or eight. There's a motel up the road a bit, the Driftwood Inn. You shouldn't have no trouble findin' a place there. They're right off th' highway, so they're open all night. I'd give you a lift but, uh, my car's in the shop an' I live in town, so..." the cook fell silent and returned to cleaning his grill.

The two-headed man sat and drank coffee while Louise and her boss busied themselves with the ritual of closing. Louise mopped the floor faster than usual, trying not to look at the stranger and his freakish papoose.

"Well, lights out, folks," the cook announced with a forced smile. The two-headed man stood up and began shouldering themselves back into the parka. "Uh, look, Louise...Why don't you lock up for me, huh? Laurie's waitin' up on me and you know how she gets."

Louise certainly did. Laurie had had enough of waiting up for her husband three years back and joined the others who'd abandoned Seven Devils, Arkansas. She nodded and watched him flee the diner for the safety of a nonexistent wife.

Gary pulled the parka's hood over his head and zipped up. All she could see was his face—that achingly handsome face—with its baby-smooth jaw and electric blue eyes.

It was bitterly cold outside, their breath wreathing their heads. The hard frost had turned the highway into a strip of polished onyx. Gary stuffed his hands into his mittens, gave Louise a nod and a half-wave and began to walk away, the parking lot's gravel crunching under his bootheels. The lump under his parka stirred.

Do something, girl! Say something! don't just let him walk off!

"Hey, mister...er, misters!"

He turned to smile at her. She felt her bravado slip. *Dear God, what am I getting myself into?* But it was two in the morning and everyone

KNUCKLES AND TALES: THE TWO HEADED MAN

in Choctaw County was asleep except for her and the blue-eyed stranger...and his traveling companion.

"I've got a place 'round back. It's not much, but it's warm. You're welcome to stay...I hate to think of you walking all the way to the motel and then it turn out to be full-up."

Gary stood there for a moment, his hands in his pockets and his head cocked to one side as if he was listening to something.

Then he smiled.

"We'd be delighted."

○ ○ ○

The frozen grass crunched gently under their feet. The dark bulk of Louise's trailer loomed ahead of them, resting on its bed of cinderblocks.

"Where are we...exactly? We've no real idea...."

"You're in Choctaw County."

"That's the name of this place?"

"No. Not really. This here's Seven Devils. Or its outskirts, at least. Not much to it, except that its th' county seat. This used to be a railroad town, back before the war. But now that everything's shipped by trucks, there ain't a whole lot left. What makes you want to drive around in this part of Arkansas in the first place? There's nothing down here but rice fields, bayous and broke farmers."

"We like the old highways...we meet much nicer people that way..."

Louise stopped to glance over her shoulder as she dug the house key from her coat pocket. Had it been Gary's voice she'd heard that time? All she could see was shadow inside the parka's hood. She stood on the cinderblock that served as her front stoop and fussed with her keychain. She could hear him breathing at her elbow.

"Welcome to my humble abode! It ain't much, but it's home. It used to belong to the boss. I keep an eye on the place for him." Why was she so anxious? He certainly wasn't the first man she'd invited back to her trailer before. She'd known her share of truckers and salesmen and hitchhikers, tricked out in their elaborate backpacks. Some of them she'd even deluded herself into thinking might be her Prince in disguise.

Each time there had been the meeting of tongues, the grunts in the dark as groins slapped together, and the cool evaporation of sweat on naked flesh. Each time she woke up alone. Sometimes there'd be money on the dresser.

She flicked on the lights as she entered the trailer. The tiny kitchen and shoebox-sized den emerged from the darkness.

"Like I said; it ain't much."

He stood on the threshold, one hand on the doorknob. "It's nice, Louise."

She shivered at the sound of her name in his mouth. She moved into the living room, hoping for a chance to compose herself. She needed to think.

"Close the door! You're lettin' the cold air in!" her voice unnaturally chirpy.

Gary closed the door behind him. She felt a bit more secure, but she couldn't help notice how worn and tacky everything looked: the sofa, the dinette set, the easy chair... For a fleeting second she was overwhelmed by a desire to cry.

Gary removed his parka, carefully draping it over the back of the easychair. He was wearing faded denims and a flannel shirt and he was so beautiful it scared her to look at him. He was so perfect she could almost ignore the Human Worm strapped to his back.

"Get you a drink?"

"That would be...nice."

She hurried past him and back into the kitchen. She retrieved her bottle of Evan Williams and a couple of high ball glasses. She poured herself two fingers, knocked it back, then poured another two before preparing a drink for her guest. She returned to the living room—he was standing in the exact same spot—and handed Gary the glass.

"Skoal."

"Cheers," he replied, lifting the glass to Carl's lips.

While his partner drank, Gary's eyes met and held hers. "We know why you invited us here, Louise..."

Her heart began to beat funny, as if she'd been given a powerful but dangerous drug. She wanted this man, this gorgeous stranger. She wanted to feel his weight on her, pressing her into the mattress of her bed.

"...but there's one thing you ought to know before we get started...and that's Carl's got to go first."

She stood perfectly still for a second before the words her Dream Prince had spoken sank in. She was keenly aware of Carl's eyes watching her. Her face burned and her stomach balled itself into a fist. She felt as if she'd awakened from a dream to find herself trapped in the punchline from a dirty joke.

"What kind of pervert do you think I am?" The tightness in her throat pitched her voice ever higher.

KNUCKLES AND TALES: THE TWO HEADED MAN

"I don't think you're a pervert, Louise. I think you're a very sweet, very special lady. I didn't mean to hurt you." There was no cynicism in his voice. His tone was that of a child confused by the irrationality of adults.

She felt her anger fade. She gulped down the rest of her drink, hoping it would fan the fires of her indignation. "I expected something kinky out of you—like maybe letting th' little guy watch...But not, y'know..."

"I see."

Gary moved to retrieve his parka. Before she realized what she was doing, she grabbed his arm. She was astonished by the intensity of her reaction.

"No! Don't leave! Please...it's so lonely here..."

"Yes, it is lonely," he whispered. His eyes would not meet hers. "Go stand over there. By the sofa. Where we can see you."

Louise did as she was told. Everything seemed so far away, as if she was watching a movie through the wrong end of a pair of binoculars. Her arms and legs felt so fragile they might have been made of light and glass.

Carl whispered into Gary's ear. His eyes had grown sharp and alive while Gary's seemed to lose their focus.

"Take off your blouse. Please." The words came from someplace far away.

She hesitated, then her hands moved to the throat of her blouse. The buttons seemed cold and alien, designed to frustrate her fingers. One by one they surrendered until her shirtfront fell open, revealing pale flesh. She shrugged her shoulders and the blouse fell to the floor.

Carl once more whispered something to Gary, never taking his eyes off Louise. "The skirt. Take it off."

Her hands found the fastener at her waist. Plastic teeth purred on plastic zipper and her skirt dropped to the floor, a dark puddle at her ankles. She took a step forward, abandoning her clothes.

Carl murmured into Gary's ear. She unhooked her bra, revealing her breasts. Her skin was milky white and decorated by dark aureole. Her nipples were painfully erect and as hard as corn kernels.

On Carl's relayed command she skinned herself free of her pantyhose. When the cool air struck her damp pubic patch, her clitoris stirred.

Gary moved towards her, bringing Carl with him.

She gasped aloud when Gary's hands touched her breasts. His thumbs flicked expertly over her nipples, sending shudders of pleasure through her. Then one hand was between her legs, teasing her thatch and gently massaging her.

Louise felt her knees buckle and she grabbed hold of Gary's shoulders to keep from falling backwards. Her eyes opened and she found herself staring into Carl's dark, intense eyes. She felt a brief surge of shame that her orgasm had become a spectator event, then Gary worked a finger past her labia and sank it to the second joint. Louise groaned aloud and all thoughts of shame disappeared.

He moved swiftly and quietly, wrapping her in his powerful arms and lifting her bodily. She felt a different form of pleasure now, as if she was once more within her father's safe embrace.

He moved down the narrow hall, past the cramped bathroom alcove and into the tiny bedroom at the back of the trailer. He lowered her trembling body onto the bed, draping her legs over the edge of the mattress.

His left hand continued to trace delicate patterns along her exposed flesh while his right loosened the harness that held Carl in place. He only halted his exploration of her body when he moved to free his burden.

Louise saw that Carl was dressed in a flannel shirt identical to Gary's, except that the empty sleeves had been pinned up and the shirt tail folded back on itself and fastened shut, just like a diaper. Gary removed the shirt and Louise swore out loud.

Even on a normal man's body Carl's penis would have been unusually large. It stood red and erect against the thick dark hair of his belly. Louise was so taken aback she scarcely noticed the smooth lumps of flesh that should have been Carl's arms and legs.

Gary positioned Carl's naked torso between her spread thighs. His gaze met and held her own so intently Louise almost forgot the absurd perversity of what they were doing.

"We love you," said Gary and shoved Carl on top of her.

Louise cried out as Carl penetrated her. It had been a long time since she'd last been with a man, and she had never known one of such proportions. She involuntarily contracted her hips, taking him in deeper. Gary's right hand kneaded the flesh of her breasts. His left hand helped Carl move. She could also feel something warm and damp just below her breasts. She suddenly realized it was Carl's face.

Gary's face was closer to hers now, his eyes mirroring her heat. She snared a handful of his hair, drawing him closer. His mouth was warm and wet as he clumsily returned her kiss. She felt the quivering that signaled the approach of orgasm and her moans became cries, giving voice to an exquisite wounding. Her hips bucked wildly with each spasm, but Carl refused to be unseated.

KNUCKLES AND TALES: THE TWO HEADED MAN

As she lay dazed and gasping in her own sweat, she was dimly aware of him still working between her legs. Then there was a deep groan, muffled by her own flesh, and she felt him stiffen and then relax.

Louise rarely experienced orgasms during intercourse. She had been unprepared for such intensity; it was if Gary had stuck his finger in her brain and swirled everything around so she was no longer sure what she thought or knew.

No. Not Gary. Carl.

The thought made her catch her breath and she raised herself onto her elbows, staring down at the thing cradled between her thighs. Carl's face was still buried in her breast. She touched his hair and felt him start from the unexpected contact. It was the first time since their strange rut had begun that she'd acknowledged his presence.

She felt Gary watching her as she moved back further onto the bed. Carl remained curled at the foot of the mattress, his eyes fixed on her. Gary stood in the narrow space between the bed and the dresser, his hands at his side.

"What about you? Aren't you interested?" Her voice was hoarse. Gary did not meet her gaze as he shifted his weight from foot to foot.

"What's the matter? Is it me?"

His head jerked up. "No! It's not you. You're fine. It's just..." He fell silent and looked to Carl, who nodded slightly.

Gary took a deep breath and loosened his belt buckle. His manner had changed completely. His movements had lost their previous grace. Biting his lower lip and tensing as if in anticipation of a blow, he dropped his pants.

Gary's sex organs were the size of a two year old child's. They lay exposed like fragile spring blossoms, his pubic area as smooth and hairless as his face. His eyes remained cast down.

Louise's lips twisted into a wry smile. She had willingly serviced a freak in order to please her long-awaited Prince, only to find him gelded. Yet all she could feel for the handsome near-man was sorrow.

"You poor thing. You poor, poor thing." She reached out and touched his hand, drawing him into the warmth of her arms. Surprised, Gary eagerly returned her embrace. To her own surprise, she reached down to pull Carl toward her. The three of them lay together on the bed like a nest of snakes, Louise gently caressing her lovers. After awhile Gary began to talk.

"I've known Carl since we were kids. My mama used to cook and clean for his folks and I kept Carl company. His mama and daddy were real rich; that's how they could afford to keep him home. At least his mama wanted him home. Carl's daddy drank a lot and used to say how it wasn't his fault in front of Carl. I knew how he felt. About having your daddy hate you because of the way you was born. Maybe that's why me and Carl made such good friends. You see, I can't read so good. And I'm really bad with math and things like that. My daddy got mad at my mama when they found out what was wrong with me and ran away. I never really went to school. When Carl was five, his daddy got real mad and started kickin' him. And Carl hadn't even done anything bad! He kicked Carl in the throat and they took him to the hospital. That's why Carl can't talk too good. But he's real smart! Smarter than most people with arms and legs! He knows a lot about history and math and important stuff like that. Carl tells me what to say and how to act and what to do so people don't know I've got something wrong with me. If people knew I wasn't smart they'd be even meaner to us." He exchanged a warm, brotherly smile with the silent man and squeezed him where his shoulder should have been. "Carl looks after me. I'm his arms and legs and voice and he's my brain and, you know." He blushed.

"You're lucky. Both of you. Not everyone is as...whole ."

"But we're not!" He folded her hands inside his own. "Not really. That's why we've been traveling. We've been trying to find the last part of us. The part that will make us whole."

Louise did not know what to say to this, so she simply kissed him. Sometime later they fell asleep, Carl's torso curled between them like a dozing pet.

The alarm went off at eight-thirty, jarring Louise from a dreamless sleep. She lay there for a moment, staring at Gary then Carl. She should have felt soiled, but there no indignation inside her. She gently shook Gary's beautiful naked shoulder.

"It's morning already. The filling station must be open by now. You can get your tire fixed."

"Yes." His voice sounded strangely hollow.

She got out of the rumpled bed, careful to keep from kicking Carl, and put on a housecoat. Now that it was daylight she felt embarrassed to be naked. She hurried into the kitchen and made coffee.

Gary emerged from the bedroom, dressed, with Carl once more harnessed to his back. She handed him two mugs, one black and one with cream and sugar, and watched, a faint smile on her lips, as they repeated their one-as-two act.

KNUCKLES AND TALES: THE TWO HEADED MAN

After they'd finished, Gary picked his parka up and laid it across one arm. He glanced first at her then angled his head so that he was as close to face-to-face with his passenger as possible. After a moment's silent communion, he once more turned to look at her, and his eyes lost their focus. Carl's lips moved at his ear and Louise could hear the faint rasping of his ruined voice.

Gary spoke like a man reading back dictation.

"Louise...you're a wonderful woman...I know you're not attracted to me, that's understandable...but I see something in you that might, some day...respond to me too..."

As Gary continued his halting recitation, Louise's gaze moved from his face to Carl's. For the first time since she'd met them, she really looked at him. She studied his plain, everyday face and his brown eyes. As she listened the voice she heard was Carl's and she felt something inside her change.

"We'll stop back after we get the tire repaired...It's up to you...We shouldn't be more than a hour at the most. Please think about it."

Gary began to put his parka on, but before the jacket hid Carl completely she darted forward and kissed both of them. First Gary, and then, with great care, Carl. They paused for a second and then smiled.

Louise stood in the middle of the trailer, hugging herself against the morning cold, as she watched her lovers leave. Funny. She'd always imagined her Prince having blue eyes...

THE CONFEDERATE STATES OF DREAD

THE KILLER

In Ferriday, Louisiana, September 29th, 1935, a woman went into labor in a tiny clapboard house, a mad dog howling outside the window. The delivery was a difficult one, lasting several hours. The beast bayed like one of Satan's own hounds as the child entered the world, then disappeared as mysteriously and suddenly as it first appeared.

Jerry Lee was his parent's second son, born into a household already troubled by economic hard times and domestic violence. He was a frail, sickly child the first few years of his life. Slender and pale, with golden curly hair, he bore a strong resemblance to his mother, Mamie. His father, a robust and masculine figure, clearly preferred his first born son and namesake, Elmo, Jr. Mamie doted on Jerry Lee, refusing to cut his long, blonde curls for the first three years of his life, and often dressing him as a girl, complete with petticoats and hair ribbons. However, in 1938, his life changed forever, putting him on the left-hand path that he would follow to its dark conclusion, thirty years later.

Little is known about Jerry Lee's relationship with his older brother, outside of what he himself has admitted to in interviews. Apparently young Jerry Lee adored Elmo, Jr., who was five years his senior, and did not resent him being his father's favorite. During the in-depth psychiatric examination given to determine his sanity after his arrest for the Presley-Montessi murders, Jerry Lee spoke warmly of his elder brother and showed what appeared to be genuine emotion when recalling Elmo, Jr.'s fate.

"Junior was my bubba, you know? I looked up to him on account of him being bigger and stronger than me. I used to be a real tag-along, following him and his friends when they'd go out crawdaddin' or stealin' apples from Old Man Pritchard's orchard. It used to bug him sometimes, since I was just a squirt and couldn't run as fast or climb as good as him, but I think he was flattered, too. He hardly ever told me to stay home, even though some of his friends made it pretty clear they didn't want no snot-nosed young'un taggin' after them."

"I was with him the day it happened. I saw it happen. We was walking down the dirt road that lead into Ferriday. It was a Saturday and mama had dipped into the egg money so's we could go into town and watch us a movie. Hopalong Cassidy was playing and we both were hurtin' to see it. We was walking down the road, well onto the shoulder, each of us with a quarter in our pockets, when this old Ford Model-T comes barreling down on us. Junior was walking on the outside, and damned if that Model-T don't strike him dead on.

"I remember seeing Junior fly up in the air all of a sudden and land hard, his arms and legs twisted all funny. The bastard driving the car stops for a second, looks back over his shoulder, and then speeds off. Turns out he was drunk and later that day he plowed his car into a tree in the next parish over, punching the steering wheel through his chest. It comforts me knowing God punished that sinner straight and true."

Elmo, Jr.'s untimely death at the hands of a drunk driver disrupted the already troubled household even further. Distraught over his loss, Elmo sought to turn Jerry Lee into a substitute for his dead son. After the funeral, ignoring Mamie's shrill protests, Elmo took a pair of pinking shears to Jerry Lee's locks. Elmo's skills as a barber were somewhat impaired due to his consumption of moonshine, and he accidentally severed Jerry Lee's right ear. When Jerry Lee began to scream, Elmo slapped the five-year-old boy and threatened him with castration if he continued to "complain" and was ordered to "take it like a man".

Things proceeded to get worse after that initial attempt at bonding. Elmo was dismayed to discover his surviving son did not share his elder brother's interests in sports or hunting, preferring to spend his time picking out tunes on the old up-right piano in the parlor. One day, in a drunken rage, Elmo slammed the lid of the piano onto his five-year-old son's hands, breaking most of his fingers. While Jerry Lee eventually recovered, he never played the piano again.

As Elmo's drinking worsened, so did the family's economic and social standing. By the time Jerry Lee was ten, the family had come close to hitting rock bottom, even by Ferriday's standards. Elmo worked occasionally in the Louisiana oil fields, drinking what little he made, while Mamie took in laundry.

Since he was often called upon to help supplement the family's income by working in the fields, Jerry Lee's education was equally sporadic. Then, in 1947, the second traumatic formative episode in his young life occurred.

KNUCKLES AND TALES: THE KILLER

There is no record of what went on that night. All that is known for sure is that by this time in his life, Elmo was a notoriously mean drunk, quick to take out his anger on those around him. In March Elmo came home from a three-day bender, out of his mind on cheap whisky, and proceeded to brutally rape and beat his wife to death in full view of his son. Elmo was arrested for his wife's murder and was sentenced to twenty-five years in Angola Prison. Twelve-year-old Jerry Lee was sent to live with relatives, ending up with his mother's older sister and her husband—both of whom were devout Pentecostals.

Where his original home life had been punctuated by his father's fits of drunken rage, Jerry Lee's adopted home was dominated by his aunt's religious fervor. Originally, she had entertained thoughts of her firstborn son, Jimmy, becoming a man of the cloth, but these hopes were crushed upon his birth, since the boy was born sporting a parasitic twin. And in a community where birth defects were seen as evidence of sin, this proved to be something of stumbling block to becoming a preacher.

The twin, which existed from the waist down, appeared to be female and grew out of Jimmy's side, forcing him to wear shirts two sizes too large for him. The twin—which was baptized as Loretta—occasionally twitched and kicked its legs and possessed working bowels, making it necessary for it to wear diapers.

Embarrassed by her natural born son, "Aunt Maisie" soon moved her dreams of having a successful preacher in the family from Jimmy to the handsome, golden-haired Jerry Lee. And, to every one's surprise, the boy took to the pulpit like a duck to water. He enjoyed having the attention of the congregation focused on him, and he especially enjoyed frightening them with graphic descriptions of the torments meted out to unrepentant sinners who fall into Satan's hands. Later, he would confess to having experienced orgasms during these hell-fire and brimstone sermons.

What no one in Ferriday knew was that the whole time young Jerry Lee was making a name for himself in the Church of Christ pulpit on Sunday mornings, he was secretly indulging in pastimes such as clandestine drinking, arson, and shoplifting, or that he was sowing his wild oats amongst the more comely members of the congregation.

In 1950, a second orphaned cousin came to join the brood—this one from nearby East Texas. Mickey was younger than both Jerry Lee and Jimmy, but this did not keep the three from forming a triumvirate that would last over twenty years and a series of crimes unparalleled in modern history.

In 1951, Jerry Lee was caught in the act with one of the ladies in the choir, effectively ending what could have been a very promising preaching career. However, while he might have lost his congregation, Jerry Lee still had his two younger cousins, both of whom looked up to and deferred to him, letting Jerry Lee set the tone and pace of their activities. And those activities more often than not proved to be cruel and dangerous.

In 1952 Jerry Lee, Jimmy, and Mickey were arrested for setting fire to a neighbor's garage. Because of their tender years, Jimmy and Mickey were set free. Jerry Lee, however, was sent to reform school for six months. When he was released in 1953, it was to discovered his father was out of prison, paroled for "good behavior".

Uncertain as to what to do next, Jerry Lee moved in with Elmo. His father was unprepared for the changes that had occurred while he was away in prison. Gone was the frail, golden-haired mama's boy he used to beat, replaced by a seventeen-year-old who stood six feet tall and was strong as coiled steel wire, with a temper that might, at best, be called hair-trigger. It didn't take long for the two to begin arguing. Elmo had returned to his hard-drinking habits, this time joined by Jerry Lee. Both men would drink until they blacked out. It was during one of these episodes—or so he claims—that Jerry Lee killed his father with a shotgun blast to the head at point-blank range.

While he claimed that he shot his father in self-defense, all evidence shows that Elmo was lying on his bed at the time Jerry Lee pulled the trigger. Since he was still underage, Jerry Lee was not tried as an adult. He spent the next three years in a juvenile detention center, where he spent most of his time with other hardened delinquents. Released in 1957, Jerry Lee returned once more to Ferriday. There he hooked up with his younger cousins, both of whom had been busy during his absence, adding various petty crimes to their records.

Within six weeks of his release, the bored trio—probably under Jerry Lee's instigation—stole a car and took a joyride to Baton Rouge. During the week the cousins spent in Louisiana's capitol city, the bodies of two prostitutes were found in different motel rooms. Each corpse showed evidence of recent intercourse with multiple partners, although it was impossible to determine whether or not rape was involved. One woman was shot in the head with a small caliber handgun, while the other had been strangled to death. While there is no evidence to tie Jerry Lee and his family to these killings, it is possible this was the beginning of their adult criminal careers.

KNUCKLES AND TALES: THE KILLER

Later that year, Mickey returned to Texas to avoid marrying a Ferriday girl he'd succeeded in making pregnant, prompting Jerry Lee and Jimmy to follow him to the Lone Star state. While there, they occasionally worked as roughnecks in the oil fields and raised hell on their days off.

The early months of 1954 found Jerry Lee back in jail for parole violation after being picked up in Nacogdoches on a drunk and disorderly. This time he landed in an adult prison facility, where he spent time learning the tricks of the trade from career criminals. One thing he learned while he was locked up was the fine art of pimping. It was a skill he would later put to good use on the outside.

During the seven years he spent in prison, Jerry Lee developed an acute—some would say decidedly unhealthy—interest in the career of rock star Elvis Aron Presley. Jerry Lee saw Elvis as a hero—a poor Southern boy born under circumstances not unlike his own, who somehow managed to break free of his poverty-stricken surroundings and make good.

While still in the joint, Jerry Lee took to sculpting his unruly blonde locks into a pompadour and affecting a sneer. This look, while hardly unusual for the time, did display Jerry Lee's missing ear. One fellow inmate who made the mistake of making fun of Jerry Lee's handicap was later found badly beaten in the shower.

Paroled once more in 1961, Jerry Lee soon hooked up with his cousin Mickey, who had recently finished time for writing bad checks in Texas. The two looked up Jimmy, who was living in Shreveport, Louisiana. It wasn't long before Jerry Lee was putting his pimping skills to use, bringing home teenaged girls and turning them out.

With his dirty white-boy good looks and native charm, there was no shortage of candidates for exploitation. Once Jerry Lee was bored with a particular girl, he would hand her over to his cousins for their amusement. It wasn't long before Jerry Lee was able to afford a second-hand Cadillac, painted fire engine red. It was during this period that Jerry Lee began writing songs. He would boast to friends that he was "writing songs for Elvis", claiming that Presley's manager, Colonel Tom Parker, had shown interest in several of his tunes.

While it is acknowledged that Jerry Lee actually sent copies of his songs to both Parker and Presley, there is no evidence the performer or his manager were interested in recording his work or had even responded to his initial requests for an audience. In the summer of 1962, Jerry Lee loaded up his Cadillac with his cousins, some of his girls, a case of whiskey, and took an impromptu road trip to Memphis "to pay ole Elvis a visit."

Their drunken spree came to an abrupt halt at the ornate Music Gates of Graceland, where Elvis Presley's cadre of bodyguards, the notorious Memphis Mafia, confronted Lee. A fight broke out when the inebriated Jerry Lee—insisting he had an important meeting with Presley—refused to leave the grounds of the mansion. The Shelby County police were called and Jerry Lee found himself up on charges once more, this time for trespassing, resisting arrest and violating the Mann Act.

During the next four years, Jerry Lee brooded over the injustice done him by Elvis—who hadn't even bothered to show up in person at his trial. Embittered, his former adulation of the singer turned into a vitriolic hatred, and Jerry Lee had more than enough time to plan his vengeance against the King.

Upon his release in late 1966, Jerry Lee elected to remain in the Memphis area. A great deal had changed during his last imprisonment—a president had been assassinated, college students were protesting the war in Viet Nam, and America's taste in popular music had been radically changed by the likes of The Beatles and the Rolling Stones. Elvis, the sneering bad boy with the gyrating hips, had been pushed from center stage, reduced to performing in substandard musical comedies about singing race car drivers and surfing champions.

Rockabilly was out, psychedelic was in. Jerry Lee, quick to realize the need to blend in with the crowd he hoped to exploit, abandoned his out-dated drake tail in favor of long hair and a beard. With his flowing blonde locks successfully obscuring his missing ear, he looked like the pictures of Jesus found in Southern Baptist homes.

While hanging on the local scene, utilizing his old pimping skills, Jerry Lee quickly corralled a small stable of teenaged girls. He rented a large house and began dealing crank and acid, throwing wild parties, with plentiful supplies of sex and drugs readily available. Mickey—now going by the name of "Tex"—and Jimmy showed up to share in the bounty. Surrounded by willing teenaged girls and easily influenced flunkies, Jerry Lee became the focus of more attention than he'd even known before in his life. In 1967, Jerry Lee finally put into motion his revenge against the society that he felt was responsible for keeping him down.

The assault on Graceland involved members of Jerry Lee's family and his most loyal girls: thirteen year-old Lurleen, fifteen-year-old Yvette, and seventeen-year-old Dee-Dee. In retrospect, his plan for

KNUCKLES AND TALES: THE KILLER

gaining access to the King's inner sanctum was as childishly simple as it was unrelentingly brutal.

It was ten o'clock in the evening the night of November 23rd, 1967, when Dee-Dee approached the solitary guard stationed in the gatekeeper's booth outside of Graceland. Dee-Dee, pretending to be an Elvis fan, struck up a conversation with the guard. The guard suggested that if she was willing to perform fellatio on him, he would arrange for her to see the King. Dee-Dee agreed. Once in the booth, Dee-Dee produced a knife and slit the unsuspecting guard's throat as he unbuckled his pants. She then took control of the gate mechanism and opened the way for her compatriots.

Testimony at the trial revealed that Jerry Lee and his family had come well armed on their second visit to Graceland. Each girl carried a butcher knife, while Mickey and Jimmy were armed with .38 revolvers and Jerry Lee packed a 9mm. semi-automatic pistol, all of which were equipped with silencers.

Once inside the gates of Graceland, entering the house was relatively simple. The intruders came in through a side door, surprising the maid and one of Elvis' bodyguards in the kitchen as they were sitting down to a light snack. Both were shot through the head at point-blank range.

The killers located their prey in the basement recreation area, known as the Jungle Room because of its rattan furniture and Polynesian wall decorations. There they surprised Priscilla, Elvis' young bride, six months pregnant with their first child; Andreas Cornelius van Kuijik, a.k.a. Colonel Tom Parker, Elvis' manager; Khang Rhee, the King's personal karate instructor; his father, Vernon, and his identical twin brother, Jessie Garon Presley.

Khang Rhee tried to disarm Jimmy using his martial arts skill, only to be shot through the head by Jerry Lee. Mistaking Jessie for his brother, he then proceeded to rant and rave about the injustices done to him and his family while the others busied themselves with tying up the terrified hostages.

Once satisfied their victims were immobilized, Jerry Lee and his gang helped themselves to the contents of the liquor cabinet, growing progressively hostile and abusive with each drink. At some point during that horrible night, Priscilla Presley begged her attackers to show mercy on her unborn child. This enraged the already unstable Jerry Lee, who began to scream obscenities and kick the trussed woman. When he tired of the sport, he turned it over to the girls, who continued to pummel the hapless mother-to-be until she miscarried.

NANCY A. COLLINS

It is uncertain, even now, which family member was responsible for which murder, but it is generally accepted that Jerry Lee killed Jessie Presley, and that his was probably the only murder Jerry Lee actually committed himself. Jessie Presley was found hogtied, a makeshift hangman's noose knotted around his neck, his tongue cut out and with multiple stab wounds to the groin. According to the autopsy, Elvis' twin brother died choking on his own blood.

Col. Tom Parker was bound hand and foot, his throat slit from ear to ear. Vernon Presley was shot in the back of the head at point blank range and had to be identified by dental records.

By all accounts, it was thirteen-year-old Lurleen who killed Priscilla Presley, clumsily slashing her throat and writing the infamous slogan "Acid is gruvee kill the pigs" on the walls of the murder sight.

Having slaughtered what they believed to be the entire Presley clan, the killers amused themselves by trashing parts of the house, stealing the gold records for *Hound Dog* and *Blue Suede Shoes* displayed on the walls and one of Elvis' Grammy Awards. Their bloodlust finally sated, Jerry Lee and his family left the grounds shortly after one o'clock in the morning.

When Jerry Lee eagerly scanned the next morning's Memphis *Commercial-Appeal* and *Press-Scimitar* for news of the crime, he was stunned and outraged to discover that he had failed to do the one thing he'd set out to do: kill the King.

According to the newspaper accounts of the tragedy, Elvis had not been at Graceland that night, but actually in Hollywood, filming his latest movie, *Speedboat-A-Go-Go*, with Anne-Margaret. A photo of the King, looking dazed as he climbed aboard his private jet in preparation of returning home for the funeral services of his father, brother, wife, unborn child and assorted friends and employees, dominated the front page.

Jerry Lee was so angry he came close to suffering a stroke, falling down on the floor of his apartment and shrieking at the top of his lungs. Once this fit of rage passed, he became convinced that the media was covering up the "truth"—that he had, indeed, slain the real Elvis, and that the impostor seen on television and heard on the radio was none other than Presley's brother, Jessie.

In order to force the conspiracy's hand, Jerry Lee concocted a second, equally heinous crime. One that would both flush the "truth" about Elvis into the open and place the blame for the Graceland murders on someone else.

KNUCKLES AND TALES: THE KILLER

Jerry Lee picked as his sacrificial victim Fred Montessi, the owner of a local supermarket chain. Under direct orders from their cousin, Tex and Jimmy, accompanied by Yvette and the resourceful Dee-Dee, broke into the Montessi's posh Germantown home in the middle of the night, surprising the hapless grocery magnate, his wife and their three children in their sleep.

Each victim was bound and gagged, their throats slit, and the walls smeared with slogans written in blood. Jerry Lee's plan was to make both the Graceland and Montessi murders to look like the work of radical black activists, such as the Black Panthers or Nation of Islam. Unfortunately, Jerry Lee and his followers were ignorant white trash, and the slogans they chose to leave scrawled in the Montessi family's blood, proved it: *All hale Alla! Kill whitie! Praise Martin Luther King!* plus the otherwise cryptic *Where is Elvis?* were so obvious not even the Shelby County Sheriff's Department was fooled into mistaking the crime as racially motivated.

In the weeks following the highly publicized murder sprees, paranoia was rampant in Memphis, resulting in brisk sales in home security systems. Elvis, shattered by his loss, became even more reclusive than before. However, he seemed to draw some comfort from the multitude of fans that thronged the fabled Music Gates day and night, seeking to console their idol in this, his hour of grief.

Meanwhile, the authorities were busy sifting through the mountains of crank mail accumulated over the years by both Elvis and his manager. In January of 1968, roughly six weeks after the first murders had occurred, they found Jerry Lee's rejected songs. While crosschecking him for priors, they uncovered his attempted "visit" to Grace land in '62. Suddenly, after weeks of red herrings and dead ends, they had a prime suspect.

When the deputies appeared at Jerry Lee's residence, they were greeted by a noticeably pregnant Lurleen, who, upon seeing the police on the front porch, freaked out and slammed the door. Interpreting this as suspicious behavior, the deputies kicked open he door and entered with guns drawn.

What they found was a three-bedroom apartment littered with countless empty liquor bottles, used syringes, dirty needles, and spent condoms. The piece de resistance was the kitchen, with its stacks of filthy dishes heaped in the sink, a plate shellacked to the wall at eye-level by dried baked beans, and a tangle of yellowed fly strips that hung from the ceiling like the tendrils of a mammoth jellyfish.

They found Jerry Lee sprawled across a soiled mattress in one of the bedrooms, naked except for his undershirt, a terrified Yvette cowering in one corner, wrapped in a dirty sheet. Jerry Lee was going for his semi-automatic when the deputies tackled him. Tex and Jimmy proved to be less troublesome, since both were still sleeping off a drunk from the night before. Any question as to who they were dealing with was answered when, while handcuffing Dee-Dee, one of the arresting officers found the stolen Grammy award being used as a doorstop. Case solved.

Dubbed "The Killbillies" by the press, Jerry Lee and his family became glommin' geeks in a media circus without precedent. And, seven years after his initial attempt to breech the gates of Graceland, Jerry Lee was finally in the same room as his idol, free to vilify him from the witness stand in front of every news service and television camera in the nation. Although the trial dragged on for three months, the verdict had never once been in doubt.

Since all three girls were both underage and pregnant (all by Jerry Lee, supposedly) by the time they went to trial, they were given the relatively lenient sentences of thirty years each. Lurleen became eligible—and won—parole after seven years, when she turned twenty-one. She has since changed her name and is the wife of a Pentecostal minister in Alabama.

Yvette died of peritonitis from a ruptured appendix in 1975 while still serving time.

Dee-Dee is still in prison, although she is currently up for parole. Failing that, she will still be released in six years, having served her sentence.

Jerry Lee, Mickey, and Jimmy were not so lucky. Each was sentenced to death, only later to have it commuted to life without parole.

Jimmy never made it past the first six months of his sentence. He was taken out of General Population and hospitalized, only to die from internal injuries after several of his fellow inmates attempted to gangbang his parasitic twin.

Separated from his older cousin's influence, Mickey was quick to find Jesus and became a jailhouse preacher. A collection of his prison gospel songs, performed by popular Country & Western recording artist Chuck Manson and his wife, Lynette, is currently enjoying modest success on the Christian radio charts.

Jerry Lee, probably the most notorious killer of his generation, spends most of his time answering fan mail and submitting to long-distance interviews. Over the years he has metamorphosized into a cult

KNUCKLES AND TALES: THE KILLER

figure, revered amongst the country's alienated youngsters as the White Trash Death God, a born loser who grabbed Life by the lapels and forced it to pay attention to him.

Twenty-five years after the fact, Jerry Lee still insists that the man he killed that night in 1967 was the real Elvis Aron Presley, and not his twin brother. Considering that after the trial and the ensuing publicity, Elvis retired from performing and lived the last nine years of his life in complete seclusion, releasing the occasional studio album, one wonders if there isn't something to this claim.

Many have often commented on the irony of how Jerry Lee—a man originally condemned to death—-succeeded in outliving the man he'd tried to kill. Jerry Lee, when questioned in his cell, does not refrain from gloating. When Elvis' wasted, anorexic body was found in his bathroom, dead of a coronary in 1977, Jerry lee was rumored to have bragged to his fellow inmates:

"He's dead, god damn him! I killed him once, now he's dead a second and last time! It took me ten years, but the King is dead! Just call me the Killer."

CANCER ALLEY

WITH THANKS TO JOHN CLARK & THE DELTA GREENS

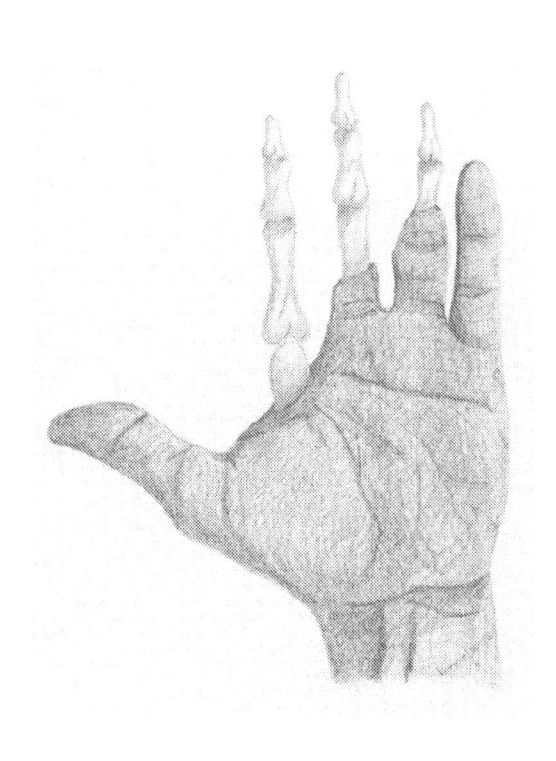

The volunteer stood in the meager shade provided by the tar-paper shack's front porch and rapped her knuckles once more on the screen door's wooden frame.

"Hello? Hello, Mr. Marsalis? Is anyone home? Hello!"

The volunteer scanned the front yard while waiting a response. A handful of rumpled chickens scratched near the dirt road, while a slat-thin hound slumbered under a partially demolished Buick. She frowned and cupped her free hand over her brow, pressing her nose to the rusty screen, and peered inside. The interior of the Marsalis home was dark and redolent of countless meals of fatback and mustard greens.

"Can I help you, young lady?"

The volunteer jumped, startled by the appearance of a slightly built black man standing at the corner of the house.

"Oh! Sorry about that! You surprised me!"

"That's awright, honey. Didn't mean to scare you none." The old man pulled a clean white handkerchief from his back pocket and mopped at his brow.

"Are you Mr. Marsalis? Mr. Homer Marsalis?"

"Have been for the past sixty-five years. You with Parish Services?"

"No, sir, I'm a volunteer worker for the Louisiana Chapter of Ecology Now. We're an environmental group trying to control pollution by America's big corporations... Maybe you got one of our flyers in the mail?"

Marsalis shrugged. His face was broad and expressive, the color of teak. The sweat beading on his brow and cheeks made him look like he'd recently been polished. "Wouldn't do me much good if I did, ma'am. I can't read except to make out m'own name."

"Oh. Well. Uh, the reason I'm here is to tell you about a meeting we're having in the town hall this evening. I'm sure you're very much aware of Redeemer Parish's high cancer rate, and that research has tied it to the chemicals dumped into the Mississippi by the companies up-river and from contaminants seeping into the groundwater from supposedly 'safe' toxic waste dumps in the area..."

The old man nodded, his eyes unreadable. "Yeah. I know something about it."

"Well, together we're having a meeting and representatives from Arcadia Petrochemicals are going to be there. They're the largest—and most notorious—polluter in the whole state."

"I know about Arcadia. I worked for 'em for close to thirty years." The hostility in the old man's voice was unmistakable.

"Oh. Well, uh, we'd really appreciate it if everyone who can make it would come to the meeting... There'll be reporters from both the Baton Rouge and the New Orleans dailies, plus a camera crew from Channel Four."

The old man nodded slowly. "I'll be there. Don't you worry 'bout that, ma'am."

The volunteer smiled nervously. There was something about the way the old man's eyes gleamed that made her antsy. "That's good to hear, Mr. Marsalis... Be sure to bring your family and friends with you. We'll need all the local support we can get."

"I'll be sure to do that."

Homer Marsalis stood in his front yard and watched as the activist climbed into her little compact car and headed down the dirt road, leaving a pall of yellowish dust in her wake.

o o o

Funny how everything was so green; how everything looked so alive. Homer Marsalis paused to stare at the field of sugar cane flanking the road. In the distance he could hear the roar and rumble of the diesel harvesters. The smell of fresh-cut sugar cane drifted on the humid breeze.

He remembered how he and his brothers used to steal sugar cane; chopping it open with their pa's machete to get at the sweet insides. He could still recall how it was made even more delicious by the knowledge he would be beaten should the overseer discover the theft.

Back then life was sweet as the syrup from stolen sugar cane. As sweet as the words that dripped from the tongue of the Father of Lies. But that had been long ago. Homer wasn't fooled. The lush fertility of the Mississippi Delta hid many dangers; cane rattlers, water moccasins, alligators...cancer.

Homer closed his eyes as the pain resurfaced once again, blotting out his surroundings. He'd become adept at riding it, like a veteran

KNUCKLES AND TALES: CANCER ALLEY

bronco buster. His one regret was that the pain would never be enough to kill him.

Despite what the songs and movies say, no one has yet to die from terminal grief.

o o o

"Sorry I'm late, folks, but I got hung up at the house."

If Homer Marsalis' family and friends noticed his tardiness, they kept it to themselves.

"There was this li'l white gal talkin' bout a meeting down at the town hall. It's about Arcadia."

Homer paused to let the words sink in for effect. He'd always had a flair for the dramatic. He pointed a finger at his brother Nestor's headstone.

"You recall that time you woke up and found that orange dust all over the yard? That stuff that looked like rust an' smelt like rotten eggs? I tole you to move then, that it weren't healthy to be livin' downwind of Arcadia! But would you listen to me? No! Just cause yore my big brother don't mean you'll *always* know more'n me, Nestor!"

Nestor said nothing. He never did.

Homer pulled his handkerchief out of his back pocket and wiped the tears from his face. He shuffled over to a badly listing gravestone and leaned against it. He knew he must look a sight; a small, banty rooster of an old fool dressed in his Sunday best, chattering away at the Dead like a washerwoman gossiping at the fence.

Not that he was in any danger of being seen. To Homer's knowledge, he was the only one who still bothered to visit the bone yard. Most of the others who had loved ones planted in its dark ground were either lying directly underfoot or had moved on.

Move on. That's what his son-in-law had told him. That he ought to move on.

That was well and good if you were young and still had some life left to you. But there was no way Homer could bring himself to leave Redeemer Parish. After all, his whole family was here.

Over to his left were the headstones that marked his parents' final resting place. His daddy had died when Homer was twelve, killed in a farming accident. His mama had lived another twenty years without her man, dying during the winter of 1957 from double pneumonia. Homer remembered how old she'd seemed at the time, and then realized—with a start—that at her death she'd been eight years younger than he was now

Flanking his parents' graves were those of his brother Calvin and his sister Esther. Calvin had died of pancreatic cancer back in '83. He'd been sixty-one at the time. No one really thought anything about it. Same with Esther, the oldest of his brothers and sisters, who developed cancer of the colon the next year. Folks didn't grow very old in Redeemer Parish. Leastwise, not the poor ones. The best someone like Homer could shoot for was seventy. Maybe seventy-two, if his luck held.

By the time Nestor died of leukemia in '86, Homer knew that whatever was carrying off his family wasn't natural. As bad as losing his big brother had been, what came next had been a thousand times worse.

It started with Ernestine. His baby.

She'd got herself married to a fellow up in Detroit back in '83. When she finally got herself pregnant she came back down to be with her mama. She'd been so excited. Gussie, Homer's wife, had been tickled to death by the idea of having a baby round the house again

Ernestine hadn't been home a week before the well water started stinking. They kept on drinking it, of course. What other choice did they have? It had happened before, but it usually went away on its own.

Then the baby came. Early. Way too early.

Homer stared at his daughter's head stone. His grandchild's name was also on there, although it had never really been alive. Homer wasn't even really sure if it had even been a baby. What Ernestine had birthed that cold winter night in '87 looked more like a tumor with a head on it. For form's sake, they'd given it a boy's name. Ernestine died a week later in Charity Hospital. They'd cut out her womb trying to save her.

Her husband took the first bus from Detroit he could find, but he was too late. By the time he reached New Orleans, she was gone. Homer could still see the emptiness in his son-in-law as he watched his wife's coffin lowered into the delta's rich dirt.

Shortly after the funeral a couple of white folks dressed in lab coats came out to the house and asked his permission to take samples from his well. They wore plastic gloves and were real careful not to get anything on their clothes. A couple of weeks later the same two men came back out and told Homer he needed to move his well. They showed him some papers and said that his well was contaminated. Then they left.

Homer might have been illiterate, but he'd worked for Arcadia Petrochemicals long enough to recognize their corporate logo on the papers. He showed the report to his son Nolan to see what he could

KNUCKLES AND TALES: CANCER ALLEY

make of it. Nolan had graduated from the vo-tech school and worked out on the oilrigs as a mechanic.

Nolan said the reports talked about stuff called Phenols and HHCs and Benzene Hexachloride and Cadmium. There was also stuff about carcinogenics and other words Homer did not fully understand. After he'd finished reading the report aloud, Nolan had looked his father in the eye and said; "Daddy, they're saying the water's poisoned."

"How can that be? That well's been there since my daddy was a boy! It's a good well! With good water! How can they say its poison?"

"Cause they're the ones that poisoned it, daddy. They knew exactly what they were looking for, and they found it."

"But—But—It'll cost money to dig a new well!" Homer had never felt so stupid and helpless before in his life. The knowledge that the water that his family had relied on for more than seventy years was no longer safe hurt him like a blow. How long? How long had it been like that? Weeks? Months? Years? The realization that Ernestine had drunk from the well, not to mention Nestor, Calvin and Esther, made his soul knot up inside him.

He'd been so proud of himself. Of his job. He'd been working as a janitor at the main Arcadia plant since it opened in 1959. Decent jobs were scarce in Redeemer Parish. Most men either busted their backs working in the cane fields or they didn't work at all. A lucky handful landed jobs in the oil fields or at the chemical plants that lined the last fifty miles of the Mississippi River before it emptied into the Gulf of Mexico. Homer had counted himself amongst the lucky. He brought home enough pay to keep a roof over his family's heads and put his son through school. He didn't see any reason to question the source of his good fortune.

Oh, he'd heard the rumors about illegal dumping procedures. You couldn't work at the Arcadia plant and not hear something. Back during the Sixties, the papers had taken to calling the stretch of river the Chemical Ditch. But in the last ten years the name had changed to Cancer Alley. But he'd paid it no mind. It had nothing to do with him.

And now the company he'd worked for the better part of thirty years was telling him he couldn't drink from his well anymore. That it was poison.

He went to the man in charge of public relations at the plant and demanded to talk with the president. He told the public relations director about the poison in his well and how his sister and brothers had died of cancer; of how the poison made his daughter miscarry.

The P.R. Director gave Homer a hard, cold stare and said; "Look, it ain't our fault if you people have sex all the time! That's what causes miscarriages. You people are always trying to blame us for your mistakes! Now get back to work!"

Two days later Homer lost his job.

Six months after that Nolan started losing weight. By Christmas he was diagnosed as having leukemia. He managed to hang on until the spring of '89. Homer thought he'd never feel a greater sorrow than that of burying his only son. But six months later, Gussie, his wife and helpmate for the past forty years, followed her son into the ground.

Gone. They were all gone. Everyone he'd ever loved or cared for lay beneath his feet. The last three years had been busy ones for the tiny graveyard. The mortal remains of Bordelons, Tanners, Watsons, and Johnsons lay cheek by jowl; good Baptists all, and each laid low by cancer of some kind.

Homer turned to stare at the towering twin chimneys of the Arcadia plant, looming over the landscape like an industrial volcano. Yellowish-brown smoke billowed from the funnels. Gussie's monument was not yet a year and a half old, but already the inscription was unreadable, the limestone badly pitted.

The pain blossomed again and Homer gasped. There was no pretending what he felt was simple grief. Not now. Not here. He needed no doctors to tell him the agony in his stomach was cancer. He leaned heavily on the tilting headstone and fumbled with his breast pocket.

"Forgive me, darlin'," he whispered under his breath. "But I can't let what they did go unpunished."

The flute was made from bone and it was very, very old. Older than Homer. Older than his mother, who had given it to him on her deathbed. It had come from Africa, and it was carved from the thighbone of a powerful wizard-king. Homer did not know if these stories were true. It did not matter. The flute held power, that much he did know.

His mother's family had been witchy as long as anyone could remember. His grandmother, dead these fifty years, had claimed to be descended from a powerful Obeah man and that, as a young woman, she had once ruled as New Orleans' reigning voodoo queen. Homer had inherited his mama's witchy ways, just as she'd gotten hers from granny.

When he met Augusta Timms, everything changed for Homer. Gussie was a devout Baptist. For him to win her love, he had to put aside what she called "heathen ways". And, because he loved her, he'd done as she asked. He never really developed a taste for church or preachers, but he agreed to their children being raised Baptist and never mentioned the old ways to them. Not that it mattered. Both Ernestine and Nolan seemed to be more their mother's children than his. Homer had not glimpsed the gleam that burned in his mother's eyes. The same that touched his own. He'd prayed that one of his grandchildren might carry on, but even that hope had been destroyed.

"I know I promised you," Homer told his wife's grave. "And you know I wouldn't go back on my word less it was important! They don't *know*. None of them knows what it's like to suffer and die the way you and the young'uns did! There's no way the Livin' *can* know the sorrow of the Dead. They don't *want* to know. And they never will. Unless they're *shown*. It's time for the Dead to speak their piece."

Homer placed the bone flute in his mouth and closed his eyes, squeezing tears onto his seamed cheeks. And he began to play.

The music was the sound of grief. The notes pierced the late-afternoon air, carried high and far by the wind. Men toiling in the cane fields paused in their labors, their eyes burning with sudden, unexplained tears. A truck driver carrying a load of gypsum to the Arcadia treatment plant found his vision abruptly blurred and was forced to pull over to the side of the road as great, wracking sobs shook his body.

The thick green carpet that covered the graves of Homer Marsalis' friends and loved ones rippled like an uneasy sea. Tombstones toppled and cracked as the earth split itself asunder. First there was the smell of freshly turned dirt; then a far more pungent reek.

Nestor was the first to rise, the powder-blue polyester leisure suit he'd been buried in looking little worse for the wear, despite clumps of grave mold. Esther clawed her way free, one skeletal hand clutching the tattered remains of her burial gown. Esther had always been modest. Beetles dropped from her wig as Nestor helped her to stand.

Calvin pushed his way through the topsoil like a plant eager to meet the sun, scattering dirt with a mighty shrug of his shoulders. Although death and decay had whittled him down, he was still a big man.

Ernestine cradled her misshapen son to her worm-eaten breast, staring at the sun with withered eyes. Nolan, his gaunt frame made even more so by two years underground, teetered uncertainly in the afternoon light, looking like a dreamer awakened from a deep sleep. Gussie wore the same green dress he'd last seen her in, her sweet face ravaged by worms and decay, but Homer could not find it in him to be repulsed by the sight of her. Anyone else would be frightened witless by the things that stood before him, but to Homer Marsalis, they were his family. It felt good to see them again.

The graveyard continued to surrender its dead, as more and more of its occupants—all of them familiar, all of them friends or family—stood up to be counted. Homer nodded his appreciation as each new recruit moved to join the others. While he had provided the power to reanimate the Dead, it was up to each individual whether or not to rise. Homer did not believe in forced solidarity.

When they were fifty strong, and the afternoon shadows had lengthened, Homer motioned for them to follow him. And they did, swaying on unsteady limbs. Those who were too decayed to walk alone were aided by the more recent dead.

Homer reached out and took Gussie's hand in his own. It was cold and its texture reminded him of soft soap, but he didn't really mind. He'd missed her so much. It was as if they'd buried a part of him along with her. And now it was back. At least for a while.

It would take them an hour or two to make it into town. The meeting would already be under way by the time they got there.

Homer hoped the fat-faced fool from Arcadia's public relations department would be there. Homer had a lot to say to that man.

And this time he'd listen.

THE WORST THING THERE IS

I almost didn't see her, even though I must have been staring at her for at least a minute or two. I was standing beside the car, looking off into empty space while I pumped the tank full of premium unleaded. It wasn't until I screwed the gas cap back on that I heard her cough that I realized I was looking straight at her.

She was standing next to the phone booth on the corner. She was dressed in a pastel pink polyester waitress's uniform—the type that could make Gwenyth Paltrow look like a sack of potatoes—and those unflattering chunky white sneakers. I recognized her as one of the waitresses from a nearby diner I occasionally stopped in for lunch. I knew she was named after a Grand Ole Opry queen, but that's about all I could recollect about her. Although it was chilly out, all she had was a thin sweater wrapped about her shoulders. She clutched the purse hanging from her shoulder tight against her hip, as if trying to hide it.

"Do you need a ride, ma'am?"

She didn't say anything at first, just watched me with that wariness you see in dogs that have caught a boot one time too often.

"I was waitin' on the bus," she said flatly, gesturing at the sign on the curb. "I live on the Old Highway, near the gas works."

"I work the graveyard out there. I'd be more than happy to give you a lift."

She stared at me for a long moment, then nodded and moved to enter the passenger side. We rode for a minute or two in dead silence, and then I decided to make some small talk.

"It's sure lonely out this way past eight o'clock. Don't you have anyone who could come and fetch you after work?"

"Not really."

"Waiting on a late bus by yourself in this kind of weather-that's gotta be the worst thing in the world."

"No it ain't," she said, in that same flat, tired voice. "The worst thing in the world is wakin' up one day and findin' out you been sleepwalkin' instead of livin' your life. You don't got no future—you ain't even really got no past. You ain't goin' nowheres and you ain't been anywheres, you're just there, damn it, with nothin' to show for it but stretch marks and fallen arches and gray in your hair. Everything you ever hoped for, ever dreamed about, is wasted. You've been lied to, tricked, and played for a big fat, ugly, stupid jerk.

"Like, pretend you been savin' up all your money. Putting a little bit aside for years an' years, so's you can get yourself a nice double-wide, with one of them wrap-around decks you can barbecue on, and be able to put it in a nice park, like the ones where there's trees and grass instead of gravel an' dirt. Then, after scrimpin' and savin' and workin' yourself damn near to death, you come home and find someone's been into your savings jar. And when that someone comes back, he's stinkin' drunk and drivin' a shiny new pick up and towin' a brand spankin' new bass boat. That would be worse than standin' in the cold waitin' on the bus, don't you think?"

"I reckon so."

"You can let me out here."

I pulled off onto the shoulder, the gravel crunching under the tires. I glanced through the windshield at the shadowy collection of decrepit trailer homes set a couple hundred yards from the highway.

"Are you sure you don't want me to drop you off a little closer to home?"

"It's okay. I live right there." She pointed to a trailer with a sagging screen door, cinder block front step, and a shiny new pick-up truck with a boat hitched on its rear bumper.

As she climbed out, I leaned across the front seat and looked up into her face. "Are you gonna be alright, lady?"

She smiled, and it completely transformed her face. The result was startling—like your aged auntie flashing a beautifully proportioned calf encased in a sheer black stocking.

"Oh, *I'm* gonna be all right. There's no need to worry about *me*," she said with a laugh. "Thanks for the ride, mister. " And with that she shut the passenger door, turned, and walked up the gravel road that lead to the trailer park.

I sat there for a long moment, wondering if she knew I'd seen the handle of the butcher knife sticking out of the corner of her purse. For all I knew, she carried it every night for protection while waiting on the bus.

KNUCKLES AND TALES: THE WORST THING THERE IS

As I threw the car back into gear, I thought about what she'd said, and decided that if there's one thing worse than a shattered dream, it's a pissed-off dreamer. As no doubt someone was going to be finding out real soon.

Nice bass boat, though.

CATFISH GAL BLUES

Flyjar is the kind of Southern town where time doesn't mean much. Maybe that's because there's little in the way of change between the seasons—the difference between winter and summer a mere fifteen degrees on average. And when you're as poor as most folks in Flyjar, there isn't a whole lot of difference between one decade and another—or century, for that matter.

The two constants in Flyjar are poverty and the river. The town clings to the Mississippi like a child to its mama's skirt, and its fortunes—for good or ill—have been tied to the Big Muddy tighter than apron strings. At one time it had served as fueling stop for the riverboats that once traveled up and down The Father of All Waters. But those days were long gone, and all that remained of "the good old days" were some deteriorating wooden piers along the riverbanks.

Since most of the wharves extended several hundred feet into the river, there were plenty of crappies, channel cat and garfish free for the taking, provided you had the know-how and patience to catch them, as Sammy Herkimer, one of Flyjar's better fishermen, was quick to tell anyone who'd listen.

There were several docks to choose from, but Sammy's favorite was the one at Steamboat Bend. It was a mile or so from town and, because of that, was not in the best of shape. Since that meant keeping an eye on where you walked, not many of the locals used it, which suited Sammy just fine. Then one day, while he was sitting on the dock, sipping iced tea from a thermos, he was surprised to find himself joined by, of all people, Hop Armstrong.

Hop was the closest thing Flyjar had to a fancy man, since the good Lord had seen fit to bless him with good looks, but had skimped in the ambition department. When it came to playing guitar and getting women to pay his way, Hop was second to none. But when it came to physical labor...well, that was another story.

"Lord A' mighty, Hop!" Sammy proclaimed, unable to hide his surprise. "What you doin' here? Someone set fire to your house?"

"You could say that," Hop grunted. "My woman said I had to bring home supper."

"That a fact?" Sammy said, raising an eyebrow.

Hop's most recent sugar mama was Lucinda Solomon, the proprietoress of the local beauty parlor. Lucinda was a good-looking and well-to-do, at least by Flyjar's standards. She was also notoriously strong-willed, and rumor had it that in living off Lucinda, Hop had finally met up with something approximating hard work.

Sammy glanced at the younger man's gear, noting with some amusement that while Hop had remembered to bring along his guitar, he hadn't bothered to pack a net. He returned his gaze to the river, shaking his head. After a long stretch of silence between the two, the older man spoke up abruptly.

"You know why they call this stretch of the river Steamboat Bend, Hop?"

"I figgered on account of it bein' a bend in the river and there was steamboats that used to come down it," he replied with a shrug.

"That's part of it, but it ain't the whole reason. A long time ago there was this big ole paddleboat that used to cruise up and down the river called *Delta Blossom*. She was a real fancy pleasure boat, with marble mantelpieces and crystal chandeliers and gold door-handles. When folks heard Delta *Blossom* was coming, they ran from the houses and fields to watch her pass. Anyways, one day, without any warning, *Delta Blossom* went down with all hands right about there," Sammy said, gesturing towards the middle of the river.

"Why did she sink?" Hop asked, a tinge of interest seeping into his voice.

"No one's rightly sure. Some said the boilers blew out th' side of the boat. Some said there was a fire below decks. Maybe it got its hull punched open by a submerged tree. Who can really know, after all this time? But my old granny used to swear up and down that *Delta Blossom* was scuttled by catfish gals."

Hop scowled at the older man. "You funnin' with me, ain't you, Sammy."

"No, sir, I ain't!" he said solemnly, shaking his head for emphasis. "Before there was any white or black folk, or even Indians living in these parts, there was catfish gals here. They live in the river, down where it's muddy and deep. They got the upper-parts of women and from the waist down are big ole channel cats. They keep their distance from humans, and, for the most part, are peaceful enough. Some folks said the catfish gals sank the *Delta Blossom* on account of one of them gettin' caught in the paddlewheel and crushed."

KNUCKLES AND TALES: CATFISH GAL BLUES

Hop turned to fix the older man with a curious stare. "You ever *seen* one of them catfish gals, Sammy?"

"No, I ain't. But I ain't gone lookin' for them, neither. But my granny said they was why no one ever finds folks who are fool enough to go swimmin' in the river. They take the drowned bodies and stick 'em deep in the mud, until they get all blote up. That way their flesh is easier to eat…"

Hop grimaced. "Hush up about that! Its bad enough my woman's got me out here without you goin' on about catfish eatin' daid folks!

"Sorry. I didn't realize you was sensitive on the subject." After another stretch of silence, Sammy nodded towards the guitar. "So—if you're here to fish, why the git-box?"

"Man can do more than one thing at a time, can't he?"

"I reckon so—but I don't recommend it. You'll scare off the fish."

"Mebbe I'll just charm me a catfish gal instead," Hop grinned.

"If anyone could, I reckon it'd be you, " Sammy sighed as he reeled in his line. "Well, I caught me enough for one day. I better get on home so's I can clean this mess of crappies in time for supper. Good luck on charming them catfish gals, Hop. Y'all take care."

"Y'all too, Sammy," Hop replied absently, his gaze fixed on the river.

o o o

Hop had to admit that being out in the sunshine on a day like today wasn't all that bad. It wasn't too hot and there was a nice breeze coming off the water…plus, there was the added advantage of being out of his woman's line-of-sight.

Lucinda was far from an easy woman to please, and an even harder one to live with when riled. And she was most always riled. Hop knew the signs well enough by now to realize that his days of leisure at the feisty Miz Solomon's expense were drawing to their close, but he didn't like to jump ship unless he had a new girlfriend lined up. Unfortunately, for a man of his tastes and inclinations, Flyjar didn't have much in the way of available lady folk for him to choose from—so it looked like was going to have to make do with Lucinda for awhile longer. At least Steamboat Bend was remote enough that the chances of Lucinda actually finding how hard he was—or wasn't—working at making sure there would be supper on the table come sundown were in his favor.

Hop pulled a forked stick from his tackle box and wedged it between the loose planks of the dock. After baiting the hook, he cast the line into the murky waters and propped the reel against the stick. Keeping one eye on the bobber, Hop leaned against the nearby wooden pylon and picked up his guitar.

There was not a time in his memory where music didn't come easy to him. Ever since he was knee-high, he'd been able to make a guitar do whatever it was he wanted of it. It's pretty much the same with women, too. Playing guitar came as natural to him as breathing and eating—and felt a lot more pleasant than chopping cotton or driving a tractor.

Hop scanned the deceptively calm surface of the river. It was so wide the current's strength was difficult to gauge with the naked eye. The only way to figure out just how powerful the river truly was by the size of the driftwood and the speed at which it went past. There were days when full-grown oak trees raced one another to the Gulf of Mexico. Today was relatively placid, with only a few deadfalls the size of railroad ties headed down river.

Hop found his mind turning once again to the story Sammy had told him. Not about the catfish gals—that was pure hokum if ever he heard it. What piqued his imagination was the *Delta Blossom*. Hop wondered what it must have been like back in those days, when the steamboats cruised the river, bringing glamour and wealth to pissant little towns like Flyjar.

To think that one of the grandest of the old paddle wheelers had come to its end a stone's throw from where he was sitting, taking its entire splendor to the Mississippi's silty floor. All Hop had ever seen gracing the river were flat-bottomed barges and the occasional freighter or small leisure craft. These were hardly the kinds of boats that sparked the imagination and quickened the heart. Folks didn't flock to the levees just to watch a barge pass by.

Hop wondered if there was still anything left of the old *Delta Blossom* at the bottom of Steamboat Bend. There was no way to know. What secrets the river held it did not give up readily. Still, it didn't keep him from idly hoping to spot the sunken pleasure ship's outline.

In his mind's eye, he could see the long-lost floating pleasure palace, white as new cotton with towering double-smokestack puffing away like a rich man's cigars as she made her way along the Mississippi. He could picture the southern belles in hoop skirts lining the ship's second story promenade, silk fans fluttering like caged birds, while riverboat gamblers in pristine linen suits and wide-brimmed hats tossed silver dollars and gold-pieces onto the felt of the gaming tables. Hop saw himself dressed like Clark Gable in *Gone With The Wind*, tipping his hat

KNUCKLES AND TALES: CATFISH GAL BLUES

to the young ladies of fashion gathered in the Delta Blossom's grand salon for the evening's entertainment. What a swath he could have cut back then!

As his well-dressed phantom-self began to dance underneath the swaying crystal chandeliers with a young woman who looked a great deal like Vivienne Leigh, Hop's nimble fingers were quick to provide the music. Granted, *Goodnight Irene* wasn't around at the time, but it was his daydream, after all, wasn't it?

As he played, a sudden movement in the middle of the river caught Hop's eye. From where he was sitting, it looked as if a swimmer had surfaced in the middle of the bend, near where Sammy said the *Delta Blossom* had gone down, then just as quickly submerged. But that was impossible.

Swimming in the Mississippi was only slightly less hazardous to your health than brushing your teeth with lit dynamite. Every so often some fool would get drunk enough to try and swim the river—and disappear without a trace ten feet from shore. If the family were lucky, the body would turn up a few days later, fifty miles down stream, snagged in the branches of a tree on the flood plain, looking more like a drowned pig than a human being. But what Hop saw hadn't looked anything like a floater popping to the surface. For one thing, it stayed in one place and didn't follow the current. Hop shaded his eyes against the sun, trying to get a better look, but there was nothing there. His attention was brought back closer to shore as the bobber on his line registered a strike. Hop dropped his guitar and snatched up the fishing rod, reeling in a ten-pound catfish.

It looked like Lucinda wasn't going to have anything to scold him about tonight that much was for certain.

But as he headed back home, his fishing pole draped over one shoulder and his guitar slung over the other, Hop couldn't shake the feeling that he was being watched—and by something besides the catfish hanging from his belt.

o o o

That night as he was lying in bed, Lucinda snoring beside him, Hop got to thinking.

Maybe what Sammy Herkimer said about catfish gals wasn't all hogwash after all. He remembered reading in one of them yellow-backed magazines down at the barber shop about some kind of fish everyone thought was extinct being found in some foreign country a few years back. Besides, who was he to decide there weren't no such things as catfish gals, when he didn't know a soul who'd been to the bottom of the Mississippi and lived to tell the tale?

The very next day Hop went fishing without Lucinda telling him to.

He decided to try his luck again at Steamboat Bend. When he arrived at the dock, he was relieved to find he was alone. Hop set himself up on the dock just as he had the day before, but after a half- hour of sitting and waiting for something to happen, he put down the fishing rod and picked up his guitar to pass the time.

Halfway into *"Moanin' at Midnight"*, Hop heard what sounded like a fish slap the water near the pier. When he glanced up to see what had caused the noise, what he saw caused him to nearly drop his guitar into the water below.

There was a human head bobbing in the water a hundred feet away from the dock. At the sound of his astonished gasp, the head ducked back down beneath the muddy surface without leaving so much as a ripple to mark its passing. Just as suddenly, there was a strike on Hop's line so powerful it nearly yanked his fishing pole into the river.

o o o

Although Lucinda was extremely pleased with the fifteen-pound catfish he brought home that evening, Hop didn't say anything about what he'd seen on the river. Something told him that whatever it was that was out at Steamboat Bend was best kept to himself.

The next day Hop didn't even bother casting his line into the river. He knew what was drawing the thing in the river to the dock, and it sure as hell wasn't the shiners he was using for bait.

He made his way to the very end of the landing, careful to avoid the loose and missing planks, and sat so his legs dangled over the edge. After a moment of deliberation, he decided *"They Call Me Muddy Waters"* would be an appropriate choice.

Just like before, the thing surfaced halfway through the song. Hop's heart was racing so fast it was hard to breathe, but he forced himself to keep playing. He didn't want to scare it off, so he kept playing, switching to *"Pony Blues"* once he'd finished with his first song.

While he played, Hop kept his head down, ignoring his audience as best he could. As he launched into *"Circle Round the Moon"* he risked glancing in the thing's direction, only to discover it was almost directly underneath his dangling feet, staring at him with big, dark eyes that seemed to be all pupil.

KNUCKLES AND TALES: CATFISH GAL BLUES

Hop was surprised at how human the catfish gal looked. From what Sammy had said, he'd pictured a fish in a fright wig, but that wasn't the case. Hell, he'd seen worse looking women in church.

Her upper lip was extremely wide, with the familiar whiskers growing out of them, and she had slits instead of a nose, but outside of that she wasn't *too* ugly. Her hair was a real mess, though, with everything from twigs to what looked like live minnows caught in the tangled locks. He couldn't see much of what she looked like below the waterline, although he did glimpse vertical slits opening and closing down the sides of her neck.

Hop couldn't help but smile to himself when he saw how the catfish gal looked at him. Half-fish or not, he knew what that look meant on a woman's face. He had her hooked but good and now was as good a time as any to reel her in

Hop looked the catfish gal right in the eye and smiled. "Hello, lit'l fishie. You come to hear me play?"

The catfish gal's dreamy look was replaced by one of surprise. She glanced around, as if confused by her surroundings, then shot backwards like a dolphin walking on its tail.

"Please! Don't go!" he shouted, stretching out one hand to stay her retreat.

To his surprise, the catfish gal came to a sudden halt, regarding him curiously, bobbing up and down in the Mississippi, as easily as a young girl treading water in a swimming pool.

"You ain't got nothin' to be scared of, lit'l fishie," Hop said, smiling reassuringly. "I ain't gonna hurt you none. Do you want me to play some more for you?" he asked, holding up his guitar.

The catfish gal nodded and lifted a dripping arm and pointed at the guitar with a webbed forefinger. Hop smiled and obliged her by picking up where he had left off on *"Goin' Down Slow"*.

By the time the sun was starting to go down, Hop's hands were cramping and his fingertips bloody. He'd played a little bit of almost everything –blues, bluegrass, honky tonk, camp songs, even a couple of nursery songs—trying to figure out what the catfish gal liked and didn't like: turned out she was partial to the blues—which made sense, seeing how the blues was born on the banks of the Mississippi.

When he finally put aside his guitar, the catfish gal disappeared beneath the river's muddy surface. A few seconds later a large catfish came flying out of the water as if shot from a sling and landed on the dock beside him. Hop picked up the floundering fish and shook his head.

"I appreciate the thought," he said loudly. "But this ain't what I'm lookin' for." After he tossed the fish back into the water, Hop reached into his pocket and pulled out a silver dollar, which he held up between his thumb and forefinger, so that it caught the sun's fading rays. "If you want me to keep playin', you got to feed th' kitty. And this here is what the kitty eats."

The catfish gal popped back to the surface, stared at the gleaming coin for a long second, then submerged again. Hop shifted about uneasily as first one minute, then another elapsed without any sign of the catfish gal. Maybe he pushed his luck a little too far too early…

Something heavy and wet struck his chest then dropped to the deck with a metallic sound. Hop picked up the flat, circular piece of slime-encrusted metal at his feet with trembling fingers. He scraped the surface with his thumbnail and was rewarded not by the gleam of silver—but the mellow shine of gold.

He gave out a whoop then looked around to see if anyone might have witnessed his good fortune, but he was alone on the landing, at least as far as human company was concerned. Talk about falling in a honey pot!

And all for the price of a song.

o o o

As summer wore on, Hop Armstrong became a regular visitor to Steamboat Bend, showing up early and staying till late, and always leaving with heavy, if somewhat damp, pockets. On those occasions Sammy Herkimer was fishing off the dock, Hop was forced to wait the old angler out, but for the most part he didn't have to worry about being found out.

At first Lucinda had been suspicious of his newfound interest in fishing, but since he never came back smelling of perfume or wearing another woman's shade of lipstick on his collar, she eventually accepted his pastime as genuine. Of course, Lucinda had no way of knowing about the Folgers can full of old gold and silver coins he had stashed out in the garage, or of the bag of gold door-knobs hidden in the woodpile behind the house. Hop didn't see any need to tell her about his new found wealth, because that would lead to her asking him where he got it from, and then where would he be then?

If he told Lucinda about the catfish gal, every man, woman and child in Flyjar would be lined up on the dock playing everything from a banjo to a Jew's harp trying to muscle in on his gig. The way Hop saw it, there was no call for him to ruin a good thing before he had to.

KNUCKLES AND TALES: CATFISH GAL BLUES

Once there weren't any more goodies coming his way from Lit'l Fishie, as he called her, he planned to take his Folgers can full of antique coins and gunnysack of doorknobs and head off to the big city—say Jackson or Greenville. Hell, he might even go as far as New Orleans—maybe even Biloxi! He didn't really care where he ended up, just as long as it was some place where the women were prettier and younger than those in Flyjar, and you could buy beer on Sundays. Judging from how Lit'l Fishie was behaving during his more recent serenades, something told him it wouldn't be long before things dried up on her end, so to speak.

She kept swinging back and forth between acting skittish—disappearing every time a bullfrog croaked—and making kiss-kiss noises with that saddlebag mouth of hers. Hop might not know much, but he sure as hell knew women, and Lit'l Fishie was showing all the signs of a sugar mama running short on cash.

As he set out for Steamboat Bend that day, Hop decided it was going to be his last serenade for the catfish gal—and his final day as a citizen of Flyjar. Now that he'd found his fortune, it was time for him to strike out into the world and collect his fame.

o o o

Hop scanned the sky, frowning at the approaching clouds. It had rained off and on since sunrise, and there were puddles all along the rutted cow path that was the only road that lead to the derelict landing at Steamboat Bend. As much as he disliked tramping through the mud, going out on foul-weather days meant he didn't have to worry about anyone snooping around.

Tightening his grip on his guitar strap, Hop hurried down the levee embankment and onto the deserted dock's wooden surface. He sat down on the end of the pier, as he always did, dangling his legs over the open water, and began to play *"See My Grave Is Kept Clean"*.

Normally Lit'l Fishie broke surface about fifty yards away the moment he started to play then moved in until she was staring up at him like a snake-tranced bird. Hop knew that look all too well. He saw it all the time in the eyes of the women whenever he played at the juke joints. He knew that if he said the word, Lit'l Fishie would roll in cornmeal and gladly throw herself in a red-hot frying pan.

He finished with the Blind Lemon and started into Leadbelly, but the catfish gal had yet to put in an appearance. Hop frowned. Maybe she couldn't hear him. He didn't really know where she lived, exactly, but he was under the impression she didn't stray that far from the Bend. He changed from Leadbelly to Son House, on the off hand chance that she didn't care for *Cotton Fields*. When Lit'l Fishie still didn't show herself, Hop's frown deepened even further. It was time to pull out the stops. He began to play one of her favorites: *Up Jumped the Devil*.

There was a bubbling sound directly below where he was sitting. Hop smiled knowingly at the shape lurking just below the murky water lapping against the pylon. Robert Johnson worked like a charm on women—whether they were two-legged or had gills.

"Why you so shy all of a sudden, darlin'?" he called out. "Why don't you show me that sweet face of yours?"

The bubbles at the end of the pier grew more intense, as if the water was boiling. Hop scowled and leaned forward, staring down between his dangling feet at the muddy water below.

"Lit'l Fishie—is that you?"

There was less than a heartbeat between the moment the thing with bumpy skin and gaping mouth filled with jagged teeth leapt from the water and when its powerful jaws snapped closed on Hop's legs. He was only able to scream just the once—a high, almost womanly shriek—before he was yanked, guitar and all, into the river.

The last thing Hop saw, before the silty waters of the Mississippi closed over him, was the catfish gal watching him drown, a sorrowful expression in her bruised eyes.

o o o

When Hop Armstrong went out fishing and never came back, most folks in Flyjar were of the opinion he'd found himself a new girlfriend and left Lucinda for greener pastures. A smaller group thought the handsome ne'er do well had gotten drunk and fallen through the dilapidated dock into the river below. In any case, no one really gave a good god damn, and after a couple of weeks there were other things to talk about down at the barber shop.

About three months after Hop disappeared, Sammy Herkimer snagged his line on something underneath the pier at Steamboat Bend. At first he thought he was just caught it on some waterlogged reeds. But when he reeled his line back in, he found Hop's git-box hanging off the other end.

KNUCKLES AND TALES: CATFISH GAL BLUES

The guitar that had charmed so many ladies out of their drawers and their life's savings was now dripping slime; it's neck splintered and body badly chewed up. Sammy shook his head as he freed the mangled instrument. He really wasn't surprised by what he'd found. In a way, he blamed himself for what happened to poor Hop. After all, when he'd told him about the catfish gals, he'd forgot to mention they weren't the *only* critters that made Steamboat Bend their home.

One thing about them gator boys: they sure are jealous.

BIG EASY

"Hurry! Hurry! Hurry! See Big Easy the Gator Boy! He swims and dives like no man alive! See him devour a fish with one snap of his mighty jaws! He hisses! He growls! He crawls on his belly like a rep-tile! Is he man or is he beast? You make the call! See Big Easy, the Amazing Gator Boy, for the astonishing low-low-low price of one dollar! Four quarters! Ten dimes! One hundred pennies! A Marvel of the Ages! The Lost Wonder of the World! Don't miss a once-in-a lifetime chance to feast your eyes on the One-and-Only Gator Boy! Hurry! Hurry! Hurry! "

The Colonel paused in his spiel to take a breath and mop his dripping brow. The Cotton King Carnival in Memphis was one of their big moneymakers, but as he grew older, the heat and humidity seemed to grow more and more oppressive with each passing year.

He glanced over his shoulder at the canvas stretched behind the bally platform. There wasn't even enough of a breeze to make the belly dancer's banner shimmy. The Colonel fished a flask from his seersucker suit and knocked back a quick slug. Five Roses wouldn't help with the heat, but it certainly tamed the twitch in his hands.

Most of the acts in the ten-in-one were as authentic as his claim to the title of Colonel. Fire-eaters, pain-proof men, snake-charming belly dancers, even the midgets and the six-legged cow were nothing nowadays. Hell, most of the yokels trawling the midway had as many tattoos as ol' Picture Pete. Easy was the only reason they were still able to land bookings like this one while their competitors had long since bottomed out. Even though most of the marks, and even fellow showmen, thought Easy was a gaffe, there was no denying that the Gator Boy was boffo. Real or not, you just didn't see acts like Big Easy everyday.

The Colonel glanced down from his elevated perch at the ticket booth at a pair of suckers staring slack-jawed at the canvas banners arranged along the length of the tent. They were dressed in matching Harley Davidson tank tops and sunburned pinker than the cotton candy the girl chewed like a sugared cud.

"The Amazin' Gator Boy?" the man read aloud, not without difficulty. He wore a more worldly expression on his pockmarked face, along with a gimme cap on his head that sported the name 'Jimbo'. "I bet its just some weirdo with bad skin, like that Human Crocodile I seen at the State Fair in Nashville."

"My good sir!" The Colonel replied indignantly, slapping his bamboo cane against the banner so hard it sounded a lion tamer's whip. "I'll have you know that Big Easy is not some unfortunate afflicted with the "heartbreak of psoriasis", as Madison Avenue has so politely phrased it! No, the Gator Boy is unlike any human oddity to ever grace the midway—even during the golden age of the great P.T. Barnum! He is the sole survivor of an ancient race of beast-men! Captured and brought to civilization at great danger and expense for your edification and enlightenment!"

The couple exchanged glances and after a moment's hesitation, Jimbo shoved his hand into his pocket and brought out two crumpled dollars.

"I still say its just some feller with bad skin—but what the hell, I'll take a peek, anyways."

o o o

The interior of the ten-in-one had a floor of straw and sawdust, with the individual acts presented on raised platforms separated from one another by canvas walls. There were a couple of acrobatic dwarves who called themselves The Tumble Bugs, a tattooed man named Picture Pete who also doubled as a blockhead and fire-eater, a bearded fat lady whose stage name was Hairy Etta, and a handful of similar novelty acts.

The Gator Boy, however, occupied an area in the back of the tent usually reserved for the blow-off. Befitting his star status, Big Easy's performance space was three times that of the others, and there was even a set of wooden bleachers for the audience. The seats were arranged before a large platform with what looked like an aboveground pool fashioned of metal panels with glass panels the size of picture windows set into them. Wooden ramps on the far side of the tank lead to a wide-bodied fiberglass slide, and to one side of the tank was a workman's ladder, atop which rested a Styrofoam cooler. As the audience took their seats, the Colonel stepped out from behind the curtains at the back of the stage.

KNUCKLES AND TALES: BIG EASY

"Now, ladies and gentlemen, we have reached the part of the show for which you have all waited most patiently! But before we begin, allow me to explain to you how such an enigma of the ages happened to fall into my humble hands! Thirty years ago, a Cajun fisherman trawling the bayous of the Mississippi Delta caught something in one of his nets. It was heavier than anything he's ever snared before, and fought like a demon as he struggled to pull it into his boat. At first the fisherman thought he had caught a huge catfish, or a giant gar, both of which have been known to grow to hundreds of pounds. But, imagine his shock and horror when he finally wrestled his catch aboard his tiny boat—only to discover it was no fish—but what looked to be a child! Yet, this was no drowned little boy! No—it was very much alive—and far from human! It had scaly skin, sharp teeth, webbed hands and feet, and eyes that glowed red in the dim light! The frightened fisherman realized that what he had unwittingly captured was a Gator Boy—one of the legendary creatures that have haunted the swamps and bayous of the Mississippi since before Atlantis was lost to the waves!"

"Big Easy is the last vestige of a mighty race that walked the Earth when the dinosaurs roamed free and wild and Mankind was nothing more than an insignificant, shrew-like creature, cowering in their awesome shadow! These shadowy lizard-men were both gods and demons to the ancient Caddo tribes who built the mysterious burial mounds that line the waterways that feed into the Mississippi Delta—some say in imitation of the nest-cities of the Gator Men, hidden deep with a haunted lost bayou!"

Jimbo, seated closest to the tank, blew a raspberry then snickered.

"Laugh if you like," The Colonel warned. "But once you have seen the Gator Boy—it is a sight you will not soon forget!" With a dramatic flourish of his cane, the Colonel turned and gestured to the heavy velvet curtains behind him, his voice booming forth like an Old Testament patriarch's. "Ladiezzzz and Gentlemennnn—Behold! The One! The Only! Big Easy—The Amazing Gator Boy!"

The curtains parted and out stepped a large, square-shouldered figure dressed in a hooded silk dressing robe, like a boxer entering the ring. The Colonel stepped towards the very edge of the platform, his demeanor archly serious.

"If there is anyone in this audience who suffers from a nervous condition, heart ailments, or is in the family way, the management of Red Lion Midway Amusement strongly suggests that they vacate the premises now, as they refuse responsibility for whatever breakdowns, seizures or birth defects that might occur as a result of viewing the Gator Boy in his natural state!"

That was Easy's cue to slip out of the robe while simultaneously pushing back its hood, revealing his face to the audience. The crowd gasped, as they always did.

The Gator Boy was not just bald, but genuinely hairless. No eyelashes, no eyebrows—not even nose hairs. His skin was thick and covered with heavy scales the color of fresh mud. He raised his arms and spread his fingers, displaying the thick webbing between the phalanges, then made a slow, shuffling turn, so the marks could see the knobby crest that started at the back of his head and ran down the length of his spine, disappearing into his black swim trunks. When he was once again facing the crowd, Easy flashed them a smile, displaying jagged, razor-sharp fangs.

A woman near the back of the tent voiced a small, sharp cry of genuine horror. Easy ignored it. Cries of shock and revulsion were as much a part of his daily life as birdsong. The Colonel jumped to fill the uncomfortable silence that always followed Easy's unveiling, filling it with his showman's ballyhoo.

"The fisherman who caught the Gator Boy did not know what to do with his find. He was both uncertain of keeping it, yet fearful of setting it loose. So he brought his strange find to a nearby carnival—and as fortune would have it, I was the one he bargained with! The price was dear—but well worth the investment, as you can well see!"

Following the second cue, Easy trudged up the inclined ramp to the top of the slide, pausing at the top to allow the gaping audience as good a look as their one-dollar ticket allowed. Then, with surprising speed, given the painful, arthritic movements it had taken to climb the slide, he threw himself belly-first on the slide's downward slope, tucking his arms tight against his side, and slid with a resounding splash into the water below, sending a huge wave over the lip of the tank, soaking the paying customers closest to the tank.

Upon making contact with the water, Easy went into his aquatic routine, performing backward somersaults and corkscrew backstrokes, all while completely submerged. The audience held its collective breath as they leaned forward to watch him through the glass walls of the tank. Despite his grotesque appearance and ungainly manner on land, there was a balletic grace to the Gator Boy's underwater movements.

The Colonel moved to the ladder propped against the tank and began to climb the rungs while addressing the audience. "When the

KNUCKLES AND TALES: BIG EASY

Gator Boy first came into my possession, he walked on all fours. It took years of careful training and immense patience on my part to teach him to stand erect. Even now, his gait is still awkward, like that of a child just learning to walk. He eats nothing but raw flesh—preferably fish, although he has been known to consume frogs, snakes and the occasional turtle—as you will witness for yourself!"

The Colonel opened the lid on the Styrofoam cooler and withdrew a ten-pound bass from a bed of ice cubes. With a practiced flick of his wrist, he tossed the dripping fish into the tank. Easy shot straight up and caught the bass in a webbed hand before it could strike the water. There was a collective gasp, followed by applause, which quickly turned to squeals of terror as Easy grasped the lip of the tank and pulled himself upright so that he was clearly visible to the paying customers.

Brandishing the fish like an oversized cigar, he quickly snapped off its head with his bared teeth then he swallowed it with one neat snap of his jaws. The Colonel glanced down at the crowd and was rewarded by the sight of Jimbo's sunburned face turning pale. The fish gag was what made the rubes come back, time and again, dragging along their sisters and their brothers and their cousins by the dozens.

Before he could launch into the final patter, The Colonel felt an invisible hand reach into his chest and squeeze his heart like a ripe tomato and he toppled headlong into the Gator Boy' tank. The audience, thinking it was part of the act, started to laugh and clap their hands, until the Gator Boy exploded to the surface, clutching the spluttering, ashen-faced Colonel in his scaly arms.

"*Get the doc!*" Easy bellowed, his throat sac making his voice to boom like a kettledrum.

The stagehand looked almost as stunned as the audience then ran to fetch the carny doctor.

As he struggled to keep the dying man afloat, the Gator Boy turned his lambent gaze on the gawking rubes perched on the bleachers. "*What are you looking at?*" he roared "*Show's over!*"

o o o

A large, shadowy figure stood at the end of one of the docks lining Memphis' riverfront. During Cotton Carnival it was not uncommon to find people enjoying an evening stroll or watching the muddy waters roll their way towards the Gulf of Mexico. However, the stranger's winter-length coat and wide-brimmed felt hat were more than a bit unusual, given the time of year.

But if anyone was staring at him, the stranger did not notice. After all, being stared at was his business.

Everyone was so used to bunkum and hokum from the talkers that it never once occurred to them—not even Easy himself—that the Colonel had been giving them the straight dope the whole time. Or straight enough.

As the old showman gasped out his last few breaths in his star attraction's arms, he had finally come clean with him. Back in 1970, when the show was pitched near Vicksburg, a local showed up with something to sell. The yokel was frightened by what he had in his possession—but not so scared he couldn't see dollar signs.

The Colonel followed the yokel out to his truck and looked at what was tied up in the back. The Colonel, ever the sharpie, managed to convince the fisherman that all he had was a freak alligator and paid him three hundred bucks to take it of his hands. Even if the fisherman didn't know what he was looking at, the Colonel sure as hell did. The minute he laid eyes on him, he saw easy green. Hence the origin of Easy's name.

As to Easy's origins, the old showman had his suspicions, which he passed along as he lay dying. As a boy he had grown up along the river, listening to folk tales handed down from the settlers, who got them from the slaves, who learned them from the Indians who first dwelt in the bayous and swamps of the delta. He remembered the stories about the catfish gals and the gator boys, and how they held cotillions on the bottom of the river during the full of the moon. Were the stories true? Who was to say? But what else could explain something like Big Easy the Gator Boy?

As the only person he had ever trusted and relied on died in his arms, Easy decided it was time to leave the world of carnies and the rubes and return to the murky world that had spawned him. The Colonel had raised him to stick to his decisions, no matter what. There was no going back...only forward motion from here on in.

Easy took off his hat and sailed it into the river. When he yanked on the lapels of his coat, it sent the buttons flying like tiddly-winks. With a flex of his powerful legs, he dove straight into the waiting Mississippi. Someone on the shore called out in alarm, mistaking him for a suicide.

The undertow caught him instantly. Had he been a human, he would have been dead within moments, instead of surfacing almost a half-mile from where he first entered the water. He spotted a small group of passersby gathered on the dock, shaking their heads in bewilderment. Easy's jaws constricted in what passed for a smile.

KNUCKLES AND TALES: BIG EASY

The journey would not be without dangers. He had not navigated open water since he was a child. There were submerged snags that could snare and drown him, not to mention the propellers of pleasure craft and the churning blades of the giant barges that traveled the river. He glanced up at the moon, hanging three-quarters full in the muggy night sky. If the current was with him, he might even make the cotillion on time.

o o o

The Steelhead was a wide, squat, ugly muscle of a ship. Its job was to push cargo, in this case sealed containers of tractor parts, down river to the New Orleans docks, where they were to be lifted onto a freighter bound for Europe. No, *The Steelhead* wasn't a flashy vessel, but she knew her job and performed it beautifully. It was that homely strength that attracted Bill to life on the river in the first place.

This was only his second trip as a working hand on a barge, so he did not have the indifference to his surroundings that his fellow shipmates shared. While the others spent their off-hours playing cards or watching television, he preferred to stroll the decks and keep an eye out for local fauna. Having grown up in suburbia, he still experienced a thrill of discovery whenever he glimpsed deer grazing on the levees or piles of turtles sunning themselves on driftwood.

As *The Steelhead* slowly made her way around a bend in the river, he lifted the binoculars to check for sandbars. He spotted one located just outside the mouth of a tributary on the opposite shore. It was too small and out-of-the way to be a hazard to the barge, but there was something about it that seemed odd. With a start, he realized he was looking at what must be a family of wild alligators sunning themselves on the wet sand.

A deep, strong, bass voice abruptly boomed forth. Bill craned his head to look at Joe, who was standing watch atop the bridge, only to find his shipmate looking down at him with an equally quizzical look on his face.

"Did you sing out?" Joe called down to him.

"No! I thought it was you!"

Joe shrugged. "The Mississippi's strange that way. The old timers say sometimes you can hear the ghosts of old river captains, calling out the soundings."

Bill nodded without saying anything, then glanced back in the direction of the sandbar. The gators were gone, apparently frightened by the approaching barge. As green as he was, even he knew that sailors, whether they navigate salt water or fresh, see and hear things no landlocked soul would ever dream of. So spectral riverboat pilots shouting out warnings from beyond the grave wasn't that hard to accept.

But whoever heard of a river ghost yelling *"Hey Rube?"*

BILLY FEARLESS

Lester McKraken was a miller who lived in the town of Monkey's Elbow, Kentucky, which is somewhere's near Possum Trot, which is a hundred miles north of Paducah, more or less.

Now Lester had himself two sons he had to raise on his own when his wife fell to her death after the neighbor kids moved the McKraken outhouse back ten feet one moonless night. The older of the two boys was a fine young figure of a man, with a good head on his shoulders and a strong back and the gumption to make something of himself. The younger boy was—well, let's just say he was Billy.

Now, there weren't nothing seriously wrong with Billy upstairs. He wasn't feeble-minded, not like the washerwoman's young'un. It's just that Billy, well, Billy tended to take things at face value, regardless of the face. I guess you could say he lacked imagination, more that anything else. Old Lester saw it as a case of being mule-stupid. And maybe he was right. But one of the strange side effects of Billy's thick-headedness was that the boy was immune to fear.

From the day he learned to crawl, Billy was always getting himself into some fix or another, like the time he came home leading a dog on a leash thinking it was in need of a shave because of the foam on its jaws. It wasn't long before his schoolmates were coming up with all kinds of outlandish tasks to try out on him, which Billy would dutifully perform. By the time he was nine years old he'd gotten the nickname of "Billy Fearless", which most folks called him more than his rightful name of McKraken. Much to Old Man McKraken's relief.

Billy's father had tried his best to school the boy in common sense. When Billy was no bigger than a grasshopper he told him that there were things he should never do, for fear of his life.

"How will I know when I should be scared, daddy?"

"You'll know you're scared of something if it gives you a shudder."

Unfortunately, Billy didn't know what a shudder was. He was under the impression it was something not very nice, but he wasn't sure. He was afraid to ask his father for fear of the old man's temper, so he never did find out.

When Billy turned sixteen he was put out of school, like most boys his age. Billy figured he'd end up working at the mill, just like his elder brother had before him. But Old Man McKraken, while he loved his son, as a father should, had pretty much worn out his worrying bone on Billy. He figured it would be better if his younger son found himself employment somewheres beside the mill. So Billy went knocking door to door, looking for work. When no one wanted to hire him in Monkey's Elbow, he walked the ten miles to Possum Trot and knocked on doors there.

One door he knocked on belonged to the town gravedigger, a fellow by the name of Shanks. Shanks looked Billy over and saw that he was young and strong and eager to work. But he also knew that even strong men often turned weak when it came to digging graves in a lonely cemetery late at night.

"You seem to be a right enough sort," Shanks said. "But I have to ask you one thing before I can hire you—are you skeered of ghosts?"

Billy blinked and thought and blinked again. "Ain't never seen a ghost, I reckon."

"Would you be scared if you did see one?"

Billy shrugged. "I don't know."

Shanks wasn't sure if Billy was putting on being brave or was out-and-out lying to him, so he decided he would test the boy to discover the truth. Later that afternoon he handed Billy a shovel, a pick and a Coleman lantern and pointed to the most remote section of the cemetery, where the grave markers were old and leaned at strange angles.

"Billy, I just got word from Reverend McPherson that there's to be a funeral the day after tomorrow. I need you to dig me a grave six long and six deep over yonder, near the weepy willow. I have to go to town to see to some business and I might not be back til the morning. I want you to work on that grave until midnight, understand?"

"Yes, sir, Mr. Shanks," replied Billy. And without any word or complaint, the boy took up his tools and set off to do as he was told.

Shanks went into town and sat at the local bar, drinking with a couple of his friends until it got dark. Then he snuck back to the cemetery, where he dressed himself in a cast-off shroud and whitened his face, hair and hands with flour. Then he snuck out to where he could see the light from Billy's lantern.

It was very dark and the night air crisp with the coming autumn as the gravedigger darted from gravestone to gravestone. The cemetery smelled of dead leaves and lichen, with the ever-present odor of rot

KNUCKLES AND TALES: BILLY FEARLESS

lurking just under the surface. Somewhere up in the weepy willow an old hoot owl cried out. Shanks had to bite back a drunken laugh as he thought of how frightened the new boy was going to be when he laid eyes on him, white and ghostly, standing on the edge of the freshly-dug grave. As he reached the plot where Billy was working, he could see that the grave was almost finished. Indeed, Billy—smeared with dirt and sweat—was in the act of boosting himself out of the hole. Shanks waited until the boy was reaching in his pocket for a bandanna to wipe the sweat from his face, then stepped out from his hiding place, moaning like a lost soul.

"Ooooohhhhhh!"

Billy looked up from his labors and frowned at the white-faced stranger who stood on the opposite side of the grave he had just dug. "Who's there?' he called out.

"Whooooo!" Shanks replied, waving his arms a little to give his performance a most ghostly effect.

"You better answer me proper or you better git," Billy said, getting to his feet with the aid of his shovel. "You got no business here at this hour, mister."

Shanks wasn't sure whether to be pleased or irked. He'd been expecting the boy to turn white and wet his pants with fear or, at the very least, flee, as any sensible person might do when confronted by a ghost. Still, the boy's bravado might not be as strong as it looked, so he decided to continue his little masquerade.

"Oooouahhh!" Shanks moaned again, shaking imaginary chains at the boy.

"What do you want here?" Billy demanded, this time starting to sound angry. "Speak if you're a honest man, or I'll whup you upside the head!"

Shanks was convinced that Billy's threat was mere bluster, so he stood his ground, waving his arms and moaning and groaning to beat the band. So Billy hefted his shovel and struck him upside the head with the flat of the spade, knocking him into the grave. Billy then packed his tools and headed for the gravedigger's shack to await his employer's return from town so he could show him the nice new grave he'd dug and tell him about the strange fellow who'd pestered him.

The next day there was a knock on Old Man McKraken's door. When he answered it he found Shanks standing on his front porch with a plaster on his head and two black eyes. Sitting in the back of the gravedigger's mule cart was Billy.

"What in tarnation is going on here?" he demanded.

"I'll have you know, McKraken, that boy of yours ain't nothing but bad luck on two legs!" Shanks snarled, wincing as he spoke. "He whopped me on the head with a shovel and left me to lie in an open grave all night long! I'll be lucky if I don't get the rheumatism from the damp!"

Aghast, Old Man McKraken promptly grabbed Billy by the ear and yanked him from the back of the mule cart. "What kind of mischief are you up to boy? The devil must be in you, child, to play such unholy pranks!"

"It weren't my fault, daddy!" explained Billy, fighting back the tears as his father gave his ear another twist. "He stood there in the night, all covered in flour, and wouldn't talk when I asked him to. I thought he was some rascal, out to do me harm—"

Old Man McKraken might have had his doubts about his son's mental strengths, but he knew the boy was incapable of lying. So he gave Shanks five dollars for his trouble and brought the boy back into the house. After a couple of days he called his son to him and sat him down in front of the fire.

"Billy, I'll be blunt, son—while I love you as the flesh of my flesh, I can't take any pride in you. Its time that you went out into the world. I'm giving you fifty dollars cash, a cart and horse, a turning lathe, and a carving bench so you can go forth and master yourself a trade. But tell no one where you come from or who your father is, for I am ashamed of you."

Billy didn't seem to take his father's words badly. He simply shrugged and said; "If that's all you want out of me, daddy, I reckon I can do that."

So that very same day Billy, dressed in overalls and a red flannel shirt, wearing his only pair of brogans, took the fifty dollars, the cart and horse, the turning lathe, and the carving bench
his father had promised him and rode out of Monkey's Elbow, never to be seen again.

During his sixteen years Billy had never gone any farther than Possum Trot. Although he knew there were other towns and villages outside the valley of his birth, he'd never once visited them. He'd also heard tell of other states besides Kentucky, although he had a hard time picturing them. But now, true to his father's wishes, he found himself heading into the world.

By dusk Billy was two valleys away from his home, passing through scenery that was both strange and familiar to him. He came to a cross

KNUCKLES AND TALES: BILLY FEARLESS

roads with a huge oak tree in the middle. As he was tired and his horse weary, Billy decided this was as good a place as any to stop for the night.

Billy made himself a small fire at the base of the tree and set about making himself comfortable for the night. As he ate his simple meal of cheese and bread, he heard a creaking sound coming from the branches over his head. Looking up, he saw a man hanging from his neck by a rope.

"Howdy!" Billy called up to the hanged man.

The hanged man didn't say howdy back.

"It looks to be a chilly night," Billy observed. "Ain't you gonna get cold up there?"

The dead man didn't say anything, but a gust of wind blew him to and fro, making the rope creak all the more.

"Lordy! Look at how you're shaking and shivering!" Billy said. And because he had a good heart, he shinnied up the tree and used his knife to cut the hanged man down and lower the body to the ground, so it could share his fire.

Billy had hoped he would have some company to while away the hours before he fell asleep, but the hanged man didn't seem very appreciative—or talkative. In fact, all he did was stare at Billy with his tongue sticking out black and bloated. He also smelled a tad high and was missing an eye, which looked to have been pecked out by a bird.

"You don't seem to have a lot to say," Billy sighed, poking the fire with a stick.

As if in answer, the one-eyed corpse fell headlong into the fire, setting its hair ablaze.

"Watch out!" Billy cried. When the dead man made no move to pull his head out of the fire, Billy quickly leapt to his feet and yanked the body clear, stomping out the burning hair.

Billy clucked his tongue in reproof, much the same way his father used to do. "Tch! If you can't do no better'n that, friend, I'll put you back up in the tree."

The hanged man just lay there and smoldered, looking the worse for wear after Billy had stomped out the fire. Disgusted, Billy went to sleep.

The next morning the dead man still hadn't moved. Billy had been thinking of offering the stranger a ride to the next town, but decided not to, seeing how unfriendly the fellow had turned out to be. So he hitched his horse back up to its cart and headed on his way.

After traveling most of the day, Billy finally came upon a little town on the edge of a big lake. In the middle of the lake was an island dominated by a huge mansion made of gray stone. It was getting on to late afternoon and Billy was hungry and thirsty and didn't cotton to the idea of spending another night under the chilly stars, so he decided to stop at the inn near the lake.

The sign over the door said The Ghost Lake Tavern. When he entered every one turned as one to stare at him, their faces showing a mixture of curiosity and dread. When they saw it was just Billy, they let out a collective sigh and returned to their drinking and tiddlywinks.

Billy eased himself into a seat and signaled to the barkeep that he wanted a drink. In the wink of an eye a pretty young girl with hair the color of a new penny set a tankard of ale in front of him.

"You're new to town," she smiled.

Billy nodded, his cheeks coloring. He couldn't help but notice how pale and fine the barmaid's skin was and how her hair shimmered in the lamplight. She was the most beautiful thing he'd ever laid eyes on in his short life.

"What brings you to our village, stranger?"

"I've just left my home and I'm out to seek my fortune."

The barmaid nodded sagely. "A fortune is a good thing to have if a man wants to find himself a wife. Youth and good looks play their parts, as well—but a fortune is the most important of the three."

"Do you have a room for the night?" Billy all but blurted, his face now so red it felt as if he was hiding live coals in his mouth.

"You'll have to ask my father," she said, gesturing to the heavy-set man behind the bar.

Billy cleared his throat, hoping his voice would not crack. "Do you have a room to let, innkeeper?"

"Sorry, lad. I'm full up."

Billy glanced out the window at the island in the middle of the lake with its huge house.

"What about that place?" he asked, pointing in the direction of the lake. The entire tavern had fallen quiet as a church, their own drinks and conversations forgotten.

The innkeeper looked up from rinsing out the tankard, frowning at Billy. "What place?"

"The big house on the island, yonder. Do they have any rooms?"

"Aye, they have rooms enough, I suppose," the innkeeper replied slowly. "For those foolish to stay there."

"Is there something wrong with it?"

The innkeeper looked at Billy as if his head was made of mattress

KNUCKLES AND TALES: BILLY FEARLESS

ticking. "Son, haven't you ever heard of the house on Ghost Lake?"

"I'm from Monkey's Elbow," Billy replied as if this explained everything. Perhaps it did.

"There once was a man named McGonagil who sold his soul to the devil for the riches of Croseus. Once he got his wealth, he started worrying about people stealing it, so he bought himself that island and built himself a mansion, so's he wouldn't be bothered by thieves. When Old Scratch finally came for him; he refused to go unless the devil promised to protect his gold for all eternity. So the devil granted his dying wish and dragged the old bastard to hell."

"McGonagil's treasure is still somewhere in that house. The story goes that anyone who can spend three nights in the house shall claim the gold for his own. But the house is haunted by all manner of ghosts and goblins and of the dozens of fortune-hunters who have braved the island, none have survived the first night!"

Billy listened to what the innkeeper said and looked back at the empty house standing on the island. He then looked at the barmaid, who was smiling at him. "Would you marry me if I had a fortune?"

"I might do it even if you did not," she replied, a twinkle in her eye.

Billy looked back out the window at the island, then stood up and announced to the tavern; "I really don't like sleeping in the open this time of year. It don't agree with my bones. I'd be more than happy to pay someone to ferry me and my belongings to the island yonder."

There was a rumbling of excited voices and a broad-shouldered man stood up. "I'll ferry you over and back, lad, for three dollars. But its got to be cash on the barrel-head, as I don't cotton to taking money outta dead folk's pockets."

"Fair enough," replied Billy, handing over three silver dollars. He turned to the innkeeper and said; "Can I keep my horse and cart stabled here? I'll pay you for their keep—"

The innkeeper shook his head. "I won't take your money, son. If you live to the third day, then you may pay me. If not, I'll keep them for my own. Before you go—tell me your name, so I can send word to your family of your death."

"I swore I'd never tell my true name, but I've been called Billy Fearless."

The innkeeper did not seem terribly impressed. "Have it your way," he grunted.

As Billy followed the ferryman out of the tavern, the barmaid hurried to him and threw her arms around his neck.

"Be safe, my brave Billy!" she whispered, planting a kiss on his cheek.

Billy blushed even deeper than before, muttered thank you and hurried away, leaving the barmaid to watch after him, a tear glimmering in her eye.

o o o

Billy had the ferryman load his carving bench and turning lathe into his launch, along with enough food and drink for three days. By the time they reached the island it was near dark, and the ferryman was loath to do more than unload Billy and his things at the old wharf.

The front door of the house was unlocked and Billy placed his carving bench and turning lathe in a large room on the first floor that had a fireplace at one end and an old canopied bed in the corner. While the house was very dusty and smelled of mouse shit and mildew, it didn't seem to be in such bad shape. So Billy set about building a fire in the old chimney, found himself a stool, and prepared a simple dinner of black bread and sausage.

As he sat in front of the fire, chewing on the last of his bread, there came a sound like a tormented soul.

"Tch! Such a noisy wind," Billy said, shaking his head.

Just then the fire in the grate blazed incredibly high, filling the room with exaggerated shadows, then fell to a tiny flicker. Billy jumped up and grabbed the bellows and began fanning the flame.

"Tch! Such a drafty room!"

There was a noise in the far corner like that of someone crackling paper and a strange, high-pitched voice cried out; "Meow! How horribly cold are we!"

Billy, who had returned the fire to its former strength, turned in the direction of the voices and squinted into the darkness. "If'n you're cold, come sit with me by the fire."

Out of the dark corner paraded not one, but two, coal-black cats, walking on their hind-legs as nice as you please. The cats had huge yellow eyes and little red boots on their feet. They sat themselves down on the stool next to Billy and warmed themselves by the fire.

After awhile one of the cats turned to Billy and said; "It looks to be a long night, friend. How about a nice game of cards?"

This didn't take Billy aback none. He reckoned if a cat could walk on its hind legs and wear boots, not to mention talk, why shouldn't it want to play cards?

KNUCKLES AND TALES: BILLY FEARLESS

"Why not?" He replied. "But first, let me see your nails."

The cats exchanged looks, shrugged, and stretched out their claws.

"Boy-howdy, y'all sure got long nails!" Billy exclaimed, grabbing them by the scruffs of their necks. "Here, let me shorten 'em up a tad before we commence to playin'!" With that he placed them on his carving bench and screwed down their paws very firmly.

The cats began hissing and spitting and cursing him in cat-talk, which isn't very pleasant to the ears. Billy picked up one of his carving knives and with four clean strokes, severed the cats' legs. Instead of blood, a substance that looked and smelled like tar boiled forth from the wounds and the cats vanished in a cloud of foul-smelling brimstone.

Billy looked about and scratched his head. Finally he shrugged his shoulders and said "Tch! Well, I didn't really want to play cards with them, anyways!"

As Billy returned his attention to the fire, there was a horrible commotion—as if the gates of hell had been thrown wide open and all the attendant demons sent forth. Suddenly the room was filled with huge black dogs with eyes the color of fresh blood. The hounds launched themselves at the fire, digging at the burning logs with their great paws and snatching burning embers between their massive jaws and worrying them like rats. Billy stood and watched the dogs, not sure what to make of what was going on. Then, one of the hounds started digging at the hearth, sending hot embers and soot flying. One of the cinders got into Billy's eye, making it water and burn.

"That's enough! Now you've gone beyond a joke!" Billy said, and seizing the poker from the fire, cracked one of the dogs across the head, killing it instantly.

The rest of the pack came to a dead halt and stared at their fallen companion, whose crushed skull oozed the same foul-smelling tar as the cats. Then, as one, they raised their heads and fixed their blood-red eyes on Billy.

"Git, you mangy critters!" Billy yelled, raising his arms and waving the poker at the hellhounds. "You heard me—go on and git!" With that he took a swing at the nearest hound, who yelped and promptly turned tail and fled the room. The other dogs followed suit, leaping out windows and even climbing up the chimney in order to get away from Billy and his slashing poker.

After the last dog had disappeared, Billy carefully picked up the pieces of his scattered fire and put them back in the fireplace. He then caught himself yawning and decided it was time to go to bed. He kicked off his shoes and climbed, fully dressed, into the four-poster bed in the corner. The bed was made out of solid wood, with little clawed feet clutching carved balls, and although the bedclothes were a tad musty, he was quite comfortable.

As he drifted off to sleep he fell into a dream that he was riding a horse. At first the horse would only go slow, clip-clop, but soon it was going faster, clippity-clop, then even faster still,
clippity-clip. Billy opened his eyes and was surprised to find the walls and ceiling of the mansion speeding past him. Sitting up in bed, Billy discovered it wasn't the house that was moving—it was him. The bed's legs were moving as fast as they could, hurrying him from room to room, up stairs and down, over thresholds and around corners as if it was drawn by six strong horses.

Billy clung to the mattress the best he could as the bed shot down the long, dark corridors, sheets flapping behind them like pursuing ghosts. Finally, with a great bound, the bed flipped over on itself with a crash, landing atop Billy. He struggled out from under the tangle of blankets and pillows, rubbing his bruised rump and shaking his head. The bed's feet were still peddling at the air, like a turtle trying to right itself. Billy laughed and patted the bed appreciatively.

"Thanky kindly, old thing! That was the damnedest ride I've had since I rode the Flyin' Jenny at the county fair last year!"

And, with that, he gathered up his pillow and blankets and made his way back to the room on the first floor, where he curled up in front of the fire and fell sound asleep.

o o o

Early the next day the innkeeper, at the prodding of his daughter, paid the ferryman to take him to the island to check up on this so-called Billy Fearless. In the thirty years since old McGonagil was given his just reward; he'd seen the house take its share of victims. Most were young fools like the boy, all of them with dreams of treasure. Each and every one of them had been removed from the old house feet-first, stiff as boards and whiter than milled flour, the very life scared out of them. He figured the same would prove true of the latest boy. It was too bad his daughter had taken such a shine to this one. It was going to break her heart...

The innkeeper entered the mansion and opened the nearest door off the great hall and saw Billy sprawled before the fireplace. He shook his head sadly. "What a pity!"

KNUCKLES AND TALES: BILLY FEARLESS

"What is?" Billy yawned, sitting up.

The innkeeper was so surprised to see Billy move he clutched at his chest. "Lord A'mighty, boy! I never thought I'd see you alive again!"

"Why shouldn't I be? Granted, I had some bother with cats and dogs and my bed disagreein' with me, but I had a nice enough night."

The innkeeper could only shake his head in disbelief. Maybe there was something to this Billy Fearless, after all.

o o o

The second night began uneventfully enough for Billy. He set up his fire and fixed himself a simple meal from the sausage and cheese the inn-keeper had been kind enough to leave for him, believing it to be his last meal. It was nearing midnight, and Billy was settling down to a pipe of tobacco before going to sleep, when, with a horrible, blood-curdling scream, half a man from the waist down fell from the chimney and landed on the hearth at his feet.

Billy craned his neck to look up the chimney and yelled; "Hey, up there! There's another half wanted down here—that's not enough!"

Presently there was a second, even more hideous scream and the top half of the man dropped from the chimney.

"There, that's better," Billy said. "Here, let me stir up the fire for you." So he got off his stool to prod the fire. When he turned back around the two halves had somehow joined into a whole man with an ugly face. Actually, ugly was being kind. The stranger's skin was the color and texture of a mushroom, the nose whittled down to nothing and the lips withered and black. One of his ears was missing and the other was hanging by a flap of skin. But to make matters worse, the ugly man was sitting on Billy's stool.

"Here now! You're sitting in my spot!" said Billy. "Get up and find your own place to sit!"

The ugly man growled something in a low, liquid voice that sounded like his chest was full of honey, and shoved Billy away.

"There's no point in being rude," Billy admonished. "And I am the soul of human kindness, taught to turn the other cheek as the Good Book says. But I was also raised to defend what's mine and stand up for myself." And with that he grabbed the stool and yanked it out from under the ugly man, sending him sprawling.

The ugly man got to his feet, rubbing at his rear end and looking at Billy as if he'd just jumped over the moon.

Billy, having reclaimed his seat, settled back down to smoking his pipe. But before he had time to take a decent puff, another man dropped down the chimney. And another. And another. Within a couple of minutes there were six men, each uglier than the last, sitting in front of the fire. One of them got up and opened a closet door and produced nine skeleton legs and a human skull and began setting them up like ninepins.

Billy watched with great interest as the six ugly men rolled the skulls at the leg-bones. While he did not hold with their manners or their looks, he did have a fondness for ninepins. After a couple of sets he asked the ugly men if he could play.

The ugly men looked at one another then one of them smiled, displaying rotting teeth and blackened gums. "You can play if you have money."

"I've got money enough." Billy pulled a wad of bills out of his pocket and showed it to the ugly men, who muttered amongst themselves.

"Very well. You bowl first," the leader said, and handed Billy the skull. The others stood aside and tittered amongst themselves, waiting to see what Billy's reaction would be.

Billy hefted the skull and frowned. "Tch! Your ball isn't very round. I think I can fix that, though." He went to his turning lathe and worked the skull until it was completely smooth.

"There!" he said, holding it up to admire his handiwork. "Now it'll roll much better."

So Billy played ninepins with the six ugly men until the break of dawn, losing a dollar or two along the way. When the cock crowed morning the ugly men seemed genuinely startled, as if they had lost track of the time, and rushed about the room in a panic. Then, as the first light of morning broke through the window, they set up a racket like a gaggle of frightened geese and disappeared in a foul-smelling gust of wind.

Billy, glad his strange visitors had finally left him alone, yawned and curled up by the fire. As he drifted off to sleep, he wondered what he might expect in the way of guests for his third
and final night in the house.

o o o

His third day at the old house had proved uneventful. The innkeeper had stopped by again and was even more amazed than before to find Billy in the land of the living. This time he left behind a roasted

KNUCKLES AND TALES: BILLY FEARLESS

chicken and some wine for his dinner. As night fell, Billy sat by the fire and whittled a toy whistle to bide the time. He had almost finished putting the final touches on his whistle when he heard what sounded like footsteps in the hall outside his door. He looked up from the fireplace to see the door swing slowly open on squeaky hinges and six skeletons dressed in the top hats and black crepe of pall-bearers, march into the room carrying a coffin. The skeletons carefully lowered their burden to the floor then, without a word, turned around and filed back out of the room.

Billy, curious to see what the skeletons had brought him, got up and opened the coffin. Inside was a man his father's age, dressed in his best Sunday suit, his hands folded atop his chest, his mouth stitched shut with black thread and his eyes covered by gold coins. Billy touched the body and quickly drew his hand back.

"Tch! You're colder than stone, friend! Come; let me warm you by my fire."

Billy reached into the coffin and lifted the dead man by his armpits, dragging him free. As he did so, the coins fell from the dead man's eyes, causing the lids to fly open like window shades. Billy paused in his labors long enough to scoop up the coins and stick them in the pocket of his overalls. "Tch! That's a funny place to keep your money, cousin. Here, I'll keep track of it for you until you're feeling better."

After some considerable grunting and groaning, Billy managed to wrestle the dead man over to the fire. He lay the corpse on the hearth, thinking the warmth would unfreeze its joints and put the color back into the stranger's cheeks. Satisfied he'd done the best he could, Billy resumed his whittling.

An hour passed and the dead man was still as cold and stiff as when Billy first touched him. Billy frowned and thought on what he should do. He recalled how his daddy had once said how two people laying in bed together could make enough heat to spark a fire, so he decided to put the stranger in his makeshift bed and warm him with his body.

Billy took the body and placed it on the pallet he'd made for himself after the bed had run away, lay down beside it, and drew the covers over the both of them. Presently, he felt the body beside him grow less and less stiff and began to move. At first Billy didn't think much about it, but then he felt the dead man's hands creeping about below the covers, feeling up his thigh.

"Here now!" Billy cried, sitting up. "I'll have none of that! I stopped that foolishness when I was twelve!"

The dead man cast aside the covers, his eyes staring wide and sightless. "Give me back my gold!" the corpse wailed, tearing loose the stitches that held his mouth shut. "Give me back my gold!"

"Are you accusing me of being a thief? Is that all the thanks I get after trying so hard to make you warm and comfortable? Then you can have your old gold—and you can go back to where you came from!" With that Billy grabbed the dead man by the hair, forced open his mouth, shoved the gold pieces under his tongue, and threw him back inside the coffin.

As suddenly as they had first arrived, the six skeletal pallbearers reappeared, marching two abreast, picked up the coffin and left the room. Billy watched them leave and scratched his head. People sure acted different outside of Monkey's Elbow.

Just as he was ready to shrug it off and go back to bed, a cold wind came rushing down the chimney, extinguishing the fire. Billy dug around in his pockets and found a book of matches, which he used to kindle another, smaller fire in its place. As the light from the fire grew stronger, Billy saw that he was no longer alone in the room.

Standing in the corner was an ogre. He was taller than Billy even though his back was hunched, and he had a hooked nose with a wart on it and horrible crooked teeth that stuck out of his mouth like the tusks on a boar. His arms were so long they almost touched the floor and his legs were bowed and ended with feet as broad and calloused as a bear's. The ogre glowered at Billy with an expression of the utmost hate.

"Howdy, stranger," Billy said. "Who might you be?"

"I am the haint in charge of scaring folks away from this place. You are a troublesome man-child," the ogre said in a voice that sounded like two rocks being rubbed together. "You've given me more problems than all the others of your kind put together. What is your name, human?"

"I'm called Billy Fearless."

"Billy Too-Damn-Stupid-To -Know-When-To-Be-Scared is more like, if you ask me."

"You sound like you been talking to my daddy. You ever been to Monkey's Elbow, mister?"

The ogre shook his head in disgust. "Old Scratch put me in command of the ghosts and ghouls that haunt this house more than thirty years ago. Up until now there ain't been a soul that survived the first night! Why, if the hellhounds didn't do 'em in, the bed finished 'em off! But you—you! You kilt my cats, skeered my dogs and wore out

KNUCKLES AND TALES: BILLY FEARLESS

my bed! If Old Scratch hears of this, he'll have me back in Hell muckin' out the harpy nests! I worked hard to get myself a nice, cushy job haunting the upper world—I ain't about to let some no-count hayseed such as your self ruin it for me! Say your prayers, boy, because I'm going to choke the life outta you!"

The ogre straightened up as best he could, lifted his arms, and advanced on Billy, grimacing and growling like a beast. And, to his surprise, Billy commenced to laugh. This non-plussed the ogre something awful.

"What in tarnation are you laughing about, boy? Can't you see I'm going to kill you?"

"That's a good 'un!" chortled Billy, wiping a tear from his eye. "A wretched old thing such as yourself thinking he can kill the likes of me."

"I can kill you three times over, boy!" bellowed the ogre.

"I wouldn't be so sure of that," Billy warned. "I'm stronger than you might think. So don't go boastin' you can kill me."

"Oh, is that so? Well, we'll soon see if'n you're stronger than me or not. I'll show you a thing or two, you pesky turnip-seed!" Grabbing Billy by the straps of his overalls, the ogre dragged him through the house to the stable around back, which had once—judging from the stone-cold forge and the anvils laying about—boasted its own blacksmith.

"See that anvil lying yonder?" the ogre asked, pointing at a particularly large specimen. "Watch this, boy." Spitting in his palms, the ogre grabbed up a nearby axe and, with one mighty swing, split the anvil in two as cleanly as a hot knife through butter.

"That's nothing!" Billy snorted. "I can do better than that!"

"Can not."

"Can too."

"Can not."

"Just hand me an axe and you'll find out."

Chuckling to himself in anticipation of rending the smart-aleck country boy limb from limb, the ogre handed his victim an axe. "So what are you gonna do, boy?" he sneered.

"Gonna do the best I can," Billy replied, and promptly brought the axe blade down on the ogre's head with all his strength.

The ogre fell like a pole-axed steer, brains leaking from the huge split in the middle of his head. The foul, tarry material that had oozed from the dogs and cats in place of blood now bubbled out of his ears, nose and mouth.

"Maybe now a fellow can get some decent shut-eye," sighed Billy, dusting off his hands as he returned to the house.

o o o

The next morning Billy woke up to find a huge chest of gold at the foot of his humble bed. He took the chest, along with his carving bench and turning lathe, and carried them out to the dock, to await his passage to the mainland. He was sitting on the treasure chest, smoking his pipe, when the ferryman arrived at noon. When he saw Billy waiting for him on the dock his jaw dropped clean to his chest.

"You did it! You survived the three nights!" exclaimed the ferryman.

"Aye, that I did."

"What about the treasure?" the ferryman asked quickly. "Did you find the treasure?"

"Aye, that I did."

The ferryman scratched his chin and eyed the chest Billy was sitting on. There was no one here to see what would become of a nameless young man, or to discover the truth of what had happened to the miser's treasure. But what thoughts he might have had concerning disposing of Billy and shanghaiing his gold quickly disappeared. Any man—no matter how young—who could spend three nights in the company of ghosts and hobgoblins and come out off it with both his wits and life intact was not a man to tangle with, no matter what the reward.

So Billy Fearless returned to the Ghost Lake Tavern and showed the barmaid his chest full of gold coins and asked her father, the innkeeper, for permission to marry her. Of course he said yes. They put on a real big do and the whole valley was invited to dance at the wedding.

Billy had a nice big house built for his wife and the family that was soon to follow. His father-in-law, now one of the richest men in Ghost Lake, bought the old haunted mansion and, after some renovating, turned it into a big fancy hotel that attracted visitors from far and wide on the strength of it being a "real, live haunted house". Ghost Lake became a fat and happy little resort town, with everyone ending up with electric lights and indoor flush-toilets. And they all had Billy Fearless to thank for their newfound prosperity.

Still, Billy was still Billy, no matter how rich and famous he might be. And although his wife was a patient soul, she was only human. One day, after he'd brought home yet another wolf as a pet, she asked, as they lay in bed, how it was he didn't know enough to recognize danger when he saw it.

KNUCKLES AND TALES: BILLY FEARLESS

"Well, I was told by my daddy—the Lord keep him—that I'd know when to be scared of something because it'd give me a shudder. And to this day I have yet to shudder—or even know what such a thing as a shudder is."

"Is that all?" Billy's wife kicked back the covers, slipped on her shoes, grabbed up a coal shuttle and trotted own to the creek that ran behind their house. Once back in the house, she crept up on her husband as he lay in bed and dumped the scuttle full of minnows down the flap in his long johns. "Now, Billy, do you know what a shudder is?"

"If that's the case, then I'll be damned if I weren't scared the whole time!"

After that Billy Fearless was renowned throughout the valley as the soul of prudence and common sense. And if his wife knew better, well—she lived happily ever after anyways.

ABOUT THE AUTHOR

Nancy Collins is the author of several novels and numerous short stories, as well as having served a two-year stint as a writer for DC Comics' Swamp Thing. A recipient of the Bram Stoker Award, The Brittish Fantasy Society's Icarus Award, and the Deathrealm Award, as well as an nominee for the World Fantasy Award. Her works include Dead Roses For A Blue Lady and the novel Darkest Heart both of which feature her cult character Sonja Blue. Forthcoming works include a Weird Western novel, published by White Wolf, titled Dead Mans Hand.

   Ms Collins currently makes her home in Atlanta, Georgia with her husband, underground artist/provocateur Joe Christ, and their two dogs, Scrapple and Trixie.

Nancy A. Collins
www.concentric.net/~Sylabub/trueblue.htm

CONTRIBUTERS

Biting Dog Publications
www.bitingdogpress.com

JK Potter
www.thebluedot.com/potter/home.html

Bonnie Jacobs
www.bonniejdesign.co

*The following is an excerpt
from the upcoming
White Wolf release of*

DEAD MAN'S HAND: FIVE TALES OF THE WEIRD WEST

by Nancy A. Collins

Hell Come Sundown

"It begun when Merle went and dug himself a new well. You see, he'd bought a parcel of land off this Meskin feller, name of Garcia. Merle already had him a place, but he wanted to build a little house on its own plot so he could bring his mama and the rest of his family up from back east. He needed the new well, on account of the old one being too far away. Garcia's old grandpappy gets all riled up when he hears what Merle's doin'. He rides out and tells Merle he can't dig where he's diggin'. Merle tells him that he's bought the land off his kinfolk fair n'square, and if he wants to dig straight to hell, there ain't nothin' the old man can do about it. Then Old Man Garcia tells Merle that his grandson had no right to sell him the land without talkin' to him about it first. Merle says that's tough, but they've already signed papers on it and money has changed hands, so the sale is legal. Then Old Man Garcia offers to buy the land back from Merle—and at a good price, too. But Merle ain't havin' none of it. So Old Man Garcia, he goes home, packs up his family, and next thing you know they're gone—after bein' in these parts since the time of Cortez.

"After a few days diggin', Merle's about eight feet deep, I reckon. He's far enough down that he's got to use a ladder to get in and out of the hole. And he's got a couple of good ole boys from town, Billy McAfee and Hank Pierson, out there helpin' him haul the dirt and rocks up topside. Then his spade strikes something made of metal, but its too dark for him to see what it is.

"Merle yells up to Billy to lower him down some light. So Billy sends down a lantern. Merle lights it and bends over to get a look-see. What he finds looks like the lid of a large iron box. There ain't much showin', but from what he can see it looks like it's the size of a steamer trunk. Merle and them get to talkin', and they decide that it must be buried treasure—maybe gold the Aztecs tried to hide from the Spanish, way back when. At first they mean to keep it to themselves, but as they get to uncoverin' the metal box, they realize it's too big and too heavy for just the three of them to pull it free of the hole.

"That's where I come in. I lived down the road apiece and Merle knew I had me a string of mules. At first I didn't believe a word he said, but then he takes me over to where he's got the well started, and tells me to climb down and take a look for myself.

"I have to admit that once they put the notion in my head, all I could think of was gold. I kept thinkin' that if that box was full of treasure, it would go a long ways to settlin' debts and makin' life easier for me an' mine. So I ran and fetched the mules and brought them back to the well. By this point, the boys had uncovered the whole damn thing. It was about four foot long, three foot high, and three foot deep, with an old-fashioned hinged iron padlock.

"I hitched up the mules and wrapped the box in a set of chains I use to pull stumps. But when I laid my hand on the top of the box, I jumped back and hollered on account of it being so cold. My hand tingled and burned like I'd just stuck it in a bucket of ice water. Merle figgered it was cold like that because it had been buried so deep all them years. That didn't make much sense, but I was in too big a hurry to lay claim to my share of the treasure to give it much thought.

"I fastened the chains around the box and then climbed up top to fix them to the team. Usually my mules are pretty easy to work with, but that day they was givin' me fits, stompin' the ground and rollin' their eyes like they do when they smell somethin' fierce nearby, like a cougar or a bear. I really had to lay into them with the whip. Their rumps were runnin' red before they finally gave in and started to pull. But once they did, that ol' box was out of the bottom of Merle's well, just as easy as yankin' a rotten tooth. Still, it took all four of us to lift it up and put it in the back of Merle's buckboard.

"By the time we finally managed to get the chest over to Merle's place, it was gettin' on dark. Since the danged thing was so heavy, we decided to just pull the buckboard into the barn and open it out there, as opposed to tryin' to drag in into the house. Billy and Hank wrassled the bastard off the back of the wagon and set it on the barn floor.

"While Merle was busy fetchin' his chisel and pry-bar, I took a few seconds to study the padlock on the chest. It was a big rascal—as large as a baby's head—and when I looked at it close, I could make out some kind of symbols through the rust and the dirt caked on it. The funniest thing about the lock, I noticed, was it didn't have no keyhole. Once that critter was locked, it was meant to stay shut.

"Merle came back with the tools he needed to open the box, along with a lantern, so he could see what he was doin', now that the sun was set. Merle weren't a small man, and he sure as hell weren't a weak one, but it took him several good swings with the hammer before he knocked that lock open.

"When the padlock finally broke and dropped to the ground, we all stared at it for a couple of heartbeats, then looked up at one another. I don't know if it was the light from the lantern or somethin' else, but the others seemed to be lit from inside with a terrible hunger that made their eyes burn like those of animals gathered around a campfire. I reckon I didn't look no different, though. Greed is a horrible thing.

"The lid of the chest was so heavy Merle had to take the pry-bar and wedge it under the lip of the box and lever it open enough so that Billy and Hank could grab hold and throw it all the way open. We crowded around, lantern held high, eager to sink our arms up to our elbows in gold coins and precious gems. But there weren't no treasure buried in that chest. Not by a long shot.

"The only thing the iron box contained was the body of a man lying on his side, knees drawn up and arms folded across his chest. Save for a thin covering of yellow-gray dry skin, and wisps of hair that were still stuck to the scalp, it was basically a mummified skeleton. Going by the rusty chest-plate and helmet it still wore, the dead man had once been a conquistador. The only thing of any possible value was a silver medallion set with a highly polished stone hung about its neck.

"Merle reached in and yanked the necklace free, holding it up to light. Merle was always one for lookin' on the sunny side of things, so he tried to put a good face on it, so we wouldn't be so disappointed.

'At least it ain't a complete loss. This has to be worth at least fifty dollars...' That was the last thing I ever heard him say, at least that weren't screamin'.

"At that point we all had our backs turned to the box, as we was lookin' over Merle's shoulder at the necklace he took off the Spaniard's carcass. Suddenly there was this cracklin' sound comin' from behind us, like someone walkin' through a pile of dead leaves. So I turn around, and I see—sweet Lord Jesus—I see the dead thing in the box stand up.

"I know what you're gonna say, now. That I must be crazy. But if I'm crazy, it's on account of what I seen in that barn. The thing that got out of the box weren't nothin' but bones with dry skin the color and texture of old leather stretched over 'em. But it still had eyes--or something like eyes--burnin' deep inside its sockets. And when the thing saw us, God help me, it grinned—peeling back black, withered lips to reveal a mouthful of yellow, sharp teeth.

"We was so flabbergasted we was froze to the spot, just like a covey of chicks hypnotized by a snake. I was too scared to swaller, much less scream. The dead thing, it made this noise, like that of a screech owl, and jumped on poor Merle. It sank its fangs into Merle's throat like a wolf takin' down a lamb. It sure as hell was spry for somethin' that had to have been dead three hundred years.

"Billy grabbed the thing and tried to wrassle if off Merle, but it was like tryin' to pull off a tick. Even though it weren't but a bag of bones, it swatted Billy aside like he was nothin'. Hank snatched up an axe handle and laid into the thing, but just ended up splinterin' the axe-handle on the iron chest armor it was wearin'. Still, he must have got its attention, cause it dropped Merle and turned on him instead.

"Things was happenin' and movin' too fast by this point for me to get a clear picture of what exactly was goin' on, but I remember that once the thing was finished with Merle, it didn't quite look the same. There seemed to be more meat on its bones, an' more juice in the meat. It was like the blood it had drained from Merle was fillin' its own veins.

"Billy starts screamin' 'It's got Hank! It's got Hank! We gotta save him!' He grabs up pitchfork and charges th' thing, but it's too fast for him. It drops Hank and sidesteps Billy, snatchin' the pitchfork away like it was takin' a toy from a kid. Now Billy's screamin' for help, and—Lord, help me—instead of tryin' to save him, I ran away.

"I fled the barn and jumped on my horse and high-tailed it to town, not lookin' back once, for fear of what might be gainin' on me if I did. Billy McAfree's death screams were echoin' in my ears the whole way."

To be continued in

DEAD MAN'S HAND:
FIVE TALES OF THE WEIRD WEST

by Nancy A. Collins

Coming Fall 2004
from
Borealis, *division of White Wolf Publishing*

www.white-wolf.com/fiction

ISBN: 1-58846-875-5

bonniej
graphic design, inc

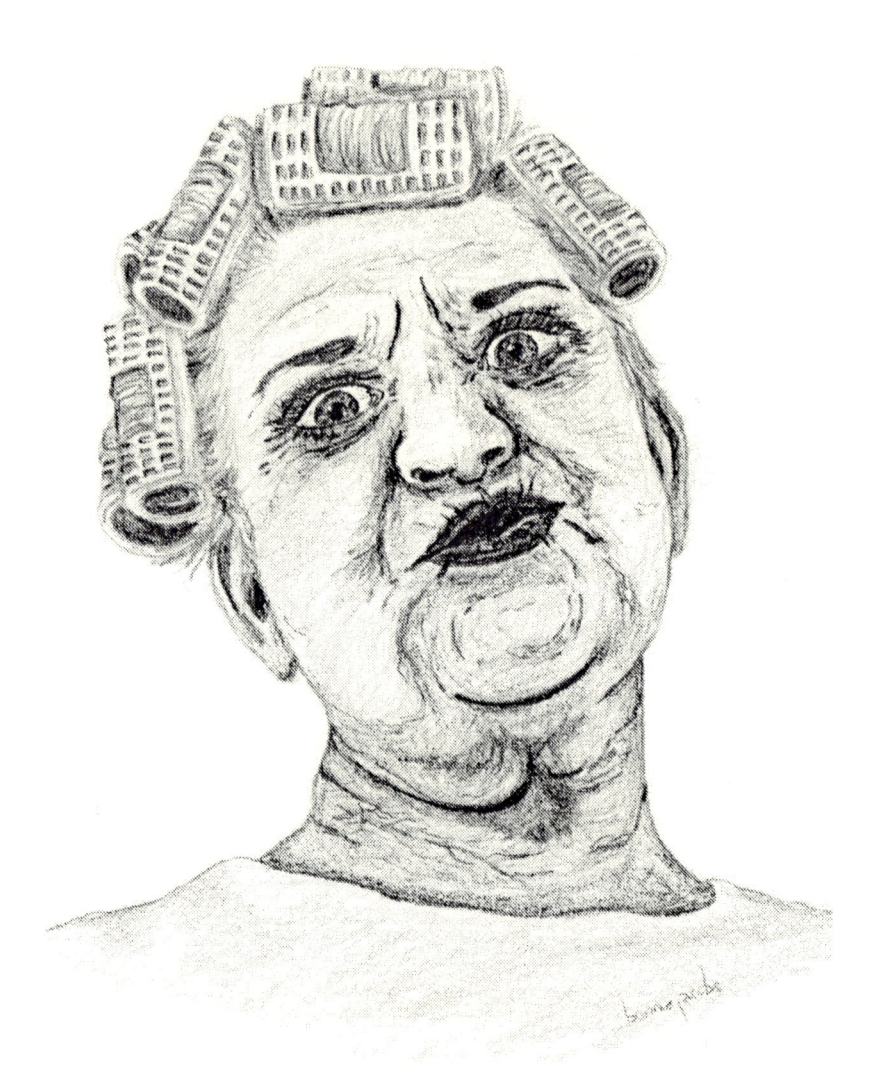

Print Design
Traditional Illustration
Digital Painting & Illustration
Web Design

w w w . b o n n i e j d e s i g n . c o m

New from Biting Dog Publications

In the fall of 1931 Max Belote kisses his wife good-bye as he promises to be home for supper. At the precise moment she anticipates his return he steps into the path of a train... In 1977 convicted murderer Jeffrey Michael Roberts shares his final words, "The best time for me was just before the screaming stopped and their voices hit that pitch," describing the unusual measures taken in his quest to perfect his soul... In 2001, Edward Paine excelled as head coach at an alternative high school in Quinley, Texas. Few knew that he fought the embraces of a dark side compelling him to fulfill its evil desires... Separated by seven decades, Max, Jeffrey and Edward are connected through the power of Virago, whose indestructible evil manifests itself within each as it seeks domination of their souls.

John Paul Allen takes his readers into a world where death only delays the inevitable. A journey of one soul through three lives, Gifted Trust lifts the reader to a new level of horror.

Gifted Trust
by John Paul Allen
Edited by Nancy A. Collins
Cover by Alan M. Clark
ISBN: 0-9729485-0-3
$15.95

BITING DOG
PUBLICATIONS

www.bitingdogpress.com

Handmade Books from...

Each and every one of our books are painstakingly handmade. From the engraving of the original artwork on wood blocks to the handpulling of each print and finally to the handsewing and casing of each book. Thats why our books are limited in quantity and high in quality. They are immediately rare because our limited editions are no more than 300 copies.

BITING DOG PRESS

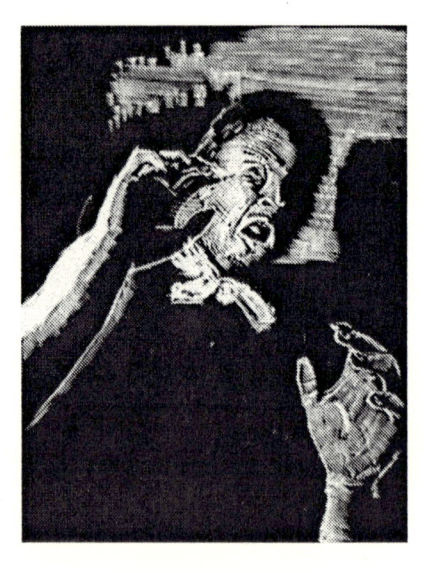

Illustrations from Nancy A. Collins, Absoloms' Wake, a limited edition handmade book, coming fall 2003.

www.bitingdogpress.com